Praise for Lulu Taylor

'Don't you just want to grab this, switch off the phone and
curl up on the sofa? Winter bliss from Lulu Taylor'
Veronica Henry, top ten bestselling author of
Christmas at the Beach Hut

'Pure indulgence and perfect reading
for a dull January evening'
Sun

'Told across both timelines,
this easy read has a sting in the tale'
Sunday Mirror

'Utterly compelling. A really excellent winter's story'
Lucy Diamond

'I raced through this gripping tale about secrets and lies and
long-buried emotions bubbling explosively to the surface'
Daily Mail

'Wonderfully written . . . this indulgent
read is totally irresistible'
Closer

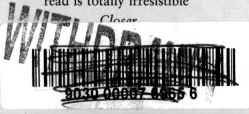

A
WINTER
MEMORY

Lulu Taylor's first novel, *Heiresses*, was nominated for the RNA Readers' Choice award. It was followed by a string of *Sunday Times* bestselling novels including *Her Frozen Heart*, *The Winter Secret* and *A Midwinter Promise*. She lives in Dorset with her husband and two children.

www.lulutaylor.co.uk
🐦 @misslulutaylor

By Lulu Taylor

A
WINTER
MEMORY

LULU TAYLOR

PAN BOOKS

First published 2021 by Pan Books
an imprint of Pan Macmillan
The Smithson, 6 Briset Street, London EC1M 5NR
EU representative: Macmillan Publishers Ireland Ltd, 1st Floor,
The Liffey Trust Centre, 117–126 Sheriff Street Upper,
Dublin 1, D01 YC43
Associated companies throughout the world
www.panmacmillan.com

ISBN 978-1-5290-2968-0

A

t

Visit **www.panmacmillan.com** to read more about all our books
and to buy them. You will also find features, author interviews and
news of any author events, and you can sign up for e-newsletters
so that you're always first to hear about our new releases.

To Lucie

Prologue

The telephone rings, and I wake at once. I leap out of bed and dash across the hall to the upstairs landing, where the table lamp casts a soft glow across the shrieking phone. I grab the receiver. 'Hello?'

'It's me,' he says.

My breath catches in my throat. I can hardly believe I'm hearing his voice. 'Yes?'

'I can't do this anymore. I want to be with you.'

Suddenly exhilarated, I see the life I've longed for drop into my hands like a gift from heaven. Will he actually leave? Come to me, into my arms? Then . . . grey reality consumes it. 'You can't leave. The children . . . they need you.'

'It's too late for that. I can't undo the damage. I can't bear to see it. I've been weak, stupid . . .'

He sounds utterly bleak, desperate.

'They still need you,' I say, but less firmly. The truth is that I agree with him. He's right – the damage has been done.

'But I need *you*,' he says, his voice low. 'I see that now. Forgive me. Is it too late?'

The gift is still sparkling in my hands. Its promise has not been doused. My heart is racing. I glance at the hall clock and see that it is one o'clock in the morning. 'Perhaps you should wait until tomorrow. Sleep on it, darling. Don't make any hasty decisions.'

'That's not what I mean. Is it too late . . . for us? Will you still have me?'

I close my eyes, standing there in the hall in my nightdress, everything in me rejoicing that, at last, I've heard the words I've longed for. 'You know I will.'

'Then I'm coming, darling. Right now. Tonight.'

'Are you sure? Do you mean it'

'I've never been more certain. Wait for me.'

'Always.'

When the phone is replaced, I cannot go back to bed. I go down to the kitchen, wide awake and bubbling with happiness, my very fingertips feeling full of magic, and I make tea. I will wait. How long will it take? Six hours? Seven?

If only I could sleep, then I would wake to find him here with me. I can almost feel it now: the warmth of his touch, the slight roughness of his stubbled skin on mine, his lips pressing against my mouth as he murmurs. He likes to do that: to place words of love onto my lips as though pressing them into my soul. He'll reach for my hair with those hands I love so much: broad, the palms almost square, the fingers long, blunt-ended and capable; he'll wind my long hair around them and say, 'You're my sea witch, my Beira, my queen.' I'll feel the soft wool of his faded, holey jumper and inhale the scent of woodsmoke and cedar, and then those

2

strong arms will wrap around me and never let me go. Because he's going to leave her, he's going to come to me.

Whatever awaits us in the future, we can face it together. Her wrath will be terrible. She's already taken whatever rage has possessed her since birth and used it to terrorise him and their children. When she knows he's finally broken free, what will she do? To him? To me? What form will her revenge take? What will she destroy?

I pace the kitchen, wondering where he is now on his journey. I will wait for as long as it takes. And when he arrives, I will give him all the strength that comes from my love and, together, we will face her.

I wait for the dawn, longing only for him.

PART ONE

Chapter One

HELEN

2018

From the moment we returned to Ballintyre, I couldn't understand what had happened to Sylla.

We arrived late one night after a fractious journey that had started very early, both Hamish and I quick to snap at each other all the way. I was exhausted from packing up our entire lives and the horrible, draining stress of everything we had just lived through. We finally pulled to a stop in front of the house in the pitch dark, the children white-faced and asleep in the back of the car, our belongings pulled in the trailer Hamish had hired. Charlie, Hamish's older brother, crunched over the drive towards us, gruff and bluff as ever.

'Here you all are! I thought you'd never get here!' he shouted. 'I was about to turn in.'

I got out of the car. 'Hello, Charlie. Please, don't shout – the children are asleep, I'd like to slip them straight into bed before they wake up—'

'Hello, Hamish,' he bellowed, ignoring me. 'How was the traffic?'

Hamish, getting out of the car, started to murmur about the M6.

'Where's Sylla?' I asked, looking about for her, shaking out my stiff legs. She was the calm to Charlie's tempest, a piece of centred soulfulness in the heart of the storm. I'd wanted to see her, *needed* to see her. Where was she?

Charlie didn't reply, busy directing Hamish here and there, explaining the water pump system he'd had installed when we were barely five minutes in the door. Later, with our suitcases stowed in our rooms, the children tucked away in their attic bedroom, we three adults sat down in the kitchen to beans on toast and glasses of red wine, which Hamish gulped down gratefully.

'Where's Sylla?' I asked again, in the relative calm.

Charlie looked at me, fixing me with that blue gaze he shared with Hamish. The pale blue could have looked insipid but, illuminated by the Ballintyre intelligence, it became interesting, almost intriguing.

'She's away,' he said briefly.

'Away?' I was surprised. 'She didn't say.'

'She doesn't tell you everything, does she, Helen?' Charlie asked peevishly.

He was right, she didn't. We were sisters-in-law, not best friends. We went long periods without being in touch. It was true I'd been out of contact for a while, taken up by the whirlwind of events that had engulfed us, but I'd sent her a message the day before yesterday saying we were coming and why. I'd been so busy packing that I'd hardly noticed that she hadn't replied. Why hadn't she let me know she wouldn't be here? 'When will she be back?'

Charlie shrugged. 'I don't know. Soon, I suppose.'

'Well, where's she gone?'

'I don't know. She needed some time away, that's all. She's an adult. I'm sure she's fine. We don't live in one another's pockets, you know.'

I felt a tiny sting of rebuke. Was he saying that I was being nosy? Or perhaps implying that I was too possessive of Hamish? It occurred to me to wonder what Hamish had told him about what had happened and why we were there. Surely his brother knew the circumstances that had brought us back to Ballintyre in such a hurry, with nowhere else to go.

But the way this family communicated had always been a mystery to me. Who knew what they had said, and what they had hidden?

Charlie had already changed the subject, back to his new pump system and the challenges he'd had installing it. Hamish was nodding away, his eyes droopy with tiredness. It had been a long drive that day. The last week alone had been exhausting, let alone the time before that. We were drained.

I looked around the kitchen. I knew it well: the chilly flagstones, the old preparation table in the middle of the room, its wooden top scrubbed to ivory over the years, the range sending out a welcome heat. Shelves were stacked with Queensware china and old-fashioned kitchenalia: huge tureens, old platters, earthenware jugs, jelly moulds and antique jars. Under the prep table, the shelf was loaded with Mason mixing bowls, saucepans and stockpots, cast-iron casseroles in all sizes, griddles, omelette pans, and roasting tins stacked up with the smallest nesting inside the larger all the way to a vast old thing only brought out for the biggest of feasts. Over the range hung ladles, fish slices, slotted spoons, mashers, scoopers, spatulas; and in the big terracotta jug was a large collection of spoons, spread like a spiky wooden bouquet.

All so familiar, and yet, without Sylla, not quite right. This was her place. The kitchen and garden were her kingdoms: if she wasn't in one, she would be in the other. Whenever we visited – usually twice a year – she was here, the glue that held the house together, serene, smiling, sweet, offering tea and something delicious she had made. But that, I reminded myself, was before the accident. She had not been like that Sylla for a while. Instantly, I felt pulled up by my own selfishness. My life had absorbed me so much lately that I had almost forgotten what she had been through. Did I imagine all she had to worry about was listening to my troubles?

I would text her as soon as I got a minute.

But where on earth was she?

We got to bed late but I still woke very early the next morning, puzzled for a moment about where I was. Then I remembered that I was in the four-poster bed in the old familiar bedroom we always had at Ballintyre. I knew it as well as I knew my bedroom at home.

Except that now there is no bedroom at home. This is where we live for the time being. I sighed. *At least the bed is comfortable.*

Hamish was still asleep, but I needed to check on the children so I got up and padded along the corridor to their bedroom, where Jamie was awake, wide-eyed and curious in his little white bed, whispering to his hedgehog toy, and Lilac was still fast asleep, one arm flung out of bed and hanging limp. She woke up as I got Jamie dressed and I took them both downstairs for breakfast.

'Is it the holidays?' Lilac asked as I put a bowl of cereal in front of her.

'Yes, I suppose in a way it is.' I poured the milk into her bowl and made sure Jamie's toast was cut up the way he liked it. 'It's the holidays for now.'

Lilac ate thoughtfully. I could see she was a little confused. Holidays usually followed the end of term and yet now life had changed very fast. Within a short space of time, she'd left her school, we'd left our house, and now here we were.

At least we have this place, somewhere she knows and loves, to escape to.

'I miss Marmalade,' Jamie declared, munching on his toast.

'Me too,' Lilac said.

'Marmalade will be fine with Katie, you know that. We'll have him back before you know it. But it's not fair to bring a cat to a new place when you don't know how he'll settle in.' I wasn't going to say that we had no idea how long we'd be at Ballintyre. They didn't need more uncertainty right now.

11

I went to the range and made myself a cup of coffee, taking a deep breath as I leaned against its comforting warmth. Even at the height of summer, the kitchen needed the heat from the range.

'Where's Auntie Sylla?' Lilac called from the table.

I wrapped my fingers around the coffee cup. 'She's away for a while.'

'Will she come back?'

I hesitated. 'Yes, of course. I don't know when. But she will.'

I hoped it was true. The place felt so strange without her. She was always standing here at the range in the mornings, cooking up something delectable for us all, turning ordinary food into a feast. My eye was caught by a photograph on the shelf over the countertop, pushed up against a row of recipe books. I went over and looked at it.

There she is. Beautiful Rose.

Rose's face gazed back at me, fresh and clear, her tawny eyes candid. Long red-gold hair fell over one shoulder. The Ballintyres all had a touch of ginger in their brown hair. It came out in Hamish's beard, when he grew one, and Charlie had a chestnut tint to the last remaining curls on his head. My children had my dark hair but with russet lights. And in Rose, it came out strong and pure, perhaps with the addition of Sylla's Nordic fairness.

Sylla, where are you?

I had a horrible feeling that she had needed me, and I hadn't been there. Sylla had so few people to turn to, with no family of her own. Ballintyre was no place to make intimate friends, out here on the coast, the nearest village a drive away and the neighbours separated by acres of woods and rolling hills. Half the houses were empty most of the time anyway, used as holiday homes or rented out in the summer. It was lonely. I felt suddenly that I hadn't been there enough for Sylla at her time of crisis, I'd been lost in my own world.

But, I told myself, Sylla had never shared her life with me the way I had with her. I was a gushing conduit of water, letting everything pour out, and she was the calm bowl that received it, held it a while and let it flow onwards. I had never met anyone who was not only as good a listener as Sylla, but one who was as adept at turning a subject away from herself. After I had poured out my heart to her, I would often get a card or email, reflecting on what I had told her and offering encouragement. But when I tried to get to the heart of her troubles, she was strangely elusive. And I had let her be like that. I had given her the space she seemed to desire, and allowed her to set the pattern for our relationship: me, the tempestuous wind, her the firm oak at the centre of it. Why had I allowed it? It could never have been that simple. I should have tried harder, especially when Rose went. Why didn't I?

I poured another cup of coffee. There could be a perfectly rational explanation for Sylla's disappearance. She might turn up tomorrow, back from some walking trip or visit to a garden on the other side of Scotland, with fresh seedlings for her greenhouse. Charlie wasn't bothered. She was an adult, as he said. Why should I be worried?

And yet I was.

Hamish came into the kitchen still in his pyjamas, his hair askew, showing the ripples of grey under the brown. He looked tired, his eyes lined and puffy, and he yawned heavily as he shuffled in. When had he stopped picking up his feet?

'Morning,' I said. 'Did you sleep all right?'

'Yes,' he said. 'Did you?'

'Yes.'

He shuffled over to get some coffee, glancing towards the children. 'Kids all right?'

Once there had been the two of us. Then the children came and now they were the things that both bound us together and kept us apart, like a pendant hanging between two links on a necklace. Lately, they had become our almost obsessional focus, as though by clinging to them, everything would be all right. Sometimes I felt that there was nothing else to join us together.

'They're fine.' I put down my coffee cup as he tipped the pot to fill his. 'They can watch some telly when they've finished their breakfast as it's Saturday. Make yourself some toast.'

'What are you going to do?'

'I'm going to stretch my legs. I still feel cramped from the drive.'

'Will you be long?'

'I shouldn't think so. Charlie will be up soon, I'm sure. You'll have plenty to catch up on with him.'

I went for my jacket. It was spring but this was Scotland and it was still cold outside; the light was pure, the sky a watery blue.

'Helen, are you going far?' Hamish called after me.

He seemed to need me more these days – or at least, he seemed to want to stay close to me. It didn't translate into a real concern for my safety or whereabouts, but more that I was a security blanket he craved in order to feel comforted. I could understand that. He was traumatised still. I had to be the strong one for now, while he was going through this dark period. But he would have to come out of it soon, surely, and put it behind him. The whole thing was over, and besides, our situation could have been so much worse. It was lucky we'd had Ballintyre to come to. What would he have done if there hadn't been that option? Would we just be homeless?

I already knew the answer to that. He would have looked to me to solve the problem, just as I'd been solving the problems for us both for so long now. I remembered the nights at our kitchen table in Stourhaven, when he wept and talked ceaselessly about how much he'd let us down, how badly he'd failed – but how he'd been set up, exploited and made a scapegoat.

'I didn't do anything wrong,' he'd say. Sometimes he'd take my hand and stare into my eyes. 'You do believe me, Helen, don't you?'

'Of course I do.' I'd squeeze his hand in sympathy, to show him I was on his side.

'I need you to be strong for me.'

'I will be. You can rely on me.'

I'd done my best, just as I always had.

Now, I turned back to him with a smile. 'Not far, honestly. Don't look so worried!'

I went out of the back door and skirted the house, crunching on the gravel as I passed the large oil tanks and the outbuildings. It took a while to walk the length of the rear of the house. The main rooms were on the other side, facing out towards the loch, and this rear side was the shaded, concealed part so I was invisible until I emerged out onto the turning circle and spotted a figure marching up the drive towards the house.

Josephine.

She was striding along in her unstoppable way. She seemed to have grown larger since I last saw her, hefty with the roundness of age and inactivity. But it wasn't only those things that were settling a great belt of body fat around her middle, I knew that. Even though she was a way off, I could see that her face was broader, a little swollen almost, and her hands looked vast and purple. The sight of her gave me a shiver. I ducked behind a bank of rhododendron and strode out behind the trees towards the kitchen gardens. Instead of the granite and stone of the house, the walls here were mellow red brick, which seemed to create a warmth within their confines where plants and trees were protected from the tempests that came off the loch, and flourished.

I opened the iron gate and went in, feeling almost like a trespasser. This had been Sylla's place for a long time now, though I could remember it from before, when it had been bare but for a few stubborn fruit trees bearing tiny bullet-hard apples and pears, and when the glasshouse had been a sad, collapsing mess of rotten wood and shattered panes infiltrated by ivy, creepers and weeds. I stood just inside the garden and looked around. I had grown accustomed to its neatness and air of being well tended, and while it was still far from what it had once been, it was now shabby at the edges, and I sensed neglect. The weeds had begun to encroach once more, there were no lines of vegetable tops in the raised beds, and the wicker wigwams were askew. At the far end, Sylla's polytunnel looked droopy and leaf-covered. Creepers had left curtains of twiggy strands over the walls that Sylla would usually have been cutting off, cursing their indestructibility.

'What is it about weeds, Helen?' she would exclaim. 'Why are they so invincible, while my poor plants expire from one frost? You wouldn't believe the tenacity of these brambles, you really wouldn't. Old Andy tells me to use chemicals on them, but I can't bring myself to.'

I missed her most in this place, I realised. I'd found her here so often, in her dungarees and cut-off gumboots, soft linen shirts, a striped jumper if the days were colder, wearing her gardening gloves, streaks of dirt across her forehead where she pushed her hair out of her eyes. 'Come and see!' she'd cry. 'Come and see what's growing!'

It was the only place she could be happy, after the accident.

I walked among the raised beds, examining what was there.

'Where's your mistress?' I asked the garden out loud, and waited. There was no reply, but distant birdsong, the cluck of a pigeon nearby and the whisper of the morning wind through the treetops. I felt helpless and also filled with a deep alarm. This was Sylla's place. She had made it her own. She ought to be here. I couldn't imagine Ballintyre without her.

I heard, quite suddenly, a cuckoo and squinted out over the pines beyond the garden walls to see if I could spot it. I couldn't make it out in the mass of dark treetops but I saw the top of the kirk, the plain battlements that topped the square tower.

It was all so familiar now. I knew this place so well; it was my home as much as anywhere was. How odd it was to remember what it had been like to arrive here as a stranger all those years ago, when I first met Hamish, and Sylla herself. That was when everything had started.

Chapter Two

HELEN

2001

'I think this must be some kind of mistake,' I said, staring at the stiff invitation card that I held with an almost fearful delicacy. It had come in that morning's post, arriving in a large envelope addressed to Miss Helen Spencer in a confident copperplate hand. I'd found it propped up against the teapot when I came down for breakfast.

Dad glanced over the top of his glasses, dragging his attention away from the paper. 'What? What's a mistake? Read it out.'

'Mrs Josephine Ballintyre, at home for Charlie and Hamish, for Hogmanay.' I looked at Dad, puzzled. 'At home?'

'It's a very old-fashioned way of saying "please visit". It's a bit pretentious, if you ask me.' He looked at me jokily. 'Unless you're becoming one of the crème de la crème? You'll be too grand for your poor old dad before I know it.'

'As if.' I shook my head. 'But I don't understand why I'm invited to her house.'

Dad frowned. 'Don't you know them?'

19

'Well, yes . . . I know them, but only vaguely. Well, not Hamish. I only know Charlie because of Rollo.'

Rollo had been my older, glamorous boyfriend at Edinburgh, where I was reading History. During our brief relationship, I'd mixed with his set of smart Anglo-Scots students, with their boarding school accents, huge houses in the remote Scottish wilderness and fearless determination to wear kilts and dance reels despite the dripping scorn of the students who sounded properly Scottish. Rollo's friend Charlie Ballintyre had been one of them: loud, good-natured and very entitled. He hadn't appeared to notice me, and Rollo had dumped me unceremoniously months ago, and yet here I was, invited to his Hogmanay.

'Ah, mystery solved, you do know them.' Dad turned back to his paper.

'Yes, but . . .' I frowned. Dad wouldn't get these things but it was extremely odd that I would even cross Charlie Ballintyre's mind when he had never apparently noticed that I was alive before now, even though I'd spent whole evenings with him and his crowd, at Rollo's side in Charlie's flat or at the pub or in various drinkeries in the town. 'It's a bit late to invite me. Hogmanay's only four weeks away.'

'You should go,' Dad said. 'It might be interesting.'

'Mmm. But . . .'

'But?'

I thought of the unfamiliar terrain of the country house party. 'I won't know anyone.'

'You do. You know this Charlie. And you'll certainly meet people if you go up there.'

'I'm worried about fitting in.'

'Nora will help you with that. It's her area of expertise.'

'Yes.' I brightened. 'Nora will help. I'll go and see her today.'

Nora was in her studio, a paintbrush in her teeth, another in her hand as she dabbed at her canvas, and specks of white on her face where she had rubbed it. Her rather wild hair was piled up into a tawny cushion bound about by a crimson scarf to keep it out of her eyes. She wore a long multicoloured kaftan belted with a curtain tassel, Turkish slippers and ropes of pearls at her neck, and she looked like an exotic 1920s spy. She turned as I came in, brightened and removed the brush. 'What's up, doc?'

Her accent was cut-glass, though her voice was as smooth as silk, and that made the way she used slang very funny. Nora's voice, gentle and yet direct, was just one of the things I loved about her.

Dad and Nora had been seeing each other for about three years. At first, I'd been conflicted about it – on the one hand relieved that Dad had found someone just as I was leaving home, and on the other protective of our close bond, our team of two. My mother had left us years before, in search of excitement and experience, and after many adventures had ended up in Arizona, where she married a deeply religious man who wanted nothing to do with her past, including me. As a result, I rarely saw her. The divorce had cost us our house and we'd scraped by for years, moving from one rented property to another, Dad working hard to support me and see me through school. I didn't want him to be with someone who might dilute us, or even break us apart by making him choose between us. I also felt, vaguely, that it was unfair to like Nora when I couldn't stand Mr Arizona, even though Mum had abandoned us, leaving Dad to bring me up, and rifled through a pack of boyfriends before she got married again, while Dad had barely had a drink with a woman. Nora, kind and wise, had sensed all this and gently overcame my initial chilliness with diligence and quiet persistence, until I warmed to her and we became good friends united not just by our affection for Dad but by our affection for one another. Now my only real worry was that Nora might break up with Dad – I didn't think either he or I could bear it – but so far, she was a fixture, and she brought light and sparkle into my life. She was clever, exotic and different, with her old-fashioned voice and eccentric tastes, and the way she called me Hélène in the French way, which I didn't mind at all.

'I've had an interesting invitation,' I said, and pulled it out of my pocket. She took it and regarded it thoughtfully.

'Ah,' she said. 'Well, well. Ballintyre.'

'Do you know it? You're from Scotland, aren't you?'

'Yes . . . a long time ago. Come on, tea first.' She put down her brushes and went to her little Primus stove to heat up the water. The electric kettle I'd given her for her birthday was still in its box. Nora preferred to boil her water over the gas flame, her brown teapot ready with four teaspoons of Fortnum and Mason's Assam, milk in a little Spode jug, and proper cups and saucers. 'From my old home,' she'd said once, when I'd admired the delicate floral china cups with their rim of gilt.

I sat down in an armchair, horsehair and springs spilling from its torn velvet seat, and looked about while Nora busied herself with the tea things. The studio, at the bottom of the garden of her tiny Victorian terraced house, was a place of fascination for me. It was crammed with Nora's collections: books, antique objects, plaster cameos in cases, old toys and bits of silver. A marble bust of a goddess was festooned in costume jewellery and wearing an original 1960s pillbox hat. Next to her, the wagons of an old tin train were loaded up with antique marcasite brooches. A pile of art books was topped off with a vase of drooping orange tulips. Around the room, canvases were stacked and hung, some half finished, some completed. A pile of square brown paper packages were ready to be dispatched to their owners. Nora painted portraits, mostly of children, and the studio was full of angelic faces, wide-eyed, cherry-lipped, glowing with the soft tones of childish skin and hair. It was, I sometimes thought, like a silent nursery.

'So, tell me everything,' she said over tea, and I did. She sat back, smoking one of her little brown pungent cigarillos, and frowned. 'I think it's obvious. Rollo has asked Charlie to invite you. He wants to see you again in a gorgeous romantic setting.'

'Really?' I was doubtful. 'Do you think he'll be there?'

'Don't you?' Nora let a trickle of smoke emerge from her pursed lips. 'Perhaps he's realised what a mistake he made and wants to relight the torch.'

'I find that hard to believe.' Rollo had chucked me without any regret and rather cruelly at the end of the term before last, actually taking me out for a romantic Valentine's dinner with roses, chocolates and a gushing card, followed by a passionate night at my place. In the morning, he'd stretched, yawned and said that it wasn't working and he needed space to work out where his head was at. He was off before I'd quite realised I was being dumped. He'd shown no interest at all in getting back with me. It had hurt but the relationship had been far too young and casual for it to be a deep wound. 'And I don't particularly want to see him, to be honest.'

She smiled at me. 'But even if he is there, you simply must accept if only for the pleasure of turning him down. You can't miss the opportunity of a Hogmanay in Scotland.' She stubbed out her cigarillo and said, 'Honestly, darling, I'm quite jealous. Ballintyre is beautiful. It's half house, half castle – granite walls, huge windows, turrets, rather austere. I believe it was an eighteenth-century hunting lodge that got expanded into a very grand house. I haven't seen it in years, but I doubt it's changed much. How funny that you're going up there.'

'But . . .' I wrinkled my nose at the stiff card and looked at her anxiously. 'I'm nervous about fitting in.'

'Don't worry about that,' Nora said breezily. 'My finishing school is officially open. You're my first and only student, Hélène, and you'll get all the benefit of my wisdom. And remember my motto – if in doubt, smile and say, "How *marvellous*." It works nearly every time.'

Nora helped me write my acceptance – *Miss Helen Spencer thanks Mrs Josephine Ballintyre for her kind invitation . . .* – and took me on a shopping trip to Bristol.

'You need a dress for the party,' she said as she nudged her little VW Golf into a parking space. 'It'll be black tie for the evening, long dresses for the girls. Luckily you don't have to worry about tartan sashes and the like, not having a family tartan.' She gave me a sideways look from her clear grey eyes. 'Steer clear of fake tartan, thistle brooches and paste tiaras, won't you?'

'Er, yes, I wasn't really thinking of going anywhere near them,' I said faintly.

'Good. But you'll be there the whole weekend, so you'll need a few other things too. Come on!'

We went to three big department stores and found a black velvet evening gown that was the stuff of fairy tales as far as I was concerned: a full skirt with netting beneath, a sweet-heart neckline and long sleeves cleverly cut so I could raise my arms.

'Very important for reeling,' Nora said. 'You're going to spin and all the rest.' When she saw my face, she added, 'I'll show you some moves when we get home, but don't worry too much, the boys will be in charge. They just push you about. It's easy.'

'Is it fun?' Being pushed about and having to spin did not sound it.

'The best fun. You'll love it. But we must get you some flat shoes. You can't dance in high heels – not only will you fall over but you could very well spear someone through the foot.'

We went home loaded with packages, and Nora gave me a crash course in fine dining, cooking an elaborate feast for me and Dad with a properly laid table, napkins, candles and four different glasses.

'All nonsense, really,' Dad said, laughing as he filled the largest of his wine glasses.

'No, Gordon, not nonsense,' Nora said firmly. 'You've just poured wine into your water glass. Doesn't matter here, not a bit. But it might make Helen feel ill at ease if she saw she'd done something like that at Ballintyre.'

Dad laughed again and shook his head. 'It's all so silly. It really doesn't matter.'

Nora looked cross. 'I'm sorry, Gordon, it does matter. Fitting in matters. Manners matter. No one will tell Helen if she does it wrong, but they'll notice. It can't do any harm to know the accepted form.'

I knew Dad was right, it was rather silly. But I agreed with Nora: knowledge was power. Why put myself in a position where I might look a fool? 'I'm with Nora.'

She smiled at me. 'Good girl. Now, I've made soup and we've got shellfish and all the tricky things. So let's get started.'

Nora was round at ours when another thick envelope arrived for me. She stayed over a few times a week and I was used to seeing her at the breakfast table, resplendent in her turquoise silk robe, a bandana around her mad, lion-coloured hair. The coffee was always twice as strong when Nora was there, and she got the special marmalade out too, as if it was for everyday. Dad didn't say anything to stop her either.

'Oh!' I said, when I'd opened it. 'I'm not going to Ballintyre after all.'

Nora looked up from her toast, startled. 'You're not? But why?'

'Well, I'm going to the party, but look – they've sent me this! Lots of information about trains and maps, and what to bring . . . and I'm staying somewhere else.'

Nora nodded sagely. 'Ah – that's quite normal. Ballintyre is big but I expect they're having a very large gathering. So some of the guests will go and stay with friends of the Ballintyres. Where are you off to?'

I consulted the sheet. 'A place called Tie-glack-ack. I think. That's so weird, it sounds like someone clearing their throat.'

'Oh – Tighglachach.' Nora gave it the Scottish lilt, changing the hard 'k' sound to a soft one and stressing the 'glach'. *Tie-GLACH-ach*. A smile curled her mouth.

'Do you know it?'

'Yes, I do, as it happens. I used to go there as a girl. It's a house owned by a family called the Drummonds, very close to Ballintyre. I thought it might have been sold by now. But if you're staying there, perhaps not. They were a slightly eccentric family; it's funny to think that they're still there.' She looked rueful. 'How time marches on.'

'How do you know all this, Nora?' Dad asked, surprised, finally roused from his copy of *The Economist*.

'My family comes from that area,' she said with a shrug. 'I told you that, Gordon, you've forgotten. I knew it when I was young. But I expect it has changed a great deal since then.'

'I don't know how I feel about staying with complete strangers,' I said, worried. 'It was bad enough when I thought

I was staying at Charlie Ballintyre's house.' I glanced at Nora. 'How eccentric are they?'

'Don't be nervous. They were sweethearts, really, and there'll be other partygoers there. Besides, you'll only go there to sleep.'

I was only slightly comforted. It felt as though there was a whole new hurdle to cross, another obstacle to tackle. But Nora had promised it would be fun, and I had the feeling that going to this party was something I had to do. At the very least so I could wear my wonderful new dress, nestling in tissue inside its stiff paper carrier upstairs.

How marvellous, how marvellous, how marvellous.

As I travelled north on the train in the dank days after Christmas, my suitcase packed to the gills, a dress case for my ballgown and a bag for boots and shoes all safely stowed (*so much for one weekend!*), I was mentally rehearsing Nora's instructions. She had got quite carried away in the end, giving me no end of advice and information. I stared out of the window, saying 'how marvellous' under my breath every now and then and watching as the landscape grew rockier and more magnificent and the short day began to turn grey and purple. After I had changed train twice, spending a few hours in station cafes over cardboard sandwiches and instant lattes, it was getting dark when I finally arrived at the station nearest Ballintyre on the western edge of Scotland.

I staggered off the train, weighed down by all my luggage, into the freezing air of the darkening afternoon. The platform was empty except for a slender young man loitering at the station entrance. He had a mass of black hair, an intense dark gaze and a moody mouth, and he watched, smoking, as I disembarked and hauled my things down the platform. When I finally came up level with him, panting from the effort, I said, 'Excuse me, do you know where I can get a taxi?'

'Where do you want to go?'

I'd expected him to sound Scottish but his accent was more English than anything. 'I'm going to Tighglachach. Do you know it?'

'Yeah.' He threw down the end of his rolled-up cigarette and crushed it under the toe of his boot. 'You must be Helen.'

'Yes,' I said, surprised, as he began to take my bags from me. 'How did you know?'

'I'm Sebastian Drummond. I've come to collect you. Come on, the car's over here.'

I gaped at him as he strode off towards the car park. 'But how did you know when I was arriving?'

'Only one connection arrives at this time of day. You have to come on this train unless you set off last night and no one does that. Easy.'

I followed him to a battered old estate car, still bewildered by the fact he'd turned up to collect me. He slung my bags into the boot, not much caring what might be in them, before turning to face me holding a pair of old slippers. 'You might want these. The heating in the old banger isn't up to much.'

'Oh, er . . . no thanks. I don't think they're my size.'

Sebastian shrugged. 'They're probably not, but that doesn't matter. Still, your choice.'

I knew I didn't want to put on someone else's slippers, and didn't want to put them on even more, if that were possible, when I slid into the passenger seat, brushing a load of rubbish into the footwell first, where there was already a mass of newspaper, discarded food wrapping and empty plastic bottles. The car smelled powerfully of dog and I had a feeling that, before too long, my luggage would too.

Sebastian climbed into the driver's seat. 'There's a blanket in the back if you want it.'

'I'll be fine, thank you,' I said stoutly.

'You really won't. Scotland's cold.'

'I know.' I shivered slightly. The train had been cosy and the icy air outside had come as an unpleasant shock.

Sebastian started the engine. 'Take the coldest you think it can be, and double it. Then add some wind chill and frost.' He grinned at me. 'Let me know if you want those slippers.'

A moment later, we roared out of the car park and bombed down the road, taking the corners far too fast.

'I'm afraid it's a bit grim at home at the moment,' he called over the sound of the engine.

'Really?' I remembered Nora's remark about the family's eccentricity and felt anxious.

'The electricity went off this morning. Bit of a bore. Someone's overloaded something, I expect. The old place finds it hard to cope with a houseful when we're all charging phones and the rest. Dad thinks I've got some kind of cannabis farm in the attic and I'm using super strong heat lamps or something. I've told him it's just because he's too arsing tight to upgrade the system.' His black eyes slid across to me as if to see if I was shocked, but I wasn't particularly. I was thinking about my hairdryer, and said nothing.

We proceeded in silence for a while, leaving the small town and taking a road that ran between a loch and a huge hillside. I turned to observe the glorious scenery as we sped along the winding roads. In the splendid barrenness of winter, it was granite and grey, and the water of the loch had tints of khaki and charcoal as the colours leached away with the sun. In the distance a great ferry was ploughing slowly out towards the islands.

After a while Sebastian said, 'So, how do you know Charlie Ballintyre?'

'Well, I don't really, except that we're both students at Edinburgh. I was quite surprised to be invited actually. I went out with a friend of his last term, so that's the connection.'

'Ah. I thought you might be a friend of Hamish.'

'No. I don't know him.'

'Good. Hamish is a prize twat.'

'Oh. Is he?'

'Incredibly wet. He's got the biggest crush on my sister Daphne and for ages my greatest fear was that she would actually go out with him. She seemed to fancy him for a bit; they would sneak off at parties to do their pubescent experimentations on each other. He'd dance with her, panting all over her, grooving away like a dad. Thankfully she grew out of it, but he hasn't. Still goes all moony over her whenever she's around. Hamish hasn't got a chance now, thank God, she's got another bloke. He's staying with us now and if they don't stop pawing each other every five seconds, I'm going to be physically sick.'

'Hamish is younger than Charlie, isn't he?' I asked, trying to make sense of it all.

'Yeah, but they're pretty close in age. I think he's a student in London. If you're lucky, you might not meet him.'

'You don't seem to like him very much.'

Sebastian shrugged. 'Oh, he's all right. Just not my cup of tea. He's fine if you like soggy, wet blankets.'

I felt almost sorry for this Hamish. Sebastian's sneering made me wonder if Hamish was actually just a gentle, kind sort, the type who could make other men scornful. Perhaps Sebastian was even jealous of him. Didn't it work that way sometimes?

I would have to make up my own mind, if I ever did meet him.

With his eyes fixed on the road and one hand on the steering wheel, Sebastian scrabbled with the other in a pocket for a tobacco tin, which he deposited on his lap and opened, taking out a roll-up and putting it between his lips. Next he retrieved a lighter and sparked up the roll-up, releasing a plume of thick, pungent smoke into the car. I discreetly lowered my window an inch, shivering as the icy air came in, and we went along in silence, following the soft curves of the loch.

The afternoon light was almost gone and I was beginning to wonder how long we would be travelling and how much colder I would get – even starting to think positively of the grimy old slippers – when Sebastian took a sudden turn off the road, steering the car nimbly through a pair of pillars topped with lichened orbs, empty rusting hinges showing where gates had once hung.

'Here we are,' he announced as we followed a bumpy grass track past huge copses of pine trees and then turned at a high stone wall, before coming to a wide entrance in front of a large, square house, its rows of windows illuminated from within. The electricity was back on then.

'Tighglachach. It's a dump, but we like it.' Sebastian switched off the engine and bounced out of the car, tossing his cigarette end into a round ornamental pond with a fountain in the centre, which sat in the middle of the drive. He opened the boot and began unloading my luggage. I tried to get out of the car, only to find my feet had frozen into unwieldy blocks. By the time I had managed to get up and stamp some feeling back into them, he was taking my bags across the drive and through the front door of the house. I hurried after him, afraid to lose sight of him.

Inside, he was depositing my things onto the floor.

'I've got her,' he announced to no one. The interior of the hall was messy, crammed with objects – furniture, pictures, shoes, coats, bags, piles of newspapers and assorted bits and pieces scattered everywhere. Wherever I looked there were large glass cases of Victorian taxidermy: kestrels on the branches of trees, owls gazing through amber glass eyes, rabbits sitting upright on artificial moss, trouts, stiff and varnished, swimming motionless behind convex glass. In one enormous display, a fully grown fox stood outside a burrow, where other woodland creatures had been frozen mid-frolic, as though a spell had been cast on them. It was eerie. Only a vase of peach roses on the central table looked serene and alive. Sebastian waited, then shouted, 'Eve!' He glanced at me. 'She'll be here soon.'

He stalked off and I was alone in the musty-smelling hall, wondering what on earth I was to do and who Eve was. I took off my coat and put it on a chair. No one came, and I stood for some time, debating my next move. My phone had no signal, I couldn't even call a taxi to get back to the station. At last I ventured tentatively into the dark corridor Sebastian had disappeared down and peered into the gloom. There was silence. 'Hello?' Nothing. I tried again, louder. 'Hello?'

'Over here,' said a voice suddenly behind me, and I turned to see a girl standing in the hall, sulky faced and bored looking. She was around fifteen or sixteen, in jeans and a sloppy hoodie with enormous earrings dangling over her shoulders. Like Sebastian, she had dark hair, spiralled up into a messy bun at the back of her head.

'Ah! Hello.' I was relieved. 'Are you Eve?'

'I am actually,' she said crossly, as though I'd deprived her of a punchline. 'You're one of the Ballintyre guests.'

'Yes, I'm Helen.'

She shrugged. 'Come on.' She immediately set off and I scrabbled for my luggage and followed. She led the way up a staircase illuminated by a large hanging lantern and then along a corridor until we reached a door. 'Your room,' she said. 'The bathroom's over there.' She gestured across the hall as she opened the door for me. 'Come down when you're ready for a drink. Dad said six thirty.'

'Thank you.' I went into the room with my things, and turned round to ask her where I should go for the drink when the door slammed shut. She had gone.

For a moment, I felt indignant, even tearful. What kind of welcome was this? Then I swallowed, and laughed. Who cared? I was, at least, where I was supposed to be, and had a shabby but comfortable bedroom to myself. They weren't the most welcoming people in the world but I wouldn't let it spoil things. The main event was New Year's Eve, after all.

I thought of Nora. *Be brave*, she had said. *No matter what happens.* So, despite being alone, I smiled brightly and said airily to my empty room, 'How *marvellous*.'

Half an hour later, changed into a smart dress, I emerged into the corridor and retraced the earlier route until I found the staircase and started down it. As I descended I heard a rumpus and then a roar.

'You're all brats! Brats, do you hear? Especially you, Eve!'

'Fuck off,' came a shrill, fainter retort. 'You're a disgusting old man.'

'You little monster, come here and say that.' The speaker came into view as he lumbered across the front hall to pursue Eve. Then he saw me, looked up and spoke in a completely changed voice. 'Oh, hello. Are you a friend of Daphne?'

'No. I'm here for Hogmanay. I'm Helen.'

'Of course you are.' He was a huge man, with enormous, slightly stooped shoulders, a thatch of dark grey hair, a gingery beard and deep-set black eyes. His face was lined and craggy, and he was dressed in well-worn, rather stained clothes: a mustard waistcoat over a blue-checked shirt, baggy cord trousers and hiking boots. 'We've got a couple of others as well as you. One of them is a president of somewhere, would you believe. Very grand. Quite an honour. I'm looking forward to learning the ways of his country.' His eyes brightened and he beckoned conspiratorially. 'Come here, I must show you this, it's my newest acquisition.'

I followed him down the gloomy hall passage to a door, which he opened before turning on the light inside. 'There!' he said proudly.

I looked inside and saw an old-fashioned lavatory with a high cistern and a dangling chain. A speckled old mirror hung over the basin and the floor was littered with more piles of discarded shoes and boots, as well as a collection of cricket bats, tennis rackets and lacrosse sticks.

'Very nice,' I said, bewildered.

'I think it's my best yet,' he said proudly.

'Lovely,' I agreed, wondering what we were talking about.

'Isn't the pattern splendid?' he demanded. 'It's miraculous, if you ask me.'

I looked at the curtains at the window. They were striped, so not particularly patterned but what else could he mean? 'It's . . . very, very nice.'

He followed my gaze. 'Not that! *That!*' He pointed at something by the lavatory. 'That!'

A long, narrow strip of what looked like thin leather hung from a hook high on the wall almost to the floor; it was pale with an intricate pattern of black lines and diamonds running down it.

36

'It's a very fine specimen,' said my host, going to stand beside it and eyeing it with satisfaction. 'The bugger must have been eight feet long. Quite a beauty too, a big old solid Indian python. And look.' He pointed upwards to the top of the strip. 'See those holes? Two bloody great bullets, right in the head. Apparently a bloke came out to find the snake had swallowed his dog, so he got the gun and gave it two blasts in the skull. One would have done the trick. He must have been *furious.*'

'Oh,' I said faintly, trying to banish the gruesome mental image. 'Well, yes, understandable.'

Sebastian put his head around the door. 'You're not showing her the snakeskin, are you?' He looked over at me sympathetically. 'You'll have to excuse him, he loves doing that. You love to shock, don't you, Dad?'

He shrugged. 'It's worth seeing.'

'Absolutely,' I said, trying not to look at it.

'Come on, Dad, you're needed. The president's just arrived.'

I went after Sebastian, grateful for a familiar face, and his father followed us in turn, coughing noisily, until we reached a drawing room and went in. There were young people lounging about everywhere, or so it seemed. Eve was by the fire, lolling on a sheepskin rug, plugged into an MP3 player. On the sofa sat a girl who looked a little older than me, and was extremely beautiful. She had the family's trademark dark hair cut into a sharp bob, the fringe low over big black eyes that had a slight downward swoop at the edges and were heavily rimmed in liner and spiky lashes. She had pale skin and a slender elegance given character by a slightly kooky knock-kneed charm. She sat close to another young man on the sofa and was holding his hand and stroking his hair with great fondness; I guessed she must be Daphne, and the man must be the boyfriend that so irritated Sebastian. She did seem to be completely fixated on him. A boy who appeared to fit in age between Eve and Sebastian was sitting on the arm of the sofa, sketching in a large notebook, oblivious to everyone else. In the middle of the room, looking faintly surprised, was a man in immaculately casual clothes: a green cashmere sweater over a checked shirt and velvety rust-coloured cords, his fair hair carefully greased and flattened, his feet in a pair of black suede Gucci loafers.

'Ah, Your Excellency.' Sebastian's father went marching up to him, holding out his hand. 'Alastair Drummond. How do you do?'

'Good evening.' The man took the proffered hand and shook it with a smile. 'Arthur Bell. How do you do?'

'Bell, Bell.' Mr Drummond frowned. 'Now that rings something, can't think what . . .' Then he burst into huge guffaws of laughter at his own joke. 'Glad to see you here in our wet little country. You'll need to tell me something of your own place over dinner.'

'I came up from London today,' said Arthur Bell, trying to look unperturbed, but I could tell he was puzzled.

'A fine city,' said Mr Drummond heartily. 'I hope you found time to visit its many sights. Now, can I get you something from the grog tray? What's your poison? Gin? Wine? Sherry? I know – we'll have a Benedictine. Sebastian, get some drinks, will you?'

'Get them yourself,' retorted Sebastian, and left.

'Little shit. Children are ungrateful, aren't they? Don't have any if you can possibly help it, that's my advice – maybe too late, but that's your business.' He went over to the drinks tray on the sideboard and poured three measures of a spirit into rather dusty glasses and brought them over. 'Chin-chin!' He knocked his back in one, and coughed loudly before saying, 'I'd better not have too much of that, as I'm driving.'

'Where are you going?' I asked, wondering whether to sip the murky liquid in my glass. Mr Bell was sniffing his, frowning.

'I'm taking us all to Ballintyre, of course. For dinner.'

'I thought we were going tomorrow night,' I said, suddenly panicking I'd got things very wrong. It wasn't New Year's Eve yet, was it?

'That's for Hogmanay. Tonight, we're going for dinner. Get to know the crowd. Nothing fancy, according to Josephine – so that means the second-best silver and the Meissen with the cracks. I would happily give it all a miss but the children insist on going. We'll leave in five minutes when the other chap is here. Goodness knows where he is. I'll have to ring the bell if he doesn't come soon.' He cast a sideways look at his other guest and said, 'Not you, Bell, don't worry.'

'I've heard all the bell jokes, actually,' said Arthur Bell politely but Mr Drummond's attention was already taken by the door opening and the other guest arriving.

'Stand down! Here he is.'

I turned and saw Rollo walking towards me. In an instant I guessed it all. So, Nora had been right. He had arranged to stay in the same house as me and he must want to start things up again, just as she'd suggested. Despite myself, I felt a burst of satisfied pleasure. He must have remembered and missed my special qualities, and repented of treating me so horribly. I wouldn't let him close to me immediately but perhaps if he were very repentant and adoring, I might let him kiss me. He was very handsome, after all; I'd forgotten quite how handsome with his dark quiff and hazel eyes. I began to prepare a casual yet ever so slightly coquettish greeting.

But Rollo's smile faded as he saw me and then he did a not-so-subtle gaze around the room as if looking for someone else. 'Er . . . hi, Helen. I wasn't expecting to see you here.'

A nasty clammy feeling crawled over my skin as I readjusted all my ideas. Thank goodness I hadn't tried to be flirtatious. I said in as dignified a voice as I could muster, 'Hello, Rollo. I wasn't expecting to see you either. Charlie must have put us in the same house by mistake.'

Rollo was blinking quickly as if thinking it over rapidly. 'Um . . . yeah . . . I don't understand it . . .' He frowned. 'I mean . . . did Charlie actually *invite* you?'

'Yes, he did,' I said, a hot flush of embarrassment appearing on my face. 'Of course he did. I'd hardly be here if he hadn't.'

'But . . .' Rollo's frown deepened and he shook his head in bewilderment.

'Drink, young man?' interrupted Mr Drummond.

Rollo remembered himself. 'Yes, please, sir, that would be fantastic. Beer, if you have it.'

'I have but you'll have to drink it quickly. Or bring it with you. We're leaving sharpish. In fact, I'm off to get the bus now. Daphne, bring everyone out in five minutes, will you? And get this young man a beer!'

Daphne, in the middle of lighting a cigarette, nodded, and her father put his glass on the side and headed out. I was collapsing inside in an agony of mortification. What if everybody here thought I was a gatecrasher? I was definitely invited, I told myself firmly. I had an invitation upstairs. Rollo was just being cruel.

'So you two know each other, how nice!' said Arthur Bell, smiling enthusiastically.

'In a way,' Rollo said briefly, and pulled his phone out of his pocket. He flicked a gaze up at me. 'I still don't understand what you're doing here.'

My face was now scarlet. 'Well, I'm sorry if you're not happy about it.'

Rollo ignored me, clamped his phone to his ear and wandered off, out of the room entirely, not seeming to mind that he didn't have his beer.

'What a rude young man,' Arthur Bell remarked. 'You mustn't let him upset you. You've every right to be here. He won't speak to you like that again, not if I can help it.'

'You're very kind,' I said, feeling crushed and yet comforted. Then added quickly, 'I *was* invited, you know!'

'Of course you were, I never thought otherwise.' He leaned towards me and said confidingly, 'Don't let him see he's got to you.'

'Thank you.' I returned the smile weakly. 'I won't.'

41

Outside there was a strange roaring, rumbling sound. Daphne, hearing it, stood up and pulled her boyfriend up after her, the cigarette dangling from her scarlet lips. I could see now that she was wearing a tight black dress that stopped at the tops of her thighs, with fishnet tights and heavy black biker boots. I felt suddenly very prim in my silk navy dress with the sensible wool wrap and kitten heels.

'Come on,' she said to the room at large in a smoky voice. 'Time to go.' As the boy with the pad closed it and put down his pencil, Daphne wandered to the hearth rug and kicked Eve lightly on the leg. Eve pulled out her headphones. 'Come on, we're off.'

Sebastian put his head round the door to chivvy us along and I followed him out.

In the hall, Rollo was pacing about and talking furiously into his phone.

'No, not *her*, you idiot. I chucked her ages ago! I gave you Bella's number, you were supposed—' He cut off quickly when he saw us. I lifted my chin and tried to act as though I didn't mind at all, though my heart was sinking harder than ever. It was obvious that Rollo had thought this Bella would be waiting in the drawing room here at Tighglachach, because he and Charlie had cooked up a scheme, and Charlie had got it wrong. I was not meant to be at the party at all. It was a stupid mistake. No wonder he hadn't been able to hide his dismay at seeing me.

Oh God, what a humiliation. I wanted to run back upstairs and hide under the bed until it was all over. But I couldn't. Not only would Nora have killed me if I'd been such a coward but something inside me – perhaps helped by Arthur Bell's words – was turning my spine to steel. I wasn't going to let Rollo see how I felt. If I made him uncomfortable, then good. I bet he'd thought he'd never have to bother with me again, and now he did. All right then – fine. I'd see it through with spirit and not let him know how crushed I was.

With this in mind, I walked with dignity back through the hall and into the cold night air, picking up my coat as we went from where it still sat on a chair. Outside, the roar was louder and I could see from the light of the house that on the driveway was an ancient school bus, its engine thudding away as it idled there. In the driver's seat, I could just make out Mr Drummond. He hit the steering wheel and a loud, raucous horn sounded. 'Get in!' he yelled. 'All aboard!'

I followed Sebastian across the gravel, past the old fountain, and we climbed in. I chose a seat halfway along, pulling on my coat as I sat down. Rollo came on, studiously ignoring me, which was fine with me. He chose a seat near the back. Daphne and her boyfriend followed, her cigarette glowing in the gloom, and they nestled together on the back seat. When everyone was on, Mr Drummond shut the doors and off we went, the engine juddering so noisily there was not a chance of anyone being heard if they spoke, except Mr Drummond, who yelled at the top of his voice: 'Ballintyre, here we come!'

Chapter Three

When the old bus roared up the driveway of Ballintyre all I could see were its lighted windows and the large arched front door open to welcome us in. A moment later we were clambering off the bus and crunching over the gravel towards it.

Now I had finally arrived, I was gripped by shyness and hovered near Arthur Bell as we went inside, following in the wake of the exuberant Drummonds. We were in a grand hall with a Victorian tiled floor and stags' heads mounted above the doors. A large staircase lined with family portraits curled away upstairs and the sound of voices and music came from the various rooms leading off the hall. It was grand and intimidating where Tighglachach had been shabby and full of junk.

A woman in late middle age stood in the centre of the hall, ready to greet us, resplendent in a frilly purple dress, her grey-blonde hair fluffed out into a smart do, diamonds glittering in her ears and at her neck.

'Josephine, hello,' said Mr Drummond, as he lumbered up to her. He stopped short for a moment, as though suddenly overcome with shyness, before landing a hesitant kiss on one of her cheeks. 'You're very kind to invite us.' He had put on a jacket to smarten himself up but still looked very shabby in his boots and baggy cords.

She laughed but subtly pulled away from his embrace as if worried he might muss her up. 'Hello, Alastair, so lovely you could make it.'

'Of course we wouldn't miss a Ballintyre party. All the brood are here.'

'Under-eighteens are eating in the back, where there's a film showing,' Mrs Ballintyre said quickly. 'Eve, Sholto, you know where to go!'

Eve and the boy who'd been sketching in the drawing room at Tighglachach, who was obviously Sholto, scampered gratefully off.

'Daphne's brought her bloke, hope that's okay,' Alastair Drummond said, as Mrs Ballintyre blanched but smiled bravely, murmuring it was perfectly all right. 'And I brought the president, just as you wanted.'

'Arthur Bell.' The immaculate Arthur bowed over Mrs Ballintyre's hand. 'Charmed to be here, Josephine.'

'Delighted you could come, Arthur. Why is he calling you the president?'

'I'm afraid I've no idea—'

'You know me, Mrs B,' Rollo cut in. 'Hello, lots of love and I'm just going to find Charlie.'

'And this is . . .' Alastair Drummond frowned at me and then said triumphantly, 'Elsie.'

'I'm Helen Spencer,' I said meekly, and just stopped myself from curtseying as Mrs Ballintyre smiled, though her eyes were beady.

'Ah, yes, I remember you on the list. Welcome. You're a friend of Hamish's, are you?'

'Um, no, Charlie invited me.'

'Did he?' She looked surprised. 'Are you a friend of Sylla's?'

Cilla? Who's that? 'No,' I said, feeling like an imposter about to be unmasked. Desperate to get some provenance, I added, 'A friend of Rollo's.'

'Oh.' She still seemed incredulous. 'I see.'

Mr Drummond interrupted. 'Excuse us, Josephine, Ellie needs a drink and so do I. I have to process it all through the old liver before we drive home, so I need a double.' He leaned towards me as we walked away and whispered loudly, 'Ignore her. She's a gorgon.'

I smiled as I went into the drawing room behind him, but I felt depressed. I was a fraud, only invited here by mistake, and Mrs Ballintyre had spotted it. I should have realised, and refused the invitation. I'd known it was an error, I'd let myself be talked into it by Nora and Dad. And now I was going to look like a prize idiot. I took the very strong gin and tonic I was offered by someone with a tray, and loitered near the curtains, trying not to feel too intimidated by the crowd of sophisticated guests, some of whom I recognised from my time as Rollo's girlfriend but was far too shy to talk to. Everyone looked impossibly smart and confident and I wondered if I could actually hide inside the curtain and go completely unnoticed, perhaps for the entire evening. Instead, I pretended to be looking at the view, which was ridiculous as it was completely dark outside. I seemed to be getting away with it, though, until the boom of the gong sounded through the house and everyone began filing out of the drawing room. I followed them across the hall to the dining room, which was set up with a vast table laden with plates and cutlery. On a sideboard, hot trays held huge dishes of steaming food, where a tall, slender girl with poker-straight fair hair was removing lids and putting ladles into the dishes. Name cards on the plates showed where people should be sitting and I went along the table looking for mine.

'Oh *no*,' I said crossly, when I finally saw my name, right next to Rollo's.

'Sorry you're so disappointed.' It was a light, pleasant voice and I looked up to find myself staring into a pair of pale blue eyes under a thatch of brown hair. The face was unremarkable but attractive, with a long nose and a narrow mouth that was smiling at me. 'There's still time to switch the cards, you know, if you're desperate to escape.'

I looked at the name on the other side of my place. It was Hamish Ballintyre. I flushed. 'I didn't mean you. It's not you I want to escape. It's Rollo.'

He raised his eyebrows. 'Really? You've been put next to him on purpose so he can chat you up. Is he already dead in the water?'

'It's all a mistake. A complete misunderstanding. He doesn't want to talk to me and I don't want to talk to him!'

'Oh dear.' Hamish looked amused. 'Then we've got our-selves in a bit of a mess, haven't we? You'd better tell me all.'

Before there was time for that, Rollo appeared at my other side to stand by his plate. 'Hello again, Helen.' He looked bored and unhappy to see me.

I gave him a frosty nod, like a Victorian miss standing on her dignity. To my relief, another girl came and stood next to him. He could talk to her. She introduced herself as Penelope in a raspy, enthusiastic voice that seemed to indicate she'd be good, chatty company who would keep him occupied. A moment later, we were all sitting down and Hamish poured wine into my glass from one of the many bottles on the table, murmuring, 'I think you might need this.'

The meal was clearly informal, and people began lining up for plates of stew from the sideboard.

'Come on,' Hamish said, nodding towards the queue. 'Let's get some dinner.'

I realised, gratefully, that he intended to look after me and I followed him with relief. The blonde girl was still by the sideboard, helping to hand out plates and keep the queue moving along. 'There's bread in the baskets on the table,' she was saying as we filed past her. 'Help yourselves.'

'This is an amazing spread, Sylla,' Hamish said to her as we started to ladle the stew onto our plates.

'You're very kind,' the girl said with a smile. 'It's pretty standard but, you know, hearty.'

So that's Cilla. She's so pretty. I wonder who she is . . . His sister? No, that doesn't seem right.

Back at the table, Hamish worked to keep me occupied as we ate, asking me questions about Edinburgh and how I was finding university. I blossomed under his attention and gained confidence when he seemed genuinely interested in my answers. Sebastian had been so scornful about him, but he seemed very nice to me – kind and attentive, listening carefully to what I said, and asking questions.

'What about home?' he asked. 'Where's that?'

I told him about my mother living in America, thinking it was the most interesting thing about me.

'You never see her?' He fixed me with his intense, light blue eyes.

'Not since her wedding. She doesn't want me to visit. It upsets things for her with her husband. She emails me and we talk on the phone a few times a year – Christmas, birthdays, that sort of thing.'

'That's awful. I can't imagine a mother behaving like that.'

'Well, I'm not a baby anymore, so it's not so bad.'

'How old were you when she left?'

'Ten.'

'God.' He looked almost personally pained. 'That's shit, it really is.' He glanced down the table to where his mother was holding court, talking effusively to her neighbours. 'I can't imagine my mother ever doing anything like that. She could never have left us. After my dad died, I don't suppose she had much choice, but she never made us feel like it was a chore for her. She couldn't do enough to keep me and Charlie happy.'

I felt a pang of sympathy. 'I'm sorry to hear that – about your father.'

He was still just for an instant, then said in a slightly flatter tone, 'That's all right, you know. It was ages ago now, when I was seven. But thanks.' He smiled, cheery again. 'I'm going to get some seconds. Want some? There's shedloads. Sylla never knowingly under-caters.'

'Is she a friend of yours?'

'She's my brother's new girlfriend. An actress. And a bloody good cook. That's why I'm off to get some more before it runs out.'

By the time the main course came to an end, the conversation had moved up considerably in volume, fuelled by the wine that was disappearing at a startling rate. I hoped Mr Drummond was managing to resist.

'Smokers, *outside*,' Mrs Ballintyre called, waving her hands in the direction of a man who'd lit up, his eyes a trifle glazed. 'We won't be able to see a thing if you all start, let alone breathe!'

There was a general exodus outside, including Rollo and Penelope. Hamish was chatting to a friend who'd come over to say hello. I got up to help clear the plates, taking armfuls of them to where Sylla was serenely piling crockery on the edge of the sideboard.

'You're an angel, Sylla!' Mrs Ballintyre called from her place but she did not get up. 'Charlie's getting the pudding, isn't he? He's so clever!'

Sylla smiled at her, then at me as I brought over my load. 'Thanks for helping.'

'You're welcome. Where do they need to go?'

I followed her back through the house to the kitchen and then to a scullery where a flustered woman was loading two dishwashers with mountains of dishes and cutlery. Charlie was in the kitchen, shouting questions to Sylla as she helped to load and I scraped plates.

'Where's the cream? How much should I use? Where's the beater? Good God, how does this thing work? Where are the mixing bowls?'

'You wouldn't think he lives here,' Sylla said dryly between shouted replies. 'I've only visited twice.'

'He's bloody useless,' declared the other woman in a rich Scottish accent. 'Can't be bothered to learn either.'

'But he made the pudding?' I asked.

'Not exactly. He's whipping the cream.' Sylla winked at me. 'I don't think we've been properly introduced. I'm Sylla. Not like Cilla Black. Like the Scylla from Greek myth, but without the "c" because people kept calling me Skilla. My father's a Classics academic so he named me after an actual monster.' She laughed and shrugged. 'Thanks, Dad.'

'I'm Helen. Your name's much more interesting.'

'Ah, but you launched a thousand ships with your beauty, whereas I ate sailors alive. So I think you won as far as names are concerned.'

Just then Charlie bellowed, 'Come on then, it's ready!' and we were recalled to the dining room, where Charlie brought in the huge pudding topped with cream to much acclaim.

'Charlie, you're a miracle!' cried Mrs Ballintyre. 'Oh, it looks delicious! Isn't it marvellous, everyone? Isn't Charlie clever?'

During pudding, Hamish turned and talked to the girl on his other side, while Rollo remained lost in conversation with Penelope. Further down the table, I could see Sebastian and Daphne, and Mr Drummond deep in an intense talk with his neighbour. Mrs Ballintyre was laughing flirtatiously with a young man. More wine was needed. Somehow we'd sunk all those bottles and fresh supplies were demanded. I didn't mind having no one to talk to, it gave me a chance to look at all the people seated around the table and wonder who they were and what on earth I was doing having dinner with them, in the depths of Scotland, in a strange house with people I barely knew. I let the waves of noisy chatter wash over me, tasted the softness of cream on my tongue with the tartness of Scottish raspberries and the crunch of something almond along with them, and felt suddenly as though I was on the cusp of trans-forming into someone quite different, although who, I had no idea.

When the plates were empty, I got up to help clear again, feeling distinctly woozy myself and glad of the cooler air of the kitchen and scullery. Sylla was making big pots of coffee when Charlie came swaying in.

'Where's the bloody port, Sylla?'

'I think we finished the last lot. You'd better get some more.' She nodded her head over her shoulder and Charlie stumbled off in the direction she indicated. I left them to it, still feeling dazed and floaty, partly from the wine but also from something else: an obscure sense of destiny knocking on the door and wanting to be let in.

Back in the dining room, smokers were impudently lighting up from the candles, dropping ash into dirty pudding plates, and now the port was circulating.

'A game, a game!' proclaimed one of the girls, her eyes glittering with wine. 'We have to play a game.'

There was a chorus of agreement and a barrage of suggestions.

'Nothing where we have to write!' shouted Charlie. 'I'm too pissed!'

People laughed, while others shouted more suggestions.

'I know!' Penelope declared. 'We're going to play sardines. This house is made for it.'

This caused a lot of excitement. I wondered if Mr Drummond wanted to be getting back, but he seemed perfectly happy with the idea of us playing something.

'And with that,' Mrs Ballintyre said, rising in a stately way to her feet, 'I, and the other oldies, will retire to the drawing room for coffee and civilised talk. It's out of bounds to you youngsters. And so is my bedroom.'

The young men started up at once.

'Boo, Mrs B, you're no fun!'

'I want to hide under your cosy blankets!'

'Come and play with us, Mrs B, you know you want to.'

She seemed to revel in their drunken shouts. 'Naughty! Don't you dare. I shall see you all tomorrow night for the party. Don't drink too much and spoil yourselves for Hogmanay.' She went out, followed by the more sedate grown-ups, including Mr Drummond.

'Who's the sardine?' cried someone.

'We'll draw names from a hat,' decreed Penelope, and a piece of paper was found, all the names scrawled on it, and ripped into pieces that were thrown into a hat. 'Charlie better draw, as he's the king of the castle.'

Charlie dipped a hand in, rustled it and pulled out a scrap. He squinted at it. 'I can't read it.'

'Give it to me.' Penelope snatched it and stared for a moment before she said, 'Helen?' and looked around.

'That's me,' I said.

'You're the sardine.'

All eyes in the dining room turned to me and it felt as though I was being seen for the first time. It was uncomfortable, almost too much, as though the walk-on part had suddenly become the lead.

Hamish leaned over to me and murmured, 'Don't worry, there're lots of places to hide. Try the attics.'

'You've got ten minutes to find somewhere, then we come looking!' Penelope said, hamming it up to sound sinister. 'Off you go!'

I got up and slipped out of the room. I had only played sardines once before at a friend's house and I thought I remembered how it went: one person hides, the rest seek. When a seeker finds the hider, they squash into the hiding place as well, and it goes on in that way until the last person discovers the hiding place, which should now be full of closely packed bodies. Hence the name.

I have to find somewhere a lot of people can hide. I mean, a lot.

I could only think vaguely of under a bed somewhere. And I also felt an obligation to be a good sardine, who hid in a decent place and didn't get discovered too easily. But time was already running out. Soon the hordes would be on my tail. I needed to be tucked away somewhere before they burst out of the dining room.

I hurried upstairs and opened various bedroom doors, before retreating down a corridor. The bedrooms were off-putting, full of other people's possessions and too personal, with half-made beds and discarded clothing. I stood at the bottom of a small steep staircase that appeared to lead to the attics but they seemed too obvious. My time was running out.

On impulse, I ran downstairs to the kitchen, wondering if I could hide in the larder or the scullery. As I entered, I had a sudden flash of memory.

Where's the bloody port?

And I remembered Charlie walking drunkenly towards a bookcase by the sofa in a large recess of the kitchen that had been turned into a nook. And then, I had for a moment glimpsed him reaching out towards the bookcase.

I hurried over, and examined the bookcase. It looked normal enough. I ran my finger down the left-hand side and felt a catch there. I lifted it and the bookcase began to swing open towards me. Beyond was darkness but as the light from the kitchen hit it, I saw shelves inside holding dozens of bottles. It must be the wine store.

This was surely an excellent hiding place. There must be room for a dozen people inside.

I heard a raucous sound from the dining room and that decided me. I would find nowhere better. This was my hiding place. I slipped inside and pulled the bookcase shut behind me, making sure the catch was not quite closed.

Darkness descended and I felt suddenly nervous. It was musty in the wine cupboard but not overpowering. I reminded myself that I was still in the heart of the house, still connected to it all. And surely someone would come to get more wine before too long. Perhaps I didn't have to worry about the catch.

I sat down on the hard floor, wondering how long it would be before someone found me. Then the noise from outside got louder. The ten minutes were up. They were on the hunt.

Chapter Four

I don't know how long I waited alone in the dark of the hidden wine store. At first there was no sound at all and I guessed that the herd had dashed upstairs. Then they must have separated out into smaller groups and lone seekers, and I heard the occasional sound of footsteps and voices, or doors and cupboards opening as they looked for me. Sometimes I'd make out a shout:

'Where is she?'

'Have you found her?'

'No one's seen Bruno for a while, do you think he's found her?'

But no one came near the bookcase.

It seemed to go on for a very long time and I began to wonder if I'd been too clever. Perhaps I'd come out to find the Drummonds had left without me. I was on the brink of emerging when the bookcase door opened and a sliver of light broadened and hit my face. I blinked into it, blinded temporarily.

'So here you are!'

The next moment, someone was inside and the door was pulled shut, the latch clicking into place.

'You're a cunning one.'

It was Hamish, who sat on the floor beside me, his body warmth radiating out and making me realise I was cold in my silk dress, despite my wrap. Without seeing him, I was suddenly very aware of him: the smell of woodsmoke and wine, the musky sweetness of his skin under his shirt.

'So,' he said conversationally, 'how did you know about this place?'

'I saw it earlier when Charlie got the port. I hope it's okay to hide here.'

'It is, but it's a little too good a hiding place. I don't think anyone knows about it, except Charlie, and he won't think to look here. He's probably gone and had a lie-down by now anyway.'

'Whipping the cream probably took it out of him.'

Hamish chuckled and I felt a flare of pleasure at making him laugh.

After a moment I said, 'Sylla knows about it. The cupboard.'

'Yes. But I'm not sure she's all that into this game. She keeps herself apart a bit.'

'Perhaps she just doesn't like games.' After a moment I said, 'But you like her?'

'Oh yes, she's amazing. We all love her. Poor kid's alone with no family, and Charlie's become her knight in shining armour, rescuing her from the big bad world. Of course, it helps that she's stunning and a brilliant cook. But . . . I can't help wondering what she sees in old Charlie. I mean, of course, he's my brother and I think he's great, but he's very solid and ordinary in lots of ways. He likes nothing more than a party with his mates, getting shit-faced and ending up playing naked rugby. She's . . .' I could almost hear him frowning in the darkness. 'She's sort of arty. An actress. All about spirit and mood. Not like him.'

'Opposites attract,' I offered, feeling it was rather a lame response.

'I suppose they must, in their case. Lucky Charlie, that's all I can say. He'd better grow up and deserve her.'

I smiled into the darkness. 'I'm sure he will. All men go through their caveman stage, don't they?' I hoped I sounded wise and mature but added hastily, 'Although I'm sure you haven't.'

Hamish laughed. 'I'm not the caveman type at all. I don't like those crazed macho types – Charlie isn't really like that, only when he's pissed. I avoid alpha males. They hold no appeal for me.'

'Nor me!' I said heartily.

'Really? Well . . . that's good.' He paused. 'So. You and Rollo. What's going on there? It was like there was the Great Wall of China between you at dinner. I thought we were helping to hook you two up.'

'I'm the wrong person. I was supposed to be someone called Bella. Rollo's a bit cross about it, actually. He chucked me a while ago and I don't think he expected to see me again. I think Charlie must have got mixed up.'

59

Hamish laughed, his mirth growing as he realised the mistake. 'That's pretty rubbish for you but . . . it is funny.'

I started to laugh as well. He was right. It was ridiculous. 'And here I am,' I said ruefully. 'At a party where I don't know anyone and where, actually, I'm not really wanted.'

'Come on,' he said comfortingly. 'You know me. I'm glad you're here. There's only one person I'd rather be shut in a cupboard with.'

'Do you mean Daphne?'

A tiny pause and he said, 'How did you know that?'

'Sebastian said you liked her.'

'Did he?' He sounded a little cross. 'Well, he shouldn't shoot his mouth off. I don't know how he knows anyway.'

'He seemed to imply that everyone knows – you've been keen on her for years? First snogs and all that.'

There was a pause and I wondered if I'd hurt his feelings. Then he said with a slightly false jollity, 'Well, you know – it's not surprising. She's just your average perfect woman. Beautiful, intelligent, mysterious.'

'That's perfection?'

'Close.'

'Maybe she should make you laugh as well.'

'That doesn't go amiss.' After a moment he said, 'Daphne's funny too.'

'Oh good,' I said stoutly. 'So she is perfect after all.'

He laughed lightly. 'Yeah. Everything's great. Apart from the liking me bit. She's not too interested back, unfortunately.'

'Then maybe you should give up on her and look for something a bit less . . . perfect.'

Another strange pause melted into the darkness. I was flirting, but why, I didn't quite know. Hamish was attractive but he hadn't instantly appealed to me. He was keen on someone else and had shown no interest in me. But he'd been kind at dinner when he didn't have to be, and he had gone looking and actually found me where no one else had. And something about sitting so close to one another in the velvety blackness was creating a bond between us. That, and the warmth radiating from his skin and the scent of his jumper close to me.

'I don't know,' he said quietly. 'My dad always told me to hang on for what I really wanted.'

'Then it's a question of what you really want. Once you know what that is, you're sorted. Sounds simple when you put it like that, doesn't it?'

'Yeah.'

After a moment I said softly, 'I'm sorry about what happened to your dad.'

'That's okay. It was years ago. A car smash on the loch road.'

I hugged my knees tight to me, my breath coming short in my chest, hoping I wasn't being insensitive. 'Tell me about him.'

He was silent and I wondered for a moment if I'd gone too far, but then he started talking as though the blackness enabled him to say things that would have been impossible in the light.

'God, I miss him. Dad was one in a million. A hero, you know? I suppose every boy thinks his father is a hero, but mine was. He could do anything, and he filled our lives with adventure and fun. And he was a lucky bastard, right up to the end, when his luck ran out. When I was little, it looked like we were going to lose everything, including this place. Charlie and I heard my parents arguing at night when we were supposed to be asleep, so we knew what was going on. We were going to leave our schools, sell Ballintyre and move somewhere else. Then, just when it was all going to shit, something happened. A shower of gold or something, and we were saved. Everything was okay. Jam for tea. The thing was, something had changed, I could feel it, but I never knew what it was. Dad took me for a walk once, out around the fairy glen, and he tried to talk to me about something but I was too dense, too young, to take it in. I remember plain as day he said to me, "I'll talk to you about it when you're older, Hamish, then you'll understand." So I relaxed and thought, *Yeah, I'll find out later.* As long as my world carried on the same way, as long as I could follow the football score and the test matches, everything was okay. And then, bam. He was dead.'

'In a car accident.'

'Banal. Avoidable. The roads here can be treacherous, because they're so empty. People speed along as though they're on a private racing track. Add in the hairpin bends, some darkness, an icy road . . .'

'So it was nearby?'

'On the road to Loch Fyne. Late at night. Christ knows where he was going.'

'That's terrible, I'm so sorry.'

Hamish's voice dropped low. 'I woke up because there was a blue light flashing on my bedroom wall. I looked out of the window and there was a police car down there, and then Mum was in a total state, getting dressed, and Sian, our housekeeper, turned up to look after us while she went to the hospital – bloody miles away. All I could think was, *What about the football?* Dad was supposed to be taking me to a match that day. What about the football? I was sadder about missing that than the fact he was in hospital. Kids are so selfish.'

I put my hand out and touched his arm. 'You were only little. You couldn't have understood.'

'Maybe.' He sighed. 'He was gone anyway. Everything changed again. It's just been us and Mum ever since.'

'You should be proud of yourselves for coping so well. I'm sure your dad would be proud of you too.'

I sensed him turn towards me. 'Thanks.'

'You're welcome.'

After a moment, he said in a changed voice, 'Well, that was depressing! And I don't think anyone's looking for us. Let's get out.'

He went to push the door open but the catch had dropped. 'Oh. Oh shit.'

'What?'

'We're stuck.'

'Can't you push it open from the inside?'

'I don't think so.' He sat back down and said in a jolly voice, 'Well, it looks like we're here for a bit longer. We can't even open a bottle without a corkscrew.'

'That's okay. If we drink, we'll only need the loo,' I said, feeling a little worried in case that happened. 'Can you try your mobile phone?'

'If it wasn't on the dining room table, I would, even though it wouldn't work in the cupboard. Phones at Ballintyre only work out on the drive, pointed east with a fair wind in daylight hours. Another joy about living in the wilds of nowhere.'

'Mine's in my bag – also in the dining room.'

'Well then, let's get comfortable. Once someone comes to the kitchen, we can start banging on the door till they let us out. Squeeze up. I'll keep you warm.'

I edged towards him, a tiny squirm of excitement in the base of my stomach at our enforced intimacy. He put his arm around me. He was warm and comforting, and I inhaled the smoky sweet smell in his clothes and closed my eyes. He started to talk, a long story about something that had happened in London the previous term. I listened and my head grew heavy against his shoulder. I rested more against his solid warmth and felt strangely peaceful. My eyelids drooped with the combined effect of wine at dinner, the dark and the low buzz of his voice. I began to slide in and out of sleep and then suddenly I was awake: a click, a presence, the snap of a light switch and the room flooded with musty yellow light from a bare bulb overhead.

'Here you are,' said a soft voice. 'I did wonder.'

It was Sylla.

'Come on in, turn off the light,' Hamish said as I blinked in the sudden glare. 'You're supposed to hide with us now.'

Sylla was a silhouette against the bright kitchen beyond. 'The game's over, I'm afraid. They all got bored after twenty minutes, and now there's a game of strip poker in the library and a sing-song in the music room.'

'Drunkards,' Hamish said with a laugh. 'Can't concentrate for long enough to find us.' He stood up and helped me to my feet.

'There is that.' Sylla smiled at me. 'And more to the point, the Drummonds are about to leave. You'd better hurry, Helen, or you'll miss your lift.'

I had a sudden sense of wanting to stay where I was, with Hamish and Sylla, but that was quickly overtaken by a need to find the others and not delay their return to Tighglachach. 'Yes, I'll find them now.'

'You rescued us,' Hamish said heartily as we stepped into the kitchen. 'I thought we might be stuck all night.'

'Yes, thank you, Sylla,' I said, looking up almost bashfully into her navy eyes. 'Everyone else forgot us.'

'Not me,' she said lightly. 'I don't like loose ends. I couldn't really relax until I knew you were okay.'

When Hamish and I entered the drawing room to a few rowdy cheers and catcalls from the people on the sofas, I saw that Daphne noticed us at once, her black eyes going quickly from Hamish to me and back again. Mr Drummond came in, rounding us all up for the return trip.

'There you are, Elsie!' he bellowed. 'Apparently you've spent the evening in a cupboard, you strange girl. Come on, we're going home in the bus, so chop chop – off you go and get on board. Your friend Rollo isn't coming, he's staying here tonight.'

'See you tomorrow,' Hamish said with a grin.

'If we make it back in one piece,' I replied, and went to get my coat for the journey back to Tighglachach. Daphne stared at me as I went.

I woke the next morning in my bare bedroom at Tighglachach, a wintry light creeping between the gap in the heavy curtains, my mouth a little dry and eyes a bit heavy. It was not exactly early but I couldn't hear any noise from the rest of the house. I went to the window, opened the curtains and gazed out over raggedy gardens, a high stone wall, fir trees beyond, and a shimmer of water through the green. In a moment, I'd decided. I dressed quickly and, boots in hand, tiptoed downstairs, although the house was still shrouded in sleepy silence. I found the room where we'd had drinks the previous evening and, just as I'd remembered, there were French windows leading out to the gardens I'd seen from my window. Outside on the chilly terrace, I shivered, pulling on my boots, and wrapped my coat tight around me before putting on my gloves. It was cold, biting and hard, and I was glad of the scarf and hat Nora had advised me to bring, as I set off towards the outer edges of the garden and the flash of water I'd seen from upstairs. A rackety wooden door almost bare of its peeling green paint stood ajar in the wall and, once through it, I was out into a wilderness of high, dry brown grasses that were brittle, sapped carcasses of their old summer selves, and dark copper ferns with slimy wet roots, cut with bare pathways that had been tramped through them over the years.

I passed a long, low stone building with dusty windows thick with cobwebs within, rubbish and detritus in the scrub outside it, and wondered what it was and why it was so neglected, and then the path led gently downhill and I found I was approaching the curved horseshoe of a small cove. A stream led from the edge of the hillside along the sandy, pebbly and shell-thick beach to join the loch, its water dark brown, almost bronze. Rims of black seaweed along the beach showed where the tide had washed up. The dark grey water spread out before me, opening up into a huge vista that ended in the misted shapes of distant hills almost lost in lowering cloud. A brisk bitter wind cut across the water and into my coat and gloves. I stamped my feet, and puffed out cloudy breaths. It was beautiful but more than bracing. I marched around the beach, looking at the washed-up scallop and oyster shells, far too many to count. Then the view took my attention again, the sky now a haze of purples, greys and the faintest lilacs as the sun climbed a little higher.

'It's beautiful,' I whispered. 'I've never seen anywhere so lovely.'

I wondered what it must be like to live with such beauty all the time. Did one get used to it? Bored with it, even? How was that possible? Surely it was easy to spend a lifetime just looking at the changing skies and the endless variations of light and colour.

'Hi there!' A figure was standing on the top of the hill, silhouetted against the pines behind. 'Do you want some breakfast?' it yelled.

I recognised Sebastian.

'Yes!' I roared back, and started towards him.

As we headed up the hill to the house, he said, 'So, where were you last night? You vanished.'

'I found a very good hiding place.'

'You must have. Dad said you were in a cupboard?'

'The wine cellar cupboard. Sylla found me in the end.'

'And Hamish.'

'Yes.'

Sebastian's black eyes slid towards me. 'Don't go falling for the Ballintyre charm, will you?'

I laughed. 'Of course I won't. But why not? What's wrong with it?'

'The whole of Ballintyre is fake. And I told you,' he said roughly. 'Hamish is an idiot.'

'He seemed all right to me. Quite nice actually.'

'That's the way it works.' Sebastian was frowning at the grass as we tramped through it on our way back to the garden. 'You girls. You either like the arrogant shits, or the weak ones who let you walk all over them – and you can't see that even though you think you're in charge, really they're just sucking the life out of you.'

I looked at him, surprised. He seemed very young for this kind of cynical wisdom about what girls wanted. 'That's a bit sweeping, isn't it? We can't all be the same! And there must be more types of men than that.'

'There are. If you open your eyes.'

'Ones like you,' I said, a little mockingly, but I was indignant to be so easily dismissed.

He shrugged. 'Maybe. I could be the arrogant shit type. I probably am. I can just see things quite clearly, that's all. I can see it all clear as day.'

'How handy for you.'

He seemed not to have heard me. 'Take Daphne. There's no way she would be interested in Hamish, he's far too dull for her, even though he'd probably suit her. She likes that other idiot instead but anyone can see he'll dump her because she won't pony up what he needs.' He shot me a look. 'You're the same. You don't want what you think you want.'

'Enlighten me further, oh guru,' I retorted. 'What's wrong with me? Do you think I'll go for either you or Hamish?' I could believe he was arrogant: how could he not be, with those dark good looks and obvious charisma? Hamish, though . . . From what I'd seen, he had warmth and kindness and if that was a weakness, it was the kind of weakness I thought should be valued, like the ability to cry or feel or empathise. The sort of weakness that was often really strength in disguise.

Sebastian shot me a look that was almost angry. 'No, I don't think you'll go for me. You're two years older than I am, for a start.'

I laughed again, which seemed to make him even more furious.

'All right,' he snapped, 'go for it with Hamish and see what happens, that's all.'

'I'm not interested in Hamish,' I said loftily, and we walked on in silence. But I was aware that wasn't true. My heart raced with pleasing excitement when I thought about him, and our time in the intimate darkness of the cupboard played itself over again in my imagination.

Back at the house, we went straight into breakfast. Eve and Sholto were already there squabbling.

'But I knew it would be good weather because of my spell,' Eve was saying as she shovelled cereal into her mouth at a furious rate. 'It always works.'

Sholto was rolling his eyes as I took my seat and reached for toast from the rack. 'Yeah, right. All the little pixies come along and sort it out.'

'What's the spell? It sounds useful,' I said politely.

Eve looked over at me as if registering my presence for the first time. 'The day before I want good weather, I get the statue of St Swithun, which Dad keeps in the alcove at the bottom of the stairs, take him outside, decorate him with flowers and sing a special bidding song to beg for fair weather – because he's the patron saint of weather. Dad got him to guard against storms on the loch. Then I leave him out all night and take him a nice hot cup of tea in the morning. And we always have sunshine after that.'

Sholto looked up from his coffee. 'Guess what, he's also the patron saint of the mentally ill, so that's two birds with one stone for you, isn't it, Eve?'

'Shut up, shithead, no he isn't,' she rejoined. Then smiled at me. 'It always works.'

'That sounds very impressive.' I buttered my cold toast, wondering if Rollo had come back from Ballintyre and if he had stayed away to avoid me. Just then, Daphne came in, striking in a huge red velvet dressing gown and trainers, her black hair mussed, her eyes smudgy and sexy with slept-in eyeliner. Even her yawns were elegant and when she lit a cigarette over her toast and marmalade, it looked sophisticated rather than seedy. My spirits swooped as I remembered how Hamish considered her his perfect woman. How could I compete with her? But, I consoled myself, as Daphne's boyfriend sauntered over, draped himself over her and kissed her thoroughly despite her mouthful of toast, she wasn't interested in him and that meant, surely, that I had a chance.

'I'm too tired to party tonight,' Daphne announced, yawning again.

Arthur Bell was standing in the doorway, incredibly neat and well turned out again in glossy bright cords – pink ones this time – and a bright green jumper over a red checked shirt. 'Surely you'll have time to recuperate before this evening!' he said in a jolly tone, going over to an empty place at the table. 'You won't want to miss the party, Josephine is going to make it a truly wonderful affair.'

'Don't worry about Daphne,' Sebastian said. 'She comes awake as the sun goes down, like a vampire.'

His sister made a face and then said, 'You're right. So we're going back to bed.' She took her lover by the hand and they strolled out together.

'We all hate Daphne's boyfriend,' Eve said vehemently once they were out of the room.

'What's his name?'

She shrugged. 'We never bother to find out. We hate them all equally no matter what. Not that it matters, as she chucks them once she's had her fill.'

'She really is a vampire,' Sebastian said darkly.

'She abandons their bloodless corpses to the rubbish tip,' Sholto said in a low voice, leaning towards me. Despite myself I felt a strange chill as he said it. No doubt Daphne enjoyed playing up to her own Gothic looks – the black hair, red lips and pale skin – but there was something a little discomforting in the way her siblings talked about her. 'Once she's drained them dry.'

'Ah, the original vamp!' Arthur Bell said, getting himself a bowl from the pile on the table. 'That, of course, was the name of the femme fatale of the early silent cinema. Theda Bara was, famously, the vamp . . .'

He was off, talking happily and not caring if we were listening. I poured myself a cup of coffee and slipped away to my room.

The rest of the day passed quietly, and I kept apart, losing myself in my thoughts and anticipating the evening. Yesterday I had seen Rollo and thought I was destined for embarrassment and misery. Now, I was full of a simmering excitement and wondering what might happen. I lay dreaming on my bed, remembering the cupboard and everything we said in it. In the early afternoon, after a light lunch, I started my lazy preparations for the coming night, beginning with a soak in the bath across the hall from my room. Once I got out, I realised I was feeling a little trembly and nervous about the evening.

What on earth do I think will happen? I asked my reflection in the dressing table mirror as I sat down in my underwear to do my make-up. My fingers shook slightly as I rubbed foundation into my pale face. *I barely know Hamish. I've only met him once. I'm working myself into a state over nothing.*

But I wasn't trying to work myself up – this odd state of apprehension was just happening. My nerves seemed to be jumping and twitching under my skin as though my subconscious was aware of something I was not, like a dog sensing an approaching storm. I concentrated on my make-up, painting thick black lines of liquid liner across my lids and into bats' wings, then coating my lashes with mascara until they stood out spikily, bringing my hazel eyes to life. My eyes were my best feature. My nose was too long with a bump in the middle from a childhood fall, and my chin was too short, but I knew that emphasising my eyes and making my brows thick and full would draw attention away from my flaws. I blasted my hair with the dryer, then let it cool around the curling brush so that it fell in soft brown waves. Then I gathered it up and pinned it back to fall over my shoulders, leaving my neck bare.

'You'd better borrow these,' Nora had said and gone to one of her treasure chests. 'Let me see. Yes.' She'd taken out a velvet pouch, tipped it up and let a rippling river of pearls drop into her hand. 'You'll need pearls. Be careful of these, darling, they're real. They were my mother's.' Then she'd

73

pinned them round my neck, where they glowed. 'And something for the ears. Emeralds, I think. Not real this time, but no one will know, they look very convincing. They're Edwardian paste for some lady trying to pass herself off as richer than she really was. If anyone asks, they were an eighteenth birthday present from your godmother.'

I held them up to my ears now, and slipped them through the lobes. They glittered, the green matching the lights in my eyes.

I have nothing to be afraid of. It's going to be all right.

I descended the staircase, Southern Belle style, in my black velvet gown. Sebastian, who was loitering at the bottom in a dinner jacket, bow tie and tartan trousers, looked up and his expression changed when he saw me. 'You look very nice,' he said shortly, in a way that I took to be quite a compliment.

'Thank you. Are the others ready?'

'They'd better be. We're leaving as soon as Dad gets down.'

'Did Rollo come back?'

'Charlie drove him over to collect his stuff this afternoon, then he went to Ballintyre. I think he's jumped ship.' Sebastian shrugged. 'I can't blame him, who wants to deal with the insanity here, when you can live in luxury at Ballintyre?'

'I like it here,' I said stoutly, deciding I wouldn't tell him the real reason that Rollo had left. 'It's got character. And charm.'

'It's utter bedlam.'

'I like your trousers. Are they your family tartan?'

'Yes. And they're called trews.'

74

Just then, the thud of footsteps on the stairs announced Mr Drummond and he appeared in full rig: lace at his throat, a bottle-green waistcoat with brass buttons, a kilt in the same tartan as Sebastian's trews, with a swinging sporran. He had high socks and gaiters, a knife tucked into one by his knee.

'Aha!' he roared, as he came down, his kilt rippling with every step. 'We are ready to party! It's Hog-ma-bloody-nay! Is everyone here? Well, look at you! You're a little stunner, Elsie. Promise me a foursome later?'

'It's a dance,' Sebastian said with a laugh, seeing my expression. 'The foursome reel.'

Mr Drummond was already heading out of the front door, no doubt to collect the school bus.

'Where are the others?' I asked, looking around the hall, its collection of glass-eyed creatures staring back at me.

'They'll be here.' Sebastian went to a huge gong hanging by the stairs, picked up a stick and banged it hard so that the air was full of thrumming noise. 'Get a move on!' he yelled.

Then he came up to me and said loudly, to be heard over the gong, 'I've got some champagne for the bus. Come on.'

We were the first aboard the bus, and we sat at the back while Mr Drummond shouted at everyone else to get a move on. Sebastian popped the cork of the champagne, which was inaudible under the roar of the engine, and poured out fizz into plastic glasses and handed one to me. I sipped it, feeling reckless. Champagne in the driveway, sitting in an antique bit of junk not dissimilar to an old lawnmower, before the party had even started? I giggled. I had not imagined this in all my daydreams of what this night might be like.

'It'll keep you warm in any case,' Sebastian said, gulping his. 'Though you can have my jacket if you get really cold.'

'Thanks.' I sipped more of the champagne. 'This is lovely.'

The others started climbing aboard, though I couldn't see them in the darkness, and then we were off, roaring along the loch road to Ballintyre. The house, when we saw it, was a riot of light. The drive had been illuminated by torches all the way up and the outside was festooned with fairy lights. My excitement grew. This was it. The point of all this planning and anticipation. It was New Year's Eve and I felt as confident as I could that I looked good.

I could almost hear Nora's voice in my ear: *Now, don't be frightened, just enjoy yourself. Relax. Have a wonderful time.*

Chapter Five

The house showed no sign of the ravages of the previous evening. It was polished and beautiful, with large flower arrangements in every room, all the fires lit, everything glowing and perfectly in place. Sebastian was right: it was luxurious here at Ballintyre, all softness and frills and sparkling cleanliness. I was sure Mrs Ballintyre would never allow dusty boxes of stuffed rabbits and strips of snakeskin. I could see that she ruled it all with strict discipline. She stood again in the hall to greet her guests, but this time resplendent in a striking red silk ballgown, a tartan sash draped across her chest and pinned with a glittering brooch. A tiara glimmered in her grey-blonde hair, which was set in big hairsprayed waves with the ends flicked out. New arrivals went to greet her with air kisses, which she accepted graciously, turning a powdered cheek first one way and then the other.

Perhaps it was the champagne and the effects of the bumpy ride, but I felt only half present as I went up with the

Drummonds to say my hellos. The other half of me floated above, watching proceedings with interest and laughing that here I was, in this beautiful house, wearing a velvet gown, like something from a film.

'You scrub up all right,' said someone cheerfully, and I saw it was Penelope, the girl on the other side of Rollo last night. She looked exactly the same except that she'd brushed her hair and put on some bright pink lipstick. Her dress was a short plain green number and she had flat shoes on. I worried at once that I'd made too much of an effort, but Penelope chattered on, dragging me off to get a drink from one of the waiters in the drawing room, so I followed her, trying to relax. While we were standing as near to the fire as we could get, sipping on our champagne, I saw Sylla come in. She looked like a dream in a silver 1920s-style dress of sequins, chiffon and fringing, her fair hair tucked to look like a bob and a silver band around her forehead. Charlie was not far behind, his dinner jacket too tight across his shoulders, his cheeks already pink, slurping from a glass of champagne as he went. Then I saw Hamish and my stomach flipped again and burned with that strange nervousness. He was wearing a kilt in the same green and plum-coloured tartan that Mrs Ballintyre wore as a sash, a sporran of white fur sitting jauntily in the centre, and a dark jacket like Mr Drummond's but in velvet, cut high at the waist with brass buttons. I thought he looked wonderful. He saw me, but only for a second and then he was lost in the crowd. I talked to Penelope and sipped my drink slowly to make it last. Then suddenly, he was beside me, smiling, his blue eyes warm.

'Hello, you look nice.'

'Hello, thanks so much.' I tried to seem sophisticated, blasé and completely at home, rather than the overawed bumpkin I felt. I also didn't want him to register the way his presence made me shaky with a mixture of nerves and excitement.

'Very nice. Do you want a top-up?' He held out a bottle of champagne. 'I took this off one of the waiters. They looked like they could do with a hand.'

'I'm fine, really.' I gripped my glass tightly to hide my shaking fingers. 'How are you?'

'All the better for seeing you. I like your dress.'

'Thank you. And I like your kilt.'

'I've got the full works on.' He gestured to his sporran. 'Three cats gave their lives for this. Only kidding, it's not real. Are you looking forward to the dancing later?'

'I'm a bit scared. I've never reeled before.'

'I'll give you a turn if you like. It's easy once you get the hang of it.'

'That's what people say about skiing and horse riding too. They also break their necks attempting it.'

He laughed. 'I'll make sure you don't get hurt. I'll make it go like a dream.' His expression changed suddenly and I followed his gaze to see that he was looking at Daphne, who was standing across the room, laughing with a group of guests. It was the first time I'd seen her not in the dark of the bus, and she looked exquisite in a low-cut figure-hugging red dress and black satin peep-toe shoes, her hair glossy and her lips scarlet. Her eyes were heavily kohled and her lashes were so long I suspected she had false ones on. She looked like a Hollywood pin-up.

'The perfect woman,' I said in a low voice.

'Well.' He grinned at me. 'Perfect-ish. You're a close contender.'

'Oh – er . . . thanks?' I looked at him but his gaze had gone back to Daphne.

'Excuse me a minute,' he said, 'I ought to go and say hello. See you later for a dance.'

And he was off, weaving through the crowd towards her. I turned back to the fire and Penelope, determined not to show I cared.

In contrast to the previous evening, the dining room was formal and lavish. The table was laden with gleaming silver, crystal and china, candles glowing and porcelain vases filled with flowers. On the sideboard, bottles were nestled into huge ice buckets or standing in neat rows. Waiters in black waistcoats stood at the edges of the room staring into space until they were needed.

These people are rich, I thought with astonishment. It made me think of a very smart hotel Dad and Nora had taken me to for my twenty-first, no doubt at Nora's suggestion, and I had a feeling the gold watch I got for my present was her idea too. The hotel had been luxurious in that discreetly lavish way: nothing overdone but everything of the highest quality from the heavy linen napkins to the delicate tea-spoons. We had been waited on attentively, and treated like royalty, and it had been a pleasant, affirming kind of experience that made one feel worthy of one's place in the world.

No wonder people like Nora, like the Ballintyres, had so much self-confidence. Their worlds shaped around them for their comfort, so it was no surprise they were sure of their worth. I found it dizzying; beautiful but overwhelming. I followed the others, looking for my name, and there it was on a card held up in a tiny silver pineapple: Miss Helen Spencer. I mattered too. I was like them tonight. I had the sudden and overwhelming feeling that this evening was a kind of hinge on which my life would turn. Last night I'd felt as though destiny were pushing me towards a door. Now Fate seemed to be looking down from her wheel, staring directly at me and nudging me through it with her finger. The idea made my innards clench. It was all very well to be noticed by Fate, but it didn't guarantee happiness. As well as the Hollywood hoofers who get their chance of stardom or the lottery winners who scoop a jackpot when Fate takes a hand, there are the unlucky ones who step in front of a bus, or who stand on the edge of a cliff at the same moment as a landslide occurs. Fate is not always kind.

Ouch.

Another nasty sensation gripped my stomach as I took my seat. I tried to take my mind off it by looking at all the accoutrements on the table, things I'd never seen before: silver-topped crystal jugs of red wine, tiny pots of mustard with miniature ladles, bowls of salt, silver pepper pots, pretty sauce boats of gleaming jus, and, most oddly, silver birds standing here and there on the table, as though pecking at the damask tablecloth. I was disappointed to see that Hamish was far away, hidden by a vase of flowers, although, to my

81

relief, Rollo was nowhere near either. In fact, he was next to Daphne and was already talking animatedly to her cleavage, though I knew he didn't have a hope there with her boyfriend on the other side of her. I had a young boy on my right, sitting very straight next to his mother and obviously at his first proper evening party, while the space to my left was empty. Next to that was perhaps the oldest lady at the party, hunched over with age but with bright eyes and a flashy silver dress that showed she was up for having fun.

Just as I was watching her attacking her glass of white wine with gusto, the chair next to me was roughly pulled back and Sebastian slid into it, smelling of cigarette smoke, his bow tie already askew.

'Christ,' he murmured, looking across me to the boy on my right and then to the lady on his left, 'when you're with the grannies and the children, you're either as boring as they are, or so charming the host basically thinks you'll be their entertainer for the evening.'

I was glad to see him. He would keep my mind off Hamish and the party later. 'Well, I hope we're the entertaining ones.'

'I am.' He fixed me with a smoky black gaze. 'I'll let you know about you later.'

We began to talk, Sebastian oblivious to the lady to his left, and me blatantly ignoring the boy on my other side who had his mother next to him in any case. The waiters put our starters in front of us, poured wine into our glasses and the meal began: scallops on pea puree with curving pea shoots to decorate it; Scottish venison with scallion potatoes, carrots and parsnip fondant. Sebastian told me about his life at art school.

'Though I'm not really the talented one. That's Sholto. But I can't think of anything else to do for now, so I'm having a shot at conceptual art. A trainer in a bin. A light switch connected to a bird cage. That sort of thing.' He shrugged. 'I quite like it. God, I want another fag.'

'You'd better not, I think Mrs Ballintyre wouldn't like it.'

'Fuck her,' he said, 'she's a pompous old gasbag.' But he stayed. I warmed to him as he talked on, asking me sometimes about what I was studying and why. He was very good-looking, a male version of Daphne, and though I knew he was a couple of years younger than me, I was beginning to like his sulky, flirting ways and was flattered he wanted to direct them at me. He was straightforward, I could tell. He had no airs about him, and no sense of pomposity. He might at times seem arrogant but he was not stuck-up.

The atmosphere was more formal than the night before, but as the contents of people's glasses disappeared, refilled and disappeared again, the mood relaxed and the volume rose. Mrs Ballintyre was in gracious hostess mode, overseeing the bounty of her table, talking to her neighbours with the poise of a head of state. Pudding came: an iced nougat with raspberries; then cheese and biscuits, then fruit, then, to my surprise, hot oysters in bacon on toast.

'A savoury,' said Sebastian. 'A little touch of Victoriana.' He rolled his eyes. 'Typically pointless.'

'Haven't we eaten enough?' I said, eyeing the savoury, my stomach gurgling unhappily at the weight of food. I had only nibbled at pudding and barely managed a biscuit but still felt stuffed. I could not inflict oysters on it now.

'Of course, it's just showing off. It's always a big act here.' Sebastian sighed.

'Do you know this place well?'

'I've been coming here since I was a kid. I hate it. You'd think I'd prefer it to the dump we live in but I don't. It doesn't feel real to me, that's why.' He nodded towards Mrs Ballintyre. 'I think it's her. She's the one who's added all the fringes and tassels and velvet and fancy stuff. It wasn't like that before. That's because she's not really part of it.'

I felt suddenly alien. If Mrs Ballintyre wasn't a part of it, how much more of an outsider was I? How could I ever hope to belong in a place like this, when it was all so mysterious to me? And yet, I found it enchanting: the beautiful house, the amazing scenery, the chill in the air.

Sebastian, not noticing, said, 'I'm really gasping now. Come out with me?'

He stood up, picking up his wine glass. I hesitated for a few seconds, then followed. The next moment we'd made our way out of the dining room, through the drawing room and out through the French doors to the terrace. It was freezing outside after the stifling warmth of the house.

'Here.' Sebastian shrugged off his jacket, his cigarette between his teeth. 'Wear this.' He dropped it over my shoulders and when I tried to protest said, 'I'm Scottish. I don't need it. I don't feel the cold. You're a soft southern lass, you'll catch your death out here.' He offered me the pack. 'Want a smoke?'

'All right.' I didn't really smoke, but I took one and he lit it. My troubled stomach had subsided into calm but now, after a few puffs, I felt nauseous and just pretended to smoke the rest.

'So, do you have a boyfriend?' he asked, scowling at me.

'No. Why?'

'What's the story with Rollo? You two seem to hate each other.'

'I went out with him for a while. It didn't end well.'

'Glad you saw the light, he's an arse.'

'He dumped me.'

'Oh.' Sebastian puffed on his cigarette, unfazed. 'Same result. Fortunate escape. If you're lucky, you might avoid relationships altogether.'

'If you don't mind me saying, you are very cynical. You seem to hate everyone and everything.'

His eyes glittered at me in the darkness and I thought I saw the flicker of a smile around his lips. 'Aren't I allowed my time of furious youth? No doubt I'll settle down and toe the line later. I'll be here in twenty years in a kilt with a paunch and a bit of lace under my three chins. Let me dread it for now.'

I laughed. 'Is that inevitable?'

'When you live around here, it is. You never really escape. They always draw you back one way or another.'

Someone poked their head out of the terrace doors and said, 'You'd better come back, Mrs B is about to do her thing.'

We stubbed out our cigarettes, I gave him back his jacket and we headed into the dining room where Mrs Ballintyre was speaking to the hushed table in a smooth, rich voice, like an actress's. We had already missed most of her speech and were just in time to hear the end: 'And so, please join us in the library for coffee and dancing, and we'll be on the terrace at midnight to welcome in the New Year!'

Sebastian and I had not made it back to our places, and now found ourselves leading the way along the corridor to the library: a large, panelled room with three sets of French windows overlooking the loch, one of which was open, which I soon realised was a necessity, for once we were all in there, it was very warm. The furniture had been removed to make a clear floor except that at one end of the room was a table serving coffee, whisky and port. At the other, on a small dais, was a band: a fiddler, an accordion player and a double bass, with a plump man in a kilt who was testing a microphone.

Ah, yes. The dancing.

A nervous tremor went through me and I wondered if I could avoid it. But the mood was energetic and excited and we were directed to find partners and form sets. Sebastian suddenly grabbed my hand. 'Well? Do you want to dance?'

I hesitated for a moment, wondering if I should hold out for Hamish, but then said, 'Yes please.'

'Good.' He led me over to join a group of other couples.

'But I don't know the first thing about it.'

'Don't worry. Neither do I.' He grinned at me wickedly.

'What? But you're Scottish!'

'I hate dancing. I've never learned. Don't worry, I'm sure we'll have fun.'

Before I could say anything else, the music began with a long resounding chord and we were off, the man with the microphone bellowing instructions that made sense to around half of the dancers. All over the room, people started moving. Sebastian grabbed my hand and began hopping on the spot.

'Stay where you are for now, you're couple three,' commanded a middle-aged man in a kilt with a huge hairy sporran and red cheeks crazed with tiny purple lines. He obviously considered himself in charge and, as the dance progressed, he threw out directions to Sebastian and me, sometimes pushing me to where I was supposed to be, or grabbing me, spinning me round and depositing me breathless where I had started, usually in front of a mischievous-looking Sebastian, who appeared to be doing his best to disrupt the dance, much to the other man's annoyance, his face getting even redder. He spluttered at Sebastian, who ignored him and danced as though we weren't in a Scottish reel at all, sinuously moving his shoulders and hips, sometimes taking my hands and doing the twist with me. Then, equally surprisingly, he did a few of the proper moves, only to suddenly press his cheek to mine and stick our arms out and start doing a sort of tango. It was utterly confusing and we were making a terrible mess of it, which I suddenly began to find very funny and started giggling. This only made the kilt man crosser, and Sebastian yet more mischievous. Then the dance seemed to be back at the beginning again and we went at it from the start, although Sebastian kept breaking into a Charleston, until I thought I was just beginning to get the hang of it. Then, abruptly, it was over and we stopped.

The red-faced man said crossly, 'You buggered that up, Drummond, what are you up to? No need to spoil it for the rest of us.'

'Can't be bothered,' Sebastian drawled. 'Sorry if I'm not Caledonian Ball standard, old love.' He took my hand. 'Let's get a drink.'

I tried to apologise to the man but Sebastian was already pulling me across the room to the drinks table where he got us both icy cold beers to swig. 'That was fun,' he said, smacking his lips with relish over the beer.

'Can you really not dance?'

'Well . . . my memory is ropy. It comes and goes.'

'You can, can't you? Then you were naughty to spoil it.'

'Can't stand the reel Nazis. I always want to freestyle whenever I see one. Fuck's sake, let's just have fun.' He swigged again on his bottle. Another dance had begun and I could see the cross man and his wife looking much happier now as they turned and twirled in another set, a much more capable one than ours. From the outside, the dance made sense but from within it was a rapid collection of moves that seemed impossible to perform in the time allowed. We watched until the music had finished.

'Want to do another?' Sebastian asked casually. 'I don't mind if you do. I'll behave next time, I promise. Or we could go outside and smoke.'

I looked at him and suddenly thought how young he was, with his funny, childish rebellion, all that delight in being naughty. I realised he was asking me to go outside with him probably so he could attempt to kiss me. He was very handsome, and his black hair hung into his eyes in a carefree romantic way, and I wondered what it might be like to kiss those sulky lips and thought perhaps I might like it.

There was a hand on my waist. I looked up and Hamish was smiling at me. 'I promised you a dance,' he said.

'We're just going outside actually,' retorted Sebastian, 'so you'll have to wait.'

'I think Helen can make up her own mind,' Hamish said easily, and looked at me expectantly. He was so different from Sebastian, with his height and heft, his steadiness, his far less exotic colouring. He was older, mature, sensible. He would never muck up a reel. 'So?'

'Well . . .' I looked at Sebastian who was clearly furious. But really – was I here to humour a sulky boy, or dance with Hamish? I remembered the thrill of being close to him in the cupboard last night. I knew there was no choice. Something was pushing me towards my destiny, and I was sure that destiny was Hamish. 'I'd love to dance. Thank you.'

Sebastian turned on his heel and marched away, disappearing out through the doors into the night, while Hamish, oblivious, ushered me to the dance floor, saying, 'It's about time you had a proper dance. I saw Sebastian fooling about, irritating everyone. You deserve better than that.' Once we were standing opposite one another he smiled again. 'Don't worry about the steps. I'll guide you. This is the eightsome reel.'

The music played and we were off. From the moment it started, I felt safe. Hamish, much taller than me, somehow made everything clear. I let myself be guided by him, and he moved me firmly but without force. We danced together smoothly, our hands finding each other, our feet in time, his whoops filling me with exuberance. The room seemed to be full of whirling couples, pounding feet, the swing of kilts and a billow of silk dresses, and the jaunty, irrepressible rhythm of the fiddle urging us on and on. I felt the sheer pleasure of it, like being a novice surfer who had just learned to take a wave: everything that had been bewildering was suddenly clear. All the stumbling and false moves were over, everything flowed and felt right. I wanted it never to stop, this feeling of being in perfect step with Hamish, feeling utterly safe in his confident hands. I'd never known dancing to be so exhilarating, exciting and full of the promise of something.

Then it was over. The music finished. Hamish whirled me round in a final turn, bowed, then pulled me close. He was panting, his heart thudding through his waistcoat. His mouth was at my ear. 'That was good. Like we were made to dance together.'

My heart, already racing, seemed to gather even more pace. We started to walk together towards the open doors to the terrace, seeking fresh air. Hamish picked up two drinks on the way out and a moment later we were outside, cooling our hot cheeks in the chilly night air.

'You don't fancy him, do you?'

'Who?'

'Sebastian Drummond, of course.'

'A bit.'

'He's just a kid.'

'He's nineteen, isn't he?'

'Exactly. He's just a kid.'

'He's still an adult.' I was teasing him, but I liked the feeling that perhaps he was jealous. 'But I thought you were pining for Daphne.'

'That was over years ago.'

'That's not what you said last night.'

'Things have changed since then.'

'Have they? How?'

'Because now I know you.' His voice was suddenly silky smooth. He had moved closer to me and I could feel the heat of the dance radiating from his body. 'You can't deny the chemistry between us. I know you feel it too.'

There it was – a rush of excitement, a sense of being pushed into the place where I was supposed to be. I was meant to be invited, Charlie was supposed to make that silly mistake, I was always destined to be here, in this place, on New Year's Eve, with this person. I looked up into his face. His blue eyes were inscrutable in the dark but I could sense the tension in him, hear the faint catch in his breath. Then his hands were on my arms and he was pulling me close to him. The brass buttons from his jacket started to cut into my chest where the dress left it exposed. He was going to kiss me, and I felt my legs go weak as if my body was determined to be as nineteenth century as my clothes, and was about to let me swoon into the arms of the handsome Scotsman in his ancestral home.

Just then, an ear-splitting noise ripped through the air, and a piper blowing with all his might on a set of bagpipes stepped out from the library onto the terrace, and everyone began to pour out after him.

Mrs Ballintyre, leading the charge, was shouting, 'Come on now, it's time!'

Hamish pulled away from me, then said with a laugh, 'It's only bloody midnight.'

The piper blew on and on, as everyone gathered, their excitement growing, and then suddenly the music stopped. 'One minute to go!' shouted someone.

The crowd began to count down. Hamish took my hand. I looked up at him in a rush of bliss.

'Three, two, ONE! Happy New Year!'

Cheers, whoops, explosions of party poppers, the sound of bells from the church over the hill. Couples embraced, kissed, shouts of 'Happy New Year!' filled the air. Hamish looked down at me. 'Happy New Year,' he said in a low voice, and kissed me. It was dizzying: brief yet meaningful, a kiss with potential, a kiss with promise. I gasped for air as he pulled away even though he hadn't really kissed me properly.

I realised a great circle was forming on the terrace, and we were part of it. Our hands were seized and the singing started. 'Auld Lang Syne'. They were bellowing it out, their arms moving in time, everyone joyous and excited. Hamish had my hand in his and we were singing too. Mrs Ballintyre was laughing as she struggled to keep her balance, pulled by the large gentlemen on either side of her. Sylla was there, but not singing, her eyes huge in her pale face, her expression not quite happy or sad, but more stunned, and her silver dress glittered. She made me think of a shimmering salmon in a dark stream, or a bolt of starlight. She held Charlie's hand and he was pumping her arm up and down with his own, his eyes squeezed shut as he bellowed out the words.

The singing came to an end in a loud cheer and another round of kissing and hugging, and then suddenly, a massive whistle and bang and a flower of pink and white exploded in the air, lighting up the loch and the lawn that stretched down to it. It was followed by another, and another, and the faces on the terrace all turned to watch the display, pops and bangs of coloured stars whizzing through the night air.

I turned to watch as well. Hamish was close behind me, his arms around my waist, his big hands clasped in front so that I was pulled close to him. For a moment, I thought I saw Sebastian scowling at me from the lawn but when I looked over, it wasn't him. In the darkness at the edge of the terrace, Hamish pulled me round so that I was facing him and while everyone was enraptured by the display in the sky, he kissed me properly and thoroughly until I was aware of nothing else except how naturally we fitted together and how wonderful it was. Destiny had brought me here. The door had opened and I had walked through it. There was no point in fighting it. I knew that this was just the beginning.

PART TWO

Chapter Six

TIGS

1968

What could be more romantic than a wedding at Ballintyre?

It was early summer and Scotland was ravishing, showing off its artistic skills with the colours of June: cerulean skies that melted into turquoise and dissolved into pinky lavender late at night; the greens that covered the spectrum from cool dark, almost black, to the brightest, juiciest neons and acids. The sea loch wore its prettiest hues, misty blue and chalky green, behaving like a perfectly docile little lake, as if it hoped to be invited to the wedding as well.

On such a beautiful day, I ought to be happy. The Ballintyre wedding was the biggest social event here in years, and the whole village and every house along the coast road had been buzzing with excitement about it for weeks. But I was utterly miserable.

James Ballintyre had been my hero since the day that Al had got the idea to send a lighted raft out over the water. We were on the beach in front of Tremewan, the house on the coast road where I lived with Dadda, Mumma and my older sister Serena. If you were in this neck of the woods and you headed out alongside the great sea loch, you'd come first to Ballintyre, set back and looking out over the water. You'd gasp when you first saw it, it's so glamorous and like something from a Walter Scott novel of Auld Bonnie Scotland, with its pointed turrets, arched windows and towers. Then, continuing on towards the west, you would pass Tighglachach, though you probably wouldn't know it, as the house is hidden down a long driveway where it's falling into mellow disrepair as the years roll on, but you might notice its lichened pillars, the ones with the big empty hinges where gates once hung. Then you'd reach St Mungo's, the village that isn't much more than a collection of cottages, small houses and a general store, all along the coast road in a little line. After that, you'd only see trees and some farmland until you crested a hill and there, suddenly, majestically, would be the sea, into which the loch flows, and the misty islands in the distance. Then, at last, you'd see Tremewan, white and elegant, with tall windows looking out over the silvery sea. That was my home, not grand like Ballintyre, or imposing and Gothic like Tighglachach, but somehow, to me at least, more beautiful, pure and pleasing in its symmetry and simplicity.

'Good bones,' Dadda would say. 'Like you, Tigs. The house has good bones.'

It was lucky it had that, because it did not have much else, except for the view of the sea and the lawn that led directly down onto the beach and my lookout rock, with its smooth shelf seat, the perfect place for thinking. That day, we had been picnicking on the beach, our sandwiches getting gritty and the orangeade tipping over to make a dark sticky patch in the sand. In the far distance, misty and vast, was a giant oil tanker making its hulking way to some industrial port, to fuel the mysterious activities of the grown-up world.

'We should explode it,' Al said.

'Don't be daft,' James replied. He had the unassailable air of his three years' seniority over Al and, at sixteen, was almost grown-up himself. 'How would we?'

'Make a raft with driftwood, drench it with oil, send it out.' Al lifted his chin proudly. 'I've done it before.'

James looked quizzical.

Interested, I said, 'Did you explode anything?'

'I was aiming for the ferry and I got pretty close but it burned out before it got there.'

'Why would you want to hurt the ferry?' I asked. 'All the people.' Everyone knew we needed the summer trippers.

But Al was glaring at James. 'It worked all right apart from that. It went out for miles.'

'On the loch,' James replied. 'That's easy. This is the sea. How will you get it over the waves?'

Al leaped to his feet, angry. I wished he wasn't always so quick to get cross. He was good-hearted but his passions were so close to the surface, and there was something about James that seemed to set him off quicker than almost anything. I thought it was partly because really, he worshipped James and longed for his approval. Anything that smacked of criticism from James made Al so defensive and that came out as crossness.

'I can do it!' Al cried. 'You watch. I'll go and get some oil now.' He ran to the edge of the beach and dragged his bicycle out of the sandy dune grass. 'Wait here,' he shouted. 'Or get some wood for a raft.' Then he was on his bike and disappearing off on the coast road towards Tighglachach, pedalling hard.

I watched him go, and ate the dry crusts of my last sandwich, wishing I could somehow eat those bits first and keep the soft centre till last but I never could resist sinking my teeth into the pillowy succulence. Mumma made such gorgeous sandwiches: soft sweet tuna mayonnaise with the crunch of cucumber under white bread and salty butter; tangy rich cheddar with the acid of her homemade chutney and wet rounds of tomato picked that morning and tasting of sunshine. 'He's all riled up again,' I said.

James laughed. 'Typical Al. He's a nutcase. Don't know what's got into him lately, he's so touchy.'

I knew he was right. Al was pricklier than ever. We three had known each other since we were very little, and had formed a gang that had lasted despite our difference in ages – I was the youngest, with five years between James and me, and Al in-between us. I think James liked being our leader and boss because he had a load of older cousins who usually took that role. Al was also an only child, but he seemed lonelier with no brothers or sisters to play with, stuck out at Tighglachach with only the brigadier and Mrs Drummond for company. Perhaps it was because he had such old parents – a father in his seventies and a mother in her late forties; no wonder he was lonely and a little strange. And I was a tomboy, who had no interest in playing house with Serena, or settling down to knitting with Mumma. Instead, I loved to go on adventures, exploring the coast, the woods, the hills, the loch, and the endless interesting world that surrounded us. The boys were the same. All this bound us together.

James got up, brushing down his sandy knees. 'Come on, we may as well humour him. Let's collect some driftwood.'

We left the remains of our picnic and started wandering about the beach, collecting likely pieces of wood. I found some orange fisherman's twine which we could use to tie it together. We chatted easily as we went, our hair lifting in the stiff sea breeze, eyes squinted against the sand blown up and the sunshine beating its way through the wind.

Al got back in quick time with an oil can and some matches in his pannier, his good humour restored, and we spent an engrossing hour creating our raft from the best bits of wood and the twine and bits of seaweed. I wanted to put shells on it but the boys said no. We took the raft to the seashore and waded to knee level, the foam-headed waves rushing in and wetting the bottoms of our shorts.

Al was carrying the oil can, full of excitement. 'Now we prime it. Hold it still, Tigs, don't let it wash away. I'll soak it.' He unscrewed the lid and began to slosh pungent liquid all over the raft.

'You're getting the oil in the water, Al,' James said.

'So what? There'll be plenty more in it when we've exploded a tanker!'

'We can't do that,' I exclaimed. I'd forgotten our mission in the absorption of building the raft. 'We can't put oil in the water, you know that's an awful thing to do! All the seals and birds and things.'

Al blinked at me furiously, his black eyes flashing.

'Don't worry, Tigs, he won't be exploding anything,' James said with a laugh. 'It's just a game. Isn't it, Al?'

'No,' Al snapped. 'No, it's not, you'll see.' He pushed the oil can into his back pocket and took a box of matches from his shirt pocket.

'Watch out,' James said, suddenly serious, but Al wasn't listening. He pulled out a match and struck it, throwing it quickly onto the raft. The oil flared up at once with a whoosh, sending a great puff of flame outwards. James leaped back with a yell. Al staggered and fell back into the sea water just as the flames caught his hair and eyebrows. I was still holding the raft and the flame rolled to the oil on my hands and ignited.

It all happened so fast, I was in shock. I said nothing but only watched as my hands burned. I seemed to be holding balls of flame in my palms like some kind of fire goddess. Then, what must have been only an instant later, James took my hands and plunged them into the sea, dousing the fire. The flaming raft bobbed and turned over, extinguishing itself with a soggy hiss.

'You idiot!' James shouted at Al, who had emerged from the water, gasping and still sooty on his forehead, his black eyebrows burned away in places, his eyelashes gone.

'Tigs, are you all right?' Al asked urgently, spluttering and shaking sea water from his hair.

'She is, no thanks to you. Luckily it was mostly fumes on her hands, you blithering fool.'

I was gazing down at my hands, not looking at my blackened palms, which didn't yet hurt, but at James's hands grasping my wrists, holding me firmly. Then I looked up into his blue eyes, fierce and glowering at Al.

'I'm all right,' I said in a small voice, though my hands were beginning to sting. 'Don't worry, Al.'

'He's an idiot,' James said scornfully.

'No I'm not! I didn't mean to hurt her.' Al stood in front of us, almost close to tears, then turned, furious again, and waded back to shore, where he ran for his bike and home.

'Come on, Tigs, we'd better show your mother what's happened.'

The two of us went slowly back to shore together, James still holding me gently by the wrist. The remains of the raft, soggy and burnt, floated out, carried by the ebb of the waves towards the oblivious oil tanker as it continued majestically on.

That was when I knew he was my hero.

And now I was sixteen myself, and Dadda was driving us to James's wedding in his beloved 1931 Daimler, only brought out for very special occasions, and which today was beautifully polished and purring like our cat. My mother sat next to me on the raised back seat, while Serena, my sister, sat in the front, trying to protect her beehive hairdo with a scarf. She'd teased her dark hair to a splendid height and stuck it in place with a whole can of Elnett, and I was very jealous as my hair wouldn't cooperate at all, and although I'd tried to flick the ends out, it was already going limp. Serena was sporting a pair of huge false eyelashes, had painted black wings of eyeliner on her lids and was wearing a frosted-pink lipstick. She also had on the shortest dress, in yellow lace over a satin underdress, and her legs were bare all the way down to her white PVC heels. She'd stuck big white and yellow plastic daisies into her rigid hair.

Mumma had practically fallen over when she'd seen her; Mumma was very proper in a pink two-piece suit, worn in places but still smart, white shoes, handbag and a white hat, her hair set in curls that were resolutely not fashionable but had a wartime echo, as if they were done in pins overnight, which they probably were. Despite her shock, probably because Serena wasn't wearing tights, Mumma had said, 'Darling, you look wonderful. What splendid little flowers, how clever!'

Serena did look rather majestic, like something from a fashion magazine, and I guessed that Mumma was feeling a little wistful. She and Dadda had always hoped Serena might be the one to marry James Ballintyre, but I never thought for a moment that she would. My sister cared too much about her hair and her clothes. She complained that rocks were slippery and water was wet and sand sandy. She didn't like too much sun, and certainly not rain; she didn't like mud and she squealed at anything that moved, even the sweetest little fish darting in the shallows, or gorgeous tiny crabs dancing slowly sideways on the beach. She liked inside better than outside, and preferred magazines to books. James Ballintyre wouldn't love a girl who didn't want to swim in the loch or go fishing, I could see that plain as day even if no one else could. It was James who taught me how to light fires in a little ring of stones in the woods, when he and Al and I went out on our adventures. He showed us how to set traps for rabbits, and let me have a go with his air rifle. He'd never let me touch a proper gun, though, even when I begged, although Al was allowed because his father had taught him to shoot. James gave me his old penknife instead, but Mumma took it off me when I cut myself on the blade and got an infected thumb. She called it a tetanus trap and gave it to the gamekeeper, as though it didn't matter if he got tetanus and died. She said he wouldn't be so stupid as to cut himself but I knew his hands were covered in cuts from brambles and feeding pens and traps, so that showed what she knew.

We children were often at Ballintyre, taken over for picnics and walks, dances and parties. My favourite thing, though, was the long summer holidays, when James and Al and I formed our little gang and spent whole days together. Sometimes Serena came too, but mostly it was just us three. We would cycle up and down the coast road, between Tremewan, Tighglachach and Ballintyre, cutting through the woods on shortcuts only we knew. Sometimes, we'd go out mackerel fishing or seal spotting in *Kitty*, James's sweet white motorboat with the blue trim. In the summer, *Kitty* bobbed in the water on her mooring by Ballintyre, waiting for us to row out in the dinghy that we roped to the mooring, before boarding her and setting her motor chugging. We'd usually end up around the head in a deserted cove tucked away from the usual trippers and visitors, so it was entirely our own. When *Kitty* was as close as possible to the shore, before she scraped her bottom on the sand, James would throw the anchor over, turn off the engine, and we'd wade in to the beach, carrying our shoes in our hands, and our lunches in rucksacks. We'd spend happy days there, playing, lazing, exploring, eating, collecting shells and swimming, then head home in the late afternoon sun, seals sliding off the rocks where they were sunbathing to dart here and there under our boat, curious to know who and what we were.

James was always our captain and I remember seeing him, his face set against the wind, his brown hair blowing back in the gust, his hand firmly on the tiller as we putt-putt-putted through the water. He would let me steer for a while, folding my fingers around the tiller and then releasing them so that I was responsible for the little craft. I was frightened at first, then grew in confidence and felt a surge of grown-up responsibility and freedom. It was heady. What if I turned the boat round and motored it out, into the sea and away? I could, if I wanted. But I steered us for the home jetty, knowing that lemon cake and scones were waiting in the kitchen at Ballintyre.

I knew Serena would never marry James, even if he asked her. She was desperate to get away from Scotland, preferably to London, as soon as possible, and she hardly seemed to see him, let alone love him. She certainly didn't know that when he concentrated, his brow creased and his eyebrows lifted into arches, or that he had a small white scar on his chin, or that he had hands that were almost square in shape, the fingers nearly the same length. She didn't stare at his long brown legs in the boat while he was steering it, or thrill just slightly when his blue eyes lighted on her and he smiled.

I knew all that because I adored him, ever since the day he plunged my burning hands into the sea.

It was hard when James left for Cambridge. Visits to Ballintyre were much duller when they meant hanging around the house, listening to my parents talking to James's parents, leaving me to wander aimlessly about, playing the piano, or shooting billiards with myself. Al and I spent more time together now but exploring and sailing with him wasn't the same, though he said it was better with just the two of us. He had never quite forgiven James for the way he had shouted that day we lit the raft, although outwardly we were just the same as ever, a gang. And I was sure we always would be.

At least James still returned in the holidays for boat trips, walks, picnics and family gatherings. But then he came back with Josephine.

We were invited to Ballintyre for lunch to meet her, and James introduced us.

'Tigs is one of my oldest friends,' he said, evidently eager for Josephine and me to be friends as well. Josephine glanced at me, taking in my summer uniform of shorts and a striped T-shirt, her gaze lingering just for a second on my knobbly, scratched knees, and gave a little laugh as if the idea that I was James's friend was simply implausible.

She said, 'Hello,' and then she ignored me. She looked through me and over me, as though I barely existed and didn't matter in any case. I watched her covertly the whole time. In James's presence, she was coquettish and clingy, fluttering her eyelashes at him and laughing too hard at all of his jokes. To his parents, she was syrupy and oversweet, proclaiming to love everything she saw. She appeared to assess everyone else and react according to how important they were in the scheme of things. She saw Serena's blatant admiration and liked it, so she was friendly enough to her, and she also clearly enjoyed being the centre of attention, a sort of visiting celebrity as James's girlfriend, the first to be brought home. But when no one was looking, she seemed to sink into a kind of torpor as though she simply couldn't be bothered to keep the whole facade going when she didn't have to.

I began to hate her.

Perhaps it would have been worse if she were a raving beauty but the fact that she wasn't also annoyed me. What did James see in her? All the way home, Serena talked about the way Josephine was pretty, like Marianne Faithfull, but I said blonde hair didn't automatically equal pretty and anyone could cut a fringe in their hair, and if you looked properly, you'd see her eyes were too close together and her teeth were bad. 'Her thin lips make her look mean.'

'Well, James likes her,' Serena said bluntly. 'And so do I.'

That only made me crosser. Serena liked her because she was from London, and therefore was sophisticated, but I could see that there was something very wrong with Josephine.

It's like . . . like she's not a real person. But why?

We went back several times over the weeks she was staying at Ballintyre and she was always the same, at least to me – strangely inauthentic. Her charm and conversation and laughter didn't ring true but no one else seemed to see it but me. A clammy horror was growing in me. Why couldn't James see what she was really like? Was it the blonde hair and the freckled chest she displayed with her low-cut tops, the rise of her breasts showing like little brown buns poking out over the neckline? Was it her short skirts, revealing a length of tanned thigh above her bony knees? Or the fluttering false lashes and the mouth gummy with white lipstick? I thought she was disgusting, fake and weird, but he seemed to like her and it made me furious.

'What do you think of her?' I'd asked Al, whose family had also been invited to meet Josephine.

'She's all right,' he'd said with a shrug.

'Don't you think she's nasty?'

'No. She's just another boring girl, like all the rest.'

'Thanks!'

'Not you, Tigs, you're not a girl.' And he grinned at me, as though he'd delivered a huge compliment.

I tried to smile but inside, I felt dreadful. Was that why James had never really seen me? Because he didn't think I was a girl? But what really broke my heart was that now, James ignored me too. He didn't mean to, but if he talked to me, Josephine made sure to interrupt, to take him away from me, purring into his ear and hanging off his arm. And he let her.

*

When Mumma told us over breakfast one morning that James and Josephine were engaged, I felt a black cloud descend on me that I hardly understood. I slammed about sulkily all day until Mumma asked me what on earth was the matter. I couldn't tell her the bitter thoughts whirling through my mind: that Josephine was all wrong. I had seen her at Ballintyre and I knew it; I don't know how I did but I knew that she didn't feel at home there in that fundamental, crucial way. She wasn't at ease. She didn't belong to the rooms, or in the garden, but seemed in some way like a visitor to a place that set her on edge. I didn't think she liked it but was pretending that she did. But that wasn't the worst thing. It was that I didn't think she really loved James.

'What *is* it, Tigs, what's the matter?' Mumma asked, as I sighed and slumped in the kitchen.

'Nothing,' I said. Then a moment later, 'When is James's wedding?'

'Soon, I think. Elspeth says the summer.' Mumma was making lunch. We might have had a large house but there was no money at all, and she grew, raised or made virtually everything we ate. She was making a quiche from our own onions, courgettes and eggs, with a salad from our greenhouse and boiled potatoes from our kitchen garden.

'Josephine's a cow,' I announced, and was startled to see Mumma turn to me with real anger in her eyes.

'Don't be so unkind! You don't know the girl, you have no reason to dislike her, or say such a horrible thing about her. You're a crosspatch whenever we see her. I know you wanted James to marry Serena, but he's not going to and you're going to have to accept Josephine. She's going to live at Ballintyre, and be part of our lives, and she deserves a chance.'

I felt suddenly tearful, as though my own mother had joined the other side, but I bit my lip and swallowed the tears away. I said in a chastened voice, 'But do you like her, Mumma?'

Mumma said nothing as she chopped onions, then at last looked up. 'She's young. She has a lot to learn. But I don't see any reason why she shouldn't have a good heart. And James loves her, that must count for a lot.'

I felt comforted. 'You don't like her either.'

Mumma frowned and sighed. 'It was just something Elspeth told me. She said that Josephine was engaged already when she met James, but she didn't tell him or break off her engagement until they were a couple. I suppose she had no real obligation to someone she hadn't married and yet . . .' She wiped her hands on her apron. 'Well, it's all gossip and doesn't matter now. They've made their choices. We must judge on what we find, not what we hear.'

I nodded. But even Mumma's reservations about Josephine didn't do anything to heal the wound I felt.

I went out of the house, slapping along the path in my plimsolls, until I found my special rock, where I could look out at the silvery sea and watch the boats going by. I knew there was no hope for me, but I couldn't bear to see James marry the wrong person and something told me very deeply that Josephine was all wrong. Not because she wasn't from here, or from the same background as us, but because I sensed that somehow she was pretending something that wasn't real. And what would happen once she stopped? What then?

Dadda had put the canvas roof of the car back as the weather was so good. As Serena had insisted on sitting in the front to protect her hair, Mumma and I did battle with the breeze in the back. The wind blew my hair and pressed on my lids, making it hard to keep my eyes open, but I wanted to look at the glittering loch as we drove along the coast road to Ballintyre. The car was a funny, long-nosed thing in shades of tan and brown, and it made a racket as we drove, so there was no possibility of talking. I didn't have anything to say in any case. I was thinking about the wedding, now only forty minutes off. I was imagining standing up and declaring that it could not go ahead, telling everyone that the bride did not really love the groom. In my imaginary scenario, James was throwing the wedding ring he was going to put on Josephine's finger to the ground and saying, 'Thank you, Tigs. I was about to make the worst mistake of my life.'

'Here we are, at last,' Serena shouted against the blustering wind, as Dadda slowed down. He pulled the car to a halt in front of the little kirk near Ballintyre, where the lychgate was covered in a beautiful arch of white roses. Guests were milling about outside, dressed up in their wedding finery. A gathering of local people were staring over the low wall at all the goings-on, children scuttling about, hopeful for the traditional scramble.

Don't worry, said a voice in my head. *He won't do it.*

Those words helped me follow my parents and sister into the church, and we looked for our pew. It was a proper stern little kirk, a plain rectangular building in local stone with arched windows of clear glass, and inside few adornments other than the old wooden pews and the carved pulpit. But today, it was bright and pretty, decorated in white roses with pink heather and purple thistles. The Ballintyre family was already gathered at the front, James in his kilt and dress jacket with the square brass buttons, a foaming lace jabot at his neck and a traditional dagger tucked in the top of his sock. His best man, smart in a morning coat, nervously patted his breast pocket every few minutes to check for the ring box visible inside. We took our places in a pew on the right-hand side, and Serena gazed fascinated at the other side, where the bride's friends and family were gathered, strange beings from far away in London. I couldn't look. I stared at the order of service in my hands, realising with a sinking heart that not only was this wedding really about to happen but that I would not stop it, as I did in my fantasies. How could I? What, really, could I object to?

He mustn't marry her. Surely he won't.

But I had a heart-sickening feeling that he would.

The service was over very quickly. From the moment Josephine walked in on her father's arm, dressed in a long, high-necked white jacquard dress with bell sleeves, holding her bouquet of white roses, her face blurred by the stiff veil in front of it, I was in a kind of daze. Within moments, it seemed, the dreaded words were spoken, the rings were placed on fingers, the veil lifted, a kiss dropped on her lips.

I could only watch James: the happiness on his face, the pride in his eyes. Then I saw the joy and jubilation radiating from Josephine as she turned to face us, now Mrs James Ballintyre. The organ played a rollicking march as the happy couple walked out of the kirk, and we followed them. James's cousins, Clara and Roberta, were Josephine's bridesmaids, and I spotted them giggling and talking to one another as they stood to one side to let the guests out. I went over to them.

'What are you talking about?' I asked.

Clara giggled and held her posy up to cover her mouth. 'Just before we left the house . . . you'll never guess what Josephine did.'

'What?'

'She went back to look in the mirror.'

'Oh?'

'It's bad luck, don't you know that? When the bride goes back to look in the mirror after she's left the house. Very bad luck!'

'Terrible,' agreed Roberta, and they both laughed again.

'Why is that funny?'

'She has no idea. And she's been so annoying all morning, wailing and moaning and complaining. Nothing's been right. She might look radiant now, but she was throwing a fit first thing because the water wasn't hot enough.'

I gazed at them in astonishment. Water of any temperature above ice cold was considered a great blessing to be treasured. Truly hot water, and lots of it, was almost unheard of.

'Not just about the water.' Clara rolled her eyes. 'Every-thing!' She started then to mimic her in a high voice: 'Daddy, no! Daddy, I don't like it! I won't have it! That's not right, Daddy!' She went back to her own voice. 'She's been a pain from the start.'

'She's from London.' Roberta shrugged. 'I suppose it's that.'

'No excuse,' Clara replied, 'and I hope her bad luck means she gets a custard pie in the face.'

'That's not very likely, unless you've got one,' Roberta remarked.

'I can improvise.'

I thought about the bad luck. Should I wish for it, or not? Would Josephine's bad luck now mean James's bad luck as well?

A piper was standing by the lychgate and when we were all assembled, he began the wonderful half-mournful, half-joyful sound of a Highland wedding march, and then led us out of the churchyard to walk the short distance back to the house. The bride's father, briefed on the tradition, produced pocketfuls of sweets to throw to the crowd of children for the scramble, and they shrieked and darted for the goodies as we passed, first James and Josephine, just behind the piper, then the family, followed by the rest of us.

'I can't walk in these things,' grumbled Serena in her white high heels, and I was glad of my flat shoes and the ease of my flowery dress. It was done and it was almost a relief.

James is married, and that's that. I just have to accept it.

Nevertheless, back at the house, I swigged back three glasses of champagne before Mumma could notice, and was soon light-headed, then heavy with misery. There was going to be a feast in the tent on the lawn, which was laid with trestle tables, and then dancing, and I didn't know if I could stand it. I was sixteen years old and my heart was broken.

I saw Serena talking to a group of Londoners, flirting with some long-haired, bearded man in a velvet suit who looked completely out of place. I knew most of the Ballintyre guests but I didn't want to be collared by any of them, made to recite boring details of my boring life on this awful, miserable day. Al wasn't even there, in bed with a bad cold Mumma had said. Instead, I slipped away and walked down the drive towards the loch, where *Kitty* bobbed on her mooring. The day was warm and the water looked cool and inviting, so I went down to the water's edge, slipped off my shoes, lifted my dress to my knees and walked carefully in, trying not to slide on the slippery stony bottom. *Kitty* sat on the water, her nose pointed out to sea as if luring me away, and I wanted suddenly to climb on board, pull the engine cord as I'd seen James do, and make it roar into life so that she could carry me far away. I started to walk towards her, and soon the water was over my ankles. It was freezing, and the cold cut through my fuzzy champagne head and made me feel alive. Quickly it was up to my knees and I lifted my dress higher. I didn't know if I really intended to go to *Kitty*, because I would have to start swimming for that to happen, and I knew in my heart I couldn't start the engine. Midges were swarming around my legs and face, and I'd be bitten hard if I didn't get back.

'Tigs, Tigs! What are you doing?'

I turned and saw James on the shore, waving at me. My heart swelled and a rush of misery and longing coursed through me.

It's too late now. He's married someone else. I can't bear it.

'Come back,' he called, beckoning me, and after a moment I started the slow wade back towards him, feeling the waving fronds of seaweed around my legs. 'What are you up to?' He looked bemused. 'You can't be going for a swim . . . can you?'

'No . . . I don't know. Just cooling down a bit. What are you doing here?'

'I'm practising my speech. I just needed five minutes before we all sit down.' He flapped his kilt around his legs. 'But I'm being eaten alive by midges. The water is a terrible place to be. Let's go back.'

I was near him now and he watched as I stepped carefully from stone to stone. When I was almost by him, I lost my footing, slipped and started to fall, and he stepped forward to catch me. I grabbed him and his arms surrounded me, holding me up.

'I've got you,' he said softly, and I gazed into his blue eyes, his face close to mine. 'Are you all right?'

'Yes,' I said weakly. 'I'm fine.'

Is there still time? For all this to stop, for things to go back to what they were an hour ago?

But there was no going back. Our old friendship was over, the gang was dispersed, and James belonged to someone else and he didn't even seem to care, or to know how deeply I did. He helped me to the grass, waited while I put on my shoes, and together we walked back to the house, to celebrate his wedding.

Chapter Seven

TIGS

1970

'Well,' said Mumma, 'it all depends on what you want to do. Art school? Cookery school? Nursery school teacher?'

I sighed and kicked my heels on the kitchen cupboard. I liked to sit on the marble counter of the pastry bench, feeling the cold cut through the cotton of my skirts. It made me think of gravestones and statuary and the eternal chill of the mausoleum.

This whole house is a mausoleum! I've been buried alive. I'm mourning my dead youth and promise.

'Please stop kicking, Tigs,' Mumma commanded. She was making cherry brandy from the glut in the fruit garden. Anything to stop the birds from getting them. Every year, it was the same: Mumma struggled desperately to prevent the birds from plundering her fruit and, despite her nets, they always seemed to steal plenty of it. She harvested everything she could rescue from their ravages and spent balmy summer days in the hot kitchen, red-faced and sweating over the range as she boiled fruit for jam, chutneys, syrups and sauces. Today she was marinating cherries in brandy for spilling over ice cream in dense blobs or baking into almond cakes, while the brandy itself was to be served at Christmas. The jars sat triumphantly in the larder, evidence of her victory over the birds. We could hardly get through it all, and some would end up at the village fair, donated to the cottage hospital, pressed on guests and hosts and anyone who might want them.

'Well,' Mumma said, wiping her juice-stained hands on her apron. 'What's it to be?

My school had closed for good, finally unable to carry on with its tiny amount of pupils. The nuns would go off to some convent, the school sold to be a hotel or something. I had expected to go back and study for university but that was over now, and no one seemed to think that another school would be the answer. Instead, it was time to think about life beyond everything I'd known so far: home, and our corner of Scotland, with its close-knit society of families.

Whenever Serena returned, I tried to talk to her about it, curled up on her bed while she sat at her dressing table, staring at herself in the mirror.

'Honestly, Serena, I read Jane Austen and it feels incredibly familiar. I'm basically living in the nineteenth century: small social circle, everyone traipsing from house to house, knowing everyone else. The major entertainment: gossip and ritualised dancing. Claustrophobia, screaming panic, massive unease, all concealed by adherence to traditional dress and good manners. Overpowering need to keep the current social order in place.'

Serena brushed her hair with a long, slow stroke. 'What are you going on about?'

'Have you read Jane Austen?'

'*Pride and Prejudice*,' she said vaguely. 'At school.'

'A fierce polemic about the woman's imperative to sell herself through marriage.'

'Oh no, very romantic. Lovely Mr Darcy.'

'Chauvinist pig.'

She didn't listen. She had left home in any case, and only returned when she needed to recover from her life in London. She was a legal secretary and seemed to be experiencing some kind of existential bliss of youth, sex and parties. Occasionally she needed to retire from the frantic excitement to the deathly dullness of home in order to recuperate and, I suspected, save money.

'Tigs?' Mumma said crossly, stirring the cherries.

I stopped kicking. 'Yes?'

'Stop dreaming, darling. You need to think about your future.'

'I could get married,' I suggested, now that I'd thought of Jane Austen.

'Married?' Mumma wiped her hands on the apron again. 'Who to?'

I said jokily, 'I suppose there's always Al.'

'Oh.' Mumma made a pained face. 'Well . . . But really?'

On paper, Alastair Drummond was perfect: our families were old friends, he had Tighglachach to inherit, just down the coast, sitting between us and Ballintyre. He had no ambitions to sell up, or move to England, or emigrate to Australia.

But I knew what Mumma was thinking. He was Alastair Drummond. That was the main sticking point.

'We've been friends all our lives,' I said, as if I were actually considering it. 'He likes me.'

'Yes, we can all see that. He seems to like you more than ever.'

For the whole summer, since he'd got back from university, Al had been coming to the house almost every day. Now that we were more grown-up, we were doing less of our old exploring and fishing. These days, we went on walks or sat on the beach and Al, who was reading Classics at Cambridge, gave me his opinions on Graeco-Roman culture and I talked about Victorian Gothic literature, which was my current passion. I loved the Brontës in particular, perhaps because I could identify with windswept isolation.

'Oh, not the Brontës,' Al had said with a touch of scorn, as we'd sat on my rock on the shore. 'You just think they're good, because that's what you've been told.'

Since he'd grown so tall, he'd become fidgety, as though he was not very at ease in his big adult body. He'd taken up cigarettes at Cambridge and now smoked continuously, one leg always jiggling, one long-fingered hand always stroking his newly grown gingery beard.

I had learned ages ago not to become indignant with Al, it only made him more decided. So I was patient but firm. 'I think that because I think it. I've read the books. That's what I think.'

'You think that's what you think.'

'I know I think it.'

'Ah. Well, you're young yet, you'll learn.'

Only last week, when it was raining hard in great, drenching sheets, Al had come over and we'd spent the morning in Dadda's study. I took down the huge Oxford dictionary, opened pages at random, selected the most difficult and obscure word I could see, and asked Al for the definition. He got it, nine times out of ten, through considering Greek or Latin roots.

'Very good,' I'd said admiringly. 'You know a lot.'

He'd accepted my compliment with mild pleasure. The great thing about Al was that he wasn't in the least vain or conceited, nor did he have any false modesty. He did like compliments, though, even if he found it hard to give them. 'Now, young Tigs, do you remember that challenge you set me yesterday?'

'Well, you rather set it for yourself, it wasn't my idea. But yes. You bet me you could learn a book of the Old Testament in one day. What was it called?'

'Obadiah. Where's your Bible? You can test me on it now, if you like.'

'All right.' I fetched the Bible and Al found the text for me. 'Oh – it's only short.'

'Twenty-one verses long,' he said with satisfaction, and gave me a cunning look. 'You didn't specify *which* book.'

'Well, no, because I didn't actually set you the challenge at all. You chose this yourself.'

'Test me, test me,' Al insisted. So I followed the text while he recited, one leg jiggling, a cigarette in his fingers.

'Well done, you're word perfect.'

'Excellent. You owe me half a crown, that was the bet.'

I couldn't help enjoying his obvious delight in his triumph, not so much because he was clever but because he'd managed to trick me. I handed over the half crown I'd been going to keep as a souvenir of the old currency. 'You can't spend it, it's not legal tender anymore.'

'I can probably still exchange it at the bank. I'll spend it wisely, young Tigs. More cigarettes, I should think.' And he pocketed it with relish.

I sat back in Dadda's old library chair and watched him light another cigarette, the last one still smouldering in the ashtray. 'What's it like at Cambridge?'

'Good fun. Hard work. Lots of rather silly people but a few nuggets among the dross.'

'Did you ever see James?' They had crossed by two years, as Al had gone up early for his age, but they had been at different colleges. I spoke casually as though I wasn't particularly interested but actually, I was longing to talk about James in any way I could. I usually resisted the temptation with Al, but now I gave in.

'James?' Al frowned and blew out a plume of smoke. 'Who?'

'James Ballintyre, of course. Who else could I be talking about?'

Al looked instantly furious, his good humour vanishing. His dark eyes hardened, his mouth turned down, he plucked at his gingery beard while exhaling hard. 'No. He's much older than I am. I barely saw him. There are thousands of students in any case.'

'You didn't want to see someone you knew from home?'

'No. I would do my best to avoid him, actually.'

'I don't understand.' I gazed at him thoughtfully. 'We were all such friends. You don't seem to like him anymore.'

'You do,' he retorted.

'Yes, of course I do.' I tried to sound as though it was simple casual friendship and not the desperate yearning of lost love. I was sure Al had never guessed about my feelings for James, and I'd been doing my best to quell them in any case. James was married now, I had to come to terms with it. He and Josephine lived in London, where Serena was exhausting herself. There was no news on when, if ever, he would be back. I missed him horribly, sometimes to the point of tears, but I'd never told anyone. I saw Al scowling at me and shrugged nonchalantly. 'We've been friends all our lives, why wouldn't I like him? I don't understand why you don't. You always used to think he was brilliant.'

Al scowled. 'I was wrong. That's just the thing. He's overrated. We only thought he was great because we were kids and we let him lord it over us. Everyone seems to think he's the bee's knees but, in fact, he's a rather stupid child.'

'A stupid child?' I was indignant, then remembered that was pointless with Al. I needed to be firm. 'Why do you think that?'

'Because it's true.' He stuck out his bottom lip and looked stubborn.

I stared at him. I liked Al, much more than anyone else seemed to. He rubbed people up the wrong way, seemingly without intending to, and even my parents, who saw the best in everyone, found him trying. Even so, lately he seemed intent on disagreeing with me on just about everything. He'd always been odd, prickly and argumentative but I'd seen that underneath all that was a tender soul with a deep curiosity about the world. When he was in good humour, he often made me laugh while introducing me to things I'd never heard of: aspects of poetry, art and history. He had a taste for the macabre, and collected Gothic etchings of golems and succubi and incubi and things of the occult, and gave me his battered editions of ghost stories to read. Unlike everyone else, he seemed to think I was worth spending time with, and I respected his opinions. But why did he think so little of James?

'I don't understand what you've got against him. James is not a stupid child,' I said at last, wishing I could think of something more persuasive to say. No doubt I'd think of the perfect reply later, in bed, my room illuminated by the silvery moonlight reflected from the sea.

'He is. You just think he isn't. But he is.'

Mumma said now, 'I just don't think Alastair Drummond is a viable prospect, darling. I don't think you'd be happy.'

'I'm not serious, Mumma.'

She gave me a knowing look. 'I think you should spread your wings. There are more people in the world than your childhood friends, and more places than here. You should see the world a little.'

That decided me. 'All right then. Art school.'

*

I was tremendously excited by the prospect of moving to London. To get my place at Chelsea School of Art, I had to submit several pieces and I started work at once, painting furiously and littering the house with damp canvases, paint-crusted palettes and wet brushes. Now the paintings were drying all over my makeshift studio, which had once been a ballroom but now was never used, unless one of us played the piano, which was the only remaining piece of furniture. It had wonderful light pouring in through the sea-facing windows and was a perfect place to paint. I had managed to splatter the old floor with quite a rainbow of colours, despite being as careful as I could, but I thought it was worth it when I looked at my finished work.

Al came up on his motorbike to see how I was getting on.

'These aren't bad,' he said in a tone of mild surprise, when I showed him what I was doing. 'You're actually all right.'

'Am I?' I stood back to look at my latest attempt at a still life: an orange on a table next to a candlestick. I was quite pleased with it – particularly the streak of white down the side of the candlestick that made it pop out of the picture and have a real sense of actually existing. That, I'd found, was the tricky thing. Shapes were all very well, if they were flat. Giving them body and life was the art.

He looked at me with something that was almost respect. 'Yes, young Tigs, these are certainly all right. I assumed when you said you were going to art school, it was only because you thought you wanted to do art.'

127

'And when will I learn that what I think is worth nothing?' I asked tartly, but he didn't seem to hear me. He carried on looking around at the propped-up canvases.

'This is good, too,' he said, pointing at one that I'd done to amuse myself when I'd had a palette full of reds, pinks and greens to use up and hadn't intended to submit. 'I think it's your best, actually.'

I stared at it. It showed a pink vase of red tulips on a green table, against a yellow wall, and I hadn't bothered much with getting perspective right or trying to make the vase look like it was sitting on the table. In fact, I'd dashed it off almost without thinking about it. 'I think it's babyish. The others are better.'

'No, I like this,' Al insisted. 'Can I keep it?'

'If you want. I think it's . . . *naïf*.'

'Yes. That's why it's good.' He picked up the canvas.

'Be careful, it's still wet! You'll have to wait until it's dry.'

'All right.' He regarded it happily. 'It's definitely your best.'

I sighed. 'Have it your own way.'

What was the point in arguing? We would never agree on anything.

I packaged up all the other paintings and sent them off, waiting anxiously for the letter that finally came a few weeks later. I had my place and could start in the autumn.

It was decided that I would live with Serena, who had just rented a basement flat in Chelsea, and she could oversee my welfare and make sure I didn't get into scrapes. Serena, now that she was working, supported herself and I would pay my rent from the small allowance Dadda gave me.

'You've got two years' money, Tigs, then we're all out,' Dadda said, sucking his pipe over the remnants of dinner.

Mumma, sitting across the table, seemed anxious but said nothing. She looked wearied, her hair grey and soft baggy pouches under her eyes. I'd grown up hearing we had no money, and yet life seemed wonderful, our house a dream and our existence charmed. But perhaps they had meant it, and there really was no money left.

'I'll make lots of money before then,' I said with certainty. 'I'll be a famous artist and rebuild the fortunes of our house.'

Dadda raised his eyebrows and puffed out smoke. 'That would certainly be an excellent result.'

Mumma said on a sigh, 'I don't think we even really need the house now you girls are leaving.'

I was dismayed. 'What do you mean? Are you selling? You can't do that!'

Dadda said quickly, 'Not yet, don't worry. It's not that bad. But it's a big place to manage on our own, you know. Neither of you can take it on.'

'I can!' I cried, hurt to my heart to think of losing our lovely house. It was shabby, it was true, but Mumma had made it beautiful with her clever way of restoring and re-covering furniture, her eye for paint colours and the pretty curtains and headboards she'd made from salvaged materials and charity shop finds. We didn't have the kind of money they had at Tighglachach, or at Ballintyre, but our house had a charm that I liked best of all, emanating from its beautiful

Georgian bones: the large doors, the high windows, the wide polished floorboards, the gracious fireplaces. The light from the silver sea that flooded its rooms gave it a natural grandeur. It didn't need expensive paintings and fancy furniture to dress it any better than that.

'I'll save it, you'll see,' I said stoutly. 'You won't ever have to leave.'

Mumma smiled. 'Thank you, Tigs. We appreciate it.'

I could tell she didn't believe me.

The traditional Tighglachach ball was held to mark the last of the summer labour and the beginning of the autumn bounty, but we'd always seen it as the last hurrah of the holidays before we were back to school and the dull rigmarole of winter uniform and lacrosse sticks, and the dreary drudge to Christmas.

This time I was particularly looking forward to it. It would mark the start of my new life in London but more than that, I was longing to see James. Surely he would come back for the ball. He and Josephine had not returned since their wedding, except on quick visits to see the family, but the ball was a tradition like Christmas or Easter and even Serena left the excitement of London to come home for it. Perhaps this time he would be there. I had a gorgeous fantasy that he would see me and say, 'But Tigs, you've grown into a beautiful woman!' and then dance with me. Nothing could come of it, of course, but the idea of being clasped to him, having him hold my hands, being able to stand close to him and touch him was enough for me. The prospect filled me with shivery, delicious excitement and I knew I would be able to live on that contact for a while longer.

By tradition, the girls wore white. Married ladies could, of course, wear what they wanted but we virgins were supposed to dress purely. Serena and I got dressed together in her bedroom, while I tried to hide my growing excitement, convincing myself that it was now only a matter of minutes before I saw James again. Then Dadda shouted for us to come down, and we were off.

We arrived at Tighglachach wearing raincoats over our dresses, as it was already a little chilly in the evenings. The drive was packed with cars and minibuses, and the house was lit up from within. High above the great hall, in the minstrels' gallery, the musicians were tuning up.

If I could ever fancy Al, I thought, spotting him as we came in, it was when he was in full kilt and all the garb. It suited him as ordinary clothes never did. He looked majestic, his dark green jacket giving him magnificent square shoulders, like a warrior or a Viking or a clan chief, and his kilt swung about him with dignity and grandeur.

He saw us and came over, while our parents greeted each other like long-lost friends, despite seeing each other all the time. 'Hello, Serena, you look wonderful.' He kissed her on both cheeks. 'Tigs.' He squeezed my hand. 'Want to dance later?'

'Of course.'

'Don't ask me then, Al!' Serena said jokily, lighting a cigarette from her purse.

Al laughed politely. 'Ah – sorry, would you like to dance later?'

'Not really, if I'm honest, but I will if you're desperate.' Serena looked around at the assorted throng of mostly older people. She herself looked entirely out of place, polished and urban with her elaborate hair and make-up. 'God, I wish Eric was here.'

'Eric?' Al frowned.

'Her boyfriend. In London,' I supplied.

'I'm dying without him.' Serena sighed again and smoked hard.

'How unpleasant for you,' Al said politely. He looked uneasy around Serena, as though she was a creature altogether too exotic for him to handle. 'Why did you bother coming back for the ball then?'

She gave him a hard stare. 'Because we *always* come back to the Tighglachach ball, don't we?'

'Then you should have brought Eric.'

Serena shrugged. 'He couldn't come. He's working. And anyway, he doesn't want to hike all the way up here to dance reels with a few old people. It's the most tedious thing in the world.'

Al was puzzled again. 'If you don't like it, why do you come? No one makes you, and I don't think we'd miss you either.'

'Well, thanks!' She gave him another exasperated look. 'I told you, because it's the ball, of course! That's what we're supposed to do. I couldn't miss it.'

I knew what she meant. There were some things about our life here that were non-negotiable. There were rituals we had to participate in, as unassailable as the liturgical calendar: one following another marking the passage of the year, and the passage of our lives. There was no point in fighting it.

Just then, there was a call for sets, and Al grabbed my hand.

'Come on, Tigs,' he said, evidently glad of the opportunity to leave Serena. 'Let's dance.'

Serena shot me a sympathetic look.

'Yes please,' I said bravely, and off we went.

If only Al could dance as well as he looked the part. If only his height and magnificence translated into grace or even just into coordination. But he had the proverbial two left feet, he moved with a kind of inner stiffness as though his knees and fingers didn't know how to bend, and he mixed up flair with simply making huge gestures. It was almost dangerous some-times, as he underestimated his strength and could spin his partner too hard or pass her over to another partner with such a flourish that she risked being half thrown across the room. Luckily, I knew all this, and I had learned to absorb his excess energy and let it pass through me rather than resist; I learned when to let go of his hand before he gave that extra thrust that would push me over, and to avoid his flailing arms and feet. But it wasn't easy.

When, after several energetic dances, I managed to escape and went panting to join my parents, while Al went outside for a cigarette, Mumma said, 'Honestly, Tigs, you're too nice to that boy. You're encouraging him.'

I got my breath back, and said indignantly, 'I'm only being friendly!'

'I can see the way he looks at you,' Mumma said, pulling me gently to one side. 'Can't you see it?'

'He looks at me like a friend,' I said obstinately, annoyed because I knew deep down Mumma was right and I didn't want her to be. I liked Al. It would surely put an end to our friendship if I had to accept that he took it more seriously than I did. Better to ignore it.

'Then he only has one friend,' Mumma said tartly. 'Because you're the only one he looks at that way.'

'Ha ha. I would have thought you'd be glad if Al likes me like that.' I gestured around the room. It was a splendid sight, with the musicians sitting high up in the minstrels' gallery, the great wagon wheel candelabra hanging from the huge central beam, the fire blazing in the enormous open fireplace. 'After all, if I marry him, all this would be mine. That would make you happy, wouldn't it? Maybe I could save our house too!'

Mumma looked suddenly so serious and sad that I regretted my silly joke; I hadn't meant those words and they seemed to have pierced her. She said soberly, 'I only want you to be happy, Tigs. If you truly loved him the way I think he loves you, I believe you could make a success of it. But if you don't feel that way . . . it's best to leave him be.'

I stared at her, the colour in my face rising and an uncomfortable heat spreading over my skin. 'I . . . well . . .' I was confused, and defensive. 'Perhaps it's a good thing I'm going to London then. To get away from him.'

'Yes,' Mumma said, still unsmiling. 'I think it is for the best.' She took my hand. 'Darling, I know you worshipped James Ballintyre. But it was a schoolgirl crush, you do know that, don't you? He's married and you need to forget him. Is he what keeps you from falling in love elsewhere?'

'Mumma!' I was shocked and embarrassed but most of all mortified that she knew my secret, the one I thought I had hidden so well. 'I don't worship James at all!'

'Then why were you all aflutter about this evening? You look terribly pretty, you always do, but you've made an extra effort, I can see that. And why do you look at the door every five minutes as if to see whether someone you're expecting has arrived?'

'I . . . I . . .' Mortification was replaced by hurt and annoyance. 'Well, the Ballintyres always come, don't they? Is it so bad to look out for them?'

'It's not bad at all. But Elspeth tells me that James and Josephine are staying in London. They're not returning for the ball this year. Josephine is pregnant.'

I stared at her, my mouth open, trying not to show my dismay on my face.

'I'm sorry, Tigs.' She held my hand tighter. 'I know it's hard for you to hear.'

I shook my head, horrified by the whirl of conflicting emotions inside me. Five minutes ago, I hadn't known that Mumma guessed my feelings for James, now she was comforting me for learning that he and Josephine would be parents. Marriages could end in divorce. Parenthood was a lifelong bond. I couldn't bear her pity, or anyone's pity. I looked up at her, lifting my chin defiantly. 'I'm perfectly fine about it. Of course they're going to have a baby – they're married, aren't they? It was only a matter of time. And if you want to know the truth, I don't care in the least. Not in the very least.'

I turned on my heel and hurried out, making my way through the crowd that was milling about between dances, and through the great front door. I crunched over the gravel to the fountain, which played merrily, its stream lit into a silver cascade by the light from the hall. There was Al, sitting on the fountain's edge, smoking and gazing into the dark water, lost in thought. He looked suddenly like the solace, the rescue I was seeking from these awful feelings.

I went up to him, breathless, my skin goosebumping in the cold air under my white satin. 'Al . . .'

He looked up, startled, the black eyes surprised. 'Tigs, what are you doing here?'

I took a deep breath to settle myself but still felt strange, upset, reckless. 'I just wanted to say . . . if you feel anything for me . . . if you want me to know that . . . you should say it now. Before I leave. I won't go if you don't want me to.'

He went very still. His eyes dropped to the drive. I was frightened by my own action, as though I'd primed a gun to go off and was now afraid of the explosion.

'I mean, you don't have to say anything,' I stammered.

'No . . . no, young Tigs.' He gazed at me and I felt my heart wrench: he looked vulnerable in a way I'd never seen before. I felt stupid and careless to play with his feelings like this. Wasn't that what I was doing? Wasn't this just a reaction to the mortification of Mumma knowing my secret, of the knowledge that James could never be mine? I may have known it anyway but a baby made it so horribly real. The thought of the baby and the loss of James made my determination return with fresh strength. Al went to say something, but I darted towards him, put my hands around his face, and pressed my lips on his. He resisted for a moment, then I felt him relax and one arm went to my back and pulled me towards him. I felt his lips part under mine and the realisation that I was kissing Al exploded in my mind with a rush of disbelief and an overwhelming sense that this was not at all right. I pulled away, on the brink of the kiss ripening into something deeper, and pushed his arms away from me.

'No . . . no . . . I can't!'

'Tigs!' he said, his black eyes glittering in the light from the house.

'Oh dear.' My eyes filled with tears. 'I'm sorry. I really am. Perhaps it's best that I'm going to London.' I turned to go back to the house.

'Don't go!' he said, standing up, throwing his cigarette into the fountain where it landed with a tiny hiss. 'Please – I need to talk to you, you can't just leave like this.'

I turned back to face him, feeling wretched, guilty and almost wicked. 'I'm sorry, Al. Really I am. Please just forget this.'

'Tigs, stop! Come back, please . . . please come back!'

But I was already running back into the hall, where I found Dadda, and begged him to take me home.

*

When Al tried to come round to see me the next day, I pretended I was ill. I could hear Mumma apologising and making my excuses to him, and stayed upstairs in a kind of writhing agony until I'd heard his motorbike engine fade into the distance.

'What did you do, Tigs?' Mumma asked me solemnly, but I wouldn't say. I couldn't admit it to her. She sighed. 'Then it's for the best to put some distance between you.'

Two weeks later, Dadda loaded all my things into the car and we made the long journey to London, where Serena, already returned by train, was waiting to welcome me to the tiny spare bedroom in her basement flat.

More than anything I was relieved to have got away from the terrible embarrassment of what I had done. I guessed Al had returned to Cambridge, and I told myself firmly that by the time I saw him again, he would have forgotten that awful moment.

And instead I nurtured the dream that, somehow, I would see James, and that Fate would bring him to me.

PART THREE

PART THREE

Chapter Eight

HELEN

2002

I returned home from that romantic Hogmanay at Ballintyre in a whirl of giddy excitement, feeling as if I'd found the end to my fairy tale.

'You're dancing on air,' Nora said with a laugh, looking up from the portrait she was working on. And I had, in fact, come spinning into her studio, humming and happy. 'Or should I say, reeling on air?'

'Nora, it was amazing! Just like you said it would be! I can't believe I was so nervous.' I laughed and sat down to tell her all about it: the mix-up with the invitation, the presence of Rollo and Daphne, and how they had almost propelled me and Hamish towards each other, and the way we had come together that evening, dancing in perfect sync, to find our future. I'd told some of it to Dad, but I knew Nora would enjoy hearing the full version as much as I enjoyed telling it.

'He sounds wonderful,' Nora said, after I'd poured it all out, smiling at my starry eyes and joyful face. 'And Hamish is a lovely name. It's the Scots version of James. So soft and musical. You must tell me all about him. How old is he? What does he do?'

I chattered on excitedly, while she worked on the portrait she was copying from a photograph.

'And what was Mrs Ballintyre like?' she asked, dipping her brush in paint on her palette.

I curled up in the armchair that sat behind her painter's stool and easel. 'Oh, she was wonderful. Magnificent! I mean, she didn't take much notice of me because she's very grand, but she was also fun. She liked being a hostess, I could tell. Hamish thinks she's marvellous, that's a good sign.'

'Always a good thing when a young man loves and respects his mother,' Nora agreed.

I was thinking of Mrs Ballintyre again. 'She was magnificent but sort of extreme. Always over the top, always emoting. She seemed to like being one of the gang, but also the boss, like the chieftainess of the clan or something. At the party she wore a huge bright red dress and a tiara and she was like a kind of queen.'

'Did you like her?'

'Oh yes. She was so kind.'

'And she's close to the boys?'

'She seems to adore them.'

'Does she know about you and Hamish?'

'I don't think so.'

Nora nodded, painting a stripe of pale yellow on her canvas. 'Keep it that way for now. There's no need to get to know the whole family yet, it might turn out to be a lovely holiday romance and no more. You could change your mind about him, after all.'

I laughed, blushing. 'I don't think he'd be interested in me long term. I might very well never see her or Ballintyre again. Goodness, I might never see Hamish again! What a horrible thought.'

As I said it, I realised how much I longed to see him again, and how badly I wanted to go back to Ballintyre one day.

'We'll see,' Nora said, squinting at her canvas. 'No need to rush into anything. But don't talk yourself down: he'd be lucky to have you in the short or long term, and don't you forget it.'

I hugged my knees, remembering. 'It was so marvellous, Nora, it really was. So beautiful! And the dancing and the pipes and everything – it was just like you said, the best fun.'

'There you are, I told you you'd love it. It was all lifeblood to me. Tell me, what was Tighglachach like?'

'It was just as strange as you said it might be! Not like Ballintyre.' I described the anarchic feeling of the house, the beautiful but wilful brood – not dwelling too much on Sebastian as I still felt guilty about the way I'd abandoned him – and the loud eccentricity of Mr Drummond and his school bus. We laughed about Mr Bell, so proper and immaculate, stranded in the mad house.

'But he was kind about Rollo,' I added.

'And the house is still standing, at least?'

'Oh yes, though it's rickety and a total mess.'

She laughed lightly. 'Well, well. That's nice to know.'

I thought about how little I really knew Nora. Her life had seemed to start when she came into mine, but of course, she had had a whole existence before that. She'd grown up, no doubt fallen in love, had a whole life I knew nothing about. 'Do you miss Scotland?'

'Sometimes. It's so very beautiful.' She looked dreamy for a moment. 'So remote. So romantic.' Then she began to mix paint with the tip of her brush and sighed. 'But so long ago now since I saw it.'

It was a year before I returned to Ballintyre. By then Hamish and I were a couple, although we'd had a long-distance relationship most of the year, sustained by emails and texts and the occasional long and loving letter. As often as I could, I made the journey from Edinburgh to London to join him for a weekend, which were glorious times of fun with Hamish and his friends – we mostly went to gigs in grotty pubs or stand-up comedy in smelly underground clubs – with romantic walks and cheap dinners and lots of time squashed into Hamish's single bed. Occasionally he came to Edinburgh but, as he pointed out, it was less of an adventure as he knew Scotland already and besides, he always had a great deal going on. He was sweet, though: loving and caring from a distance, and smothering me with love when we were together. The only thing that bothered me was that when we were with his friends, he could sometimes ignore me. Not with malice but as though I flew completely out of his head. I would have to tug on his sleeve for attention, like a child, to remind him of my presence. And when one of his friends,

Piers, took great pleasure teasing me, Hamish joined in and I became the butt of their jokes all evening. I complained afterwards that he'd hurt me by teasing like that, and he was genuinely surprised. 'It never occurred to me you didn't like it,' he exclaimed, then laughed it off, telling me I was too sensitive and it had just been a good-natured joke. He'd kissed me and asked me to forgive him, and I had. And yet, whenever we were with that group, I felt the same sense of being subtly discarded, to be picked up again afterwards when we were alone, although he always protested he meant to do no such thing. I believed him. If I was gentle and kept reminding him not to ignore me, to consider my feelings, to notice when I looked lonely, he would eventually remember, I was sure. He was, at heart, kind, and just a little thoughtless at times. And anyway, I adored him and spoiled him with love. I liked to coo over him, admiring him, petting him, and in return he'd wrap me in his strong arms and love me back. I felt that only I could see beneath the funny, confident exterior. Inside, he was unsure of himself, sensitive, a little fragile even. His father had died when he was young and he was still a hurt boy. I knew I could make him better with the force of my love and cherishing.

The visit to Ballintyre that Christmas was very different from the previous year. For one thing, I was Hamish's established girlfriend. It was serious, and now I had a different apprehension: would his mother like me?

We arrived on a dull winter's afternoon just after Christmas, driving west from Glasgow airport into the dark. The house was as beautiful as I remembered but felt cavernous and empty without the razzmatazz of a big party. Mrs Ballintyre greeted us with shrieks of excitement, huge kisses and a torrent of questions about our journey, which we hardly had time to answer before she asked more.

'Come through, come through!' she exclaimed, leading us to the drawing room, where tea was laid out on the low table between the squishy sofas. 'We have a wonderful surprise!'

I followed Hamish. He held the tips of my fingers as we went in but let go as we came into the room to see Charlie and Sylla sitting on one of the sofas by the fire, holding hands.

'They're *engaged*!' declared Mrs Ballintyre dramatically.

There was immediate excitement, as they stood up and we exclaimed and there were hugs and kisses. When we were settled, and Mrs Ballintyre was pouring the tea, she said, 'It was so romantic!' Her eyes glistened with damp. 'The sweetest thing I ever saw!'

'Were you there, Mum?' Hamish asked in surprise.

'Oh yes, it happened right here, by the fireplace, on Christmas Day.' She smiled happily over at Charlie. 'Such a lovely way to propose.'

I looked across at the happy couple. I was still feeling very shy and only said a timid hello and 'congratulations'. Sylla seemed so glamorous to me: those navy eyes, wide-set and candid like a child's, the sprinkle of freckles across her nose, the long straight fair hair. It seemed a strange thing for Charlie to propose in front of someone else, but perhaps that was the way things were done, and I just didn't understand.

'You lucky dog,' Hamish said. 'I can't think why you said yes, Sylla, you must be a glutton for punishment.'

'Hamish!' exclaimed Mrs Ballintyre. 'Sylla is a very lucky girl!'

'Of course she is,' Hamish said, grinning. 'And it would take someone pretty special to make Charlie give up his single life. Congrats, Sylla.'

'Thanks. I'm very happy,' Sylla said, her navy eyes unreadable.

'Is there a ring?' Hamish asked.

'This one.' She held out her hand to show us a dark ruby in a heavy, old-fashioned setting, a tiny ring of diamonds glittering around it.

'It's beautiful,' I said. 'Is it antique?'

'It's a family ring,' Charlie said, looking at me. 'My grandmother's. I want Sylla to wear it, just as she did.'

'That's how I knew a proposal was on its way!' Mrs Ballintyre said jubilantly. 'When Charlie came to ask me for the ring, I knew for sure. Honestly, it was all I could do not to give away the secret, it was so exciting! I was all of a tingle knowing it was coming. Charlie said he wanted to take Sylla up to the fairy ring to pop the question. I said, don't be silly, propose outside? The poor girl will freeze! Ask her in the drawing room, by the fire, with the Christmas tree sparkling there, nothing could be nicer. I made myself scarce – well, I lingered in the hall – and I thought I'd given them plenty of time, but Charlie was popping the question as I came back in. So I got to see it! It was lovely, Charlie down on one knee just as he should be.'

I looked at Sylla. She was smiling and yet strangely serene.

'You added to the excitement, Mum,' Charlie said heartily. 'I think you were more excited than Sylla.'

'Of course I was. She's getting a husband, but I'm getting a *daughter*.' Her eyes moistened again. 'A new daughter. What more could I want?'

'The ring is lovely,' I said politely. I thought that it was lucky it had fitted and then noticed that Sylla was holding it straight on her finger with the edge of her thumb tucked underneath.

Oh, it doesn't fit then.

'Yes, isn't it beautiful?' She looked at it fondly. 'But the most important thing is that I know it means a lot to Charlie.'

'And to me,' Mrs Ballintyre put in. 'The boys' father proposed to me with that ring. Of course, it wasn't right for me, I always thought it was rather ugly, but it still means a great deal.'

We all stared at it for a moment, suddenly seeing the ring rejected, and I couldn't help my gaze sliding to Mrs Ballintyre's ring finger, where a huge oval sapphire, nestled between two fat diamonds, glowed discreetly. I looked up at Sylla and saw she was watching me, a tiny smile playing around her lips.

'Now,' Charlie said, getting to his feet and rubbing his hands. 'I think this calls for a celebration. Sod the tea, I'm getting a couple of bottles of bubbly and we can make this a proper party!'

I watched him go, puzzled by the story of the proposal, knowing Sylla had guessed that it didn't sound quite right to me.

I stayed at Ballintyre for two days. Mrs Ballintyre now had time to observe me, but while she asked me some questions about my background and my father – I managed to skate over the situation with my mother – I was grateful that her attention was mostly elsewhere, with the thrill of the engagement to keep her occupied, and Sylla the focus of her attention. She wanted to talk endlessly about the wedding and started making plans in a beautiful bound leather notebook.

I enjoyed being with Hamish in the place he most loved, and getting to know it as he did. If anything, it was more lovely empty. The party glitz and all the trappings were gone, and now the house revealed itself for what it was: grand, though a little faded now, but still dressed in the eighties glamour that I supposed Mrs Ballintyre must have applied – the frills, tassels and florals, velvet-textured carpets, shades of pink and lemon everywhere. Beneath that were glimpses of another house; strong and plain, of stone and plaster, wood panelling, granite and flagstones. It had imposing proportions, with large rooms, huge windows overlooking the loch, and many staircases – formal with polished banisters, informal winding up the back to the hidden gable rooms – and it was filled with the accoutrements of big houses: the grand piano, the room devoted just to boots, coats and fishing rods, the billiard room, the library.

We went on long walks along the loch, or up into the hills among the pine trees, and got soaked by real Scottish rain: deceptively soft and drenchingly wet. We ate Sylla's delicious food, lazed by the fire and let Charlie top up our glasses, which came out at five p.m. with a flourish and the pop of a cork, and stayed out till midnight.

I woke early on the second day, and was too alert to go back to sleep, excited to be back at Ballintyre, so I slipped out of bed, leaving Hamish fast asleep, and went down to the kitchen to make myself some tea. I found Sylla already there, working on the counter and humming to the kitchen radio. 'Good morning!' she said, looking up as I came in. 'Did you sleep all right?'

'Oh yes, thank you, very well.'

'There's some coffee in the pot if you want it.'

I went over to pour some. 'You're up early.'

'I'm prepping for lunch. It's easier to do it before every-one's up.'

'It's nice of you to cook for us.'

Sylla shrugged, smiling as she chopped carrots. 'I don't mind. It's the least I can do.' She looked up at me. 'They've been so wonderful to me. Ever since I first arrived, I've been welcomed in like one of the family. I don't have any family of my own, you see, so it means a lot to be taken in the way I have been.'

'They're so kind,' I said.

'Yes. Very. I'm sure you'll find the same.' She regarded me with her navy-blue gaze. 'I was very lost. Now I've found my home. So looking after them all is the least I can do.'

'And you're marrying Charlie.'

Sylla nodded, looking happy.

'Did you mind Mrs Ballintyre being there? At your proposal?'

Sylla laughed. 'I could see you thought it was strange. It's just her way. Josephine loves to be at the centre of every drama and I don't mind. She lost her husband such a long time ago, so all her pleasure in life comes from her sons. If I could give her the happiness of being present at our engagement, then why not?'

'That's very sweet of you. But poor woman. It's so sad.'

'It must be said, she overcompensates a bit as a result,' Sylla said, scraping her chopped carrots into a bowl on top of diced onion. 'And she can be a bit full on with the boys but it's no surprise she's overprotective when she lost her husband so young, so I cut her plenty of slack. She doesn't have a daughter and I don't have a mother, so I think we'll be good for each other.'

'That's so nice.'

She smiled again. 'You must come to the wedding.'

'Well, I'd love to,' I said, flushing. It seemed presumptuous but I hoped that I would be there with Hamish. More than anything, I wanted to be a member of the family, taken into their tight little unit, clasped to their heart, just as Sylla had been. How wonderful it would be if I could be welcomed in like Sylla, and loved as she was. *Perhaps*, I thought, *if I'm lucky, that might happen.*

I couldn't think of anything better.

Chapter Nine

It all seemed so right at the start.

'Hamish is good for you,' Dad declared after they first met, not long after my second visit to Ballintyre. 'He's a good man. You'll be happy with him.'

I was delighted. If Dad liked Hamish enough to entrust me to his care, that surely meant everything.

'What do you think, Nora?' I'd asked eagerly. She'd been there too, observing quietly, while Dad chatted away brightly with Hamish, who'd laughed appreciatively at all his jokes and generally been the charming, adorable man I knew he was. I'd been sparkling with pride and excitement.

'He's very nice,' she'd said, hugging me almost with relief, as though she'd been scrutinising him carefully and he'd passed a test. 'And you're clearly head over heels, it's lovely to see. You deserve some happiness.'

Her approval had meant just as much as Dad's. I knew that, at some level, Nora had more wisdom than Dad, and I knew that she really cared for me. I didn't have a mother – at least, not one that took an interest – and she filled that role for me. If she thought Hamish was a good thing, well, I could trust her. She would be honest, I was sure of it.

When I'd finished at Edinburgh, armed with my degree in History but with not a clue what to do, I'd gone home and got a job in a local bookshop, while Hamish stayed in London and signed up to a Master's degree. One mad weekend, not long after Charlie and Sylla's wedding, when we'd been full of joy being together and feeling very romantic after the nuptials, we decided that I would move to London and we would live together. Dad didn't mind, but Nora seemed less happy.

'Living together, so soon?' she had queried. She wasn't painting, as she usually was, but was sitting across from me on one of the old armchairs in her studio, wrapped in a silk kimono, her gaze fixed on me.

'It's nearly two years!' I protested.

'But you still don't know each other very well.'

'All the more reason to live together,' I'd said brightly. I didn't want any rain on my parade. This was exciting. I was already planning how we would furnish a flat, where I might apply for jobs, and what our lives together would consist of: endless fun, love and happiness, as far as I could see.

She tilted her head on one side. 'Yes, but once you're in that situation, it's very hard to move out of it, you know. You'll be giving Hamish everything he needs. He might feel he doesn't have to try anymore.'

I laughed. 'What on earth do you mean?'

'Well . . . where's the mystery, once you're washing his socks and cooking his food, and in his bed every night? What if he stops trying to earn you?'

I was mystified, and also slightly sorry for Nora. She was so old-fashioned. She'd never been a modern young woman like me. How could she understand? 'Hamish isn't like that. We're going to do everything fifty-fifty. And if we can't, it's only because he's so busy with his course. It's really demanding.'

'What is the course?'

'Oh, it's something to do with overseas development,' I said vaguely.

'You don't know?'

'Of course I do, it's . . . I think it's about Third World development, and Western aid and the effects of corporate involvement on it.' That sounded right.

Nora gave me a worried look. 'He does . . . *talk* to you, doesn't he?'

'Of course, we talk all the time! Non-stop.'

'And when you argue, or disagree, or fall out . . . he talks to you then?

'Yes!' I said stoutly, and then I was aware almost at once that that wasn't true. I told him frankly why I was upset, but it didn't happen the other way around. He didn't say much when I explained my feelings either but would look downcast until I relented, hugged him, kissed him and told him not to worry. But I was sure he'd learn to confide in me as we grew closer.

'Good. If you ever stop talking to one another, you must take action.'

'Don't worry, Nora. We'll be just fine. He really loves me.'

'I'm glad of that, darling Hélène.' She smiled, but with a trace of melancholy on her lips. 'It's what I want for you most of all. To be loved.'

I was delighted to be able to prove Nora's fears had been unfounded when, after only six months of living together, Hamish proposed. It took me by surprise, not least because it was at the grand lunch Josephine hosted at Ballintyre to celebrate Rose's christening in the little kirk. Sylla and Charlie's beautiful daughter had been born four months before, plump and perfect, with a dusting of red-gold hair and tawny eyes instead of Ballintyre blue. The new parents could not have been happier or prouder. We were sitting at the top of the table with his family when Hamish suddenly stood up and knocked his wine glass with a fork for quiet. I thought he was going to propose a toast to the baby's health, but instead he started talking about what a wonderful family Charlie and Sylla made, and how he envied their happiness now they had Rose.

'And that's why,' he said, suddenly looking down at me, 'I want to ask Helen if she would do me the honour of becoming my wife.'

I gasped. There was an astonished ripple among the guests; Charlie looked confused and Sylla disconcerted. Then, as Hamish dropped to his knee and produced a ring from his pocket, Josephine screamed with joy and excitement.

I blushed scarlet, more uncomfortable than I had ever been in my life; happy, of course, and certain I wanted to accept, but bewildered that Hamish had thought this was an appropriate occasion for a proposal. But what could I do but smile happily, say yes, and let him push the ring on my finger? The table broke into a round of polite, slightly surprised applause as Hamish kissed me.

'What on earth made you do it at the christening?' I asked him later, when we were alone.

'Why not?' He seemed completely unfazed. 'I assumed you'd like it. I thought it was romantic, in front of all those people when you were looking your best.'

'It was . . . lovely,' I said, and kissed him. He seemed utterly unaware that it might be regarded as stealing someone's thunder to propose at their special occasion, or that I might have preferred to get engaged without an audience.

He meant well, I told myself. I held out my finger with the diamond sparkling on it. 'I love this. It's beautiful.'

'Ah.' Now he did look apologetic. 'That's Mum's, I'm afraid. I nicked it out of her jewellery box. I'll have to put it back later, before she notices. I had a feeling she'd be too excited to give it a proper look. But don't worry,' he added, seeing my face, 'I'll get you your own one soon, I promise. I'd better take that one back now, actually.' And he put out his hand for it.

I had to laugh, even while I shook my head in disbelief. I loved Hamish, but sometimes he acted in ways I simply didn't understand.

The actual engagement ring did not appear anytime soon. Hamish said he could not afford it. He was still a student, while I'd been headhunted from the bookshop to work in an advertising company; I was very junior but the money was good, the prospects were excellent, and I enjoyed the work.

Hamish teased me about selling out. He was going to do good and save the world, not flog it junk using greed and manipulation. Until then, though, as I pointed out, he didn't mind my supporting him on the proceeds of my evil job, or my putting up more than half the cost of my engagement ring when I finally insisted on getting one, as there didn't seem to be a Ballintyre ring for me.

But all of this was part of the ebb and flow of a long-term relationship. I loved my modest ring and I was walking on air to be engaged. I did wonder why Hamish was always flat broke, though. 'Do you get any money from home?' I asked him.

He shook his head. 'Mum doesn't have anything to spare.'

'Really?' I thought about Ballintyre, so large and obviously valuable, full of pictures and furniture and silver. 'No money?'

'A house like that takes a lot of upkeep, you know. It's vastly expensive to run. It takes all Mum's cash. She shouldn't have to support us too.'

'Of course,' I said hastily. I couldn't bear him to think I might be interested in any money he might have. 'I understand.'

But I was confused as well. Why have such a large house if it was too expensive to maintain? Why not downsize? I felt protective of Hamish for one thing: he was running up huge student debts getting his qualifications. And it meant that I was working to support us both, while my father gave me extra money on the quiet so that I could pay all the bills.

'Don't tell Nora,' he would say, when he pressed a cheque into my hands. 'She'd get so cross.'

Nora had been a little distant with me since my engagement and I was worried that somehow I'd displeased her. She'd always seemed to like Hamish but when I told her about his odd ways, she didn't laugh as I thought she might. She said, 'Think carefully, Hélène. You don't have to get married just because you accepted the proposal.'

'But I want to,' I'd said firmly. 'It's what I want more than anything.'

'Then . . .' She'd hesitated and smiled. 'Then I'm happy for you.'

But I could still sense that coolness and it bothered me.

Hamish proposing to me set Dad's mind at rest, I could see that. He obviously thought that there was money in the Ballintyre family that would come to Hamish at some point and provide us with security. That was why, when he was diagnosed with prostate cancer that year, he at once gave me the money for a deposit on a flat.

'I want to see you settled,' he said firmly. 'You need a good start in life.'

'Dad, thank you,' I said, crying hard and hugging him, still reeling from his diagnosis. 'I can't bear it, though!'

'Now that's enough. I'll be fine. Apparently most men with prostate cancer die *with* it, not *of* it. I've got years left, just you see.'

But he hadn't. He was one of the unlucky ones. He lived long enough to walk me down the aisle of Camberwell register office and see me marry Hamish, and to see our first home together, but not much longer after that. My wedding day was not quite as joyous an occasion as I'd hoped for. Not only was Dad so visibly weak and ill, but at the last minute, Nora told me she could not be there. I hadn't minded that my mother did not attend, but I did mind very much about Nora.

'I'm sorry, darling,' she'd said on the phone to me a few days before the wedding. 'I'm simply not well enough at the moment. You know I'd be there if I could. Your dad has his cousin Mabel to support him, he'll be fine without me. I'm devastated, Hélène, really. But there's nothing I can do, I'm going into hospital the very same day. Now, don't be anxious, it's a routine procedure, but I can't put it off, your father is going to need me a great deal. I hope you understand. But you must come and show me all the photographs.'

'Of course,' I said. 'I hope you get better soon, Nora.'

But when she'd hung up, I cried bitterly that she wouldn't be there.

The first few months of married life were happy enough. Hamish graduated, and went into management consultancy, advising on ethical business standards. It was a relief that he was bringing in a salary at last. But my father was ill, and I gave up my job so that I could go home and be with him and Nora, as he reached the end.

It was desperately sad and I was lonely too without Hamish, who stayed in London to work. Dad went into hospital and from there to a hospice. I'd got back to Dad's house late one night. Nora was already fast asleep at her place, in preparation for an early visit to Dad in the morning, and when the phone rang just before midnight as I was eating a late supper of toast and drinking a glass of wine, I answered it quickly, worried it might be the hospice.

'Hello?'

There was a strange spluttering on the other end of the line.

'Hello?' I said again.

Then I began to make out words in a slurred voice that was spitting slightly and hard to decipher. To my horror, I realised it was Josephine.

'What kind of wife are you?' she was saying. 'Hamish is all alone. You're not six months married, and you've left him alone! I'm sorry, Helen, but someone had to say it!'

'Josephine?'

'It'll be your fault if he abandons you! You don't leave your husband all alone. You look after him. You care for him. What's he supposed to do by himself? A wife should be with her husband! You're being a bad wife, Helen, I'm saying it for your own good!'

My hands were shaking slightly. I'd never heard her talk this way to me before. 'Josephine, are you drunk?'

'What's that got to do with it? Someone has to say something, Helen! You can't treat Hamish like this.'

'Josephine,' I said firmly, full of fury. 'How dare you call me like this? Hamish is a grown man. My father is dying. How dare you?'

'How dare *you*?' she cried, slurry. 'You're a bad wife! How dare *you*?'

'I'm putting the phone down now. Never call me like this again.' I put down the receiver, shaking and furious, hearing her voice still shouting, 'How dare *you*?' as it went down.

I couldn't bring myself to tell Nora about this horrible call. Two days later, Dad died, and I put the incident out of my mind while Nora and I grieved together, offering each other what comfort we could.

Over the next few years, I saw less of Nora, with Dad gone. She still phoned me often, and visited, but we were not as close as we had been. I had a lot to cope with. We had Lilac and, two years later, Jamie. It was a happy time, but pressured and relentless too. We moved from our flat to a bigger one in a less expensive area so we had room for the children. In the volatile employment market of the recession, Hamish lost two jobs in three years, then settled down in a third before giving up on that too, walking out grandly one afternoon.

'Don't worry, I'll get lots of freelance consultancy work, you'll see,' he said.

'That means neither of us has a steady income,' I said nervously. My career in advertising had not resurfaced after I'd quit it to be with Dad, and it had been impossible to commit to a job like that with a toddler and a baby to look after. I had become a freelancer myself, working as a copy-writer, picking up work from my old agency and through my contacts. I did marketing blurbs after the children were in bed, turning clunky translations into smooth English for websites and brochures. I was always tired, but that's what parenthood was: work punctuated by joy.

We'd be fine, Hamish reassured me. He was setting up his own business and soon he'd have plenty of work coming in – it was only a matter of time before he was a success. In the meantime, we could share the childcare burden between us. Despite my fears, it seemed to work well for some months. Then, one day when Hamish had taken the children to playgroup so that I could work for a few hours, I found a loan statement that I did not recognise.

I stared at it for ages, trying to work it out. Then I checked our joint accounts. Then I waited for Hamish to come home.

'I don't know anything about it.'

'What? How can you not know?' I'd started by giving him the chance to come clean, asking him if there was anything I should know about our finances. I waited until the children were in bed, and we'd had our supper and were sitting across the kitchen table from one another, and I'd tried to open the subject very gently so he would feel comfortable about telling me whatever he'd neglected to so far. But he looked completely blank. I began to nudge him towards the area that I was talking about in case it genuinely had slipped his mind, but he affected total ignorance.

'I don't know what you're talking about, Helen,' he said, looking helpless. 'Honestly.'

I was confused. I didn't have Hamish down as a liar but surely he must remember that he'd taken out a sizeable loan, with the money nowhere to be seen in our joint account. So I decided to be direct.

'Have you taken out a loan without telling me?'

'No,' he said positively, looking me straight in the eye.

'Are you sure?' Now I really was confused. Had I misread the statement somehow? I took it out from the folder and put it in front of him across the table. 'What's this?'

He stared at it and then looked up. 'Oh, that.'

'Yes, that! Why did you pretend you'd forgotten?'

'I thought you already knew, to be honest. I thought I'd told you about it.'

'What?' I exclaimed. 'Then why pretend you didn't know what I was talking about?'

His blue gaze was clear and candid. 'I thought you must be talking about something else, as you already knew about this.'

I was more confused now. 'That's just not possible, Hamish.'

His expression cleared. 'Oh, I know why I didn't tell you. It's a business loan. For new start-ups. I didn't think it really applied to the both of us. As it's for my business.'

'Of course it applies! It will still affect us both if you don't make enough money to repay it. And you don't seem to be, from this statement. Why did you keep it a secret from me?'

His gaze slid away from me and fixed on the tablecloth. 'I didn't want to worry you,' he said, his voice low.

'There's a difference between worrying me and telling me an outright lie, isn't there?'

'Yes,' he mumbled. 'Sorry. I didn't know what else to do.'

I shook my head in disbelief. 'Anything's better than lying, isn't it?'

He looked repentant. 'Yes. I shouldn't have lied. I was just trying to protect you.'

'Okay, I appreciate that. But you'd better tell me now, what's this loan exactly? Who provided it?'

He began to tell me the story. It was hard to understand exactly what he was saying, but each time I tried to press for detail or clarification, he only got more uncertain and woolly about the facts. Eventually I managed to draw from him that he had borrowed a significant sum from a loan company in order to set up his freelance consultancy business – and pay some bills.

'What bills?'

He sighed. 'My freelancing isn't going as well as I'd hoped. I'm not getting the jobs. I keep getting promises of work and then they fall through. It's this recession, it's a nightmare. My sector is the first to go when people are cutting back.'

'You never said! In fact, you told me you've plenty to plug the gap. The joint account looks fine.'

'I told you, I didn't want to worry you.'

I was baffled. 'But I've been bringing in money. Perhaps not a lot, but enough to pay the bills when you're not earning. And the money Dad left me – I used that when the boiler needed replacing, and for our summer holiday last year. I wouldn't have spent it if I thought we needed it for bills.'

'I appreciate that, but I still had to find money for things. I've got my student loans, don't forget, and some credit cards that were building up, and I had to get on top of them. And there was all the rest of it. Meals out. Holidays. Presents.'

'But I wouldn't want you to spend money you don't have on those things! We don't need them. Oh Hamish . . . why didn't you tell me? If you needed money, we could have sorted it out together. And if it was that desperate, couldn't your mother help?'

'No,' he said sulkily. 'I can't ask her, you know that. It would worry her too much. Besides, I didn't think it was desperate. Just to cover me until more work comes in or I get a job.'

'All right. How much did you borrow? Because the statement has some hefty repayments on it.'

'I don't know! You can look at my bank statements if you like.'

'I don't want to look at your statements, I want you to be honest with me, to tell me what's going on. How much was it? Ten thousand?'

'Around that.'

'Well, was it?'

'A bit more.'

'Fifteen? Twenty?'

'Yes.'

'Which?'

'Eighteen,' he said recklessly as though picking a number at random.

I gasped. 'Hamish! Eighteen thousand! Really? How?'

'I don't know! It just happened. Look, I'll show you all my statements. You can look over it all, if you want. Then you can see.'

I felt uncomfortable. 'No. I don't want that. Just *tell* me what I need to know. Be straight with me. Please.'

'Sorry,' he said, looking away. 'I made a mistake. I'm sorry. I won't do it again.'

'Okay. Just, please . . . talk to me when things are bad.'

'I will, I said. I'm really sorry, Helen. It's been pretty dreadful for me, if you must know.' He looked miserable. After a moment he said, 'I'm not the only one to have secrets, though, am I? You got money from your dad all the time without telling me.'

I was taken aback. 'It's not the same, though, is it?'

'Isn't it?'

'Well, no.' I was confused again. Was it the same? 'I was trying to take the pressure off you without you feeling bad.'

He smiled sadly. 'Exactly what I was doing.'

'Okay. Maybe you're right.' I still felt it wasn't quite the same, but I didn't trust myself to go on without getting more upset, and what good would that do? He was feeling defensive and needed some time to think about it. It was clear that he'd been careless, then panicked over the debts and done something stupid. I didn't understand why he hadn't confided in me, but he accepted that was wrong, and I was sure that once he'd considered, he'd be truly remorseful, and understand that wasn't the right way to run a relationship. I said, 'Well, let's make a pact then. We'll be honest with one another from now on. Both of us. About everything, especially money. Okay?'

'It's a deal.' Hamish smiled at me, his good humour restored. 'Shall we watch something funny on the telly to cheer ourselves up?'

I hadn't told Nora. She was still grieving over the loss of my father, and I was reluctant for her to know Hamish had deceived me. I knew she would not approve. The important thing was to hold our family together and I was sure that by forgiving him, I would show Hamish he had nothing to fear by being honest with me. The money was unfortunate, but we'd get through it. It was a lesson and I was sure Hamish and I would learn from it and get through the blip together.

Immediately afterwards he sank into a morose depression and when I asked him about it, he said he felt guilty about how he'd treated me. I trod carefully around his feelings, took as much of the burden of our home life off him as I could, and did my best to bolster him. But it became clear that his sector wasn't going to pick up again anytime soon. He had several unsuccessful job interviews and I was beginning to get seriously worried about how we would manage just on my salary. All our ballast was gone, and Hamish's loan repayments took any money he did manage to bring in.

That was when he had his brainwave. He would train as a teacher and get a job in a boarding school that would provide accommodation.

'We'll have all expenses paid,' he said, 'and that will help us get back on our feet. Once I've got an income, we can remortgage to pay off the loan, then rent out the flat to pay the mortgage, and then we'll be quids in. After I've paid back the cost of training. But I reckon I can get a grant to help.'

'Okay,' I said. It seemed to make sense. We'd have a chance to get back on our feet. 'I think that's a great idea.'

I felt hopeful. Teaching was steady. There were long holidays, when he would be able to help with the children. Perhaps this was the answer to his flitting attention span, and he'd always enjoyed spending time with children, not like some of the fathers I knew. 'If it's what you want. I think you'd be an excellent teacher.'

'Sting was a teacher,' he said thoughtfully. 'And Orwell. And Waugh.'

'Yes?'

'It's a stepping stone. To great things. It'll give us the breathing space we need.'

I hoped it wasn't a stepping stone, but a landing place. We needed something anchored in our lives after bobbing about so aimlessly on the open sea. 'You'll be wonderful at it,' I said. And I meant it.

PART FOUR

Chapter Ten

TIGS

1970

London was overwhelming for me from the start: hordes of people everywhere, traffic, noise and bustle wherever I looked. I was used to space, endless skies, solitude and my lookout rock whenever I needed solace. Tremewan was full of air and light, but here the flat was shrouded in constant darkness, down a flight of clanging iron stairs to a front door below pavement level. At the front was the poky sitting room, then a kitchen-dining room and at the rear the one decent bedroom that opened into a tiny courtyard garden. Serena had that, of course. I was in the tiny spare room, which was next to the bathroom. It was long and narrow, probably only ever intended for storage, and just had room for a single bed and a built-in wardrobe and dressing table with drawers beneath. Lying in bed, I could reach out and touch the opposite wall if I stretched.

What also made me ill at ease was the chaos in which Serena lived. There wasn't a clear surface anywhere, and every room seemed full of abandoned objects – books, clothes, shoes, hairbrushes, curlers, make-up all littering the floor, tables, sofa and chairs. Worse, though, Serena never seemed to clean anything.

'Don't you have a mop?' I asked, looking warily at the kitchen floor, which I suspected might actually be cream rather than light brown.

'Somewhere,' Serena said airily. 'I really don't have time for that, you know.' She was the height of sophistication in her barrel-bottom jeans, mint-green jumper with a shiny red belt, her dark hair tucked into a paisley satin headscarf.

'I don't know how you can bear it,' I said, shaking my head. I hadn't realised how calm life at home was, but I now understood that Mumma worked hard to keep the house in order and that order translated into the sense of serenity that filled it. She hated clutter and chose every object carefully. She was constantly restoring things to their places and, without realising, I'd come to do the same. It didn't appear to have had the same effect on Serena, though, who went through life wading through piles of discarded things, creating an ever bigger mess.

Serena lit a cigarette and went to get her coat. 'If you want to tidy up, be my guest. I'm meeting Eric at the pub. There is a hoover in the cupboard in the hall.' She picked up her handbag, and was heading out before I could say anything more.

I sighed. It was already obvious that my room had not been cleaned for a long time and I itched, almost literally, to get rid of the dust. In the end, I had to take a trip to the shops to buy dusters and cleaning things, then I rolled up my sleeves and got on with it.

'It seems fair enough,' Serena told me the next day, when she saw the fruits of my labour. 'Obviously I could make quite a lot letting out your room. You're getting it cut price. Tons of girls would love it.'

'Would they want it? It's rather snug.'

'It's Chelsea, Tigs! So I think you doing the cleaning will help to balance it up.'

I rolled my eyes but didn't protest. I found it soothing to clean, more soothing than facing the noise and crowds and traffic outside the flat.

Serena was vaguely interested in my welfare but once we established that I knew how to get to the Underground and had my front door key, she was happy to leave me to myself. She was kept very busy by her work and social life, and I envied her hectic routines. She had a wide social circle of girls like her: well brought up, living on the edges of Chelsea, working as secretaries and waiting to meet Mr Right. But I hadn't stumbled into that world yet, if I ever would.

Art school wasn't at all what I'd expected. I'd imagined jolly sessions of painting, but so far I hadn't seen a brush. The other students came from all over the country and from all types of background, but mostly they were typical young arty types, in interesting clothes with long hair and very earnest about their calling, and I found them all highly intimidating.

I felt an idiot from the first day, unprepared, untalented and stupid. No matter what I attempted to do, it came out embarrassingly amateurish despite trying my very hardest.

'Draw what you see, draw what you see,' I muttered to myself. We were doing timed rapid-fire charcoal sketches to loosen us up and mine were getting worse at every attempt, coming out like something a five-year-old would do, while all around me the class created brilliant drawings in a variety of styles and perspectives.

'Look for shapes,' my teacher Miss Watson urged as she stood by my easel, gazing at my smudged heavy lines. 'Stop trying to see like a photograph. See with your eyes. First of all – the light. Where is it? Where is it coming from? What does it do to the objects? How do they relate to each other and to their surroundings?'

'I'm trying to get that bowl just right and I can't seem to do it,' I said, hoping I didn't sound petulant.

'You will. But relax. Look, it curves out like a half-moon; you've made it too flat and it's losing its quality of round-ness.' Miss Watson took my charcoal and added one thick, sure line to the bowl. 'There. That helps, doesn't it? And the light falls here in a great silver patch.' She picked up my eraser and with a smooth movement took out a portion of my grey smudge. Suddenly the bowl glowed.

I stared. She had brought it entirely to life. 'Yes. Thank you.'

'Keep going. You'll get there.'

It took all I had not to rip the drawing up in front of her, but I kept on, hating my efforts. I was too embarrassed to hang around with the other students when classes were over, certain they could see how untalented I was. I headed off on my own instead. I soon spent every lunchtime alone, slipping into the Tate, or walking by the river, looking for oases of calm and beauty in the busy city. At home, I was alone a great deal of the time, with Serena out at her parties and going to nightclubs. There was no television, not that I was used to watching it in any case. I spent my evenings curled up on the sofa, reading and dreaming and wondering if my life would ever really begin. I was starting to suspect I wasn't really an artist, and London was more overwhelming than I'd anticipated. Art school was intimidating. I should have stayed in Scotland, and been happy. When I felt lonely and stressed, I found I could lift my mood by tidying and cleaning, bringing order to the little flat where everything was safe.

It was Serena's idea to, as she put it, whore me out.

'Becky Ridgemont is desperate. I said you would help.'

'What?' I blinked at her, astonished. Serena had risen late on the Saturday morning, as was her habit, and I had already been out and returned from the bakery with bread and our Saturday treat of iced buns.

'Did you remember my cigs, by the way?'

'In the bag. What am I doing for Becky Ridgemont?'

Serena yawned. 'Cleaning, of course. You're quite the charwoman. This place has never looked so dazzling.' She gestured at the kitchen. I liked to tune into the radio and listen to John Peel on a Saturday, working away with my cleaning cloths and polishers. Before I knew it, I'd be washing out the fridge, or scrubbing the floor or pulling out the contents of the cupboard to clean inside. It was satisfying. I was pleased with my efforts in a way that I was never pleased with my art.

'So you said to Becky I'd clean for her?'

'Yup.'

'Oh, thanks!' I said indignantly. 'Without even asking me? Checking if I have time? I'm rather busy, actually!'

'Really?' Serena raised her eyebrows. 'Surprised to hear that, as you're always here when not at college.'

'As far as you know! You're either at work or partying or nursing a hangover!'

'Don't get so defensive. She's going to pay you. A pound an hour.'

'What?' I gaped at her.

'Yes.' Serena nodded wisely. 'You see? As if I didn't have your best interests at heart.'

'A *pound* an hour?' I'd be rich. Let's say I worked for Becky for three hours every week, that would be twelve pounds a month. It was practically my rent. All for me to do exactly as I wanted. I'd never had so much money at my disposal. 'Gosh, thanks, Serena.'

Serena shrugged. 'I had no idea she'd accept. She's got more money than sense. You would have done it for half that.'

'When do I start?'

'As soon as you like. I told you, she's desperate.'

Becky Ridgemont was not quite as bad a housekeeper as Serena but she and three flatmates did very little around the house and they clearly considered me a necessity, paying up without a qualm, and I was soon Becky's regular cleaner. She recommended me to a friend, and it wasn't long before I had several regular cleaning jobs, working in Chelsea, Kensington and Fulham. To my surprise, I enjoyed it. I found it so satisfying to go into an untidy house, full of dust, dirt and over-full bins, and to leave it spotless and sparkling, everything nicely arranged and peaceful calm returned. I would turn on the radio, listen to the music and the chat, and lose myself in the job. I often worked longer hours than I was paid because I forgot the time but I didn't mind; no one quibbled at my rate when they saw my work so I felt richly rewarded, enough to do extra without minding. I'd take my money from wherever it had been left for me and let myself out, happy that the owners would come home to the joyful sight of a clean and tidy house.

I soon started to skip college to clean. During my long walks around the city back and forth to my clients, I found intriguing junk shops and odd little antique shops, where I could spend some of my newfound wealth on treasures. I was drawn to all manner of things: unusual oil paintings, pretty porcelain, antique jewellery and, best of all, wonderful old clothes. I found an elegant 1930s jacket in olive tweed, which I wore over the denim dungarees I cleaned in, and a turquoise turban from the fifties that I tucked my hair under and wore while hard at work scrubbing.

'What funny things you like!' Serena would say when I showed her my treasures. She suggested we go shopping on the King's Road and Carnaby Street, where I could get some fashionable things. But my little cupboard bedroom filled up with my finds and I never did end up shopping in the trendy boutiques and department stores that Serena frequented.

I was enjoying myself dealing with some particularly dense dust under the radiators of a much-neglected flat when Emma, the owner, came in, carrying her baby, which had just woken from its afternoon nap.

'Oh, you are a treasure,' she said, jiggling the pink-faced, grizzling baby. 'I know it's in a state. I haven't managed to do anything thoroughly for ages, what with the baby . . .'

'Don't worry at all. It wouldn't be very satisfying if there were nothing for me to do when I got here,' I said, from my position on my knees by her sitting room radiator. I had pulled out hanks of dust and debris from behind it, including some crunchy old knickers that had clearly been drying on top, fallen down the back and hardened into a creased ball.

Emma flushed scarlet when she saw them. 'It's so hard when you can't bend over. I couldn't for ages when I was pregnant.'

'I understand.'

'In fact,' she said very fast, as though trying to distract me from the scrunched-up knickers on the floor, 'I've got a friend who's pregnant, she could really do with your help. She doesn't live far from here, just over the way. Any chance you could do her place as well?'

I sat back on my heels and considered. 'I'm quite booked up.' My cleaning was taking up such a lot of my time, I'd had to cut back on my attendance at art school to the point where a few letters had arrived at the house asking if I was ill, and if I could kindly telephone in to explain my absence. So far, I'd just ignored them but I knew it wouldn't be too long before someone pulled me up properly on my truancy.

'You'd be saving her life, I mean it. I promised her you'd at least take a look – do you think you could?'

'All right.' A little voice told me that any more cleaning really would spell the end of my art career but I silenced it. 'I can look in today, I suppose. Did you say she was near?'

'Very. She's on Gibson Street, in an upstairs flat.'

'Give me the address and I'll pop round.'

'Oh, thank you! She'll be so grateful. I'm taking the baby out for a walk now, your money's on the kitchen table.'

It was mid-afternoon once I'd finished at Emma's, having decided on the spur of the moment to clear out the cob-webby cupboard under the stairs. I put my jacket on over my dirty dungarees, grabbed my bag and headed out with my trusty A–Z to guide me to Gibson Street, which lay between the King's Road and the Fulham Road, another Chelsea street lined with early-Victorian houses, some smartened up, some a little down-at-heel. Quite a few had been turned into flats, and when I found number eight, I pressed the little buzzer on the intercom and waited.

After a while, a woman answered. 'Yes?'

'I'm the cleaner. Emma sent me?'

There was a long pause and then: 'Oh yes. Come up. Second floor.' Then a buzz and the door catch released, so I went in, climbed to the second floor and knocked on the door there. A moment later, it opened and I found myself staring at Josephine Ballintyre, her large pregnancy bump covered in an orange shift dress that ended at her knees, her fair hair held back by a wide headband in the same orange. She wore clogs. I was speechless with surprise as she gave me a quick look up and down, and then beckoned me in.

'Thanks for coming. Emma tells me you're very good. I'm afraid a pound an hour is quite steep, though. I'm happy to pay you one pound fifty a time, if that's all right. It's what I paid my last cleaner.' She was walking through the flat to the kitchen and I followed, still dumb with astonishment. She didn't appear to have realised that she knew me from Ballintyre. I'd been right, she'd simply ignored me when we'd met there.

In the kitchen, which looked pretty clean and tidy to me already, she turned and faced me, without inviting me to sit. 'I absolutely hate being here when someone is cleaning, so I'll be out when you arrive. The key will be under the mat and you're to leave it there when you go. I'll expect you gone by three hours on the dot. I'll need a thorough clean of the kitchen and bathroom, of course, and dusting, tidying and hoovering in the bedroom and sitting room. Any time left over, there's always ironing to do, the laundry basket's behind the sofa. I'll provide cleaning things, but I'll leave a list out for you to fill in for supplies, and that includes anything you spot missing in the house: loo paper, bin bags, hoover bags . . . you know the kind of thing. I'll need you on Fridays.' She looked at me with absolutely no flicker of recognition. In the mirror on the wall over the kitchen table, I caught a glimpse of my reflection: hair tucked away under the turquoise turban, my face bare of make-up and streaked with dirt from Emma's cupboard. Perhaps it wasn't surprising she didn't know me. It had been some time since I'd seen her, after all.

But here I was, standing in James's own home, talking to his wife, surrounded by his things and his life. Even his baby was growing just a few feet away from me. I felt as though I'd stepped by accident and without warning into another world entirely. It was disconcerting and confusing.

'Well?' she said with a trace of impatience.

I gaped at her, trying to take in what she'd said. She was offering me half of my usual pay and in terms that would usually have me politely but firmly declining.

'Can you do Friday?' she said slowly as if I were not very bright.

'Yes,' I said. I knew I would do it, no matter how she spoke to me. How could I not?

Josephine nodded. 'Good. I'll make arrangements to be out on Friday mornings.' She smiled at me, obviously prepared to soften now that negotiations were over and she'd got her way. 'Emma tells me you're very good, so it's a big relief to me.' She put her hands on her bump. 'As you can see, I'm not really in any condition to do housework anymore.'

'When is the baby due?'

'In December.' She smiled. 'Very exciting.'

'Yes. Very. Congratulations.'

There was a pause, then she said, 'Well, if it's all decided . . .' and began to move towards the door. I followed her. 'So you'll start this Friday?' she said as she opened it and stood back to let me out. It wasn't really a question, more of an order disguised as one.

'Yes,' I said obediently, going past her. I turned, suddenly struck by the absurdity of it, and also realising that if I said nothing now, the chance would have been lost and how could I explain myself later?

She stared back at me, her utter lack of recognition all over her face. 'Yes?'

'I . . . nothing,' I said, and managed a smile. 'I'll be here on Friday.'

I walked home in a daze. I had had the feeling that if I put out the call to the Fates to bring me to James, it would somehow happen. But now it had, I was overwhelmed and almost frightened. Josephine Ballintyre had invited me into her home. There would be a key under the mat. I could hardly believe it. I knew that I should not have accepted the post, not without telling her who I was. And I also knew that I should not have accepted it in any case. It was an invasion of their privacy.

And an invasion of mine.

There had been her manner: I would not have liked it in anyone. People who treated me with disdain or with a sense of their own superiority were few, and while most knew I was Serena's sister and so would have been polite, some did not and it made no difference. It wasn't that I expected different treatment to any other cleaner; it was that I thought no cleaner should be treated with haughtiness, as a servant to be ordered around. Someone like Josephine would usually ring alarm bells. I'd have made my excuses and turned down the job. I hadn't. I had, in some way, endorsed her treatment of me by accepting it. Why had I?

To be close to James, of course. To be near him again. For that, I had risked my life at college. Friday mornings were Miss Watson's classes, the only ones I liked. If I cut them, I would be bound to lose my place. And I was prepared to risk it, it seemed, because I could not resist the siren call of proximity to James and the appalled fascination Josephine afforded me.

It was hard to sleep that night. I only managed it at last by thinking of home, of my rock, and of riding in *Kitty* with James, bobbing along on the waves of the loch as the sunshine touched their white tops and we laughed in the salty air.

My fingers trembled as I pulled the key out from under the rough coir mat in front of the door. I had hardly believed it would really happen, but here I was at James's flat. I put the key in the lock and opened the door to the silent rooms beyond.

'Hello?' I called, just in case, but there was no reply. Josephine was as good as her word and was not there. Everything looked neat and tidy already, but that only meant that Josephine would be more demanding than most: the ones who lived in messy disorder were most grateful for the transformation. Women like Josephine had gimlet eyes, looking for tiny smears left on mirrors, the one hair left behind in the bath, the rug not lifted and cleaned under. She would have high standards and expect them to be met.

I went into the kitchen and saw the bucket of cleaning things left out, the one pound fifty on the table, half what I would usually make. Then I went straight out again and into the sitting room, walking carefully around it. It was pretty, as nice as any of the other houses of well-off young couples for whom I cleaned. It was traditional, not fashionable, with a chintz sofa, a green armchair and floral curtains swagged and tasselled in a way that was a bit over the top for such a small room. A bookcase by the fireplace held lots of history books, classic novels and lighter-hearted stuff, along with reference books. On a table in the window sat family photographs. There were James and Josephine on the wedding day I remembered so vividly. And there was Ballintyre, so beautiful against the pine-covered hills. I longed suddenly, with a wash of homesickness, for the loch and the forests and my parents. My eyes filled with tears and I turned away from the little table.

I went to the bedroom. As I entered, my heart began to thud unpleasantly, the sense of intrusion making me tremble. I was supposed to be here, I reminded myself, I was the cleaner. Josephine wanted me to be there. And yet . . . I stared at the bed, neatly made, sheets turned over the counterpane, yellow flowered pillows propped up against the mahogany headboard. My imagination supplied the images: James turning to Josephine, taking her in his arms, kissing her, making love to her – right there, in that bed. The pillows would be askew, the sheets crumpled, the counterpane thrown back, their bodies entwined, the air filled with the sound of their gasps and murmurs.

It was like standing in a torture chamber, imagining the rack being used. I couldn't bear it. I turned and hurried out, going to the kitchen to start cleaning there, hoping the work and the radio would take my mind off it. But nothing could. My head was full of James. Everything I saw was a clue telling me about his life, from what muesli he ate to what brand of coffee he drank. I could imagine him now, sitting with one of the blue and white mugs from the cupboard, munching on a ginger nut, or making toast in the green toaster. I could see everything about his daily life. His socks were drying on a rack over the hall radiator. His coat hung on a stand in the hall, with caps and umbrellas. In the bathroom, it was even more intimate: his shampoo, his towel, the shaving things on the stand, his toothbrush in the cup. The room was clean enough, but even so. Here he stood naked every day, and I could barely stand my thoughts as I polished the mirror.

What am I doing here?

Back in the bedroom, I dusted and resisted the temptation to touch anything or open drawers. I was almost determined not to do anything I might be ashamed of, and yet I couldn't stop myself when I saw a navy-blue jumper folded on a chair. I picked it up and put my nose to it, inhaling his scent. At once, he was alive for me, and the sense of his physical presence was almost overwhelming. I put the jumper back reverently, almost frightened of the potency that conjured him up so immediately. *Stop it*, I told myself firmly, and went to get the hoover from under the stairs so that I could finish the room and leave it.

At the end of the three hours, I took the money from the table and looked around. It was spotless. I had taken extra care to leave it dazzlingly clean. It was my gift to him. I had, I realised, barely given Josephine a thought.

I let myself out of the front door, slipped the key under the mat and left, knowing I would not be able to help myself returning.

Chapter Eleven

Postcards kept arriving for me.

They were often bizarre sketches of trolls or unusual monsters, illustrations of fairy tales and myths. Sometimes they showed objects from classic times: a vase, a statue, a relic. On the back of the card would be an observation in a scrawled hand. Sometimes it would just be a comment about the picture: *This was drawn in 1745. Surprisingly modern.* Or: *This is the grave of a Roman woman. The inscription warns that there is no afterlife so enjoy life while you can.*

I knew Al was sending them and I wished he wouldn't but I could hardly object. He said nothing of the dreadful thing I had done – kissing him and then running away and refusing to see or speak to him again – and yet I still felt rebuked. But perhaps that was my own guilt and regret.

I didn't think much about Al except when I got those cards. I was busy with my classes and my cleaning, and in any case, I was living for those three hours a week when I entered James's private world. Then I could step invisibly into his life, soak it in, smell it and even taste it. I was growing in courage in the silent flat: I made myself a cup of his coffee, ate one of his biscuits, touched the fruit he might eat and shared the milk from his bottle. I was like a lone worshipper allowed into an empty church, able to walk to the altar, touch the golden candlesticks, run my fingers over the carvings and across the embroidered cloths. I was reverent and yet dangerously close to the source of the magic.

I had written to my college to explain that I had a recurring doctor's appointment during my Friday classes and so had to miss them until the end of the term. This seemed to be a way to gain a little time but I knew that my place was hanging by a thread. In the evenings, usually on my own with Serena out, I sketched and drew, and tried to find my own style, my way of making things come alive, but it all looked derivative and flat, and anyway, I was more alive in my dreams and fantasies now than in my real life. I looked forward to the mindless cleaning I did so that I could lose myself in intense imaginings of James.

The season was changing in London; the streets had drifts of brown leaves in the gutters, and nights came earlier. Now I was often walking home in the orange glow of street lamps, the pavements glistening with rain and an icy wind blowing. Despite being used to the cold in Scotland, I felt the chill. I bought a duffle coat so that I could hide inside its thick warmth, and some stout boots. When I wasn't cleaning, I was walking and walking.

'Are you all right, Tigs?' Serena asked me one night. She had run out of money and so was on an economy drive, and we were spending more time together. She liked my cooking and I enjoyed some company for a change. 'You're very quiet. And I think you've got thinner. Turn around.'

I twirled on the spot, like a ballerina except in dungarees and slippers. 'Ta-da! Do I pass the audition?'

'You are thinner. Much. Are you ill?'

'No . . . just busy, I suppose. There often isn't time for lunch and then I lose my appetite.'

'I wish I could,' Serena said gloomily. 'Eric was telling me how well padded I felt the other night. It's all the evenings in the pub, drinking lager and eating peanuts.'

'That won't help.'

'And while I love Eric, he does like the filthiest food. Chips with everything! If it can be fried, it will be fried.'

'I miss Mumma's cooking,' I said wistfully, suddenly full of longing for the wonderful meals she conjured up with our home produce. I yearned for the Sunday evening supper of eggs laid by her hens, baked in milk with cheese and butter, pieces of homemade bread on the side, and a dark green swirl of spinach from the garden.

'We'll be home before too long,' Serena said comfortingly. 'I miss it too. When I'm there, I can't wait to get to London, and when I'm here, I start to miss home horribly. It seems impossible to be completely happy, doesn't it? There's always something one can't have.'

She started to talk about going home for Christmas while I went back to stirring the stew, glad she had changed the subject. But Serena was right. My clothes were loose and I could see that my stomach was getting almost concave below my ribs. Even my wrist stirring the spoon looked bony and delicate.

I'll be all right when I get home, I thought. *Mumma will look after me.*

I had a horrible feeling that I'd gone off track somehow. I'd been supposed to be a flourishing artist by now, but here I was, a cleaner, skipping classes and living for the three hours a week when I'd clean James Ballintyre's flat without him knowing. I'd been there that very day. Now, I had taken to waiting down the road, loitering by a telephone box, until Josephine came out of the house, her bump large and belted under her raincoat, and walked off. Then I went in, not wanting to waste a moment, knowing she'd be out till after lunch. I'd take my time as I tidied and cleaned, running my hand over cups in the sink, touching his shampoo bottle, looking almost in awe at his side of the bed. This was where he slept. I'd feel the smoothness of his pillow with my fingertips and brush the cotton of his pyjamas tucked beneath.

You're being very odd, I would tell myself, even while I gazed lovingly at his toothbrush. I knew I was, but it was harmless. No one knew. No one would know. It was the closest I could come to him, probably in my life. I saved up the best until last. Then I would work my way slowly through the stack of laundry, ironing his clothes with special care and taking pleasure in making them as perfect as I could, imagining them close to his skin. There were Josephine's things too, of course, and I treated them with care as well. Her association with him elevated her into a special being too, chosen by him, as baffling as it might seem to me. I was glad she wasn't present in the flat while I cleaned. I didn't want to be close to her at all. But what would happen when the baby came? Would she be there all the time? Would I be able to stand it?

I'll cross that bridge . . . I told myself firmly and went back to stirring the dinner.

We had just finished eating when the doorbell rang and Serena immediately looked guilty.

'Who's that?' I asked. 'Eric?'

'Um, I meant to say,' she said, getting up, 'I meant to say that Alastair Drummond rang up and asked if he could come round. I was going to tell you. But I forgot.'

I felt the blood drop from my face. 'Al Drummond . . . is here?'

Serena checked her watch. 'I think so, yes. He said eight p.m.'

'Serena!' I said crossly. 'I can't believe it.'

She was already out of the kitchen and crossing the hall. 'Hello,' I heard her say when she'd opened the door. 'Yes, come in. I'll get Tigs.'

As I came slowly out of the kitchen, I saw him standing in our hall, a hulking tall outline in a long, shapeless coat, his black hair overgrown and messy. He was staring at the picture I'd hung over the telephone table and looked around as I approached. 'This is good, young Tigs.'

'I found it in a junk shop in Pimlico.'

'Did you now? Well, it's a print of a painting by Honoré Daumier.'

'Is it? I just liked it.'

191

'It's lovely. You'd think it was from the early twentieth century, but he painted it around 1860. Wonderful soft quality and even though there's no background detail, it's almost as though we know they're in a smoky little bistro somewhere, singing their hearts out.'

'Al . . .'

He turned to look at me questioningly and I was struck by the vulnerability in his dark eyes, the same I'd seen there the night of the Tighglachach ball.

'What are you doing here?' I asked quietly.

'I happened to be in London and thought I'd look you up and see how you're getting along at art school.'

'Really?'

His gaze slid away from me and something in him seemed to droop a little. 'Well, not entirely. I want to talk to you. But . . . not here, with Serena earwigging. There's a pub on the corner. Can we go to that?'

'It's a bit rough, I think,' I said. I'd never been in a pub, and Serena only went to those in Belgravia.

'Don't worry about that. Will you come?'

'All right.'

We went together down the road and into the lounge bar of the Rose & Crown, which turned out to be almost deserted. One man sat obscured by the *Evening Standard*, a pint of cider on the table next to him. We could hear noise and banter from the saloon bar, which could be seen across the counter but was divided from us by a wall and entered by a different door. Thick clouds of cigarette smoke wafted across the divide and I could hear the click of balls on the pool table.

'Quieter on this side,' Al said, then went to ring a bell on the counter to alert the barmaid to our presence. When she arrived, he ordered a pint of beer for himself and a cola for me, at my request, and got a packet of crisps for each of us.

He put the crisps down in front of me. 'I hope you like cheese and onion.'

I nodded, though I wasn't hungry as I'd just had dinner.

He sat down, opened the packet and started eating them. We sat in silence while he crunched his way through the crisps, then he folded the packet up into a neat triangle and looked at my untouched packet. 'Are you going to eat those?'

'No.'

'Mind if I do?'

I shook my head. He tore open the packet and, just as before, ate the contents, crunching each one noisily. When they were finished, he made the little triangle out of the packet, lit a cigarette and sipped his drink.

'What are we doing here?' I said at last, a little helplessly. I had almost expected Al to be different in some way, but, of course, he was just the same: completely himself.

'I thought you might enjoy a bit of night life.'

I looked around at the lounge bar, empty now that the other man had folded up his newspaper and left, perhaps put off by the crunch of Al's crisp consumption. 'It's hardly the Café de Paris, is it?'

'Do you want to go there? We can, if you like.'

'No, of course not.'

'Some other disco then?'

I almost laughed at the idea of Al disco dancing, when his reeling was practically a martial art. 'No, I don't want to go anywhere. I just want to know why you're here.'

'I sent you cards and you never replied.'

'I didn't know what to reply. You didn't exactly say anything on them.'

'A friendly acknowledgement would have been something.' He stared at me. 'You don't look comfortable. Don't you want to see me?'

'Well . . . yes, of course . . . but . . .'

'But?'

I flushed and shifted. 'It was a little awkward last time.'

'I know.' He suddenly became occupied with his tobacco tin, finding his papers and preparing a cigarette, even though one had only just been mashed down into the ashtray. 'I wanted to talk to you about that.'

My stomach did an unpleasant flip. I had guessed it must be this. I'd tried to avoid it but now it must be faced. Well, I deserved it. 'Yes,' I said.

He looked me straight in the face, his dark eyes inscrutable. 'Tigs . . . did you mean it when you kissed me?'

A hot flush crawled up my neck and fired up my cheeks. 'Oh dear. I shouldn't have done it. I'm sorry, I really am.'

'Then why did you?'

'I . . . I was just in an odd way. My mother had said to me that I was being unkind to you, because you liked me, and I said she was wrong but it occurred to me that maybe she was right, and if she was, then I should see if I liked you.'

I could see the pain on his face and I could have kicked myself, but it was too late.

'So you had a go and found you didn't.' He looked at me sadly. 'It's all right. It's fine. But I needed to know. You must have guessed how I feel about you. I've always felt that way. I have to know whether there's any hope. I take it there isn't.'

'I'm sorry. I don't think there is.' I leaned across the small sticky pub table towards him. 'You're a wonderful friend to me. I love spending time with you.'

'It's cold comfort, I'm afraid.'

'It would never work, you must see that!'

'Why not?' he asked obstinately. 'It already works. At least, I think so.'

'But that's just the thing. You know what you think and you never seem to have any room for what I think.'

'What on earth do you mean?'

'You're always telling me I'm wrong or mistaken.'

'Now, Tigs, that's not true—'

'See?' I sighed crossly. 'You don't even know you do it. You never let me have my own thoughts! You always contradict me or know better. I don't mind it too much but I could never live with it, not all the time. And it stops me feeling . . . the way you do.'

He was silent for a moment and then said sadly, 'I always had the impression we were in tune about everything. I didn't realise you felt this way.'

'Well, I do. I'm sorry.'

He smoked for a while, gazing out of the murky window into the night outside. Then he said in a matter-of-fact voice, 'You can tell me, you know, if there's someone else.'

'There's no one else.' I laughed wryly. 'I think I probably have even fewer friends than I had back home.'

'So you're still pining after him.' He said it flatly without a question in his voice.

I went scarlet again but said nothing. I was about to deny it but what was the point? He had guessed. I had not been so brilliant at hiding it after all. Anyway, I couldn't bring myself to lie to him now.

The expression on his face went from sad to utter misery. 'I see. Well, I can't fight your fantasies. I know you think he's some magnificent hero, but he's just an ordinary person, perhaps even less impressive than most. And he's married that awful woman. He'd never have chosen her if he had anything about him, but he's weak and she's ambitious and look where they are now. It'll end badly, I can tell, and it would have ended badly for you too if you'd married him.' He tapped his roll-up on the plastic ashtray and expelled another stream of smoke, his leg fidgeting, his foot tapping. 'You'd not be happy with him.' He looked at me very intensely. 'You'd be happy with me.'

I stared back, almost wavering in the face of his certainty. But I remembered the kiss. The way it had made me feel. I hadn't swooned and dissolved; I'd felt awkward and wrong. He'd smelled of smoke, his skin had felt rough, his arms stiff and strange. No. It couldn't be. I didn't love him and I never would.

'I'm sorry,' I said in a small voice. 'I really am.'

'Well.' He took up his pint and drained it, then put a hand on his own jiggling knee as if to still it. 'That's that. You've given me the answer and it's all I wanted. Come on, I'll take you home.'

As we went back round the corner I said, 'We'll still be friends, won't we?'

'If I can, I will.' We were at the top of the iron staircase down to our basement flat. His expression was lost in the shadows cast by the street light. 'But I don't suppose we'll see each other for a while in any case.'

'You've finished at Cambridge, what are you doing now?'

'I'm planning to go abroad for a while. To Greece. There's a monastery at Mount Athos and I'd like to spend some time there.'

'You're becoming a monk!' I exclaimed, horrified.

He laughed. 'Not because of you, Tigs, don't worry. I'm not taking vows or anything. I want to do some study and some writing, that's all. But I'll be gone for some time, I should think, then I might go back to Cambridge to continue my studies.'

'Oh,' I said. 'I see. It sounds fascinating.'

'Read up about it, young Tigs, you'll find it enlightening. The monks are so against the presence of females that they're strictly forbidden on the mountain. They can't set foot there. Even the cats are all male.'

'I'm sure you'll be happy there then.'

'I'll fit right in.' He grinned. 'Don't worry. I'm still your friend. I'll write to you from Mount Athos.'

I felt cheered and said sincerely, 'Good, I'm glad. Write often.'

'Bye, then.' He dropped a whiskery kiss on my cheek.

'Bye.'

He turned and wandered off in the direction of the Tube station and I watched him go, a strange and solitary figure, huge in the orange light from the street lamps.

'Goodness,' Serena said, when I told her. 'I'm impressed. It's like he's gone to join the French Foreign Legion or something. He must really fancy you.'

'It's nothing like that,' I said stubbornly, but somehow I wondered if Al's whole future had turned on this evening, and what I would say to him. I hoped not. I didn't want that responsibility.

Al's brief visit into my life seemed to have woken me up from some strange dream and when I let myself into James and Josephine's flat the following Friday, I was struck suddenly by the ridiculousness of what I was doing. It was bound to come out sometime and how terrible it would look when it did. It was beyond strange that I'd never admitted my connection with them and there was no way I could not have known it. And what more could I get from these strange rituals of purification, cleansing and worship I went through there? Because that's what it was like: tending a shrine and praying at the altar.

That's it, I decided. *I'll give in my notice. I'll leave a note on the table today and explain I'm terribly sorry but I can only clean for another two weeks and then it'll be almost Christmas in any case, so it will be a natural break.*

I had the sudden thought that Josephine might tip me for Christmas, which would be embarrassing, and that she might even be at Ballintyre that year, and see me. I would have to hide from her for the rest of my life. It sent such a chill through me that I went straight to the sitting room to find some writing paper so I could write my resignation note. She'd probably forget about me before she saw me again. After all, she hadn't seen me since the day she interviewed me. I'd just sat down with a pad on my knee when I heard the door open and the sound of heavy breathing.

'Hello?' I called out.

'Oh, you're here, thank goodness!'

I got up and went out into the little hall where Josephine was standing, bulky in her outdoor coat, white-faced and panting, clutching her bump in both hands. She looked awful. 'Are you all right?'

'The most dreadful thing has just happened. I went to the bus stop, I was going to get some last things at Peter Jones, and while I was standing there . . . ' – her face crumpled and tears started to flow – 'my waters broke and it all splashed down on the ground like I'd wet myself, and people looked around and they were so disgusted! One boy started to laugh and point. It was awful.' She began to sob now and I felt sorry for her. 'But one of the older women came up and told me not to worry, told the others my baby's coming and then said I should go straight home. So I started to walk down the road, trying to hail a taxi and one stopped but when I said I was having a baby, he said, "No thanks, not in my cab," and drove off and left me there. So I had to come all the way back. And I think it's starting!' She was still panting, one hand over her bump, and I could see she was paler than ever, her eyes glassy and frightened. Her tears stopped and she sniffed, wiping her face with the back of her hand.

'I'm so sorry. Perhaps you should have gone to the hospital,' I suggested. 'Shall I take you there now?'

She looked cross. 'No, no, I can't go yet. Besides, I don't have my bag.' I remembered the overnight bag, stuffed to the gills, that I'd seen in the bedroom: her hospital bag. 'And James has to take me there, I can't go alone, I can't *walk* there, that would be absurd.'

I didn't know what to say. She had practically hobbled past the Chelsea and Westminster to get home. Why hadn't she gone there and been sure of being looked after? But I wasn't going to argue with her. I tried to think about everything I knew about childbirth. It would take hours. Perhaps days. It would hurt horribly. I really, really didn't want to be there when it happened. Josephine needed to be in the hospital, though. I was sure of that. 'Perhaps you should ring James and ask him to come home, and then he can take you to the hospital.'

'Yes, yes. Oh – wait.' Her expression became suddenly focused and intense, as though she was listening to a voice that only she could hear, and then it cleared. 'Oh my goodness, that was a contraction! Like a nasty stomach pain, that awful cramp you know means you're going to be very ill. It's gone now.'

'You're going to have a baby,' I said in awe, and then fearfully, 'You really ought to go to the hospital.'

'What's the time?' she demanded. 'We'll time it until the next one. The books are pretty clear, you don't have to worry until it's about a minute between contractions.'

I checked my watch. 'And you'll ring James?'

'Yes, I'll do it now.' She went past me into the sitting room, swaying under the weight of her bump, and picked up the telephone receiver. I watched the clock face on my wristwatch and listened as she dialled and was connected, first to an operator or secretary and then to James. 'I'm sorry, darling, the baby's coming. I know the weekend would be more convenient but I'm afraid it's on its way.'

I heard the tinny sound of his voice replying but couldn't make out the words. I felt myself blush just at the strange little distorted noise, and felt very stupid. Their marriage was real and important, and they were about to be parents. My dreams appeared ridiculous beside that.

'I'd better go,' I said quietly and went to pull on my coat but Josephine made frantic signals at me while she finished her call.

'Yes – I'm not alone, don't worry, the cleaner's here. I'll see you soon, darling, bye.' She put down the receiver and said firmly, 'You can't go. Don't leave me, not when I'm in labour. Ooh, the next one is just starting, how long is that?'

'Seven minutes.'

'Well, I'm not about to give birth, don't worry about that.' Her eyes were wide and pleading. 'But I don't want to be alone, not right now.'

'Is your mother nearby?'

'Miles away in Surrey. I'll ring her in a moment. But until James gets here, could you stay?'

Until James arrived? I gaped at her. But what else could I do? I couldn't leave her alone like this. 'All right.'

'Thank you. Now, I must change out of these wet things and get ready for the hospital. Then I'll ring Mummy. Then . . .' She looked thoughtful. 'Could you make me some tea and toast? I'm going to have to keep my strength up. Marmalade, please. It's in the kitchen cupboard.' She lumbered off to the bedroom and I went through to the kitchen.

She's going to have her baby. James is coming. How can I not see him?

I put on the kettle for tea and made the toast. If I just did this, I could probably slip away. If he was coming from the City, he'd have to get out of the office, take the Underground, walk from the station . . . half an hour at least. If I left in twenty minutes, I'd be bound to miss him.

I felt better as I put marmalade on Josephine's toast, now that I had an escape plan. From the bedroom I heard a muffled moan as the next contraction hit. By the time I took the tea and toast to the sitting room, she was coming out of the bedroom, in a fresh maternity dress, her hair brushed and pink lipstick on.

'All ready,' she said brightly, and then as she reached me, she suddenly bent double, shouting, 'Ow, ow, ow!' She reached out and grasped my hand, clutching it with bone-crunching ferocity. 'Oh my goodness, ouch!' She looked up at me, her face paper-white and sweat all over it. 'That came faster than I was expecting. How long since the last one?'

'Five minutes?'

'Oh dear, it was horrible.' She stood up, her face frightened. 'This is going to hurt, isn't it? Really hurt?'

'I'm afraid so.' I was surprised to find myself breaking that particular bit of news to her. Surely she'd already known.

'I don't know if I can!' she said in a panicked voice. My heart went out to her. There was no stopping it now, whatever she felt about it.

'Come and sit down.' I led her to the sofa, and helped her down onto it, then fetched her the toast, putting the tea on the side table. She took a bit and tried to eat it.

'I don't feel at all well,' she said. 'It's like when I drank too much whisky at New Year and woke up feeling most awfully sick.' She put the plate down. 'Oh dear. I don't know if I can eat after all.'

I felt helpless. I passed her the phone. 'Perhaps you'd better call your mother.'

'Yes.' She started to dial, and was gripped by another fierce pain as she did, crying out until it was over. To my horror, she started to cry again. 'I don't want to do this on my own! James should be here, my mother should be here! But here I am with just the *cleaner*!'

'I'm so sorry.' I checked my watch again. I ought to be going now. 'I'll leave you in peace, James will be here soon.'

She was crying hard now, trying to dial a number and not making it to the end before another contraction seized her. I collected my coat and put it on. As she recovered from the pain, panting and crying, I said, 'I really must leave.'

'Don't go!' she wailed. 'You can't leave me! Oh God, I can't sit on the sofa like this, it feels all wrong.' She tried to heave herself off the sofa but she was too far back and couldn't manage it. 'Help me!'

I took her outstretched hands and pulled. She was very heavy indeed, and my yanking seemed to make little difference. She pushed her feet forward and half rolled herself off the sofa until my counterweight stopped her and then I pulled again, so that she finally gained her feet. Then, just as she'd stood up, another contraction came and she flopped forward into my arms, landing with the most extraordinary weight. I stumbled and had the awful vision of her falling on me and trapping me under her, both of us stuck while she had a baby on top of me, but I managed to stay firm as she laid her head on my shoulder and howled loudly in my ear. The strange thing was that, with her body so close to mine, I could almost feel the contraction moving in her. I could picture the corset of muscles around her abdomen tightening and pushing to start the baby on its journey down the birth canal. I remembered watching Tinker, our dog, having her first litter of puppies and the way her body and instinct had taken over. She pushed out each pup, punctured each little birth sac with her teeth and licked it away, picking each new pup up as it arrived, putting it in front of her while the others wriggled back to find her teats.

'How do they know what to do?' I'd asked Mumma, amazed.

'They just do. They can't help it. Somehow we know what to do when our bodies demand it.'

And now, here was Josephine, also in nature's grip, her body doing what it was designed to do. The baby was coming.

'That was much quicker than the last one,' I said. It occurred to me that the labour was happening much more rapidly than I'd expected. Wasn't it supposed to take hours? Her contractions were definitely now no more than three minutes apart. Panic seized me. I could not deliver a baby. That could not happen.

Josephine was still leaning on me, panting by my ear. As I tottered a little under her weight, I could sense she was already exhausted by the experience so far.

'Can you stand up?' I asked her.

'I want to lie on the floor,' she said weakly, and began to sink to her knees, so I tried to let her down gently, though it felt like she was pulling my arms from the sockets. Once she was there, she closed her eyes and sighed heavily, her cheeks still wet from the previous tears. 'I knew we should have gone to those child birthing classes,' she murmured. Then she opened her eyes and looked straight at me, her expression beseeching. 'Can I please do this tomorrow? I really don't feel like it at the moment but I promise I will just as soon as I've had a rest.' Then her face contorted again and she shouted with pain as the next contraction wracked her. She tried to roll over but couldn't. 'Help me!' she shouted.

'What shall I do?' I cried, beginning to panic properly now. It felt as though we'd gone from Josephine in fresh lipstick and a nice dress to Josephine writhing on the floor and howling in a matter of seconds. Was that even possible? The prospect of her giving birth was very real. Perhaps I should start to undress her . . . fetch towels and whatever else I might need. Scissors? I felt sick. Then I remembered the time and gasped with horror. I looked across the sitting room to the hallway and the front door, where I could escape all this if only I could get there. But as I looked at it, the door opened and James came rushing in, dropping his briefcase as he went.

'Josie? Are you all right?'

He came rushing in, with eyes only for her. I stepped back, dipping my face down into my coat, as he kneeled down beside where she lay.

'James!' she cried out. 'You're here! It's awful! Awful! I can't believe it's going to get worse than this.'

He took her hand and held it firmly in his, stroking it to calm her. 'There, there, old girl. We're going to get you to the hospital. They'll have lots of lovely painkillers for you. We'll get you down the stairs, the car is just outside.'

'I can't,' she moaned. 'I can't!'

'Come on, up you get,' he said kindly. 'Take my hands.'

'Oooh!' She crunched forward in another spasm of pain, this one seeming to go on for a while. When it ended, she was breathless, sweating again, and wide-eyed.

I watched them, glad to pass responsibility for her over to him. He was handsome, a little older than I had been imagining him, formal in his work suit. He'd grown a beard, which I didn't like much.

James coaxed her into holding his hands and tried to pull her up but she was too heavy. I began to edge towards the door, but he looked up suddenly. 'Here, can you help me?' he said, in the kind of tone that made it clear he didn't know if I spoke English. 'Help? Help me? *Aidez-moi?*'

I stepped forward, my eyes lowered, and took one of Josephine's hands, then we both pulled. It was much easier with two of us, and she rose up from the ground, panting and whimpering. I felt terribly sorry for her as she gained her feet, sighing and looking exhausted.

'Good girl,' James said comfortingly and for a wild moment, I thought he was talking to me.

'Thank you,' I said and smiled at him as he looked at me properly for the first time.

'Tigs?' He stared at me, evidently not able to believe his eyes. 'Is that you?'

I felt blood flood my face. 'Er – yes, I suppose it is.'

'What on earth . . . ?'

'James!' howled Josephine, clutching at him. 'Stop talking to the cleaner! You have to take me to the hospital!'

'Yes, yes, old girl . . . Come on.' He put one of her arms around his neck and began to help her towards the door. Then he looked at me, his blue eyes unreadable. 'As long as you're here – though I've no blessed idea why you are – can you get the bag from the bedroom?'

'Yes,' I said, agitated. 'And I can explain—'

'Never mind that now, please just get the bag.'

I rushed to get it, in an agony of frustration and embarrassment. He and Josephine were already negotiating the stairs when I got back with the bag, so I followed them down. It was slow work as we had to stop for two contractions as we descended. Josephine bellowed so loudly that the door to the ground floor flat opened and an elderly woman popped her head out before hastily retreating when she saw what was happening. Out on the street, James and Josephine staggered to the little black VW parked down the road, and then James opened it, still taking Josephine's weight as she panted and cried out.

'Let me put this in first,' I said, pushing the bag over the front seat into the back. 'There.'

'Thank you.' James helped Josephine in, reclining the seat as far back as it could go. Her bump rose up, massive and shuddering, as though it was alive but quite separate from her.

'Good luck,' I said, as he went round to get into the driver's seat. 'I hope it all goes well.'

'Thanks,' he said, obviously working hard to keep himself under control. 'Can you lock up the flat?'

'Yes, I'll do anything. Just say.'

'That's all I need. Thanks for helping, Tigs.' But he didn't smile. Instead, he shut his door, started the engine and began to head off, all his focus now on the journey to the hospital.

I sighed, watching the car as it disappeared down Gibson Street in the direction of the hospital. I was grateful Josephine was no longer my responsibility. But now my cover had been blown, my fantasy was over and it was time to face the consequences. I would have some explaining to do.

You idiot, I said to myself. *If only you'd left five minutes earlier!*

But I knew that he would have found out sooner or later. And perhaps I'd wanted him to.

PART FIVE

Chapter Twelve

HELEN

2018

I wandered along the shore of the loch, gazing out over the dark grey water that reflected the grey sky, while the children skipped around the slippery rocks, finding shells and examining the remnants of crabs with interest.

'A leg!' Lilac said with awe, looking at one lone pincered limb tangled in russet seaweed. 'Poor crab, I hope it can still walk.'

'Let's find a walking stick for it,' Jamie said, and they amused themselves building a crab hospital among the pebbles, unfazed by the wind ruffling their hair and chilling their fingers. It was spring, and the air still had plenty of bite. I sat down on a rock and watched the huge ferry making its stately way up the loch and out towards the islands. It was lovely for the children to play here, so carefree and so untouched by our troubles.

I'd left Hamish in our bedroom, still in his pyjamas, a blueish shadow of stubble all over his lower jaw, sitting in an armchair by the window, plugged into the commentary of an international cricket match. He'd finally pulled the earbuds out when I called his name twice.

'Yeah?' He blinked at me groggily.

'I'm going to take the children out.'

'Okay.' He went to put his earbuds back in.

'Are you all right?'

'Yes. Fine.' His fingers twitched over his earbuds.

I knew he was sleeping badly and restless in the night. His low mood was showing no signs of lifting. But it was natural that, after everything that had happened, he'd be depressed. 'You should come with us for a walk. It would do you good.'

'No thanks.' He gave me a small smile. 'I'm happy here. With the cricket.'

'All right. You know where we are if you change your mind.'

Downstairs, Charlie was in the kitchen, in his usual outfit of shabby cords, worn, checked shirt and a heavy green gilet. He had his tablet open on the worktop and was tapping away at an email while he slurped on his coffee. 'Ah, Helen. Morning. There's fresh coffee in the pot if you want some.'

'Thanks but I'm heading out with the children. I'll make some more later.'

He nodded and went back to his email.

I lingered by the island and said, 'Thanks for taking us in, Charlie. We really appreciate it.'

His glance flicked up at me. I saw that his cheeks were much more crazed by red veins than they had been, and his eyes were bloodshot. 'Don't be silly. There was no question.

Hamish has had a hell of a time. He needs me and we stick together.'

'That's very kind. He has had a miserable year. I just don't know when he's going to be able to get his career back on track.'

'Don't push him, there's no need for that.'

'I mean, we might be here for the foreseeable, that's all. While there's no income.'

Charlie shrugged. 'I don't mind if you don't. Nice to have some people around. Mum will love it, especially having the kids here.'

'Charlie . . .' I hesitated, then said boldly, 'Where is Sylla?'

He said nothing for a moment, gazing intently at his screen, but a pink flush filled in the spaces between the broken veins on his cheeks. 'Bloody pump,' he muttered under his breath, as though I hadn't said anything. 'Always bloody breaking down. It costs me a fortune.'

'Charlie? Where's Sylla?'

He breathed short and sharp through his nose, then said, 'I don't know. I told you that. She's gone away.'

'And she didn't tell you where?'

'No.' He frowned, his face even redder. 'I don't need this inquisition.'

'Is something wrong between you?'

'Not more than usual.'

'What does that mean?'

'I'm sure she's told you all our secrets over the years. I expect you know all about it.'

'She's not like that. She's told me very little about your relationship actually.' It was true. Our communication had so often been those little shared looks, small smiles of support at sticky moments, a kind of unspoken bonding that came just from understanding.

'I expect she's told you plenty,' Charlie said sourly. 'She's probably told you more than she's told me. If you want to know more, why don't you talk to her yourself?'

'She isn't answering her phone, or replying to messages. Or her emails.'

'Maybe she's just sick to bloody death of you,' Charlie retorted. 'Maybe she just wants a break, have you thought of that? She's listened to your bloody problems for a year and maybe she's just had enough of it.'

I pulled in a sharp breath of hurt. 'Charlie! Why are you talking to me like this?'

He paused and looked sheepish. 'Look – sorry. I don't know where she is. And I'm worried too, if you must know.'

'Did she leave when she heard we were coming?'

'That's about the size of it. Do you mind if I get on now? Some of us have to work. We just have to trust that she'll be in touch when she wants to be. What else can we do?'

I went to get my coat, scarlet with mortification. It had not occurred to me that Sylla might have left in order to avoid me. What a horrible thought. Tears sprang to my eyes, but I didn't want Charlie to see that, so I called the children and concentrated on getting them ready to go out.

Now, down by the loch, watching the children while hunched against the stiff breeze, I felt that pain again, thinking I might have bored her with my outpourings. More than once, I'd called up and the sound of her soft voice had opened the floodgates and it had all poured out: what was happening to Hamish, to us, to our life in Stourhaven and how, suddenly and rapidly, it was all being taken away. Of course, I'd asked her how she was, but she'd always quietly reassured me she was fine, and just the sound of her moving around the kitchen as we talked had comforted me as our life began to crumble and fall around my ears. I knew what I was going through didn't compare to what she had suffered, but she was only supportive and kind, and never hinted that she thought I was being insensitive in telling her my troubles.

I pulled out my phone and scrolled back through my messages to Sylla. She had stopped replying a while ago, just after Christmas. Her messages before that were typical of her: brief yet tender, saying next to nothing about herself.

Happy New Year, Sylla! Love to you and Charlie I'd texted in January. A row of kisses was the reply, with one line: **Take care, Helen.** And nothing since then.

I tapped out a quick text:

We're at Ballintyre and missing you very much. Where are you? Please let me know that everything's all right. Helen x

When Hamish and I were first engaged, I was worried that Sylla might grow to dislike me. First there was Hamish's scene-stealing proposal at Rose's christening, although she laughed it off when I tried to apologise, and then I was suddenly promoted to Josephine's favourite golden girl. When I went to stay at Ballintyre, she gushed over my clothes, my hair, my intelligence, and my extraordinary skill at cooking. It was flattering but I felt like a fraud. I wasn't a particularly good dresser, or cleverer than anyone else in the family, and I was certainly in no way as good a cook as Sylla, so it seemed ludicrous when Josephine insisted I come to the kitchen and advise her on the best way to cook a chicken, or asked me winsomely for my recipe for roast potatoes. Sylla, who had previously been the fount of all knowledge for Josephine, was now pushed back into second place, and I felt bad about it but powerless. Josephine could not easily be resisted.

'I wish she wouldn't make such a fuss of me,' I said to Hamish.

'Don't take any notice of her,' he replied. 'She's just showing how fond she is of you.'

'I feel I should say something to Sylla.'

'Why?' Hamish looked mystified.

'In case her feelings are hurt.'

He shrugged. 'Why would they be? I'd leave it if I were you.'

But I found her one evening in the kitchen when Hamish and I were staying at Ballintyre for the weekend, clearing up while the others made inroads into several bottles of wine in front of the telly. Sylla looked up good-naturedly as I came in and grabbed a tea towel to dry the dishes she was washing. We chatted for a while, and then I plucked up my courage to address the subject.

'I . . . wanted to talk to you about Josephine. I'm sorry that she's all over me at the moment and rather ignoring you.'

Sylla laughed. 'That's sweet of you, Helen, but don't worry.' She gave me a mischievous look. 'If anything, I'm rather grateful to you. You see, before you and Hamish got engaged, I got all the attention. Now I'm out of the spotlight, and you're in it. It's a relief, actually.'

'It is a bit tiring,' I admitted, taking up a wet glass to wipe.

'It'll wear off in time, believe me. Do you remember how I told you how kind she was? On one of your earliest visits?'

'Yes.'

'Well, it's not as straightforward as that. Not at all. She's quite a complex person.'

'In what way?'

'I suppose she's not quite as kind as I thought at first. But I don't want to prejudice you, it might be different for you. Just remember, you can always talk to me about her. If you need to.'

'Thank you.' I was slightly confused, but grateful.

'And don't worry, I'm not at all put out. Not a scrap.'

Sylla was right, my reign as queen of Josephine's heart did come to an end. The first sign of my demotion came when I insisted on getting married in London, which was easier for Dad than a trip to Scotland. Josephine, her heart set on another Ballintyre wedding, kicked up a fuss but I was firm. Hamish stayed well out of it, which disappointed me, but I understood he was happy either way. When Josephine appeared at our wedding wearing purple so dark it was almost black, I wondered if she were giving me a message, but I laughed it off. Then Dad got ill and I went to be with him when he died.

The next time we were in Scotland, Sylla and I sat up late away from the others and I told her about the phone call accusing me of being a terrible wife. 'The weird thing is, Josephine hasn't ever mentioned it again. I thought she might say something, but she's acting like it never happened.'

Sylla looked thoughtful. 'She's probably forgotten. I suspect she was very drunk.'

I stared at her, round-eyed. 'She did sound tipsy, but I had no idea she was drunk enough to blank it out. I know the Ballintyres like a drink but . . . that's going quite far, isn't it?'

Sylla nodded. 'She and Charlie encourage each other. I try to make him hold back, but he's got no willpower and she offers it to him all the time.' She gave me a sideways look. 'Now that Rose is growing up a little, we're going to have some changes.'

'Really? What kind of changes?'

'I think it's time for Josephine to have some independence. Charlie's going to do up the lodge for her, and she can move out.'

'I don't know how you've put up with having her live with you for so long!' I exclaimed. 'She doesn't seem to mind interfering in our lives, does she? Do you think she'll go?'

'I think I can make it happen, with time and effort. She'll do what Charlie says.' Sylla looked thoughtful. 'But watch out for yourself, Helen. Don't let her bully you. Stand up for yourself. Tell Hamish to stand up to her too. Don't forget, you can always talk to me.'

I remembered that, as Josephine's attitude to me continued to fluctuate. Whether she had blanked out the spiteful phone call or not, I was on the downward curve in her favour, while Sylla was reinstated to her previous position of golden girl. We could stay in our relative positions for years on end, but eventually the tide would turn. Much later, when I had Lilac, I was handed back the crown, partly because Sylla had been put on the naughty step for her attempts to redecorate the house. Although Josephine didn't mind surrendering the tiresome business of running it while still enjoying its comforts when she pleased, she was not happy when Sylla began to strip away the frills and pleats and tassels, and complained so much that Sylla slowed down her efforts to the point that they almost stopped. One thing she dared not touch was the portrait of Josephine in her glory days that hung in the drawing room. It was really very bad, showing her as an eighties glamour puss in a plunging black dress, her hair swept back in layered wings, her eyes bright with turquoise shadow.

'I just yearn to put a moustache on it,' I said, which made Sylla laugh. 'If only the children could reach, I'd blame one of them.'

Neither of us had been brave enough. Even Hamish thought the picture was horrible. 'I'd put it in the attic,' he joked, 'if it weren't for the worry that it might start ageing while Mum stays the same.'

It was the closest thing to a criticism of her I think I'd ever heard from him.

Sylla and I, though, learned to be freer with each other as we laughed about our respective positions in Josephine's affections. Eventually, we both seemed to slip permanently out of favour. I felt that, despite my best efforts, Josephine hadn't developed a real affection for me, or anything like the kind of relationship I had with Nora: warm, honest and real. I seemed to fade from sight and became a totem for someone generally all-round exasperating. I felt constantly that she hardly ever saw me – not really. I was Hamish's burden, a necessary evil, needed to cook, clean and provide children for him but at the same time a sad drain on his resources and a sort of needy vampire exhausting his reservoirs of life and strength. Poor Hamish! That seemed to be the unspoken cry that filled the house when Josephine was with us, or we were at Ballintyre.

Poor Hamish, cooking the children's supper! Wasn't he wonderful?

He had put some pizzas in the oven. My carefully prepared two-course dinner for the adults merited a 'very nice, thank you' while she practically kicked chairs out of the way in her rush to stop Hamish clearing the table or helping with the washing-up.

At least Sylla and I were allies. She had to put up with 'poor Charlie' just as much as I did 'poor Hamish', and we spent many a happy hour late at night, the wine bottle open, driving ourselves into hysterics at Josephine's latest howlers. Sometimes, when I wanted to make Sylla laugh, I would just say in a voice of strangled joy, 'My *daughter*, my new daughter!'

We were sitting together one summer night, Charlie and Hamish playing on the lawn with the youngsters. I could hear Rose's shrieks of laughter. Josephine was away and we were making the most of our freedom to reminisce about her choicest moments.

Sylla chuckled. 'Oh my God, that proposal. Charlie had barely finished the whole "will you make me the happiest man . . ." bit when Josephine clapped her hands and said, "Oh, she will!" I just about managed to say "yes" before she had thrown herself into Charlie's arms.'

'Well, *poor* Charlie! He has to cope with your moods, I'm afraid. And you will keep cooking pasta when you know how much it disagrees with him.'

'Yes, the fact he loves it, asks for it, scarfs it down and takes seconds isn't the point.' Sylla's blue eyes twinkled at me over the top of her glass. 'And poor Hamish, you told him off for letting the children go out without their coats. How was he supposed to know it was freezing outside?'

I giggled. 'You're always pressuring Charlie, why can't you just lay off him? He's *very* busy. Looking after Rose is *your* job.'

'Of course it is. When I do it, it's invisible. When Charlie does it, the world applauds.' Sylla rolled her eyes. 'I'll see your "childcare is Mummy's job" and raise you "very controlling".'

'What? What does she mean, controlling?' I could still be stung by Josephine's criticism, even when I laughed.

Sylla shook her head. 'Don't you remember? You told Charlie off the other day for chucking out all the veg left over from dinner.'

'I was going to purée it for Jamie's lunch,' I protested. 'It was such a waste, all that lovely sweet potato.'

'I know that! You always save the leftovers. Anyone would. Why Charlie can't remember that you do that, I don't know. But don't forget, Josephine's had you down for controlling ever since The Slapped Hand.'

We always remembered The Slapped Hand. It had been at Christmas lunch and we had all dressed up for the occasion. Hamish's tie was sloppy as usual, badly tied, half under his collar. 'Look at your tie,' I'd said. 'Honestly, Hamish, it's all wonky.' I'd put my hand out to straighten it and – slap! Josephine had leaned over from her seat to swipe my hand away.

'Leave him alone!' she'd hissed, her eyes blazing. I'd pulled my hand back as though she'd burned it, and gone scarlet with embarrassment. Charlie had quickly started talking about something else. Hamish had stared at his plate and said nothing. He hadn't spoken for the rest of the meal, until Lilac had asked if she had to have Christmas pudding or could she have ice cream.

Sylla and I had stared at one another with knowing eyes. The Slapped Hand became the symbol of Josephine's intolerance of any criticism, even well meant, and her instant and fierce rush to protect her sons.

That was the Sylla I remembered best – my friend and companion in the murky Ballintyre waters. Sometimes I felt they were trying to draw us under, subdue us, but we helped one another stay afloat and resist their pull. Even so, the years at Ballintyre changed Sylla. They soaked into her and altered her, making her more reserved, more protective of herself. But despite what she might have felt about her relationship with Charlie and the strain of living so close to

Josephine, she seemed to be happy, getting her pleasure from Ballintyre, from gardening and cooking and, of course, from Rose, who was her world.

A shriek from Lilac made me look up, panicked. For months after the accident, I'd been nervous about the children, more vigilant and afraid of the cruelty of Fate. She was fine. She and Jamie were throwing stones into the sea and laughing at their efforts.

I had a sudden flash of memory, so vivid it felt real: it was Rose, seven years old, marching around with a toddling Lilac, holding her by the hand as they looked for shells.

'Not there, Lilac, over here, look at this!' She'd bustled around, taking the role of a little mother to Lilac, who gazed up at her with huge, adoring eyes.

Rose had always had time for her little cousins, even when she was twelve and thirteen and they were still small children. I could almost see her bright hair blowing in the wind and hear her high voice telling them stories and issuing her childish commands which they were happy to obey.

Tears sprang to my eyes. When Rose died, it was the end of Sylla's easy laughter and silliness. The pain of her loss had been unbearable for everyone. But most of all, for Charlie and Sylla. They never seemed really to look at one another again.

Sylla, where are you?

I looked out over the children's heads to the loch beyond. The water was icy and clean once you were free of the seaweed. That was the other option. That Sylla had decided that life without Rose was too much to bear. Perhaps the grief had, in the end, been too much for her and she had done something to end it. I could almost imagine Sylla, calm and unpanicked, taking her decision; perhaps filling her pockets with rocks and walking into the loch, waiting for it to swallow her up and wash her gently out to sea.

I couldn't believe that. Sylla had survived the worst, surely – those awful days in the immediate aftermath when the world turned black with grief and pain.

I remembered the phone call.

'Helen, it's Sylla. I'm calling about Rose. There's been an accident.'

'What? How bad?'

'Very bad. She's gone.'

'Gone where?'

'Helen . . . she's dead.'

'No. Oh, Sylla, no!'

'Yes. I'm very sorry.' As though she was comforting me. Then she told me everything.

When the call was over, I fell to the floor. The horror spiralled up and collapsed me. I could only guess what Sylla felt.

Was it enough to want to leave us?

I had never felt that was a possibility, even in the darkest days. Sylla was too connected to life, as though she had been granted knowledge of some of its secrets. She was so expert at conjuring it out of the ground, magicking beautiful flowers, or coaxing vegetables rich in health and vitamins into being. I'd never forgotten how Hamish had described her to me that first time: *all spirit and mood.*

Perhaps that spiritual quality had made it easier for her to join the invisible forces of the universe.

I shook my head. No. I was sure she hadn't.

Lilac came running up, Jamie panting close behind her. 'Can we have a biscuit? We're hungry!'

I stood up, shaking off my sadness. I took their hands, delighting in the gritty warmth of their fingers. 'Let's go home and have some lunch. You can have a biscuit afterwards, if you want.'

As we walked back from the loch, we passed Josephine's small lodge house at the bottom of the drive. I looked at it guiltily. I had managed to avoid her that first morning, and I had not yet paid a call and she would be waiting. It had been nearly a week now and I would have to do it soon. I couldn't avoid her forever.

Chapter Thirteen

There was still no word from Sylla. When I checked again the next morning, my message had apparently not even been delivered, let alone read, as far as I could see, which made me anxious again. This was not like her. I was beginning to get seriously worried.

There was, though, an envelope waiting for me on the breakfast table when I sat down with my coffee first thing. It was addressed in a familiar curling hand with over-elaborate loops and flourishes. I'd seen it often, frequently on thank you letters to Hamish, addressed as though I hadn't even been at the lunch Josephine had come to, let alone cooked it:

It was so marvellous to see you and the wonderful family! The children are a credit to you! How amazing you are, darling. Lots of love, your Mama xxx

'You take it too much to heart,' Hamish would say blankly when I complained at being erased.

'You don't know how it feels,' I replied. 'And nor does she. I would never write in this way. She hasn't even put my name on the card, or the envelope. Can't you see how passive aggressive it is?'

'No.' He looked over the curling handwriting. 'She says "wonderful family". That's you.'

I gaped at him, wondering why he couldn't see it. And then, little by little, I began to wonder if he was the same. Like her. The kind of person who sent birthday cards that were blank apart from the words: 'I hope you have the day you want. Josephine.' I knew what that really meant. *I hope your selfish desires don't put too much of a strain on my darling son.*

'She's outrageous,' I would exclaim, half hurt, hurt laughing.

'She's generous,' Hamish pointed out, as a voucher for a large sum floated out of the card.

'Yes, but . . . I'd rather have nothing and feel like she really likes me.'

'Don't be silly, she loves you!' Hamish shook his head, puzzled. 'She's always saying how amazing you are, how she doesn't know how you do everything! She's really in awe of you.'

'Is she?' I'd never felt it, even in my golden girl phase. It had never rung true. Now I picked up the letter by my plate. At least it was addressed to me this time, there was that. I opened it.

Dear Helen,

I can hardly believe you haven't been to see me! I don't know why our paths haven't crossed yet. Hamish has been here with the children despite being exhausted, so I'm not sure why you haven't come in to say hello. Let's catch up. I'll expect you this afternoon for tea at 4 p.m. Bring the children if you want.

Josephine

I sighed and looked up, almost as if hoping to see Sylla across the table, sending me one of her comforting looks. But there was no one there. Hamish had yet to surface, the children had been and gone, munching down their toast before heading back to their toys. Charlie was off on an inspection somewhere, and I had the breakfast room to myself. I went to the landline in the hall and rang Josephine's number, glad when she didn't answer and I could leave a message telling her I'd be there that afternoon.

Then I went to the library to get on with some copywriting work I'd taken on.

Four o'clock arrived at record speed. Leaving Hamish on duty with the children, I tramped down the drive towards the lodge. It was a freezing day. I'd lost a lot of my tolerance for the Scottish cold after my time in the balmy south coast region where Stourhaven was situated, nestling in rolling green acres with oak trees and deer. There, everything was soft and easy on the eye, well tended, gentle. Here, it was handsome, rugged and boldly inhospitable. Even beautiful days had a jagged edge to them, like unpolished diamonds. But there was a grandeur in the hills and forests and the hard-edged granite beneath the wiry ferns and heather that Stourhaven had lacked. The robust majesty felt good for the soul, and I tried to absorb its strength as I approached the lodge.

I knocked on the door, telling myself it would all be over in an hour or two. A couple of cups of tea and I could be on my way.

'Oh!' Josephine opened the door and looked about, frowning. 'Where are they?'

'Hello, Josephine, lovely to see you.' I leaned forward to kiss her cheek, which she accepted with a lift of her chin and a backwards tilt of the head. 'I'm afraid they're having a reading session with Hamish this afternoon.'

'I was expecting them. I've put out fairy bread.'

'I'm sorry, I can take it back up with me. Or they can come down tomorrow.'

'It doesn't keep, you know that.' She turned and led the way to her small sitting room. She was wearing a pie-crust-collar blouse with a pink tank top and a long blue skirt and looking, I realised, rather fashionable. The eighties were obviously making a comeback. Her grey hair was back in a bun, and she was looking well, except for that barrel stomach, and the swollen purple hands. As we went into the sitting room, she pointed at the plate of fairy bread on the tea table. 'It will ruin if it's left too long,' she said in a martyred tone.

'I'll take it back tonight, they'll have it for pudding.' It was really party food – hundreds and thousands on thickly buttered slices of white bread – but it would do for a treat. 'They can come down and play tomorrow.'

'If they can be bothered to come down and see their old grandmother. I suppose I'm too boring for them now.' She sat down.

I took my place opposite and smiled bravely. Was she in that kind of mood? 'They love you, Josephine, you know that.'

'How is Hamish?' She leaned forward and poured me a cup of tea. Her fingers looked almost too swollen to hold the teapot, more like raspberry-coloured sausages.

'He's all right, I think. Recovering.'

She sat back with her cup and I took mine from the table.

'He has suffered so much,' she declared.

'I know. It was so hard on him.'

She shook her head. 'Wicked. *Wicked*. That girl should be punished. Locked up. Making up such vile lies about my son. I wrote in very strong terms to the headmaster.'

'Did you?' I asked faintly, thinking about how much that would not have helped Hamish's cause.

'Absolutely I did. There is nothing I wouldn't have done to help him, Helen, you know that. I considered visiting the girl myself to tell her what I thought of her and to demand that she retract everything. All of it.'

'I'm glad you didn't do that.'

'No one should treat my son that way and get away with it. He, of course, has been far too good about it. He should have put up more of a fight.'

'He tried. But it's not easy in the present climate.'

'I know!' Josephine shook her head in disapproval. 'Any trollop is believed these days, over the word of a decent family man. They get money for it, I believe.'

I said nothing. There was no point trying to talk about this rationally with her. Hamish was in no way to blame as far as she was concerned. There was no nuance. He couldn't have done anything any differently except perhaps be less 'good', less 'trusting', less 'perfect' and how could he do that? She was right up to a point, but there would be no narrative but her own: Hamish was the victim here, and the only victim. Nevertheless, I said, 'It's been hard on all of us.'

'I'm sure it has. The poor children, leaving everything they knew. I don't know why you haven't put them into school. They need friends their own age.'

'I don't want to do that while we're uncertain about where we'll be living.'

'What?' She took a big drink of her tea, and put the cup down. 'You're here! Where else would you go?'

'Well, it's fantastic that we could come here, of course. But we can't live with Charlie forever. And when Hamish gets another job—'

'Another job!' she interrupted, looking appalled. 'How on earth can he get another job in the state he's in, Helen? Haven't you seen him? He's utterly drained! He's suffered! It's quite clear he's had some kind of breakdown. I would have expected a bit more compassion from you.'

'I think a breakdown might be overstating it just a little but I do know he's had a very rough time. Luckily there's no immediate hurry. Of course he must recover. But he'll need to get a job at some point, I think it would help him hugely—'

She didn't appear to be listening. Her face had flushed and her eyes blazed. 'Get another job!' she said loudly in a tone of outrage. 'Why don't *you* get a job, Helen? That's what I'd like to know! What about *you*?'

I was startled. 'Well . . . I—'

'You have had it far too easy. Hamish has worked like a slave trying to establish himself, first in consultancy and then with his own business, while you sat at home. I realised you wanted security when the children came along but perhaps you don't know the sacrifice he made when he gave up on his dreams and became a teacher.'

My mouth dropped open. That was not the story. It hadn't been like that at all. I stammered out a word or two but there was no point, she wasn't listening.

'I'm sure you thought you were on to a very good thing when you and Hamish got together, with access to all this.' She waved her arm vaguely towards the window. 'But it's not the same as ready money. It's lovely but it's also a millstone, as poor Charlie has found out. If it weren't for the subsidies, we'd have lost the place long ago. I'm afraid none of us can afford for you to sit around in the lap of luxury.'

I started to laugh in disbelief. 'I've always worked, even when the children were babies.'

'Work,' she said disdainfully. 'I don't think you can call it that.'

'Well, it certainly seemed like it to me. And it paid the bills. It kept us afloat when Hamish lost his job – not once but three times.' I paused, about to mention our own mill-stone of Hamish's loans, but I had never told anyone about them. It seemed too disloyal. 'When he became a freelancer – and that was his choice – and while he was training to be a teacher.'

'Under pressure from you.'

I felt my heart racing, my breathing quicken. *Never let her get under your skin*, Sylla had told me many times. *Never rise to her. It's what she wants. She feeds off conflict, it's meat and drink to her.* I took a mental breath. 'No,' I said evenly. 'It was Hamish's idea.'

'He's good like that. He'll always take the blame. It's no secret that you pushed him in that direction. You liked the idea of a grand boarding school.'

I stared at her, trying to sort out my thoughts. It didn't make sense. Why would I do that? The years of Hamish's training and poor pay had not been easy for us. We hadn't known where he would find a job, or where we might have to move. As it was, Stourhaven had been a wonderful place to end up, far beyond what we'd hoped for. I'd certainly never dreamed we could be so lucky. If that was my grand plan, I was certainly some kind of genius to pull it off. *Don't rise to it.* Sylla's voice in my mind again. *It's what she wants.*

Josephine stood up suddenly and went out of the room. When she came back, she was holding a bottle of Diet Coke and I had taken the time to calm down and breathe.

'Perhaps you're right,' I said, as she sat down, undoing the bottle lid which cracked as the seal broke. 'There's no pres-sure on Hamish to get a job right now. It's important he gets better first. I've got my copywriting but I'll also look around for jobs. Perhaps someone local is hiring.'

'They might be looking for staff at the hotel up on the coast,' Josephine said, apparently also calmer now. 'Tremewan House. It's rather exclusive now. I've heard they're thinking of laying out a golf course. Wonderful spot for it. You should take a look.'

'I will,' I said. I had more than enough copywriting on my plate to keep me busy for now, but perhaps it was good to know that there might be another option if that should dry up, though goodness only knew what I could do in a hotel. Chambermaid? Reception? I certainly couldn't cook, so chef was out. Maybe I could wash dishes. I watched as Josephine took a swig from her Diet Coke, glad that her fury seemed to have dissipated.

Her eyes went suddenly misty. 'It's lovely for me to have the children nearby. I've not seen them very much lately.'

'Stourhaven was a long way from here.'

'It certainly was. And Hamish's work was punishing; obviously you couldn't travel in term time. I missed the little angels. They're all I've got now poor dear Rose is gone.' Her eyes welled up.

'We all miss her so much.' I thought of my walk by the loch with the children. I felt a rush of pity for Josephine. I was sure her health had declined since the accident: her eyes were permanently reddened, her skin was dry and cracking. I had wondered if she was drinking too much. The odd phone calls I sometimes received late at night when she was tearful or slurring certainly indicated it, but perhaps it was just the wine she put away with Charlie at dinner. It was no wonder if she was drinking more in the aftermath of the accident. When I talked about it with Hamish, he brushed aside my concerns. 'Mum's fine. Her generation always drink like fishes, it's normal for them. She's as strong as an ox. Besides, everyone dies of something, so if she wants to drink, then fine.'

I found it odd that he didn't seem to mind that his beloved mother might be drinking herself to an early grave, but perhaps his attitude was normal and I was the one overreacting. And yet, when Dad had first got ill six years ago, I had done everything I could to restore him to health. Not that it had helped. But it had made me feel less powerless.

'I suppose she's broken-hearted, like we all are,' I said. 'Have you talked to her about what happened to Rose?'

'We all know how we feel. It only makes it harder to dwell on it.'

I thought of that now, as Josephine started to talk about Rose. Perhaps that was one thing she valued about me, that I would listen; when I did, she seemed to soften and we bonded, and I felt as close to her as I ever did. I sat back, letting her talk, nodding and chiming in from time to time, feeling she was getting comfort from her memories. When she seemed to have reached the end, I said casually, 'Have you heard from Sylla?'

Josephine's face turned stony and she took another swig from her Coke bottle. 'No, I have not.'

'So you don't know where she is?'

'No, I do not.'

I leaned back in my armchair and said lightly, 'When did she go?'

Josephine harrumphed slightly, shifting in her chair. 'Terrible,' she muttered. 'Just terrible. Poor Charlie.'

'Was it recent?'

'He needs her support and she waltzes off, thinking only of herself. I knew something was up. She was here less and less; goodness knows where she was going. I'd see her heading off in the mornings, in the dark sometimes. Up the road or out across the hill at the back into the woods. And she'd be gone for hours, leaving Charlie alone in that big house.'

I could just imagine Sylla walking out her grief, taking it with her on long treks, soaking up the comfort that nature could give her, looking for solace alone. What I could not imagine was Charlie being able to offer her anything. He would do what he had always done: rely on her quiet strength and inner calm, knowing she would hold things together for him. Perhaps she'd had nothing left to give him. 'When did you last see her?'

'I don't know. A couple of weeks ago? More? I don't know.' She drank some more of her Diet Coke.

'I didn't know you liked fizzy drinks,' I said.

'What?' She looked startled and then down at the bottle in her hand. 'Oh – yes. I seem to have become rather fond of this stuff. Ghastly, really. But I like it. And, you see, zero calories.' She smiled at me for the first time since I'd seen her that day. 'Guilt free.'

'Yes. Guilt free.' I smiled, took my cup and drained it. 'It's been lovely seeing you. I must be going, though. Poor Hamish has been looking after the children long enough.'

'Yes.' She stood up.

I knew that playing the Hamish card would work, though I felt a little underhand to use it. He was my get out of jail free card sometimes.

She said, 'Charlie asked me not to come up while you were settling in, but I'm going to be up at the house more. He's needed the company, you see. Rattling around there, all alone. Perhaps I can help Hamish with the children.'

'That would be wonderful,' I said politely. A job washing dishes up the coast suddenly seemed more attractive if the alternative was living with Josephine. 'I'm sure Hamish would like that. And so would the children.'

She was a decent grandmother to them, I had to give her that. She liked children. It was adults who seemed to cause the problems for her.

I said my farewells and got away, carrying the plate of fairy bread for the children. On the way down the small path that led to the lodge, I was startled by the sound of an engine approaching at speed, then a dark blue car, low to the ground like a sports car, flew past the gates in a flash, and zoomed away up the road, taking the curve of the loch without a touch on the brakes.

I'll have to tell the children to take care crossing the road.

They were so used to skipping across to the loch without looking. But there were maniacs around here, that much was obvious. I pulled out my phone as I walked up the drive, and looked again at my last message to Sylla. It was still undelivered.

Then I tucked my phone in my pocket and went back into the house.

In the kitchen, Hamish was following the cricket on his tablet while the children were painting at the table. There was no sign of their supper being prepared. He was dressed but still in the same clothes as he'd been wearing for the previous week, the jumper stained and holey with the wrists stretched and baggy. His hair was long, curling over his collar and hanging right over his ears. He was unshaven and generally had an air of weariness.

A sign of depression, I thought as I came in.

Was it only last year that he'd been looking so well? He'd told me with satisfaction of comments in the staffroom about how smart he was looking. 'Phil wanted to know if I'd had a makeover,' he said with a laugh.

'You do look good,' I'd said. 'You've lost weight.'

'A bit,' he'd said modestly, and ruffled his hand through his new short hair. 'Must be my mid-life crisis! Going to the gym in my spare periods is paying off, now that Hardeep's given me that programme to follow.'

I'd been glad to see him so happy. He seemed to have found his stride at last; he'd adapted to life at Stourhaven, made friends, found school life stimulating. He had ambitions to rise through the school hierarchy. He was well liked. Lilac and Jamie were settling into the junior school attached to the main school. I'd made friends among the families of the staff. We seemed happy and life looked bright again. Then, without warning, it had all exploded.

'I have to trust you, Hamish,' I'd said to him the day after the bombshell. We were in the kitchen of our house at Stourhaven, facing one another over the table. 'You lied to me about the debt. It's really, really important that you don't lie to me now.'

'I'm not lying!' He'd looked so anguished. His whole expression pleaded with me to believe him. 'Please, Helen. I'm telling the truth.'

'Tell me the whole story,' I'd said.

He'd explained. I already knew who she was. I'd seen her at staff gatherings, except that she wasn't quite one of them. She lived in a space between staff and pupils. A gap-year student, over from Australia on a training scheme that Stourhaven ran through some long-established connection with a college there. I'd first seen her at the start-of-year drinks, held on the lawn in the main quad before all the pupils returned; she was bright and fresh, only about twenty-five, eye-catching in a pink dress, her blonde hair flowing around her shoulders.

I'd gone over to talk to her because I liked to be friendly to new staff. It wasn't so long since I'd stood on the lawn, nervous and shy, overwhelmed by our new environment and all the strange faces who seemed to know one another and the right things to do and when. So now I was an old hand of three years, I made a point of giving a warm welcome to newcomers.

'Sharing the caring,' I said to my friend Tessa, shortly before I headed over.

'You're very good,' Tessa murmured. 'I just can't be bothered anymore. So jaded.' She took a sip of her wine and wrinkled her nose. 'Do you think the head's had his entertainment budget sliced? This is nasty, I'm sure we had better last year.'

'Look at that,' groaned Katie, coming over to join us.

'What?'

'Venus from over the sea.' She nodded her head in the new girl's direction. 'Can't you see all the boys slavering over her?'

I looked back and saw that the blonde girl now had three male members of staff hovering around her. 'It's mostly the sports department. They probably want to talk about the Ashes with her, or something.'

'Yeah.' Katie lifted an eyebrow. 'That will be it. Her cricket expertise. If I see Giles talking to her, I'm going to be very upset.'

I laughed. 'Poor girl! The last thing she needs is for us to be wary of her. I don't suppose it's so bad if the men feast their eyes for a bit. I mean, we are rather raddled old mums now, aren't we?'

'Speak for yourself,' Tessa said tartly. 'No point in showing the dog some treats, is there? When he's supposed to be happy with his supper?'

'I think I know what you're saying.' I laughed. 'Look, I'm going over. She's probably bored stiff talking to that lot.'

I'd taken a glass of the head's best fizz over for her, and got her away from the sports staff.

'Thanks for that,' she said brightly. 'I mean, I like talking about the rugby and all that, but jeez, they weren't letting up. I'm going to be getting enough of that when I do the girls' sport this term. I'm Kaya, by the way.'

'Helen. My husband Hamish teaches Business and Economics.'

'Oh right,' she said, her blue eyes widening. 'I'd better meet him, then, cos that's the department I'm working in. The sport is my added-value contribution.'

'Oh.' I felt a strange bolt of apprehension and then instantly dismissed it. I was just as bad as the others, playing along with stereotypes of temptresses and weak-willed men. It was offensive to everyone. *Get a grip.* 'Well, that's great! Come and meet Hamish. By the way, he's a big cricket fan, he's bound to ask you about it, I'm afraid.'

She rolled her eyes and laughed. 'Don't worry, all Englishmen think Aussie girls are mad for cricket. As it happens, most of us are, including me, so I don't mind talking about it.'

'That's good. I don't understand it, I'm afraid. So you'll be a gift from heaven to Hamish.'

I took her over to him and introduced her. Soon they were chatting away like old friends.

'Very brave,' Tessa said as I rejoined them.

'So cynical,' I said, shaking my head. 'I trust Hamish.'

'He's a man,' Katie said.

'You two!' I exclaimed. 'What is this, the nineteen fifties? And your husbands are perfectly trustworthy!'

'Yeah. But they're human.' Katie sipped her drink. 'Look, I'm sure Hamish is a great husband, but I don't see the point of putting temptation in his way, that's all.'

'He has to work with her,' I pointed out. 'There's not much I can do about that.'

'We're only teasing, Helen,' Tessa said with a smile. 'Anyone can see you and Hamish are as strong as a rock. You're lucky, Helen, you got one of the good ones. He's just an all-round decent man. Maria and Simon on the other hand . . . Did you hear what happened over the holidays?'

'No, I did not,' I said, glad we'd changed the subject. 'Tell me all.'

I had thought nothing more about it. Hamish rarely mentioned Kaya. When I asked, he said she was getting on well and enjoying herself. She found living in the students' accommodation a bit tough and was sometimes homesick, but was doing a good job overall.

'We must have her round,' I said, so Kaya came with some other staff to dinner, and was friendly and chatty, wanting to ask me about the children and our lives at Stourhaven.

'You're lucky,' she said wistfully. 'You've got it all sorted.'

'Have I?' I'd felt mildly surprised. I'd thought she was the lucky one: so young, blessed with looks and health, with everything in front of her.

'You've found a great guy, got married, settled down and had kids. I'm jealous. I really want a family, as soon as I can.'

'How old are you?'

'Twenty-five next June.'

'You've got plenty of time! There's no rush.'

She sighed. 'I want to get started. I don't want kids late. But all the guys my age aren't looking to settle down.'

'I'm sure you'll meet the right man soon – once you get back to Australia, maybe.'

'Yeah.' She'd smiled and I noticed her slightly crooked teeth and the gap between her two front ones. 'I hope so.'

A few days later, I'd bumped into Hamish in town. He was coming out of a shop, a look of happiness on his face, lost in his thoughts and smiling, as though they pleased him.

'Hello!' I went up. 'What are you doing here?'

Hamish looked startled, then immediately guilty, and stammered out, 'I didn't know you were going to be in town.'

'Obviously not. Aren't you in school this evening? Isn't it your late duty night?'

'You caught me out of bounds.' He grinned, looking normal again. 'I'm due there in half an hour. It's Matron's birthday and I realised I hadn't got her a present so I came into town to get her something.'

'Oh, what did you get her?' I looked at the bag he was holding, interested.

'Just a little something.'

'What? Show me.'

He pulled out a pair of white woolly slippers with cute sheep's faces on the front and black pompom tails on the back.

'They're so sweet,' I exclaimed. 'Really nice. Does Matron like slippers?'

'Loves them.'

'You've done well then. I'm just getting things for the kids' supper. They're round at Tessa's and we're cooking up some pasta for them.'

'Great. Well, I'll be back later. Late one, I'm afraid.'

'I know. As usual on duty night.'

I'd headed off to the supermarket, wondering idly why Hamish had time to go into town when usually he said that he didn't have a moment to spare on duty night.

Four weeks later, Hamish came to see me late at night, white-faced and shaking, and told me he'd been dismissed for gross misconduct.

'She says I've sexually assaulted her.'

'What? Who?'

'Kaya, of course. She's accused me of assault and I've been dismissed.'

'What are you talking about?' I'd been reading in bed. My book dropped to the floor.

Hamish slumped down on the bed, staring at the floor, his eyes wild. 'Oh my God. This is a fucking disaster.'

I began to take in what he was saying. 'But how can they do that?' A doubt hit me. 'You didn't, did you?'

He looked up at me, his eyes wild with hurt. 'Of course not! How can you even think it, Helen? I would never do such a thing! Never!'

'So she's made it up?'

'Yes! It's a complete lie! I've been kind to her, good to her! I don't know why she's done this. Maybe she thought it meant something it didn't. I've only been friendly but perhaps she misinterpreted it.'

'But sexual assault, Hamish! That's not being friendly, why would she say that?'

He went back to staring at the floor, rocking back and forward, hunched over his knees. 'I don't know,' he said, almost whimpering. 'I don't, Helen. I don't know.'

'What's her story?'

'Inappropriate touching. Making suggestions. I don't know. It's not rape or anything. But you know what it's like these days, you can't say how much you like someone's dress without being accused of something indecent.'

I'd gone cold and calm. I had no choice, when Hamish was shaking and afraid, trembling on the brink of collapse. 'Hamish, did you ever touch her?'

'No!'

'Ever? In any way?'

'No. I don't know. Maybe . . . maybe a hand on an arm or something. Innocent stuff, I promise!' He looked up at me again, his eyes filled with tears. 'I didn't do anything, Helen.'

'Then how can they sack you?' The implications were sinking in. We'd lose our home. Hamish's income. The children's school places. Our life here at Stourhaven, our friends. It would be terrible. Humiliating. Where would we go? 'We have to fight this, Hamish, if you're innocent. I just can't believe this of Kaya! How could she do this to you?'

'She's one of that generation, isn't she? Me too, or whatever they call it. Hypersensitive, easy to offend, practically professional victims.'

I shook my head. 'I can't believe that. What could she have misinterpreted?'

'I don't know!' he almost howled, and rocked again, breathing hard.

'We'll fight it,' I said firmly. 'They can't take everything from us on the word of an exchange student. You've been here years, you're well liked, respected. Never a breath of anything like this! Remember old Malcolm, he was always leering over the sixth-formers before he retired, and no one cared a jot! At least, no one did anything about it. Why should you suffer like this? It's bullying.'

'You don't understand. I had to accept dismissal. If I hadn't, they would have gone to the police. She's agreed to drop it if I agree to go. I'll be allowed to keep my pension if I go quietly and don't make a fuss. The whole relationship with the Australian college is under threat. So I've said yes. I've signed the document they gave me. It's over.'

'You signed? Without talking to me?'

'I didn't have a choice,' he said wretchedly. 'I promise. It was the only thing I could do. I'm off the staff with immediate effect. We've got a fortnight to get out.'

'What?' The full horror was sinking in. 'Oh my God,' I whispered. 'Oh no.'

'I'm sorry.' He turned to me, holding out shaking hands. 'I need you now, Helen. I don't know why everything has been destroyed like this. I don't know why Kaya would want to do this to me. You've got to stand by me.'

'Of course I will.' I took his hands and held them tight with my own. I believed him. 'Of course. We'll be all right. They're cowards. They've decided to throw you to the wolves rather than stand by you. And it's too late for us to fight it, if you've signed their ghastly document. Don't worry. We'll be all right.'

He bent down and kissed my hands. 'Thank you, Helen. Thank you. I knew I could rely on you.'

I struggled to keep things as normal as I could for the children while everything collapsed. I'd tried to stay strong and dignified, walking around with my shoulders straight and my chin up, refusing to be defeated, knowing they were whispering about us, about me. Katie and Tessa stayed firm but even they kept their distance and sometimes I wondered if they were rushing off to their WhatsApp groups and their socials and book clubs to report the latest inside news of what was going on in our household. I wondered what they knew that they weren't telling me.

Then I told myself I was paranoid. Unfairly suspicious. They were my friends. They all knew it was a pack of lies. I knew it was. I *knew* it was. Hamish might be weak at times, but he knew where the boundaries lay. He was good. If anything, he was too trusting. That was all. He could get carried away. His kind nature meant that he went above and beyond his duties, and that made him vulnerable.

I knew him so well. I'd fallen in love with his strength and simplicity. He seemed to embody those solid words. Kind. Caring. Reliable. Of course I would stand by him, even it if meant our lives were in pieces all over again.

PART SIX

Chapter Fourteen
TIGS
1972

Mumma and Dadda tried not to be disappointed when I came back from London, having lost my place at art college through lack of attendance. They put a brave face on it.

'It's nice to know you're so good at cleaning, Tigs,' Mumma said. 'You certainly showed no sign of it before you went to London.'

'Ha ha.' I hadn't wanted them to know about that, but Serena had told them all about my clandestine career with great relish.

Dadda puffed on his pipe as we sat in front of the fire. The house was freezing and we had no money to put in proper heating, so we spent most of our time in two rooms: the kitchen, which was cosy from the range, and the study, which always had a fire on, and was insulated by layers of thick curtains at the windows and wedges of cotton that Mumma had stapled around the frames to stop the wind blowing through them. 'I don't know what you're going to do, though, sweetheart,' he said, frowning into the fire. 'We're out of cash. I suppose you'll have to get a job.'

'What *can* I do?' I asked helplessly. 'I'm not qualified for anything.'

'Neither is Serena, and she's doing all right.'

'She's in London, there are jobs in the city. But I don't want to live there.'

Mumma had taken out her embroidery and was carefully stitching the shadows on the side of a stag. 'You could go to Edinburgh. Become a secretary. Teach. There must be lots of opportunities for a bright girl.'

I pulled my legs up so that my knees were tucked under my chin. I was filled with love for my parents, in their shabby clothes, surrounded by their ancient possessions, managing as best they could as their savings diminished, and feeling desperate that I might have let them down. 'I don't want to go to Edinburgh,' I said stubbornly. 'I want to stay here.'

Mumma put down her needle and looked at me over the top of her glasses. 'It's no life for a young girl,' she said. 'The farming is finished for us, we've sold off the land. The house is far too big. We meant to sell it too, in a year or so, when you were on your way, perhaps you and Serena married and settled. Then we'd downsize and properly retire.'

Dadda now worked only as a land management advisor. Big chunks of the country surrounding us were being bought up by wealthy outsiders who often weren't here most of the time. Dadda, having sold off his own land, helped them to manage it: the shooting, the stalking, the forests rich in timber, the rivers brimming with fish. But even that would soon be too much for him. They deserved to retire. The house could buy them a comfortable retirement.

'I wish I'd been a boy,' I said. 'I could have kept the house on and been a farmer like you. You could have stayed here and been happy.'

'It's ridiculous to think like that. Besides, you could have done it as a girl, if you'd ever been interested. But you weren't.' Mumma picked up her needle again. 'And there's nothing wrong with that.'

'And I'm looking forward to a nice cosy cottage,' Dadda said thoughtfully and puffed his pipe. 'Less work for you, darling, too.' He smiled at Mumma.

'Yes. But that doesn't solve the problem of how Tigs is going to occupy her time.' Mumma was stitching her stag again.

'Don't worry about me, I'll think of something. I'm just glad to be home.'

'What went so very wrong in London?' Mumma asked. 'You wanted it so badly.'

I lay my head on my knees. 'I suppose I didn't like it as much as I thought I would.'

I couldn't tell them about the awful clash between my fantasy life and reality. I still could hardly bear to think about it myself. When I remembered the terrible day of Josephine going into labour and James discovering my secret, a horrible shame enveloped me. I hadn't been able to bear it. I'd left London as soon as I could after that day. We were going back for Christmas at home in any case, but when Serena returned to our little flat, I refused. I had the letter from the college formally rescinding my offer as my excuse. Another letter had also arrived, in handwriting I knew was

James's. But I simply couldn't bring myself to open it. I was sure he was writing to tear a strip off me for a strange and unpleasant action: not telling his wife that I knew her and him, wriggling my way into his home under false pretences. He must have guessed my secret, my hidden passion for him. It was too humiliating to face. I kept the letter in my treasure box instead, taking it out sometimes to stare at my name written in his hand, and stroking it gently, but still never daring to open it. I supposed I would never see him again, and I could never show anyone my heartbreak.

He's broken my heart twice already. Not loving me. Marrying Josephine. And now rejecting even my friendship. I have to be brave and realise that love is over for me.

I felt trapped by my need to stay at home where I was safe, close to Ballintyre and James, but also to avoid seeing him. Luckily he was probably taken up with his life as a new father in London but my only way of hearing about him was from Mumma and I waited eagerly until she dropped something for me.

'Elspeth's so happy to be a granny at last,' she said one day, scrubbing potatoes at our butler's sink. 'I must say, I wasn't expecting it. But now that James and Josephine have had a little boy, she's gone quite gooey, knitting booties and cardigans that I'm sure the baby will grow out of before it's had time to wear them all.'

'Is the baby all right?' I asked, breathlessly.

'Of course.' She looked around, puzzled. 'Why wouldn't it be?'

'What's it called?'

'Er . . . Charles, I think. Or is it Colin? No – I think it's Charles.'

'Oh. Charles.'

'Apparently Josephine is taking to motherhood with great energy, although she's perhaps a little overprotective.'

'Is she?'

'Very worried about every meal, every sniffle, the contents of every nappy.' Mumma rolled her eyes at me. 'You know the kind. A little over the top. A panicker.' She turned back to the potatoes. 'Let's hope she grows out of it, for the sake of the boy if nothing else. It doesn't do a child any favours if you coddle it.'

I felt relieved that the baby had arrived safely after that traumatic morning. I wondered if Josephine ever thought about me, but I doubted it. I certainly hoped not. It was now my mission to avoid her for as long as possible.

'Are they coming to visit?' I asked, trying to sound casual.

'Oh no,' Mumma said. 'Josephine won't travel apparently. She's adamant she won't put the baby through the journey. So Elspeth and Roger have to go to them for the foreseeable.' She shook her head. 'As I said. Rather over the top.'

I went back to my room and took James's letter out of my treasure box. I wondered if I should open it but I couldn't bear it if he said something cruel. I'd rather not know. I put it away again and tried to forget. I knew Mumma was right and that I should get on with my life. But I still longed for the comfort and safety of home.

And there's my other mission. To find something I can do to help Mumma and Dadda.

*

The answer came quite by surprise and out of the blue – almost literally. I'd been at home seven months, when one summer evening there was a ring at the door.

'I'll get it!' I yelled, because I was closest and no doubt Mumma was busy in the kitchen. I hurried to the front door and pulled it open. 'Hello?'

'Well, hello there, young lady! We're the Dohertys!'

An elderly couple stood in front me, white-haired but hale, in pastel sweaters and light-coloured trousers and sensible trainers, also white. They seemed almost preternaturally clean. The gentleman had greeted me in a strong American accent that sounded Southern to me.

'Oh. Hello,' I said politely.

'We made it!' the man said jubilantly.

His wife nodded, smiling broadly at me, and adding quietly, 'Yes, indeedy we did.'

'That's good. Did you want to see my father?'

'We'd be very happy to see your father. But perhaps we should bring in our things. Do you have a porter?'

I noticed then a pile of white luggage on the step beside them. Four large suitcases and a vanity bag. 'No, no porter.' I looked at them, puzzled. 'Have you come to stay?'

'Yes, of course we have,' the gentleman said but I could see his wife starting to look uncomfortable.

'This is Trenewam Hill House, isn't it?' she said.

'Trenewam? Oh no!' I laughed. 'This is Tremewan House. Tre-*mew*-an. You're looking for Tre-*new*-am. But I can see how'd you get confused.'

Their faces fell and at once they looked anxious. The man started to fumble in the large bag he was wearing over one shoulder, while the woman said, 'I told you, Don, I told you the taxi driver hadn't really understood!'

'Oh dear, has there been a mix-up?'

Mr Doherty pulled a sheaf of documents out of his bag, including a map. 'It's all in here,' he said. 'All the information.'

'Goodness. There's a lot of it.'

Mrs Doherty said sadly, 'We're on a very big tour of Europe. And there have been one or two mix-ups along the way. I'm afraid geography is not Don's strong point.' She sighed and patted his arm with a long-suffering air.

I felt sorry for them, away from home, in a strange land and somehow in the middle of nowhere, far from where they were supposed to be. 'Please come in. You look very tired. Come and have a cup of tea and we'll sort it all out.'

Fifteen minutes later, the Dohertys were looking much happier, sitting at our kitchen table with a mug of coffee each, although they mysteriously wanted cream in it, and chattering away loudly to Mumma and Dadda. The contents of Mr Doherty's information pack were scattered across our kitchen table as he explained the complex series of misunderstandings and mistakes by which he'd ended up on the wrong side of Scotland from the hotel they were supposed to be staying at.

'Yes,' Dadda was saying, frowning at the heavily annotated map on the table, 'I'm afraid you're rather a long way away from this Trenewam Hill House. I'm not quite sure how you ended up here, to be honest.'

'Well, I looked it up in a guide to Scotland, and made the arrangements accordingly. We flew into Edinburgh last night.'

'The house is mentioned in some guides,' Mumma put in, 'but not as a hotel. It's a historic building so it does appear.'

'Going to Edinburgh was all right,' Dadda said, tapping his pencil on the map, 'but you should really have headed north and then east, you see? Here's where you wanted to be. But you've headed west. Now you're all the way over here.'

Mrs Doherty wrapped her hands around her coffee cup and looked anxious. I watched, fascinated at how people could be so old, with white hair and wrinkles, and yet seem so young and childlike. 'How on earth will we get there?' she said in a worried voice. 'Don, you've led us on a wild goose chase again. This is like in France when we found out the castle we were staying in was a deserted ruin.'

'They did not say, Nancy! I was given very bad information.'

'Or when we drove six hours in the wrong direction, missed the ferry and ended up in Belgium.'

'It's easily done in a foreign country.'

Mumma came over, wiping her hands on her apron, sympathetic. 'I'm sorry, you won't get back tonight, I'm afraid. It's just too late. The trains have stopped. The taxis aren't running now. I think the nearest pub has shut now too.'

'Why does everything close here at five o'clock?' Nancy said, shaking her head in puzzlement. 'Don't you people ever need anything or have to go anywhere at night?'

Dadda said, 'I could drive them to Lanceston. The hotel there might have a room. We could telephone and find out.'

'I don't want to put you out, not one bit,' declared Don.

Mumma said nothing but I could see that she knew they were certainly going to be putting us out one way or another.

'You must stay here,' I said quickly. 'Mustn't they? It's really the best way.'

'Oh, we couldn't!' Nancy exclaimed.

'We've got plenty of room. Two more for dinner is all right, isn't it? And while you relax from your journey, I'll prepare the bedroom.' I thought rapidly. 'The best guest room. It'll be fine, if I give it the onceover.'

Mumma bit her lip. 'I'm sure the chicken will stretch if I do some extra veg. And I've just made lots of ice cream, I had yolks left over to use up.'

'We would hate to put you folks to any trouble,' Don said hopefully.

'Don't be silly,' Dadda said. 'Tigs is right. You must stay here. We've got room. It's summer so not as chilly as it could be. I'll turn on the immersion and we'll get some hot water going. You'd better light the guest room fire, Tigs.'

'Well, goodness, this is so very kind of you,' Nancy said, beaming. 'And I can't help seeing how romantic it is here. Will you give me a tour of your house?'

'Certainly,' Mumma said. 'You're very welcome.'

Nancy turned to her husband. 'Don, you may have just fallen on your feet this time. These kind people are our good Samaritans. Maybe it was meant to be.'

I raced upstairs with the housekeeping bucket while Dadda fetched wine from the cellar and Mumma entertained the visitors. I was pleased with the guest room once I'd finished with it: Mumma's lovely touches meant there was a beautiful flowered headboard and matching curtains that framed the two windows and their stunning view of the silver sea. I'd cleaned the room thoroughly, put fresh linen on the bed, plumped the pillows, placed a vase of flowers by the bed and lit the fire in the grate. It looked comfortable and welcoming. Across the hall, I made the ancient bath look as clean as I could, although there was nothing I could do about chipped enamel and rust marks, and put in fresh towels and more flowers on the windowsill.

I nodded with satisfaction at how nice it looked, and went back downstairs in time to join everyone for drinks in the ballroom, where Dadda had put out some chairs.

'Oh, this is amazing. Wonderful!' Nancy's eyes were bright and she looked almost rapturous. 'It's so old world. We would love to see you in that kilt your wife mentioned. Would you kindly put it on for us, sir?'

'I suppose I could,' Dadda said gruffly, a little embarrassed.

'I admire what you've done with that garden,' Don said. 'Those chickens are fine creatures.'

'Thank you,' Mumma said graciously. 'If you go and put your kilt on, darling, I'll put the finishing touches to dinner. Tigs, would you mind talking to Mr and Mrs Doherty until it's ready?'

'Nancy and Don, please!' declared Don.

'Of course, Nancy, Don,' I said, smiling. 'It would be my pleasure.'

It *was* a pleasure to entertain them; even the most ordinary stories of our life seemed to fill them with joy and great amusement. I described the Tighglachach ball to their misty-eyed enjoyment and they wished they could be at such a wonderful occasion. They loved the stories of the history of the house, and the bits and pieces of furniture we had left. They were, I thought, delightful.

Dinner was typically delicious, Dadda was a hit in his slightly moth-eaten kilt, and Mumma opened up her marinated cherries to spoon over the homemade ice cream.

'This truly is paradise,' Nancy sighed as they went up to bed. 'Thank you so very much.'

'I don't know how much like paradise the spare room mattress is,' Mumma muttered, as we went to clear up.

The next day, they were still in great good humour, despite the mattress.

'It's a real home!' Don said. 'I like that! I mean, in a hotel, you get the showers, and the warmth and the comfort, but you don't get the real thing. Not like this. And I value that.'

They rhapsodised over Mumma's bacon and eggs, spent the morning walking on the beach and sitting in the ballroom looking at the view, and then Dadda said he would drive them to the station so they could get their train back to Edinburgh.

'We've had a marvellous stay,' Don said, shaking our hands heartily, as Dadda piled their luggage into our car. 'Thank you so very much.'

'Wonderful!' Nancy echoed. 'Now I've got your address written down here. Let's stay in touch! And don't forget, if you're ever in Atlanta, you must look us up.'

When the car pulled out of the drive, Mumma sighed with relief. 'Thank goodness that's over.'

'I liked them!' I said. 'And they really liked us.'

'I know. I was afraid they'd never leave.'

When Dadda came back, he showed us with amazement the envelope that Don had pressed into his hands at the station. 'Look at this! A hundred pounds in travellers' cheques!'

'A hundred pounds!' Mumma stared at it. '*What?*'

'He said they would have spent at least that at their fancy hotel, with a wonderful meal and the wine. He said he appreciated our kindness, there was no way he wasn't going to pay us. So I had to accept it!'

We all sat around the kitchen table, staring at the huge amount of money.

'It didn't cost that to feed them,' Mumma said slowly.

Dadda said, 'The cellar's full of wine. We never drink it and it needs drinking.'

I looked up at them, my eyes bright. 'I think this might be the answer. Why don't we open up for guests? It's so obvious! I don't know why we didn't think of this before!'

It took a little while before we managed to get the house running properly as a guest house. It had seemed so very easy and yet, of course, it was not. How did we let people know we were open for business? How did we provide food and all the rest? Not everyone was going to be as easy to please as Nancy and Don. And what were the regulations? Insurance, health standards, tax implications and all the rest of it? But somehow we found our way through, especially once we'd written to Nancy and Don, explaining what we were planning to do.

We think it is a marvellous idea, they wrote. *But can we offer our advice? Don't change the house into something it isn't. The charm of it is that we lived alongside you, more as friends than simply guests. That is how you should stay. Make sure you don't lose that by becoming like a hotel.*

'They're right!' I exclaimed. 'That's what we'll do! No menus, no choices – except for allergies and things – no fancy things. Just living here with us. We can offer peace and relaxation in a real family home.'

'Will it work?' Mumma said anxiously. She was not at all sure about this idea, I could tell, so my energy would be needed to carry it through.

'Yes, as long as the place is clean and comfortable. The hot water and the heating are the main things, so we should stick to summer months for now.'

'Tigs, I don't want this to become a reason for you not to move away,' Dadda said sternly. 'It's fine for now, but it's not a proper job, you know.'

'I'll look at getting a secretarial job in Edinburgh,' I promised. 'And I'll do the typing course that Gladys McMurray is running in the village hall on Monday nights so I've got more chance of getting one.'

'All right,' Mumma said, looking relieved as I'd hoped she would. 'As long as you're not letting go of your future. This is no place to waste your youth.'

I didn't agree. I was happy here. There didn't seem to be much sign of James returning, he didn't even come back for Christmas. But I was still closer to him here than anywhere else except London, and I could never go back there.

We opened for business the following year and Nancy and Don were our first guests, followed swiftly by some of their friends, and then the advertisements in holiday guides began to pay off and people started to book their stays. I managed to get articles about us in the local news and in Edinburgh papers, and soon we had regular enquiries from as far away as London. Some people didn't quite get what we were offering but most did, and they wanted to potter in the gardens with Mumma, watch her cooking and learn her techniques, or go walking and sailing with Dadda, while he explained all the wildlife and flora they were seeing. I managed it: the bookings, the housework, the supplies. It was busy but satisfying, a step on from my cleaning business, and we earned enough in the first year to invest in repairs for the house and some new furniture, and we took out a loan to pay for central heating and a huge hot water tank, which was put in during the autumn when we had no guests.

When I wasn't running our new venture, I was taking my typing course and a correspondence course in bookkeeping so that I could keep pretending to Mumma and Dadda that I intended to go off to Edinburgh one day to be a secretary. I found both pursuits a bit dull but the bookkeeping came in useful for managing the house accounts.

The only person who didn't like what was happening was Serena, who was very sulky about her room being used as a guest bedroom. All her things had been moved to an attic bedroom instead.

'It's not like home,' she complained, though she was very keen on the hot water and even got enthusiastic when I said we might be putting in a shower or two.

'It's no skin off your nose,' I pointed out. 'And it means you can still live in Chelsea and you have this place to come back to.'

'Yes. But it's hard work for Mumma and Dadda, that's all,' she said. 'I don't like to see them working so hard.'

'They actually seem to enjoy it. I think Mumma looks better now that she has people praising her cooking all the time and seeing what a marvellous job she does in the garden.'

'Hmm. Maybe. I'm just not sure. Visitors are one thing. Paying guests are something else.'

I didn't see why it bothered Serena, whose life was now, more than ever, far from home. She had dumped Eric and was now serious about a young lawyer she had met called Richard, who seemed like exactly the kind of pink-faced steady type she had been bound to end up with, once she'd tired of rockers and trendies.

At Christmas, Serena got engaged to Richard, who had been up to meet us and ask Dadda for her hand in marriage, but she wanted to be married in London, not Scotland. We decided to open at Easter that year, and close for a week in July for Serena's wedding, and soon the reservation book next to the telephone was filling up.

The air was bright with spring sunshine when the telephone rang just as I was passing, so I picked up the receiver and a pen simultaneously, flipping open the reservation book as I said merrily, 'Tremewan House, can I help you?'

'Tigs? Is that you?'

I blinked with surprise, struggling to identify the voice for a moment, when I'd not been expecting to hear it. 'Al?'

'Yes. How are you?'

'Fine! Just fine. And you? Where are you?'

'I'm back at Tighglachach.'

'I'd heard you'd decided to stay much longer on Mount Athos.'

'Yes, it turned into quite a stretch.'

'You said you'd write.'

'I did write!'

'Once or twice. Then you stopped.'

'Well, yes. But no one really sticks at that kind of thing, do they? Besides, I was busy. Once I'd left the monastery, I went to another island and stayed there for a while. I've been writing a book.'

'Oh?'

'Crime. Set in the Middle Ages. The detective is a monk.'

'It sounds very good.'

'Thank you, it is. I've actually found a publisher for it. In America. A little press that specialises in medieval crime. You can do that in America, apparently. Just publish one thing. So that's rather exciting. They don't pay much, only two hundred pounds a book. But I don't mind about that.'

'Congratulations.' It was so nice to hear his voice again. I'd missed him, I realised. 'Why don't you come over?'

'Oh no, no . . . I won't do that. But it would be good to see you, Tigs. Why don't you come over here, and I'll meet you for a walk by the cove?'

'All right.' I was surprised. Al generally liked to come here, flying over on his motorbike. He didn't usually ask me to go to Tighglachach. 'I can drive now, actually. Dadda taught me and I passed my test last year.'

'Well done, you. That will free you up. I'll see you in the cove at four p.m.'

'See you then.'

Just before four, I was happily walking down to the cove, clutching a bag full of scones cooked by Mumma that morning as a gift for Al. He'd always loved them, especially her fruit ones. The wind was low, and the tide was high, the water clear and shallow for yards, the rippled sand visible at its depth. Further out, the waves were small, their white caps rolling briefly before disappearing, and the sun picked out the many shades of blue, green and grey.

I could see Al already on the shore, his face buried in the collar of his coat, staring at the sand as he paced back and forth at the water's edge.

'Hallooo!' I cried, waving as I walked towards him. 'Here I am!'

He looked up and smiled. 'Hello.'

'Present for you.' I held out the paper bag. 'Scones.'

'What a treat. Please thank your mother from me.'

'I will. She wants to see your book – perhaps you can show her one when you have it. How are you? You look well.' He had shaved his gingery whiskers and looked much younger as a result, and he had got some colour from his time under the Mediterranean sun, which made him look healthier and his eyes even darker.

'Thank you. I feel well. Let's have a walk and you can tell me all your news.'

I fell easily into step with him and we walked around the cove while I chattered on, telling him about what had happened at home and the way we were going to save the house.

'That sounds like a very good idea,' he said approvingly. 'I suppose we'll all be going that way eventually. These old houses cost such a lot to keep up.'

'You're all right, though, aren't you?' Al's father had been a successful diplomat and then a soldier, knighted after the war. He had made some decent money and there had never been a question over the future of Tighglachach, as far as I knew. It wasn't like us at Tremewan, or Ballintyre, dependent on rents and farming and timber, gradually getting poorer and poorer as we sold off land to stay afloat.

'Yes, I suppose so. For now. But everything changes. We don't know how long we'll be here.'

'I think I'll always be here. I'll always want to be, in any case,' I said stoutly. 'Even if I have to go somewhere else.'

'As long as you're happy. It's when you're miserable that things need to be dealt with.'

I gave him a sideways look. 'You seem happy?'

'Yes, I am.' He looked back at me, a smile playing at the corners of his lips. I noticed suddenly that he was not as fidgety as he normally was. Usually he'd be rubbing his hands, twitching his thumbs, rolling a cigarette or puffing on one. He seemed, by his standards, calm. 'That's what I want to tell you about.'

'Yes?'

'In Greece. I met a girl.'

'Not on Mount Athos!' I joked.

'No. They would have had her thrown off the cliff if that had been the case. Afterwards, when I went to live in the little village to help with the olive harvest and write my book. She was the daughter of the mayor, or equivalent, and as she spoke some English, she was kind enough to help with my translating.'

'Ah.'

'And she's very lovely.'

I felt a faint echo of jealousy and was immediately ashamed of it, and suppressed it completely. I was happy for him. 'What's her name?'

'Dimitra.'

'That's pretty.'

Al nodded, his eyes misty as though he was lost in thought.

'You must miss her.'

'Miss her? Oh no. She's right here. At Tighglachach.'

I stared at him, astonished. I'd expected his heart to be lost to her but, for some reason, not that she might reciprocate.

'That's what I wanted to tell you,' he said almost impatiently. 'But you haven't really let me get a word in, Tigs, with all your excitement about your new venture. I've brought Dimitra here. We're married. She's my wife.'

Mumma was matter-of-fact and unsympathetic. 'You can't be dog in the manger about it, Tigs. He gave you a chance, you didn't want him. Now he's found someone else. Very sensible, I call it.'

I was following Mumma around the garden as she put out old kale plants for the chickens to eat. The birds were stepping carefully over the knobbly stems and pecking at the limp, faded leaves. 'But he's *married*!'

'I shouldn't think her father would have let her come under any other circumstances. Greece isn't like here, where people live together. Serena's moved in with Richard without even asking what we thought about it. It's far more traditional there. Alastair probably wouldn't have been allowed on his own with her until they *were* married.'

'I don't think that's a very healthy circumstance to propose under!'

Mumma stopped chucking kale plants on the ground and turned to look at me, her expression grave. 'Now then. It doesn't matter what you think, miss. It's Alastair's business, not yours. I think it's rather handsome of him to tell you. He didn't let you find out in some uncomfortable way. He didn't lord it over you to make you feel bad. He told you straight. Well done him.'

I felt almost sulky. 'I just think he might be making a mistake. What on earth can they have in common, besides sex?' I sighed and tossed a handful of biscuit crumbs I found in my pocket to the hens. They scuttled after it. 'And I suspect it's going to ruin my friendship with him. I don't suppose he'll be allowed to see me very often if he has a wife. He didn't seem to want to introduce me, he never even suggested I meet her.'

'I can quite understand that. And why he won't want to see you.' Mumma went back to her trug for one last plant. 'You see, Tigs, you can't have it all your own way. You can't turn him down but expect him to be on call for you whenever you want him. Life doesn't work like that.'

My eyes filled with tears as though I was being rebuked. It all seemed so unfair. Here I was, in the middle of nowhere with only my elderly parents for company and now I'd lost one of my oldest friends because I couldn't feel for him what he felt for me. How was that fair? Did I ask him to love me? I'd have much preferred it if he hadn't. Now he loved someone else, and I was no better off. And was I supposed not to care?

I turned on my heel and marched away, heading for my rock on the shore where I could gaze out to sea and think about it all in peace.

Chapter Fifteen

I wasn't exactly in a sulk but I didn't get in touch with Al and he didn't contact me. It was a busy season at the house, and I hired Carina, a local girl, to help me. She also did some mornings at Tighglachach.

'Have you met the new lady there?' I asked casually, when we were cleaning the terrace windows together. They got coated with salt blown in with the water from the sea, and we soaked it off with white vinegar and newspaper once a week.

'Oh aye, she's lovely,' said Carina, in her soft accent. 'So pretty! Really dark and romantic looking. And she's very religious, I think. There's religious stuff everywhere – pictures and crosses and things.'

'Greek Orthodox, I suppose.'

'Oh, she's Greek? I thought she must be Spanish, I don't know why. I've heard her talking a language but I didn't know what it was.'

'Does anyone else speak Greek?' I asked, scrubbing hard at some salt spots.

'Mr Alastair speaks it, I suppose. If that's what they're speaking in.'

'Does she seem happy?'

'Aye, yes! Except—' Carina stopped cleaning and turned to me. 'Why would you want to come here after living somewhere like Greece?'

'What do you mean? It's lovely here!'

'Oh, there's no doubt, but I just mean – if you're used to the sun . . . well . . .'

'There is that.'

I was glad there were lots of visitors to keep me busy and stop me from thinking about Al and wondering about his new wife. *I'm not jealous*, I told myself. *But it does seem a shame he's chosen someone who doesn't want to know me. She must have told him to have nothing to do with me.*

The spring melted into the summer, the chill in the air gradually disappearing, only coming back on those blustery, grey, rainy days we got at least a few of every summer.

The day of Serena's wedding approached. I hadn't paid much attention to it, as Mumma went to London to fit Serena for her dress and make all the other arrangements, leaving me with the cooking when she was away. All I knew was that Serena was very cross because Princess Anne was getting married in the same month.

'Stealing my thunder!' she said when she called me to talk about the bridesmaid dress I was going to be wearing.

'Hardly, unless they've double-booked Westminster Abbey.'

'Ho ho. You know what I mean.'

'You'll have all the flags and bunting up, you can pretend it's for you.'

'I don't care anyway. Though I do hope she's not wearing a dress like mine, or people will think I copied her.'

'As you're getting married first, that's not likely,' I pointed out. And as far as I could see, all wedding dresses looked pretty much the same: high-waisted, long-sleeved, faintly medieval looking. We'd had two wedding receptions at Tremewan already and both our brides had looked just like that. Mumma had shown me Serena's dress, which she was making from a *Vogue* pattern chosen by Serena, and it looked as though all of them had bought the same one, which perhaps explained it. Mumma was also making my bridesmaid dress, a long gown in sky blue with a gauzy overskirt arranged in two swoops like theatre curtains and fastened in place with pink roses. I thought it was horrible but Mumma said I looked nice in it.

'I would never choose this,' I said, as we both looked at my reflection in the long mirror in her sewing room.

'Nor would I, but it's what Serena wants.'

'I don't mind really. I just want it over with, if I'm honest.'

Mumma nodded. 'I know what you mean. It would be so much easier and cheaper to have it here. We'll have yours here when it's your turn.'

I looked at my reflection thinking how impossible that seemed. 'I don't think I'll ever get married,' I said mournfully.

'Don't be silly, Tigs, of course you will. Once you get away from here and meet someone.'

After a moment, I said what had been on my mind for ages: 'Are the Ballintyres going to the wedding?'

'No, darling. We invited them, of course. But they're busy with James and Josephine that weekend.'

'I see.' I plucked at the gauzy swoops. I'd been wondering if James would be there, yearning to see him after so long, but also dreading it. Surely by now he must have forgiven me. But I was too frightened to find out, just in case he hadn't.

We were staying in a hotel near the Chelsea church where Serena was getting married, our suite decked out in all the wedding clothes for us, and for Serena who was staying with us the night before and getting ready there. She was a bag of nerves but rather docile as a result as people bustled around her, getting her ready. Her dark hair was backcombed high and then given ends that curled upwards like the bottom of a J, and a stiff veil that fell to her waist was stuck in with a pearl-edged comb.

'You do look gorgeous, Serena,' I said, when the hairdresser and make-up girl had done their work. She had toned it down for the big day and her conservative husband, and as a result she looked very young and natural.

'Thank you.' She smiled at me. 'So do you.'

I looked all right, with my hair waved and a circlet of orange blossom on my head. The blue was Serena's colour, not mine, but the overall effect was fine. The other bridesmaid was her friend Licia, who had just arrived and looked miles better in the same dress than I did. How was that possible?

'Come on, girls, off we go,' Mumma said. She looked magnificent in a turquoise knee-length coat dress with large white buttons, and a matching turban hat. She'd brought out the last of her good jewellery: an antique cameo pinned to her lapel and a strand of pearls at her neck. A diamond hatpin glittered in her turban. 'We're walking, Dadda and Serena are following in the car.'

I felt like a fool walking the streets of Chelsea in my get-up, not enjoying the odd catcalls and whistles we bridesmaids got from passers-by. I concentrated on how magnificent Mumma looked and kept my eyes fixed on her.

At the church we lingered outside, waiting for Serena while Mumma went in to check everyone was where they were supposed to be.

'That's a relief, Richard's here,' she said, coming back out. 'So it's just the bride we need now. If you two are all right, I'll go in and sit down.'

Just then, a taxi pulled to a halt right outside and a squabbling couple climbed out, the woman in a flowery maternity dress and a purple hat with a veil that was perched on a fat page-boy cut, framing her face liked a padded blonde cushion.

'I told you we'd be late! You wouldn't listen! And now look, we're the last.'

'The bride's not here,' the man said evenly, though evidently tense. 'So we're not last.'

'Oh dear,' Mumma said. 'They've made it just in time.'

I'd gone stiff with tension. 'That's James Ballintyre,' I said faintly.

'Is it?' Mumma squinted at him. 'Oh yes. I didn't recognise him with that beard.' She glanced quickly at me. 'Are you all right, Tigs?'

'Yes, Yes . . . I just . . .' As they approached, flustered and in a hurry, Josephine almost as large as the last time I'd seen her, I held my posy up over my mouth and pretended to cough, turning away for good measure.

'Hello, James, glad you made it,' Mumma said. 'Josephine.'

They said quick hellos as they went past and I turned back, scarlet, as soon as they'd disappeared inside. 'You said they weren't coming!'

'They weren't on Serena's list,' Mumma said apologetically. 'I invited Elspeth and Roger, of course, but she declined. I was sure she said it was because she was with James and Josephine. I must have got it wrong. Oh – here's the car! Serena looks like she's going to be sick.'

I was relieved that Serena was here to take the attention off me. I followed her and Dadda down the aisle as the organ played, and all eyes were on the bride. I stared at her train, hoping I was somehow invisible to James. Why had Mumma told me he wasn't coming?

Oh my goodness. What if he tries to talk to me? I can't bear it! And has Josephine recognised me?

During the service, I was sitting at the front with my family and couldn't see anyone behind me. For those bits, at least, I could relax. I managed to pay attention as Serena actually got married, even feeling quite moved at the key moment. I sang the usual hymns and prayed the usual prayers, and it was all over far too quickly as far as I was concerned. It felt like only five minutes later that I was processing back out, my eyes glued on the train again, and we were out in the sunshine, and climbing into cars to go to the Chelsea Physic Garden, where the wedding breakfast was being held on the lawn.

There it became harder to blend in, as my bridesmaid outfit was so noticeable. Luckily I had plenty of relatives and friends of Serena to talk to, including those I'd cleaned for, and I was almost congratulating myself that I'd managed to avoid the Ballintyres altogether when I felt a hand on my elbow and heard a voice murmuring in my ear. 'Tigs, could I speak to you for a moment?'

I was more than a little tipsy on wedding champagne, and turned to see James gazing earnestly at me, his beard bushier than I remembered. He looked very handsome in his grey morning coat and a blue silk tie the colour of his eyes. 'Oh, hello!' I said with faux brightness. 'How nice to see you! I'd love to chat, but I think they're about to do the speeches, actually.'

'I'm sure we've got a minute while Josephine is talking to your mother.'

'Ah . . . All right then.'

'Come this way.'

A moment later, he was leading me off the lawn and down a winding path into the gardens themselves. We began to walk together, me keeping my eyes on the path, still too embarrassed to face him.

'How are you, Tigs?' he asked, his voice gentle. 'You look very nice, by the way.'

'Thank you. I'm fine.' I clenched my fists to hide my trembling fingers.

'Still cleaning?'

'Er, no. I'm back at home now. I have been for ages.'

'I knew that, actually. I rang Serena to find out if you were all right when you didn't reply to my letter. I assume you got it?'

'Well. Yes.'

'And what did you think?'

I said nothing, not able to admit that it was still unopened in my treasure box.

After a moment he said, 'I know things are different now we're grown up – life had to change and move on. But I thought we'd always be friends, Tigs. You and me and Al.'

'I didn't break it up!' I exclaimed. 'You did!'

'What do you mean?' He looked hurt. Being close to him was so confusing. He was so familiar, so wonderfully known and so very dear. And yet at the same time he was strange and exciting, setting my heart thudding with his nearness. I knew I was his friend and that he was fond of me, but I also felt like an awkward child, someone who had made a stupid mistake, stepped out of life and didn't know how to get back in. I'd imagined that he was angry with me all this time for inveigling my way into his home and into his life. But perhaps he didn't see it like that.

'You dropped me – us – when Josephine came along. Just like that.'

He looked stunned and then sad. 'Perhaps I did. I'm sorry, Tigs, I didn't mean to hurt you. I suppose I was taken up by my new grown-up life. You'll know what it's like when it happens to you: love, marriage and parenthood.'

It will never happen to me, I thought.

He went on: 'It couldn't stay the same, you must know that. But that doesn't mean I'm any less fond of you. I always will be. You know that could never change.'

I dropped my gaze to the ground to hide the fact that my eyes were suddenly full of tears.

James said gently, 'You know, you've never told me what you were doing – why you didn't tell Josephine who you were.'

'I . . . it was a mistake. I didn't know it was your flat when I turned up for the job. I should have said straight away, but I didn't. And she didn't recognise me. And it all got too awkward. So I wasn't brave enough to come clean.' I took a deep breath. 'If it's any comfort, I was about to resign in any case.' Then in a small voice I added, 'Does she hate me?'

'That's why I wanted to talk to you. She doesn't know. She couldn't remember much about you being there actually.'

'Oh.' I felt indignant. I'd imagined she would be forever in my debt for keeping her company, making her toast and helping manhandle her down the stairs. I'd imagined her telling people that the true heroine of the day had been the cleaner. Obviously not.

'So I thought it was best if we keep it that way. She'll not remember you working for her. She doesn't even remember me recognising you, she was far too occupied with her labour. And since then, she's been thinking of nothing but Charlie. Now we've got another on the way—'

myself firmly. *You could have had all that if
 job in London. A lawyer husband. A life in*

want that.

sat on my rock, watching the boats going by
journeys across the sea, I felt as though life
 by, just as they were, on their way to places
than this. What was I doing, really? I was
ny family home for my parents, but did they
was shutting myself away from everything to
roken by someone who knew nothing of my
'd lost my friend, who lived so near and yet
now he had his own happiness in the form of
er was embarking on her future and all the
aiting her, while I cleaned rooms, changed
lishes and managed the accounts.

l for? I asked myself.

ould see the millions of shades of blue in the
 draw my breath in again at the beauty of the
 special bit of it, full of a loveliness that was
 melancholy. Serena might be soaking up the
 and blue of the Caribbean but I was com-
pinks and greens and lucid sunshine of this

ill be here. One day not too far away.
I got my paints out of the trunk in the nursery
 them on my return from London and found
 took them down to the shore and started

'Congratulations.'

'Thank you. What I want to say is – first, thank you so much for helping Josephine that day. She's not easy, especially in times of stress, and you were so kind to look after her. I'll always be grateful to you for that. I never wanted to scold you, I wanted to thank you – and find out how you'd come to be there that day. Serena told me about you taking on cleaning to support yourself, and that you'd lost your place at art school. I was sorry to hear that. I haven't seen your artwork but I bet it's brilliant.'

'Thank you,' I said, half wretched, half pleased.

'And second – if you're happy to, then let's just let it lie, shall we? You can come and meet her again now as Tigs from home, whom she hasn't seen for years. And who has grown up to be a lovely young woman.'

A flush crept over my cheeks. 'Do you really think so?' I asked, sounding a little choked.

'Of course I do. You look so grown-up, Tigs, quite unlike my tomboy pal from all those years ago. I'd be too shy to talk to you now!'

I bit my lip in embarrassment and pleasure.

'I take it you didn't read my letter,' he said quietly. 'Or you'd know all this.'

'It was all so awful. I was ashamed.'

'Well, I can see how it happened. How you got in too deep and couldn't say anything. It's just one of those things. But I wish you hadn't been ashamed, not with me. Not with everything we've meant to each other.'

We came to a halt in a shady part of the garden and I breathed in deeply, touched to my core by his words. As I did so, I had the strangest sensation of being pulled through time and space, and I was filled with a huge sense of comfort and familiarity. 'How odd,' I exclaimed. 'What is this garden?'

James looked down at the plaque that explained its origins. 'Look at this – it's the Scottish garden. That's the heather we have all over the hills at Ballintyre. And we've got pines just like this too.'

'That's it,' I said, laughing. 'We've been taken home!' I took another big sniff. 'It smells like it too! Heather and pine and birch . . . Doesn't it make you long to be home? Properly?'

James was smiling at me, his face so familiar under that big beard even if he did look older, a married man, a father. 'That's what I was going to tell you, actually, Tigs. When this baby is born, Josephine and I are coming back. To Ballintyre. To live.'

'What?' I tried to hide my reaction of half-stunned excitement.

'Yes. Dad wants to start taking a step back from managing the estate and we won't fit into our flat once we've got two small children. And I always wanted my kids to grow up at home, like I did. With the loch. The hills. Everything we had.'

'Yes,' I said, my voice high and weak. 'I see that. I'd feel the same.'

He smiled again and took my hand. 'That's why I want you and Josephine to be friends. I want you to get on, if you're living there too.'

'Oh. Yes. Of cours[...]
James cocked his [...]
to order. They must b[...]
We'd better get back.[...]

I let him hold my h[...]
away from the Scottis[...]
dizzy from what he h[...]

*Coming back. The[...]
They're coming back.[...]*

At home, I couldn't th[...]
relaxed after all the st[...]
and free of guests for [...]

'It was a wonderful [...]
Serena is having fun o[...]

'I'm sure she is,' I [...]
Caribbean.'

'She'd better be enjoy[...]
ard a fortune. She shou[...]

'Me?' I was surprised[...]

'Without the guest m[...]
wedding. She wanted th[...]

'Oh. Well, that's nice.[...]

We were still receivin[...]
Richard, sent from relati[...]
London. They were piled[...]
return and open them. I [...]
I did, I felt more like a Ci[...]
home, while my big sister[...]

Idiot, I told [...]
*you'd wanted.[...]
Surrey.*

No. I didn't [...]
And yet, as [...]
on the endles[...]
was passing [...]
more exciting[...]
trying to save[...]
even want it?[...]
nurse a heart[...]
love for him [...]
never saw m[...]
a wife. My [...]
adventures [...]
linen, washe[...]

What is i[...]

And then[...]
endless sky,[...]
world and [...]
both joyous[...]
dazzling ye[...]
forted by [...]
northern la[...]

And Jan[...]

On imp[...]
where I'd [...]
my old ea[...]

painting the sea and the sky, and sometimes turned around to paint the house and the hills.

And all the time, the refrain went through my head that James was coming back. But really, what difference did it make? What would really change? Wouldn't my life just become more painful?

There seemed to be no way out.

I felt as if I were living vicariously. There were the guests, whose comfort was always at the forefront of my mind. I was so intent on making sure their rooms were clean and welcoming, their needs catered for, their meals of the highest standard, that I barely noticed my own room was a mess, and I was existing most of the time on sandwiches or leftovers I found in the fridge when everyone else had retired.

My parents seemed to notice that I was not myself but when they tried to ask me what was wrong, I deflected their questions and grew good at putting on a sunny disposition and a smile to put their minds at rest. Mumma said I was too thin but I scoffed and made sure I wore plenty of layers to assuage her anxieties. They spoke again of my going to Edinburgh, and Dadda talked to some of his contacts about finding me a job but I refused all of that: I wanted to be at home with them, protecting and preserving what we had. And in my brighter moments, I felt that the world was coming to me through the many guests we had, from all over. Nancy and Don came back, and sent over plenty of their friends, who insisted, to our surprise, on pressing money into our hands at every opportunity. At first we were mortified and tried to give it back but we soon realised it was hopeless and learned to accept their kind generosity in the spirit it was offered.

It was one of the Americans who asked me to paint her portrait. Alberta Cameron and her husband were in Scotland on the trail of their Scottish forebears and had ended up with us for a night as part of their adventure. It was a quiet day and I'd already finished all the evening's preparations, so I'd rewarded myself with a session painting in the ballroom. There was a gentle drizzle outside so I'd decided to copy one of our few family portraits, a 1930s study of my grandmother by a Scottish society painter of the day. Alberta, passing by, had come in to see what I was up to, and admired it.

'I don't suppose you'd paint me, would you?' she asked, standing by my easel, her head cocked to one side as she looked at the canvas. 'I'd love a real family portrait.'

I blinked at her, astonished. 'Oh! I don't think so. I'm not used to painting from life.'

'What's the difference between copying this and painting me?' She pointed at the portrait of my grandmother, laughing.

'Everything! I can see the paint strokes, the colour choices, the light doesn't change, she doesn't move. That's just for starters.'

Alberta went and fetched a chair, then sat down in front of me. 'Give it a try.'

'I can't, it'll take hours! Days even.'

'Then you'd better make a start as soon as possible.'

I'd been too taken aback to protest, but put up a fresh canvas and started mapping her face onto it. She sat, quite relaxed and still, watching the view through the windows and letting me do my work in peace. Two hours flew by before she said, 'Now I do have to get up. Let me see.'

She came around and inspected the work in progress, so far an underpainting in pale brown that sketched out her face and features, and where the light was falling.

'Oh, I like that very much!' she exclaimed.

'It's just a sketch.'

'But you've got me! I can see that. We should do a bit more.'

I put down my palette. 'I'm afraid the light's changed. It won't be any good to do more today.'

'Then we'll do some tomorrow. Same time and probably the same weather, I expect. What do you say?'

'All right then,' I said cautiously, worried about setting her expectations too high. I was no portraitist. I'd only studied objects so far, and not even those for very long. I felt wistful for the chance I'd passed up when I'd let go of my place at art school.

The next day Alberta was keen to sit again. 'This is the most perfect place to be,' she said, settling back into the same position. 'Watching the sea like this is so relaxing.'

I started adding colour now: the chestnut hues of her hair, which I suspected were dye, and the vivid green of her sweater. The peach and tan shades of her face that, now I looked closer, had grey, blue and pink in there too. I began to mix, following my instincts as I added a morsel of blue or a tiny blob of yellow into my colour. It was absorbing work but I painted as fast as I could, pulling her face out of the canvas with my brush. I was adding a line of white down her nose when she yawned and stretched. 'Oh dear, that's enough for today! Let me see how it's getting on.' Once she was in front of the canvas, she clapped her hands. 'It's wonderful!'

'It's not finished, not really.'

'I love it as it is. You must let me take it home.'

'Of course – but it's wet. It won't dry for days.'

'Then you should send it to me when it's ready.'

I laughed, tickled at the idea of my painting on a wall in a house in America. 'All right. I will.'

After the Camerons left, I did some more work on the canvas, working from memory and filling out the background in a mix of grey-green that made Alberta stand out particularly well. A few weeks later, when the canvas was dry, I carefully wrapped it and Dadda made a wooden frame to protect it during the shipping and we sent it to America. A month after that, a cheque arrived for me, for two hundred dollars.

We all stared at it when it fluttered out of the envelope. 'Gosh!' I said, stunned. 'How much is that in English money?'

'Probably about a hundred pounds,' Dadda said, impressed.

'How do you bank an American cheque?' asked Mumma. Then she beamed at me. 'You clever thing. You should do more of that, Tigs. You were much happier when you were absorbed in the portrait.'

'Was I?' I hadn't noticed but perhaps, now they mentioned it, I had been less gloomy while I had Alberta to paint. 'But I can't paint the guests! They haven't come here to sit in the ballroom for hours on end. And what if I can't finish before they have to leave?'

'Could you paint from a photograph?' Dadda asked. 'You could offer to take their photos while they're here, work on the portraits in the off season, and send them off when they're done.'

'What a good idea!' Mumma said jubilantly. 'Another string to your bow, Tigs.'

'Maybe,' I said thoughtfully, looking at the cheque on the table. 'Maybe I could do that . . . Why not?'

'I'll print a pamphlet up,' Dadda said. 'What a good thing I took a picture of the portrait before we sent it.'

'You could do me, as another subject,' Mumma offered. 'To show what you can do.'

I smiled at her. 'I don't know why I didn't think of that before.'

We heard on the grapevine – or, at least, from Mumma going to have coffee with Elspeth Ballintyre – that James and Josephine had had a second son.

'He's called Hamish,' Mumma told me. She was making bacon and egg pie, which all our guests seemed to adore, rolling out her pastry on the marble section of the bench. 'Another boy. Bouncing and healthy. Josephine is a little disappointed, apparently. She'd been hoping for a girl.'

'Maybe next time.' I lolled against the counter, eating an apple as carelessly as I could.

'Yes, she's still young. And I must say, the next generation seems to be in a hurry to arrive. Alastair and his wife are expecting too.'

'How lovely,' I said warmly, and when Mumma looked at me with her eyebrows raised, said, 'I mean it. I'm very happy for them.'

'That's nice, Tigs. But that's why I worry for you. You don't meet anyone. There's Serena, nicely settled with Richard. You haven't even had a boyfriend!'

'I'm all right. Someone will turn up, sooner or later.'

'I hope so,' Mumma said, 'because you deserve it. I don't want you yearning after what you can't have for your whole life.'

'Don't be silly,' I said, flushing. 'I'm not yearning for anyone. If you're talking about James Ballintyre, I grew out of that years ago.'

Mumma looked at me carefully. 'Good. I'd worry about you otherwise. Elspeth says James and Josephine are coming back when they've sold their London place. Roger's keen to retire from running Ballintyre now and James is planning to find a position in Edinburgh, so he's going to start taking over while he works in town.'

'It sounds like a lot to take on.'

'He's young. He'll manage. And he's got Josephine to help him.'

We looked at each other and said nothing but we could see in one another's faces what we were thinking. That Josephine might well be as much of a hindrance as a help. But there was no point in thinking it, even if it were true. It was none of our business.

Mumma turned back to her pastry, rolled to a perfect even thinness. 'Everyone comes back sooner or later. You'll see.'

PART SEVEN

Chapter Sixteen

HELEN

2018

I stood up from my chair in the library and stretched. It was good to lose myself for a while in my work, but every now and then, I had to return to the real world.

I liked to disappear into the library. It was a peaceful place to work, with all the old books providing a kind of beneficent, encouraging hum of knowledge and industry around me. *People took the time and trouble to write us*, they seemed to say. *Take it from us: you need to put the effort in if you're going to get anything back.*

I noticed a photograph propped on a table by the window in a silver frame and went over to it. It was a group shot from Charlie and Sylla's wedding; they stood at the front, smiling and happy, Josephine beside them. Just behind were me and Hamish, looking absurdly young. Sylla was radiant in her simple white dress, her fair hair carefully styled. I picked up the photograph and touched her face with my fingertip. 'Where are you?' I asked her. 'Why haven't you replied to me?'

I was beginning to feel a chill when I thought of her. It was not just the fact of her absence, but the reaction of the others. To me, she was a constant presence in my mind. I couldn't forget she wasn't there. There were the physical reminders – her coats on the pegs, boots standing against the wall, and her hats on the rack. Her pens and notepads sat by the phone, the row of recipe books had her sticky notes in their pages. A shopping list in her handwriting was still on the fridge door, held in place by a magnet. All this made it stranger. How could they just forget her like this? Why weren't they concerned? No one mentioned her. No one even seemed worried about her. It was as though she had simply dropped out of existence and I was the only one to remember she had ever actually lived here at all.

The library door opened and Hamish put his head around it. 'Coffee?'

'Yes, please. I'm going to take a break.'

He came in. 'What are you looking at? Oh – the wedding photo. God, look at me. I'm a lot thinner there! Bit more hair as well.'

I looked at him as he grinned at the photograph, his blue eyes creased in amusement.

'Hamish, aren't you worried about Sylla? Charlie was so touchy when I asked about her. Josephine seems almost angry with her.'

'Worried?' He raised his eyebrows and pursed his lips. 'Not really. Although now you mention it, it's a bit strange. Do you know what I think?'

'No. What?'

'I think she and Charlie have been having problems. It's no wonder really, loads of people split up after a bereavement. She's probably gone off for a bit of time to herself and Mum's taken umbrage. You know what she's like.'

I looked again at the photograph. There was Charlie, red-faced, hair mussed, already a few sheets to the wind. And Hamish, boyish, carefree. And in the centre of us all, Josephine. Now I looked more closely, I could see that she was holding Charlie's hand with her own, the other on Hamish's arm. She seemed to dominate everything. Sylla and I had focused on her as the cause of our frustrations and problems. But what if that were not the case? Why hadn't we talked more about the sons she'd raised, and what her inability to let them go had done to them, and to us?

'Sylla's sensible,' Hamish said. 'But it is a concern that she's just gone like this.'

'So you *are* concerned?' I asked, slightly confused by his sudden reverse.

'Of course. Have you tried to reach her?'

'Yes. No reply.'

'Then I guess all we can do is wait.'

'Will you talk to Charlie about it? See what he says about how things have been recently?'

'Yes, of course. Good idea.' He smiled at me as I put the photograph back in its place. 'Now come and have some coffee. You could do with it.'

After lunch, I decided to drive up the coast to see if I could find Tremewan House, the hotel that Josephine had mentioned. I couldn't see it on my sat nav and hadn't heard of any smart hotel near Ballintyre in all the years I'd been coming here. A few restaurants had come and gone over the years, most unable to make it through the low season when tourists were few and far between, but a smart hotel with a golf course? That was something new. It might have a spa, or something indulgent like that. The idea of a sauna seemed wonderfully appealing. I hadn't been out of bed socks since we'd arrived, and although the house had radiators, they didn't give out much heat so I usually had several layers on.

'Do you want to come?' I asked Hamish, who was lolling on the sofa with a book while the cricket was adjourned for lunch.

'Not really,' he said, and sighed heavily. His mood had turned after that morning and he seemed low again.

'Might do you good to have a change of scene.'

He made a face and sighed again. 'Can't face it really.'

'Well, at least go for a walk later. This moping about isn't good for you.'

'I'm not moping about. I'm depressed.'

'Yes . . . sorry. But walks are good for depression, it's a scientific fact.'

'I might go later,' he said wanly. 'You enjoy yourself, though.'

'Okay. The children are watching a film but it'll be over in an hour. I'll probably be back by then.'

'No worries.' He turned back to his book.

I went out to the car, frowning. How long would this go on? Hamish was insistent that he was depressed but refused to go to a doctor about it. And sometimes his depression lifted so completely, I was sure that he was recovering – if not recovered. Inactivity was part of the problem, surely. Perhaps Charlie could find him some work to do on the property. I'd ask him about it.

I drove carefully out onto the road, remembering the speeding car of the day before, and headed west, on the more unfamiliar road that led to the coast. In all these years, I'd almost never gone further than St Mungo's when we needed basic supplies from the village shop. Sometimes I walked up the hills in that direction and once or twice we'd gone to a restaurant further up the road, but my knowledge of the place really stopped at Ballintyre. We never seemed to have much need to go anywhere else when we were there.

It was a few miles further on that I passed the pair of lichened gate-less pillars that led to Tighglachach, and the memory suddenly came punching back into my mind. That New Year when I'd stayed there. I remembered Rollo. I hadn't thought of him in years. Where was he now? Married, no doubt. Where had life led him? And what about Tigh-glachach itself?

Josephine had given up on her big parties after Charlie and Hamish were settled. The house was turned over to us and our friends for New Year celebrations and we didn't go in for black tie and formal dinners. It was more about bangers and mash and turning the library into a nightclub rather than reeling and fireworks. The Tighglachach lot had not come back to Ballintyre, at least not when we were there. Josephine told us the children had grown up and gone away, leaving Mr Drummond living there alone. *They were a funny*

lot. I wonder where Mr Drummond is now? He must be old.
As old as Josephine. Seventy or so?

He'd seemed fairly ancient when I first knew him, but that
was with my ridiculously young eyes at the time. He was
probably in his early fifties then. Still relatively young. I'd
thought he was doddering on the edge of death.

As I drove up towards the coast, the woods began to clear
and soon I saw the sea glittering in front of me, and the dark
shapes of islands further out. Not long after that, I saw a sign
to Tremewan House Hotel, and turned off to follow a curving road that took me ever closer to the sea, until at last I
drew up in front of a gracious white house with elegant
Georgian windows that faced out over the water, with a
sandy strip of beach at the bottom of its sloping garden. It
felt like a home but there were the unmistakable signs of a
corporate touch: lights along the paths and around the parking area. Discreet signs. A certain polish that ordinary homes
lack.

I went along the lavender-edged path to the front door and
pushed my way in through the wood-and-glass inner door to
a smart reception area where a woman stood behind a desk,
studying her screen. She looked up as I came in.

'Hello,' she said brightly in a soft Scottish accent. 'How
can I help you?'

'I'm a local and I just wondered what services you offer to
non-residents.'

'We serve meals and drinks to visitors – our restaurant is
very highly regarded. Seasonal, local produce is our special-
ity. We also do light lunches and all the rest.'

'Any spa services?'

'I've got a full list in our brochure here.' She produced a shiny booklet. 'Why don't you take this and have a coffee in our lounge over there? You can look through it at your leisure.'

'Thanks, I will.' I took it from her, surprised at how appealing this suggestion was. It had been so long since I'd done something like this. I walked through the door she indicated to a room that made me gasp as I went in. A row of floor-to-ceiling windows let the light from the sea flood in and the decor was restrained and simple. Pale sage-green walls hung with framed seascapes, splashes of colour from lampshades, the furniture dark and simple, except for some sofas upholstered in plain linen. The atmosphere was calm and restful. I went to one of the polished tables and sat down.

The receptionist brought me a pot of coffee on a tray.

'Thanks so much,' I said as she put it down for me. 'Can I ask, was this always a hotel?'

'No, no, it was a private house, I think. A Swiss family owned it most recently, and they intended to make it into a hotel but they lost interest after a while and put it on the market. It sold about two years ago and we've been open like this for about a year.' She pointed at the brochure. 'You'll see that we're going to be offering a lot more in the next year or so – a pool, a steam room. Treatments.'

'A golf course?'

'Oh, you know about that?'

'I heard a rumour.'

'The boss is mad keen on golf.'

'And do you have a marketing department?'

She looked puzzled. 'No.'

'Who does your advertising and marketing literature, like this brochure?'

'It's all hired out. The boss uses a company in Edinburgh, I think. The manager does a lot of it as well.'

'Of course. The manager.' I guessed that's who I needed to speak to if I wanted to get some copywriting, or any other kind of work. 'Is he around?'

'Actually, that's her, just coming in now.'

I looked over, and saw a woman about my own age walking through the door, though ten times more glamorous in a smart but flowing outfit of wide-legged trousers which she wore with platform trainers, and a jacket of a loose tweed boucle that buttoned easily over a white vest top. Her dark hair was pulled back into an elegantly messy bun and she wore a slash of bright red on her lips.

'Oh,' I said, feeling suddenly weak and confused. 'I think I know her.'

'You know Daphne?' The girl looked surprised and then called over, 'Daphne, this lady knows you!'

Daphne came over, smiling and frowning at the same time. 'I'm so sorry, I don't recall . . . Have you stayed with us before?'

'Er, no. I'm Helen. Helen Ballintyre. Hamish's wife.'

She stared at me blankly for a moment, and I felt a familiar sense of inferiority returning, the kind I'd experienced when I'd first seen her. There was no reason for her to remember me from so many years before and no doubt I'd changed. I felt painfully aware of my jeans and chunky sweater, lack of make-up and my hair untouched by a hairdresser for months. These days I pulled it back damp into a ponytail and did nothing else to it. I must look a fright. Daphne's face cleared and she smiled. 'Of course. I'm so sorry. I remember you. Hamish is a very naughty boy, not putting any photos of you on his Facebook page. How are you? And the children? What a pair of cuties they are!'

'I'm fine, thank you. And you?' I was struggling to take everything in at once. Here was Daphne Drummond, some-one I'd rarely thought of in decades, standing in front of me and talking about my children.

'Oh, doing very well, thank you. Busy! It's full on, running this place.' She smiled, her expression open and friendly. 'What are you doing here? Staying at Ballintyre?'

'Yes, we're living there now.'

'Really?' Her dark eyes widened. 'I didn't know. But Hamish has been very quiet these last couple of years. Is he with you?'

'Yes. No – I mean – he's not here. He's back at home.'

'Oh, right.' She saw my cup of coffee. 'And you're getting a bit of peace and quiet, are you? I don't blame you! Listen, the coffee's on the house. I'll tell Amy' – she looked about but the receptionist had slipped away – 'and I won't interrupt you. But you and Hamish must come up and have dinner and we'll all catch up properly. My husband's not here, but he'd love to meet you both. It would be nice to have some local friends. So sorry not to have been in touch before, I thought you lived miles away. Here's my card.' She pulled one from her jacket pocket. 'Drop me an email anytime and we'll sort something out. Enjoy your coffee, Helen. Great to see you again.'

She left me staring after her, trying to process everything she'd said.

On my way back to the car park a little while later, I noticed parked at the side of the house a dark blue sports car very similar to the one I'd seen speeding past the day before. Perhaps it was Daphne's. It looked like her kind of thing: sleek, elegant and chic. I climbed into our battered old Volvo and headed back home.

'Daphne? Really?' Hamish looked astonished. 'That's weird!'

It was after dinner, and Charlie had gone to take the dog out for its evening stroll. I had cooked for the three of us, and we'd eaten dinner over a bottle of wine. Once we were alone, I'd told Hamish about my trip to Tremewan House.

'You didn't know she works there?'

'Of course not.'

'Have you been in touch with her?'

He laughed. 'Don't be stupid. I haven't given her a thought in a very long time. But it would be nice to see old Daphne.'

'You used to have rather a soft spot for her.'

'That was ages ago.' He laughed and lifted his eyebrows at me. 'You're not jealous, are you?'

'No.' I was about to say, *what about this Facebook page of yours?* But I bit my tongue. Hamish had always been scornful of social media and prided himself in keeping off it. 'A load of rubbish – show-offs and troublemakers,' he declared. 'It doesn't do any good at all, and you shouldn't go on it either.'

But I did. Not in any great way. Just to keep in touch with our old London friends, and make connections with my new ones in Stourhaven. I didn't post much, but I did scroll through the feeds from time to time, seeing what people were up to. I hadn't seen anything from Hamish.

He had perked up and was a little brighter in his eyes. 'I'd like to see her, actually. You're right, we did have a bit of a thing. In fact, I think Daphne was my first snog.' He looked nostalgic. 'Huh, the happy days of youth. How was she looking?'

'Very glamorous. Modern.'

'Tell you what, let's drop her a line. It would cheer me up to go out for dinner.'

'All right,' I said. 'Let's do that.'

I stared at him over the top of my wine glass as I took a sip. Something didn't quite make sense.

Later I lay awake as Hamish slept beside me. He'd wanted to make love for the first time in ages.

'Let's get those bed socks off you,' he'd joked.

It had been nice to see him with some of his old vigour and I was happy. Perhaps this meant some of the depression was lifting at last. But I was also troubled. I kept hearing Daphne saying that Hamish had not put photos of me on his Facebook page. I'd looked him up on Facebook when I got home and he didn't appear to be on it. There was no Hamish Ballintyre.

But Daphne had said quite plainly in a way that made me sure she was his friend on Facebook. And if that was true, why had he pretended they had not been in touch? It didn't make sense. I'd found Daphne herself but her settings were private and I couldn't see her friends.

I should just ask him.

And yet . . .

I blinked up at the pleated silk on the underside of the bed canopy. A faint light from the bedside clock and the hall light on the landing was enough to make the folds gleam a little in the darkness.

So much had been taken on trust.

I stared up now at the canopy, wakeful, while Hamish snored beside me.

I have to trust you, Hamish.

I'm telling you the truth, he'd said.

Why did I have a feeling of dread? What were these alarms going off inside me? I wanted them to switch off so that I could sleep easily.

But try as I might, I couldn't silence them.

Chapter Seventeen

Hamish had perked up since I'd told him about Daphne, and more than once during the following day he asked if I'd been in touch with her.

'You could write to her if you like,' I'd said.

'I don't have her email,' he'd said innocently, his blue eyes wide. It was on the tip of my tongue to ask him about the Facebook page but then I decided to keep it to myself. I had the feeling that if I did say anything, whatever might be there would disappear.

Working in the library that afternoon, I tapped out an email to Daphne, saying how nice it had been to see her and that we'd love to take her up on her invitation to dinner. Then I went back to my copywriting, but I couldn't keep my focus on it. However hard I tried, my attention kept wandering.

I decided I might as well go out. Most of my walks these days were with the children and they did slow things down. I rather fancied a proper stomp across the hills before darkness fell. There was a casserole in the oven, so dinner was already made. I thought about asking Hamish if he wanted to come too; he hadn't been getting enough exercise lately, and I was sure it was not good for his state of mind. But he was in the kitchen with Josephine, half listening as she rattled on, so I would just slip out and get some air on my own.

I picked up my coat and put on my boots in the boot room and let myself out of its side door, then skirted the house, breathing in the soft afternoon air. Darkness was already close by; I could sense it in the tops of the trees. It fell so fast here and so early but the consolation was that the evenings lightened earlier than they did down south. I would walk quickly and be back before the twilight deepened into full darkness.

I struck out past Sylla's walled garden, through the rough ground above it, stamping down fern and avoiding tussocks as I went, and found the footpath that led up the hill and into the pine forest. I knew this walk well. It took me through the dark woods and down to the fairy ring, a circle of old standing stones in a clear glade surrounded by dark green pines. It was a calm, sweet place that the children loved and truly believed was inhabited by fairies. When we came here for a picnic after Rose had died, they'd gone off to play among the stones and startled me by running up, both highly excited and telling me that they had seen Rose on one of them.

'Did you, sweeties?' I asked, as they pulled at my hands, chattering away. I was filled with melancholy at their childish sincerity; they really believed that such a thing would be a comfort.

'Yes, yes!' Lilac exclaimed. 'We saw her!'

They led me towards some stones on the western side of the circle. Jamie hadn't really understood when Rose died, but Lilac had, and she had wept with desperate sadness when she learned what had happened. Now her eyes were shining and she was full of excitement.

'She was over here,' Jamie said in his rough little voice. His asthma meant he had a small growly voice like a teddy bear talking. 'On this one.' He touched one of the low lichened stones.

'No, this one,' Lilac said, going to the one next to it. 'She was here! Only it wasn't her, was it, Jamie?'

He shook his head. 'It was her butterfly.'

'Not her butterfly, it looked like a butterfly. But it was her soul,' Lilac said solemnly. 'Her soul was here, and now it's all right.' And she beamed at me.

I thought of that as I emerged from the woodland path into the fairy ring, where the last light was touching the standing stones. I looked around, remembering the many times we'd been here, and wondering, as I always did, who put these stones here and why. Some pagan shrine? Or a Victorian pastiche?

It was a strangely peaceful place, as though the ring of trees around shut out all noise and weather and left this as a little oasis of calm. I stood for a while, taking in its restfulness. Perhaps Hamish should come here for some recuperation. He needed some real quiet and serenity. He needed help.

As I stood there, I thought of him and had a strong feeling, quite suddenly, that I could not help him and that he was out of my grasp. Did I mean grasp? No. Beyond my reach. Was that it? What message exactly was I hearing inside my own head?

I wanted so badly to help him. I'd devoted myself to supporting him during these horrible months. I'd stood, stalwart, by his side like an avenging angel with my flaming sword in my hand. And now this voice was saying to me very clearly, *You cannot help him.*

Perhaps that was why he was still shuffling around in his slippers, his hair messed everywhere, smelling slightly. All the energy and thought I poured into him just seemed to drain away as though he was a bucket with a hole in it. Nothing seemed to do any good. I put all my strength and everything I had into him and he sucked it away and asked for more.

Why can't I help him?

As I thought of that, I felt a sense of unease growing over me. It had been a long time since Hamish had lived here at Ballintyre. And now he was back, Charlie was here, and Josephine was here too, and it was more and more as though they were sinking back into some pattern that they were barely aware of acting out. I realised that I felt oddly invisible to them all. As if I, like Sylla, wasn't actually there. They didn't appear to need me. No . . . that wasn't quite it. It was as if they took what they needed – the children, my contribution in terms of work and money – and the rest was discarded.

I thought about Josephine telling me that she wouldn't call what I did work. 'Why don't you get a proper job?' she'd asked, as though my copywriting counted for nothing, and hadn't kept us afloat when things had got tough. As though my father's legacy hadn't gone on paying our bills when Hamish wasn't earning anything. I thought about how she never complimented me on bringing up the children unless it was along with Hamish, while he received lavish praise for everything. I thought about how she rarely asked how I was. There was something about her that couldn't or wouldn't see my input. Like those letters she wrote in which I wasn't mentioned. And I'd noticed lately at dinner that when Josephine served, as she often did from her position at the head of the table no matter who'd cooked, my portions were getting smaller and smaller until they weren't much more than I would serve Lilac and Jamie for supper. As though she wanted me gradually to disappear altogether.

Like Sylla?

It seemed as though Sylla, for some reason, no longer had any value and so they had discarded her entirely, like an empty milk carton.

But why?

I could only think of one answer: that Josephine wanted to recreate the past in some way, when she had been here in her glory day, with the boys, before they were married. Now she had my children too, of course, and there was no doubt that they were included in her new utopia, but Sylla and I were not.

We had laughed about her, Sylla and I. Her insensitive comments, her way of undermining us, her not-so-subtle attempt to put divisions between us and our husbands. We had thought she was just an over-fond mother who adored her boys to an almost comical extent.

But I knew now that she was not so funny after all.

I left the fairy ring and walked back down the hill along the woodland path. Just before I reached the road, I saw the small iron gate that led to the kirk and on impulse I went through it and into the tiny churchyard. Around the kirk were mouldering gravestones, the oldest at odd angles, and in one section were the new stones and memorial plaques. The night was falling now, coming in fast, and I'd get back to Ballintyre in the dark at this rate, but I wanted to go in. I made my way across the grass to the far side of the kirk. Here, Sylla and Charlie had been married, just as Josephine had dreamed of. She'd wanted Hamish and me to be married here too, but I put a spoke in that – the first thing she held against me. And here, Hamish's father James was buried, with a proper headstone and a bed of green gravel over his resting place.

Over by the wall I found the thing I was looking for: a shiny black plaque set into the ground with gold writing on it, still so bright and new.

IN LOVING MEMORY OF OUR BEAUTIFUL ROSE
TAKEN TOO SOON AND NEVER FORGOTTEN
SHE WAS OUR SHINING STAR

And underneath her dates, so painfully close together.

But I wasn't reading them. Instead, I was staring at something that had made my heart almost turn over inside me. On the plaque was a bunch of winter roses in pure white, tied together elegantly with twine. They lay there, perfect and quite new, neatly put so that they did not obscure any of the writing.

Of course. She would never leave Rose. She's still here.

I looked around, exhilarated.

'Sylla!' I called. 'Sylla, are you there?'

There was no answer as my voice faded in the lowering twilight. I hadn't really expected it. But my spirits had lifted into something almost like happiness. She was close, I was sure of it. No one but Sylla would leave flowers here on Rose's grave, when it wasn't an anniversary.

I started to head back to the house, feeling a rush of positive energy that almost fizzed inside me. I was going to find her soon. I was sure of it.

The response from Daphne Drummond to my email came the next day, chirpy and short, saying that she and her husband Lars would be delighted to welcome us to dinner at Tremewan that Friday. I accepted with thanks, and went to tell Hamish the news.

He was in the television room with the children. They had built a den out of cushions and blankets, and Hamish had crawled in to join them.

'Hello there!' I said, seeing the mess of furnishings and not much else. 'Is anyone home?'

'Mummy, Mummy!' The children came out to greet me with hugs. 'Do you like our den? Will you come in like Daddy?'

'I will later, when I've finished work,' I promised.

Hamish appeared, unshaven and still unwashed. 'Hi,' he said. 'This is my new hideout.'

'I've just heard from Daphne.'

'Really?' He came crawling out, and stood up, interested. 'What did she say?'

'She wants us to go there for dinner on Friday.'

'Oh, nice. Great. I could do with a bit of socialising.'

'Really?'

'You know – with people who don't know all the fuss.'

'I see. Of course.'

'Are you looking forward to it?'

'Yes, I suppose so. It will be very odd to glam up.'

Hamish looked thoughtful. 'I wonder what Daphne's husband is like.' He rubbed his hands together. 'No doubt an arsehole.'

'Why do you say that?'

'You know. Norwegian. Very rich. Hotel entrepreneur. Bound to be a twat.'

'How do you know about that?' I asked, surprised.

Hamish said easily, 'I looked her up on the internet when you told me you'd seen her. It's all there. They're quite the power couple. God knows why they wanted to end up back here.'

'You didn't mention you'd looked her up.'

'Didn't I? Well, you're working all the time. I hardly see you these days.' Hamish turned back to the children. 'Come on, kids, back in the den! The monster's coming!'

And Lilac and Jamie dived, shrieking, back into their den with Hamish roaring after them.

*

On Friday night, Josephine came up from the lodge to baby-sit, as Charlie was also out with his golf friends. She brought a handful of bottles of her favourite Diet Coke and some packets of crisps and chocolate for the children.

'You didn't have to bring your Cokes, I've got some in for you,' I said, as she unloaded her bag in the kitchen.

'That's quite all right,' Josephine said. 'I've got plenty. I don't mind supplying my own. Now, we're going to watch *Chitty Chitty Bang Bang* together, so we're making a night of it.'

'As long as they go straight to bed afterwards,' I said, 'and don't let Jamie get too frightened. Not too much sugar for them either, they won't sleep.'

'I have had children, you know,' she said tartly. 'And I think their granny can give them a few treats now and then!'

'Of course. It's very kind of you.' I couldn't be bothered to fight her on it. I'd just have to be prepared to get up in the night if Jamie had Child Catcher nightmares. I went to the kitchen door and yelled, 'Hamish! Are you ready? We should get going.'

'He won't hear you, dear,' Josephine said. 'This place is a little larger than your London flat, you know.'

'He'll be here in a minute, I expect. I'll just get the children's milk sorted, they like to have it last thing but they will need to clean their teeth afterwards . . .'

'There's no need to get upset, Helen.' She was staring at me, her eyes wide.

'I'm not upset,' I said, surprised. 'Just a little flustered. We haven't been out for ages. I must find my handbag.'

'Here's Hamish,' Josephine said happily as he came sauntering in through the door. 'You look wonderful, Hamish! Doesn't he look good? Daphne will be quite bowled over!'

I gave her a bemused look. 'I don't think that's the point, Josephine.'

'I'm just saying he looks very handsome! I don't think you see it anymore, Helen, you're used to it. He's a very good-looking man, you're lucky to have him.' She went to pick imaginary fluff from Hamish's shirt.

'Well, do I scrub up?' he asked, grinning.

'Very nice,' I said, smiling back. He was looking much better than he had for ages, freshly shaved and in smart clean clothes: sand-coloured chinos, a crisp shirt and shiny shoes. His hair was washed and combed, and I could smell his expensive aftershave too. 'Actually, it's really good to see you looking more like your old self.'

'Let's get on our way then,' he said. 'Don't want to keep Lars waiting, do we?'

'No,' I said, seeing my bag on one of the chairs and going to pick it up. 'Goodnight, Josephine. Call us if you need to, I've left the hotel number by the phone. We won't be late.'

She waved us away, already absorbed in putting the treats out on a tray. I went off after Hamish, a little awkward in my unfamiliar high heels, and wondering if I was vain for minding that no one had said I looked nice too.

*

Hamish drove us to the hotel and we arrived five minutes after our invited time.

'Perfect,' he said, bright-eyed. 'I'm looking forward to this.'

We went into the hotel, which looked smart and welcoming with a pair of carriage lights beaming out on either side of the front door, and were shown to a table in a separate part of the dining room which would have had a wonderful view of the sea if it hadn't been dark outside.

'This is nice,' Hamish said as we sat down. 'Very luxurious.'

'Did you know this place growing up?'

Hamish shook his head. 'Never heard of it. I suspect it hasn't been a hotel for long. A newly acquired part of Lars's empire.' He pulled the open bottle of champagne out of the ice bucket and poured it into our glasses. 'Let's dig in.'

'Do you think we should? Before they get here?'

'I'm sure they won't mind.' He took a gulp. 'That's nice.'

'Would you like me to drive home?'

He grinned at me. 'If you don't mind. I could do with a bit of a party.'

'That's fine. Enjoy yourself. I'll have this and that will do me.'

'Thanks, sweetheart. Oops, here they are.' He got to his feet and I turned to see a good-looking couple walking towards us: Daphne elegant in a black wrap dress, with her signature red lipstick, and a man who must be her husband dressed in shades of linen and taupe that complimented his short white-grey hair.

'I'm sorry we're late,' Daphne said, smiling as she reached us. 'I'm so glad you've helped yourselves to a drink. I had to get Lars off a conference call.'

'My apologies,' Lars said. 'It's hard to stop work when it's international and across the time zones. America is just getting going.' He had a faint Scandinavian accent, but otherwise perfect English.

'You look amazing, Daphne.' Hamish stepped forward to kiss her cheek. 'It's delightful to see you again. You've met Helen, haven't you?'

'I met her nearly twenty years ago, remember!' Her sparkling black eyes turned to me. 'How could I forget? The night you got together. And I saw her last week. Nice to see you again, Helen.'

'You too.' We exchanged kisses.

'I hope this evening isn't going to be all reminiscences,' Lars said dryly. 'I'm Lars, by the way, as Daphne has forgotten to introduce me properly. Let's sit down and order and we can get started on the trip down memory lane.'

'Yes.' Daphne sat down. 'It will make a nice change for the evening to be all about me and my friends instead of business.'

Soon we were all engaged in easy conversation while we perused the menus, and ordered our food. Daphne explained that she and Lars were living in a newly converted house in the grounds. 'It was a carriage house but now it's a really lovely home. We'll rent it out once we've moved on, which will no doubt be in our near future.'

'Will you move on so soon?' Hamish asked.

'Oh yes, once Lars finds his next project. He found this after we spent a Christmas at Tighglachach and did some exploring. I'm sure he'll find another place to add to his empire once this is properly up and running and we'll be on the move again.' She smiled fondly at her husband. 'I can't keep him pinned down anywhere for long.'

'Don't be too sure,' Lars said. 'I rather like it here. Reminds me of home. There are lots of Norwegians around as well. Scotland is popular with us.'

'I think he just wants to get his hands on Tighglachach,' Daphne said dryly.

'You've got to admit, it would be magnificent,' Lars replied. 'That house! The views. I would make it something really special.'

'You'd have to persuade Dad to sell, and I don't think he's going to do that.'

'Your dad's still living there?' Hamish asked.

She nodded. 'Oh yes. As eccentric as ever. He spends his life mending the house, keeping it in his own version of order, which is to say absolute chaos. But he loves it. I don't think he'll ever move.'

'But your brothers and sister might, once he's dead,' Lars said easily.

'You cold-hearted monster,' Daphne said, and laughed. 'Lucky for you I'm not easily upset. Oh look, here are our starters.'

The food was delicious, the ambience wonderful and everything was smooth, sleek and sophisticated. I talked a little about myself and the children when asked, but mostly stayed quiet, slightly overawed by the sophistication and obvious success of Daphne and Lars. I was impressed by their easy and straightforward manner with one another, not afraid to disagree, teasing lightly, but always with affection and always looking out for one another. Lars made sure Daphne had a drink, she passed him the bread before he asked for it. They were partners.

Hamish was a version of himself I hadn't seen for a long time: vivacious, charming, talkative and funny. It was almost a nostalgic experience to see him back, the man I'd fallen in love with and married and who hadn't been in my life for so very long. After Daphne and Lars had talked for a while about their work and life together, Daphne said, 'And what about you, Hamish? What have you been up to?'

He told them about his early career as an ethical business consultant, talking up what he had done. 'I went solo in the end,' he said. 'Probably not at the best time, but hindsight's a wonderful thing. I was just getting a bit bored with the cut and thrust of corporate life and owning your own business is a risk worth taking sometimes, right, Lars?'

Lars nodded. 'True.'

'But then I started to fall out of love with it. The children had come along. I wanted a bit of security and I felt the need to give a bit back as well. And Helen's a freelancer, doing bits and bobs that come her way so . . . well, put it this way: one of us had to get a proper job!' He laughed.

The others looked at me, and I flushed slightly. 'I'm a copywriter and marketing advisor, specialising in refining translations – but I do nearly anything. I suppose it's a bit hand to mouth. But it keeps me busy.'

I'd planned to pitch myself with confidence and here I was, doing the opposite. I hated diminishing my work but somehow I couldn't help it. Hamish had made it sound like a minor pursuit, and I couldn't contradict him in public.

Lars, though, looked over as he munched thoughtfully on his salad. 'Have you seen our brochure?'

'Yes.'

'What did you think?'

I said diplomatically, 'The photography's lovely, the layout is good. I think there's room for improvement in the text. Some areas could be polished.'

'Good. I'm not happy with it. Why don't you mark up what changes you'd suggest and send it to me?'

'Thanks. I will.' I smiled at him, grateful for the encouragement.

Daphne looked over at Hamish. 'But you're not teaching now?'

'No. I'd gone as far as I could in my last school. The head was rubbish, so I decided it was time to move on. And I wanted to be closer to Mum now she's getting on. A bit like you and your dad, Daphne.'

'I never said I want to be close to him!' She laughed. 'Only kidding, it is nice to see him a bit more.'

'Wait!' Lars put up a hand. 'I've missed something. You're a teacher, Hamish?'

I realised as he said it that Hamish had not said what his proper job was. But Daphne had known without being told.

A cold feeling filled my stomach and travelled up and out, until the ends of my fingers tingled. Neither of them seemed to notice the slip as Hamish said, 'Yes, I trained as a Business and Economics teacher.'

'Interesting stuff. Important for young people to learn.'

'I think so. I'm sure I'll find another school up here. There are some good state schools about. And one or two private ones as well.'

'I don't understand you English with your private and public schools, it doesn't make sense to a Norwegian,' Lars said.

'We're Scottish!' chorused Hamish and Daphne at the same time, and then laughed together.

I was looking at Hamish and thinking, *He hasn't even looked at me to make sure I'll confirm his story. He knows I won't say anything. He knows I'll keep quiet.*

'That was great,' Hamish said, as I drove us home later that night. 'I really enjoyed it. It's lifted my spirits.'

'Good.'

'And you? Did you enjoy it?'

I stared at the road ahead, illuminated by the powerful beam of the headlights.

'Oh Christ,' groaned Hamish. 'Come on, then. What did I say?'

'You said you had to get a proper job. As though my work isn't worth anything. Just a hobby that brings in pocket money.'

'You're upset about that? It was just a throwaway remark! It doesn't mean anything. I was just saying that one of us needed to get a job with some security and a pension.'

'I supported us while you weren't earning, with my silly unimportant work.'

'I know that.'

'It didn't sound like it. You put me down in front of them when I particularly wanted Lars and Daphne to take me seriously.'

'No, I didn't. You're imagining it. And he's going to try you out, isn't he? So I don't know what you're complaining about really. Honestly, Helen, you're making too much out of a slightly thoughtless remark. If you're that upset, I apologise, okay? I shouldn't have said it.'

I stared at the road, unhappy. I couldn't express how much I felt it. He had almost inadvertently given away not just that he didn't really esteem my work all that highly but that the financial contribution I had made – while looking after young children and our house – didn't really count either. There was a long silence while I wrestled with it.

'I see. An apology isn't good enough. Well, great. If you want to spoil the evening, go ahead,' he said and leaned back in his seat with a sigh. 'I was just beginning to feel human again.'

I bit my lip. I didn't want to bring him down. It really was very good to see him cheerful again for the first time since we'd left Stourhaven. 'Let's forget it,' I said. 'Don't worry about it. I realise you were just being flippant.'

'Good.' He closed his eyes and let his head flop against the headrest. 'I'm glad that's sorted out.'

I said nothing more. I wanted to ask him about the fact that Daphne had known he'd become a teacher before he told her, but I didn't want to start a row now, when it was late and Hamish was half-cut in any case.

I'll ask him tomorrow. When he's sober.

When we got home, the children were in bed, although a mass of empty packets and sweet wrappers all over the television room showed they'd eaten a ton of sugar before they'd gone up. The television was still on, playing some late-night news programme, and Josephine was lying on the sofa, fast asleep and snoring loudly.

'Mum, Mum, wake up!' Hamish said loudly and shook her. She didn't move but carried on sleeping, the snoring deep in her throat and making a horrible grating noise. 'She's dead to the world.'

'Hamish,' I said in a low voice. 'I think she's drunk.'

'Don't be silly, how can she be? She's been drinking Diet Coke.' He gestured at the several empty bottles on the coffee table.

I picked one up and sniffed it. It seemed all right.

'You're so suspicious,' Hamish said. 'She brings them sealed, how can she have anything in them? She's probably had a sherry or two after the kids were in bed, and it's gone to her head.'

'Then where's the glass? Look, here's an unopened bottle.' I picked up the last bottle and examined it. It was sealed, as

Hamish had said. I twisted the top and it cracked open. I took it off and sniffed the liquid inside. It smelled fine again, but the overpowering scent was of flavouring and sweetener. I put it to my lips and took a swig. 'Oh my gosh, yuk! Taste this! It's got to be about thirty per cent vodka, surely!'

I passed Hamish the bottle and he took a sip. He wrinkled his nose. 'Yeah, okay. That is quite strong.'

'She's drunk three of them! She must be doctoring them at home and sticking the seals up somehow. No wonder she didn't want any of the Coke I bought!' I was horrified. 'Hamish – this is awful!'

'I think she's going to be all right,' he said, frowning at her. 'She might have a bit of a head in the morning but I suspect she's used to it.'

'Not her! She can do what she likes, but not when she's babysitting the kids! How soon did she get drunk? Was she capable of putting them to bed or had she already passed out? This is serious, Hamish.'

He took a deep breath and ran his hands through his hair, looking tired and a bit drunk himself. He'd certainly had plenty of the wine Daphne and Lars had supplied, and, of course, kindly paid for at the end. 'I think you're making a bit of a fuss about nothing. Everything is fine, the kids are fine. We'll just tell her not to do it again.'

'Hamish!' I put my hands on my hips, my temper flaring. 'You can't seriously be saying you're all right for the kids to be looked after by your mother while she's swigging vodka! We haven't been up to check on them, we don't know what state they're in. And what about the fact that she's hiding it in Coke bottles? One of the children might decide to have a drink, if they think it's just fizzy pop.'

'They wouldn't like the taste,' Hamish said in a bored tone. 'I don't think they'd drink very much.'

'That's not the point! It's their safety we're talking about! This can't happen, surely you see that.'

He sighed heavily again. 'Look, I'm too tired for this right now. We'll have to leave Mum here under a blanket and have it out with her tomorrow. Let's check on the children and turn in, I'm bushed.'

As usual, he was diminishing what bothered me. This happened all the time. He was always acting as though my fears and worries were not real or to be taken seriously. He didn't seem to feel my concern or be anxious about the things I was anxious about. His first thought had been for his mother, not for the children. I didn't understand it.

I stared at his back as we climbed the stairs together.

I don't understand it. I don't understand him. I really, really don't.

PART EIGHT

Chapter Eighteen
TIGS
1974

'It sounds like you had a lovely time! I'm just delighted you've found someone,' Mumma said happily. She had come eagerly into the ballroom, all of a flutter to hear how my date the previous night had gone. 'It's just what you need, darling.'

'I haven't *found* anyone. It's just going out a few times, that's all.' I wiped my hands on the rag I kept by my easel.

'But you like him?'

'He's very nice.'

Mumma beamed all over her face. 'Oh *good*.'

It had all been set up by Dadda, who'd met the new land agent at the estate he advised up the coast. 'Angus is a single man,' he'd said, his eyes bright as though he'd just spotted a prize salmon or a plump grouse in the offing. 'And he'd like to meet someone, I think.'

'You didn't ask him that, did you?' I was mortified at the idea.

'Of course not! But I had to find out what his status was. And he's keen on the idea of meeting you. What harm can it do?'

I'd groaned, rolling my eyes. 'Dadda! Oh my goodness. How embarrassing.'

But he'd insisted I at least give Angus a chance, so we'd gone on three evenings out now, all to the same pub. He always came dressed the same, in a heavy tweed suit and sturdy boots, his cheeks wind-beaten, his sandy hair ruffled, and he always gave me a thorough low-down on the state of the pheasant pens and the ground quality, before we talked about anything else. I liked to listen to his deep, rolling Scottish accent as he described the soil erosion or the water pollution levels and what he was doing about them, letting myself float on top of his words rather than immersing myself in them. It was all quite relaxing and he kept my mind off James.

Mumma was so excited for me that I didn't like to tell her that it wasn't likely to end in marriage. It might end in bed – I was quite keen for that to happen. It was time, after all, that I discovered the delights of sex, and I'd already decided that a man like Angus, in touch with nature, would probably be the best person to do it with. With that in mind, I'd agreed to another date and fully intended that this time I'd really go for it and hopefully seduce him. I hoped he'd invite me back to his cottage, as it was hardly going to work if I brought him back here. Not that my parents would mind, they'd probably be all for it, which might make it worse. We'd feel the pressure in that circumstance.

'Tell me all about him,' Mumma said, practically hopping on the spot with excitement.

I gave her a few of the salient facts that I could remember from our conversations and she was delighted. 'You need some romance in your life, Tigs,' she said. 'I just can't bear to have you here, all alone with only us old people for company.'

'I'm quite happy,' I said, leaning forward to dot some white into the pupils of my portrait's eyes.

'You say that. But it isn't natural for a young woman to waste away like this. It isn't what we want for you.' Mumma tilted her head to regard my work on the canvas. 'That's very lovely. I haven't seen you paint a child before. Who is it?'

'It's one of Nancy and Don's grandchildren. She posted me that photograph' – I indicated with my brush the glossy print that sat on my table by the easel, of a grinning American boy against a lurid blue background – 'and I'm copying it for her.'

Mumma looked from the photograph to my canvas. 'Oh! You've transformed it! I mean, it's the same child. But you've made him . . . beautiful.'

'Do you think so?' I squinted at my work. 'I've tried some mixed medium. There's pastel as well as paint. Obviously I've softened the background to that light sky blue, and brought down the glossy element. I've tried to concentrate on his childishness.'

'It's really lovely.' She looked at me with respect. 'You're properly talented, Tigs. Nancy's going to love it. You'll have a stream of commissions, I'm sure.'

I smiled, wiping my brush on another bit of rag. 'It keeps me busy in these winter months when there's no one here.'

That evidently made Mumma think again about alleviating my loneliness. 'You must ask Angus here, darling, for Sunday lunch. Then we can meet him properly.'

'All right. I'll ask him next time we go out.' I assessed the painting. 'I think this is done. I'll move it to the drying room.'

Angus fell far more easily into my trap than I was expecting from an experienced land agent. I'd imagined that, with his background, he'd be wary of ensnarements and man traps but on the contrary, he was pleasingly eager to get me back to his cottage and very happy to seduce me there. The experience was what I'd hoped for: painless, natural and fun. He was very well built and enthusiastically devoted his energies to making me as happy as possible for as long as he could.

'You're a marvellous lass,' he said when we lay together under his sheets after a fresh bout the next morning.

'Am I?'

'Very nice indeed,' he said in his deep rolling voice, and showed me all over again how much he appreciated me.

'You're good at this!' I said breathlessly when we'd finished.

'It's the best way to keep warm in Scotland, you know,' he said with a smile. 'That's why we have so many bairns born in the autumn.'

'It all makes sense.' I laughed and kissed him. 'Thank you, Angus. I couldn't have wished for a better introduction to sex.'

'It's not your first time?' he said with surprise.

'Yes. It is.'

'Well, well.' He rolled over, put his hands behind his head and stared at the ceiling, considering.

'I hope you're not disappointed.'

'Oh no.' He turned and smiled at me. 'I'm honoured. Very honoured. And if I may say, you're a natural.'

'Good teacher,' I said, smacking a kiss on his cheek. 'Now, I'd better go home and look my parents in the eye somehow.'

As it was, my parents were far too embarrassed to say anything about my night out, except that they understood it was better not to drink and drive, but nevertheless I picked up that they were quietly in favour of my spending time at Angus's cottage and so I stayed there more and more. He came for a hearty Sunday lunch not long after, charmed Mumma and had a long talk with Dadda about their mutual interest in estate management, and was now my accepted permanent boyfriend.

I was happy. The affection he gave me was delicious, giving me a sense of value which I found comforting, and hadn't realised I'd been missing. He was a decent, sturdy man with a kind heart and he liked me very much as well. I made him laugh. He was always shaking his head and chortling at the jokes I made. We enjoyed spending time together and suddenly I felt more normal, as though I was being given a glimpse of the kind of lives other people took for granted, full of affection and hugs and kisses.

I also knew, deep in my heart, that I didn't love Angus, not in the same way I loved James. But perhaps being fond of someone was the safer path in any case. Perhaps I'd been mistaken when I'd thought that love was that overwhelming passion and need I felt for James. Maybe that was infatuation. And real love was the steady warmth I felt for Angus. And yet . . . I knew Angus felt more than steady warmth for me.

It was confusing.

Stop analysing everything, I told myself sternly. *You're lucky that Angus came along just when you needed him. You're lucky he likes you so much. Just enjoy it and don't overthink it. There's no need to rush anything.*

I was also glad that, when James and Josephine returned, I would have something to keep me from thinking too much about their proximity. The new baby was already close to a year old, but I heard that Josephine had not been up to the move while he was so little and that she had wanted to avoid a Scottish winter with a newborn. That made sense. But as the spring blossomed out again over the hills, the time of their return got closer. They were due in April, just after Easter, when the countryside was full of nodding daffodils and blossom was beginning to dress the trees in preparation for the summer.

I heard that Alastair and his wife had also welcomed a baby – a little girl. I knew some of what was going on at Tighglachach because of Carina, who had been absent during the winter when we had no guests, but started coming back to clean once the season was underway.

'They've called her Daphne.' Carina wrinkled her nose as we scrubbed away at the windows together. They were rimed with salt after the winter storms, and needed lots of vinegar to break it down. 'Isn't it a horrible name?'

'Is it?'

'So old-fashioned. Like someone in the olden days. I think it's ugly.'

'What would you call a baby?'

'Something a bit more modern,' she declared. 'I like Teresa, Terry for short. That's nice for a girl. Or Linda, like Linda Ronstadt. I love her music.'

'You're a country and western girl?'

'No, I like Barbra Streisand too. That's another nice name. Barbra.'

'I expect they chose Daphne because it's Greek. A nymph who became a tree, I think.'

'Well, that explains it.' She rubbed hard at the glass with a piece of newspaper. 'I still think it's ugly, though.'

It was exactly the kind of classical name I expected him to choose for a daughter. I tried not to feel hurt that I'd heard nothing from Al. I had no right to expect anything but all the same, I'd never thought I'd be so comprehensively dropped. He was no more than a few miles away, living with the wife I hadn't met, now with a new baby, and yet he might as well be living in another country. The truth was that I missed him, even when I tried not to. I knew I shouldn't really pump Carina for information but I couldn't help leading her towards telling me about life at Tighglachach and she obligingly chattered away, giving me lots of details about what was going on there. They were in love with the baby, apparently, and Al was very hands on, but they were always squabbling about it.

'I can't understand what they're saying,' Carina said frankly, 'but you can tell they're always arguing. Snip, snip, snip. And sometimes they go full on shouting and she's all fiery, shaking her hands at him and stamping about, and he's bellowing back at her. One day the baby was lying there screaming on her blanket, naked as a kitten, and they were yelling over the top of her, probably about what to do about it, I expect. Oh, the noise!'

'Doesn't anyone mind?'

'The old fella's deaf,' Carina said, meaning Al's father. 'And I think he's accidentally on purpose lost his hearing aids, if you know what I mean. He's moved out to the stables where he's quite comfortable. He doesn't like the stuffed things, I imagine, and nor do I.'

'Stuffed things?'

'The animals that keep arriving in their glass cases. I don't mind the cute ones so much, although it is a bit heartbreaking to see the little bunnies and things. But I get the creeps from the other things: nasty snakes curled around branches. Stoats in boxing gloves. Horrid.'

I could only imagine that Al had a new passion. It made sense. He'd always had a taste for the macabre.

'But I'll tell you the funniest thing,' Carina said, confidentially. 'Well, it's not funny. I came into the hall one day and I heard this muffled shouting and I looked around and couldn't work out where it was coming from. Then I realised it was inside the old bench in the hall. There was a chair on top of it, so I took it off, lifted the lid, and there was Mrs Drummond. He'd shut her in there!'

'What?' I stared at her. 'Really?'

'Yes! I let her out, she was very grateful. I think. I couldn't really understand what she was saying. I don't know how long she'd been in there. Not long, I think, though she was a bit red-faced and breathless. That might have been with anger, of course.'

I was puzzled. That didn't sound like the Al I knew. Squabbling, arguing, passionate debate – yes. Shutting a woman up in an old bench and putting a chair on top so she couldn't get out? No. That was quite out of character, surely.

I asked Mumma what she knew about goings-on at Tighglachach.

'Nothing at all,' she said with a shrug. 'It's all gone very quiet since Frieda died. You know that they've not even had the ball the last few years. I thought the new Mrs Drummond would keep it all going but it seems not.' She gave me a sideways look. 'Have you heard anything?'

'No. Well . . . Carina told me that the baby's arrived, and that Al and Dimitra are quarrelling a lot.'

'I'm sorry to hear that,' Mumma said. 'If it's true. It might be gossip, remember.'

'I'm just worried about him. And her.'

'Well, don't be,' Mumma said plainly. 'Think of your own life now, Tigs. You're spreading your wings a bit. Don't let them be clipped now. And while we're on the subject . . .' She turned away as if unwilling to face me. 'I think you should keep away from Ballintyre as well, once James and Josephine get back.'

'What?'

'You know what I mean. You're happy with Angus. You're living your own life now. Don't let yourself be pulled back into whatever there was in the past.'

I flushed even though she couldn't see me as she cleaned down the kitchen bench. 'Nothing happened in the past. Nothing. At all.'

'Good.'

'I have to be polite. If I'm invited, I'll go.'

'Of course. But keep your distance.' She turned back to face me, her expression serious. 'I mean it, Tigs. Will you promise? For your sake as well as my peace of mind?'

'Promise what?'

'Not to be around James. If it means you'll be hurt.'

'I won't be hurt! But if it makes you feel better, then I promise.'

'Good. I feel much better, darling. And it's for your own good. I mean that.'

I wished that Mumma hadn't taken that promise from me. It played on my mind for days, even when I was having fun with Angus. Now that we were in a proper relationship, he'd unbent and become much more relaxed. He was still passionate about his work but now he was at ease with me, he could communicate it better. He loved the land and all it contained and was committed to managing it for the good of all its inhabitants as well as for the needs of the owners. Hunting and shooting didn't bother him at all – he thought they were in the best interests of the animals, and if humans got pleasure and good food from it, so much the better. He preferred a haunch of honestly shot Scottish venison over imported, factory-farmed beef any day.

I admired his principles and could see what sense they made, and I spent a few days with him on the estate he managed, in thick trousers and a coat and sturdy boots, climbing through undergrowth and marching over the open hills, while he pointed out the areas of interest to me as we went.

'I'll try you on a gun one of these days, if you'd like that,' he said as we walked along.

'I'm not sure about that. It's a man's thing, isn't it?'

'No. It's anyone's thing. You might need a different gun – lighter, with a shorter stock and less recoil. Apart from that, pointing and shooting can be done by anyone.'

'I don't want to shoot a bird particularly,' I said uncertainly.

'Then we can try you on clays. To get your eye in.'

'Perhaps,' I said. 'I'll think about it.'

I was keener when he suggested a trip out in a boat on the other side of the coast, far from our coves and beaches and closer to the other side of the great estate he managed.

'That would be fun,' I said. 'I can't sail, though. Dadda tried to teach me, I never could learn.'

'We won't sail, we'll motor out there.'

'You've got a motorboat?'

'The estate has several.' Angus grinned at me. 'My boss is incredibly rich. There's no shortage of toys, you know. That's why I'm driving that top of the range Land Rover – he supplied it for me. We'll make a day of it.'

'I'll bring a picnic.'

'Lovely. We'll go on Saturday.'

The day for our trip dawned bright and clear.

'That's good,' Angus said, looking out of the window. 'I wouldn't want to do this on a bad day.'

'Do what?' I said sleepily, admiring his naked back from my position in bed.

He turned and grinned at me. 'You'll see. It's a surprise. I think you'll like it.'

We set off an hour later after one of Angus's hearty breakfasts: eggs, bacon and sausages fried up in one huge ancient saucepan, everything mopped up with crusty bread.

'I can barely move after eating all that,' I groaned as we got into the car. 'I'm afraid I'll sink the boat.'

'You'll have a life jacket on, don't worry.' He drove the car deftly out onto the roads and half an hour later, we arrived at the estate buildings, where Angus jumped out and arranged for a sturdy motorboat mounted on a trailer to be attached to the back of our vehicle. Once we set off I could feel the added weight on the car, but the brand new Land Rover managed easily. Angus turned up the radio and we sang loudly to David Bowie as he drove us over to the other side of the headland, where two large islands sat close to the coast, a narrow channel between them on the way out to sea.

'Where are we going exactly?' I asked when I had a sense of where we were heading.

'I'm taking you to see Crithcorrey,' he said. 'It's a lovely day for it and it's one of the wonders of the area. You grew up round here. You must have seen it.'

I shook my head. 'No. I know of it, of course. But we've never approached it. Dadda isn't that brave a sailor. We've been out to the isles, but from the other approach, round the coast from our beach. Dadda always said it would be madness to go to Crithcorrey.'

Angus frowned as he drove. 'I know what he means. It's no place for amateurs even when the weather is fine. But if the tides are fair, it's not that dangerous. They take tourists out there all the time.'

I shuddered. 'That's not my idea of a good time.'

Angus gave me a sideways look. 'I thought you'd enjoy yourself. I hope this isn't going to be a disaster.'

'No, no, I trust you. But I wouldn't go out on one of those flimsy tourist boats.'

'They're stronger than they look. I just can't believe you've never seen Crithcorrey, that's all.'

When the sea suddenly appeared in its glittering majesty, Angus pulled over by the side of the road so we could see it. The islands, hulking and grey, rose up in the distance, covered in a slight mist despite the sunshine, and the sea danced in the breeze that tickled its tops, bringing up foaming white ripples on its surface. He pointed out towards the channel between the islands.

'Look over there, can you see that messy bit? Where the sea seems more churned up?'

339

I squinted out through my sunglasses towards where he was indicating. Just as he said, there was a patch of sea where the waves seemed to be behaving quite erratically, breaking in all directions and yet staying where they were, far from shore and not needing to travel to turn and dissipate. 'Yes, I see it.'

'That's it. That's Crithcorrey. The whirlpool.'

'Oh. It doesn't look that bad.'

'It doesn't now, while we're here and it's over there. But once you're up close, you'll find it a bit more hairy.'

'I don't want to go too close then,' I said quickly. 'I'm sorry, I'm a bit of a coward.'

Angus grinned at me. 'You'll be safe with me. I'm trained in the sea. Once you know what's happening, it's less intimidating. For years, before people understood it, it was considered an evil place, a mystery. They said the sea witch, sometimes called Beira, did her washing in that cauldron. It was there to suck men to their deaths. But now we know what causes it. There's a great hole in the seabed, and a pinnacle of rock next to that, like an underwater cliff. When the tides move over the hole, the water descends rapidly, and then hits the pinnacle as it climbs again. The opposing forces make the eddy, and the standing waves.'

'I've heard about those. Ten feet high and roaring like tornadoes but standing still on the spot.'

'You wouldn't want to be out there then. That's when it's officially non-navigable. But it's not like that today, it'll be a gentle morass of water, fighting itself and all the different pressures, and ending up going around in a circle.'

'It doesn't sound that gentle.' I smiled at him. 'Well, I'm safe with you.' I was afraid but didn't want to show it. Besides, if dozens of tourists went out there all the time, why should I be any less brave than they were? 'Let's do it.'

Angus drove us down to the shore, unhitched the trailer and we pulled it down the stone jetty onto the beach. From there, halfway to the water's edge, we slid the boat off the trailer and dragged it to the sea.

'Life jackets on.' Angus tossed me an orange life preserver and showed me where the light and whistle were.

'I don't imagine I'd have much chance of blowing on my whistle if I get sucked into a whirlpool!' I joked.

'No,' he said grimly. 'Which is why we won't let that happen. Stay close to me, be sensible and you'll be fine. The boat is safe and strong.'

The wind was fiercer than it looked from the car, and we were buffeted already, my hair whipped about until I pulled it back with a band. I was glad of my long jeans, sand shoes and the jumper I was wearing, which kept out the cutting breeze. I put on my wind cheater for good measure and obediently let Angus tie the straps of the life preserver. Then I climbed on board while Angus pushed the craft further out into the water, and then leaped on himself, vaulting over the side, his legs and feet now dripping wet. 'I'll dry off!' he said, grinning, and pulled the engine cord. It roared obediently into life, the boat lifted and felt light and energetic, and Angus took the tiller while I sat on the other side. A moment later, we were bouncing out over the incoming waves, the small craft bumping over them until we reached gentler water a little further out, and away we went.

'I'll take us on a little tour first!' he cried. 'We'll save the best till last.'

Soon we were flying out, away from Crithcorrey, and zooming over the water to take a turn around the islands. To amuse me, Angus took the boat at an angle so that we flew high in the air when we hit a wave and landed with a bounce, which made me squeal as showers of spray came over the sides and drenched me in cold, salty water.

'It's like a fairground ride! Like a rollercoaster!' I shouted over the noise of the engine.

'Scream if you want to go faster,' Angus yelled back and I laughed.

We rode about for a while, then Angus accelerated round a rocky outcrop, before slowing down and taking us past a deserted seal colony. 'No pups. They're born in the winter, sometimes as early as August further south. They're all gone now. We might see some adults swimming about, though.'

And there were seabirds everywhere, the rocks covered in guano. The water beneath me was all colours of emerald and sapphire or dark grey, churning lacy billows of foam as we passed. The wind battered us as we went and I inhaled great, briny breaths of sea air.

'This is marvellous, what a ride!' I said. 'Dadda's boat never did anything like this!'

Angus responded by revving up the engine and taking us on another exhilarating spin across the waves, skimming over the top, more like flying than sailing. It was a world away from gentle old *Kitty*, puttering along the loch at five miles an hour. James at the tiller was nothing like Angus, who took me on a heart-stopping joyride, making me shriek by doing daredevil tricks like manoeuvring us through a narrow channel and spinning us round in the tiny natural harbour beyond.

'Oh, look!' I said, breathless from the excitement, pointing. 'That's sad.'

A small white corpse, almost rotted away, lay at the back of the deserted beach, no more than a few metres wide, inaccessible except from the sea.

'A baby seal. I'm surprised it hasn't been washed away or pecked to bits.'

'There's not much of it left. It's mostly just a patch of fur.'

'Ah, well.' Angus shrugged. 'It's the way of things. There'll be plenty more next season to take its place. Now then, I'm getting hungry and I'm keen for a bit of hot coffee too. How about we take a look at Crithcorrey and then head back?'

'How long have we been out?' I asked, surprised. It felt like about ten minutes.

'Over an hour,' Angus said, laughing. 'Come on. Let's head to the whirlpool and then we'll go back.'

He turned the boat and began taking us back the way we'd come and in the direction of churning water between the islands.

'What was that word you said before – the sea witch?'

'She's called Beira. The Winter Queen. In Gaelic she's the *Cailleach*. She raises the storms and brings winter by washing her clothes in the whirlpool. And if she doesn't like you, or thinks your soul is rotten as you're sailing by, she'll conjure up a whirlpool and suck you down to the bottom, boat and all.'

'She sounds charming!'

'Just your average magical old hag.'

'So sexist.'

'She's got all the power, love! So you don't have to worry your wee women's lib head about that!'

I laughed and squinted against the sun and the spray as we approached the churning water ahead. 'It's bigger than it looks from far away.'

'Aye, that's called perspective.'

From his chirpy tone, Angus was evidently trying to keep my fears at bay but I could already feel the boat rocking as the water beneath grew more fierce and I felt us plummet slightly and then head back upwards.

'It's so strange to have such big waves here,' I said, holding tight to the rail beside me, awed by the power beneath us. 'And they're not going anywhere.'

'We won't go too close,' Angus said, now concentrating hard. 'Just so you can see the whirlpools. There's more than one, really. They form spontaneously all around the water here as the forces act on it. We're right above a great underwater sea cliff and the hole I told you about. Although in bad weather, you'd have one great pool maybe, a real death trap. As it is now, a bigger boat could sit across one of the small ones and feel it moving underneath.'

'I don't want to do that,' I said quickly.

'Don't worry, we won't.' He pointed through the curtain of spray that was blowing up around our boat. 'See that one there? See it?'

I looked. I saw the great upwelling of water in a circle and the turning at the heart of it, white foam whirling and being consumed, then whirling up again, like cream in the mixer being taken down and folded under itself, then back over. As though being pulled downwards to a giant plughole at the bottom, the water turned and span, its movement making no sense to me, familiar as I was with the ebb and flow of normal tides. Sea water didn't do this. The forces at work on it, making it buck and turn so strangely, frightened and chilled me. I imagined we were being pulled down into that irresistible whirl and what that would feel like. I imagined it twice the size, triple the size, whirling in fury while great waves reared over it, roaring, battling themselves. Panic grew in my depths. I didn't like it. I wanted to get away.

'I want to go back!' I shouted.

'It's fine, we're safe!' Angus shouted back.

'No! I want to go. I don't like it.'

'All right.' He turned the boat, bumping us round against the churning water. Another whirlpool suddenly emerged beside us and I gasped with fear as it started roiling and moving, spinning water downwards in a white and green rush.

Angus saw my face and moved us quickly away. A moment or two later, we were out of the churning water and back into the normal sea.

'We'll go to shore,' he said. 'That was plenty close enough for today.'

Later, on the beach and feeling calmer, with the boat pulled up on the sand nearby, we ate the picnic and warmed our fingers with mugs of coffee.

'We were safe all along, you know,' Angus said. 'I'd never put you at risk.'

'I know. There was just something very chilling about it.' I shuddered at the memory despite the warm sunshine. 'That Beira person can't be very nice at all.'

Angus laughed. 'No. And I'm not underplaying it. You can imagine what that water would be like in the full flood of a winter tide.'

'A nightmare.'

'As it is, things can change quickly. You need to be careful. But did you find it interesting?'

'Yes, I did.' I leaned over and hugged him. 'Thank you. It really was great fun. But maybe we can stick to the hills and the woods for a bit?'

'Certainly, my lady.' He grinned and dropped a kiss on my cheek. 'Whatever you command.'

Chapter Nineteen

James and Josephine were back, everyone knew that, but I'd been faithful to my promise and stayed away.

I'd seen James once, when he was going into the village shop in St Mungo's, and I'd hidden behind the wall in front of the village hall until he'd come out and driven away in the direction of Ballintyre. I was desperate to see him. But I'd promised.

It hadn't been too difficult to avoid him. There was talk of the Ballintyres visiting us, but it came to nothing. And when Mumma and Dadda went there, I made my excuses and they were happy enough to let me stay behind. I heard from them that Josephine was occupied with her children and with a grand makeover of the house. She'd hired an interior designer from Edinburgh apparently, who had brought swatches and paint charts and lots of ideas of how to make the whole place the height of chic. James, meanwhile, had a job in Edinburgh from Mondays to Thursdays, only returning at weekends.

Knowing that had made it easier to keep away from Ballintyre.

'Goodness knows how much she's spending,' Dadda said, when Mumma reported Josephine's extravagant redecoration. 'I'm surprised that Elspeth and Roger are allowing it.'

'I don't think they have all that much choice,' was Mumma's response. 'I don't know if Elspeth would mind quite so much if only Josephine wasn't such a fan of yellow.'

I felt thankful that Mumma had such wonderful taste; she had never needed someone to tell her that salmon pink was the *dernier cri* for walls this year. Her own homemade interior design was so wonderful that she was always having guests beg her for the names of her fabrics and her seamstress.

'You know, I can't remember. I got it in a remnant sale in the town hall,' she would say vaguely when someone gushed over the headboard fabric in the guest room. 'And I didn't even sew it. It's stapled on. I've still got the stapler, if that's any good?'

There was no avoiding the Ballintyre New Year fancy dress party, though. It was the most glamorous social event for a long time, and there was no question of not accepting the invitation. Everyone was going. Even Angus was invited.

I had made my own costume and I was very proud of it. Dadda was in his usual kilt get-up but had thrown Mumma's sash over his shoulder, taken an old shield off the wall, and declared he was Rob Roy. Mumma looked quite normal in her usual ball dress, but I'd put white make-up on her face and blood trickling down her chin, using lipstick, and we called her the Bride of Dracula. Angus was driving us over in his Land Rover, and he was wearing a big fur coat and a fur hat and said he was the Beast of Bodmin.

I felt as though everyone else's efforts were not quite up to mine.

'You look amazing,' Angus said, admiring as I'd come down the stairs.

'Very nice,' Dadda said. 'But who are you?'

I stood for a moment catching a glance at my own reflection in the pier glass in the hall. I'd spent ages sewing my gown and making the glittering wig and the effect was what I'd hoped. The flowing white dress was covered in whirls of snow, which I'd created from a mixture of cotton wool, glue, glitter and hairspray, and belted with a chain of icicles, while my sleeves fell in jagged icicle shapes stamped with cut-out snowflakes. In my high white wig, ordered from a fancy dress shop in Edinburgh, were dozens more tiny glittering silver icicles, and a crown of cardboard and frosted tinsel.

I struck an attitude at the bottom of the stairs, raising one arm high as if casting a spell. 'I'm Beira, the Winter Queen,' I announced dramatically.

'You look very nice, dear,' Mumma said. 'You've certainly put the effort in. Now, let's be on our way.'

I felt a little flat after this response but Angus, walking out to the car with me, told me I looked fabulous. 'Really stunning,' he said admiringly. 'I've never seen you look like this. I'm proud that you're my girl.'

I put a kiss on his cheek under the fur hat. 'Thank you. You're very sweet.'

When we got to the party, I wondered if I'd gone too far, despite my many compliments. Some partygoers had pulled out the stops but many had made my family's desultory effort, paying lip service to fancy dress and wearing more or less normal evening clothes.

And then, through the crowd, I saw an extraordinary party arrive: a great bare-chested Grecian god sporting a gold laurel wreath in his hair, his skin sprayed with gold, wearing a white toga and winged sandals, carrying a tiny winged angel with black hair and enormous black eyes. Next to him was a stunning goddess, with ropes of long dark hair twisted through with gold thread. Her white gown fell in draped folds over a plump, pregnant belly and she also wore sandals. She did not look happy, though, her beautiful face anxious and her mouth turned down.

'Bloody hell, they must be cold,' Angus muttered as he saw them. 'Though to be honest, I'm sweating in this get-up.'

'It's Al,' I said, staring. 'And that must be his wife Dimitra. She looks miserable.'

'You would be too, pregnant in the middle of a Scottish winter wearing just a sheet.' He laughed. 'Let's hope he gets her a nice warm cardy.'

I was staring at the little angel sitting in the crook of Al's arm: a ravishing girl of about two. It was very like Al to bring such a young child to an evening like this, if it looked right. But it was more than that.

They're a family.

Families were building all around me. There were the two little boys asleep upstairs here, the baby on the way for Al and Dimitra as well as their angel. Serena was expecting her first, down in Surrey, and hadn't made the long journey up here as she said it was too uncomfortable to sit in the car.

When would it be my turn? I wondered. I glanced over at Angus who was looking round for a drink. I knew quite suddenly and clearly that it would not be with him. He was a good man, but I did not love him. And if I didn't love him, then I should let him go so that he could find someone who did, no matter how painful that was and how much I would miss him.

I was being selfish, I realised, with a sharp pang. Angus loved me and gave me so much warmth and affection; and I took all of that, while my heart was elsewhere.

Then I saw him, walking towards us. The beard was gone and he looked young and handsome, a broad smile on his face, his blue eyes strong and bright. He was wearing a tam o'shanter, a chunky sweater draped in bits of net, and rough baggy tweed trousers. *James.*

'Tigs, is that you? Oh my goodness, you look simply stunning.'

He was beside me, and then stooping to kiss my cheek, one hand softly touching my arm. The imprint of his fingers seemed to burn my skin, as if I really were made of ice and he was melting me with his human touch.

'Hello, James,' I said faintly.

'You make the rest of us look insipid by comparison. I'm just a lowly Scottish fisherman. You're so regal and lovely—'

'How do you do?' Angus cut in, curtly. 'I'm Angus McLachlan.'

James seemed startled, as if seeing him for the first time, but turned and shook his hand politely. 'James Ballintyre. Welcome. Have you got a drink? Good. My wife is coming down in a moment, she's settling the boys. You must meet her.'

He turned his gaze back to me. I was still overwhelmed by being so close to him after so long. Everything I had ever felt for him came rushing back with a tidal force, rushing through me with equal measures of pleasure and despair. How could I still feel like this for him, when I'd done my best to stay away for so long? What was the hold that he had over me? All I knew was that I responded to him in a way I did to no one else, with a deep longing and need. The touch of his fingers on my arm aroused utter yearning in a way that hours in bed with Angus never had. I was powerless over it.

'I've missed you, Tigs,' he said. 'Where have you been?'

At that moment, there was a murmur of appreciation and a general hush, and we all turned to see that Josephine was descending the stairs, stately and magnificent, dressed as Cleopatra. Her hair was hidden under a black-fringed wig hung with turquoise jewels and with a snake crown on top. She wore heavy eye make-up with great kohl wings around her eyes. The costume below it, though, was more like that of a belly dancer than an Egyptian queen, with an embroidered bra top under a transparent blouse, gauzy harem pants and curled toe slippers and a chain of gold discs at her waist. Nevertheless, the effect was startling and impressive, and as she made her way towards us, there was a smattering of applause, which she received graciously with little waves very like those of the Queen herself.

'Here she is,' James said in a blank voice and I saw that his face, too, was devoid of expression. No – that wasn't right. He was staring at her as though he hated her.

I managed to avoid talking to Josephine the whole evening, still not entirely sure she wouldn't recognise me as her erstwhile cleaner. James had left us, taken up by greeting his guests and making sure everyone was fed and watered. Angus was soon heartily drunk and enjoying himself discussing his favourite subjects with other keen hunters and fishermen, of whom there were plenty at the party. The older guests, including my parents, occupied the drawing room sofas and talked about gardens and grandchildren. I chatted to neighbours, aware all the time of James, shadowing him from room to room as he moved about. I couldn't help myself. I was drawn to his presence with some irresistible force.

I don't know when I'll see him again, I thought, as if to excuse my actions. *This might be my only chance for ages.*

It was hot in the house, filled as it was with people, and I needed air, so I wandered out through the French doors in the library, to breathe in some of the icy cold night beyond. A glitter of gold startled me and Al emerged out of the shadows, smoking.

'Oh my goodness, aren't you freezing?' I said, clutching my chest in shock.

'I'm a god,' he said shortly. 'I don't feel the cold. And you're the Snow Queen, so I imagine you don't either.'

'Beira. The Winter Queen.'

'Ah. The sea witch. Luring sailors to their doom.'

'Both, I suppose.'

'Fitting. You look very nice.'

'So do you. Where are your goddess and godlet?'

'Gone home, the sprog couldn't take the pace.'

'She looks very young.'

'She's only two.'

'So beautiful.'

'Yes.'

There was a pause and then Al said, 'I think I'll go home too, in a moment.'

'Before midnight?'

'I don't care about that. We shouldn't have come really. Dressing up was the fun part. I see you're with someone now.'

'Yes. Angus. He's very nice.'

'Good. At least you've given up your hopeless crush on James. I always hoped you would. I mean, I'm glad you didn't before because I'm very happy now. But I think it's best for you. If that matters.'

'I know you always wanted the best for me,' I said in a small voice.

He turned away towards the loch and puffed swiftly on his cigarette, sending billows of dark smoke into the night air. When he spoke he said, 'I don't think we can be friends right now. I'm sorry. It doesn't mean I'm not fond of you. But it's not right.'

'I guessed. You haven't spoken to me in years.'

354

'No. I suppose I haven't. Well, this is me saying it formally. So . . . goodbye, young Tigs. Good luck with the man in the fur coat, he looks reliable. Take care of yourself.'

He stubbed out his cigarette on a stone plant pot and was gone in a shimmer of gold paint.

The dancing had started in the library and I realised why people had taken it easy on the costumes. It was impossible to reel in my intricate outfit. I could only watch. Josephine, though, had no problem, and bounced around with her chest shaking, the gold coins at her waist jingling, adding a belly twist to her moves while howling with laughter. I stood at the edges of the dancing for a while, sipping on my glass of punch and wondering where James was. I couldn't see him in the reeling sets and, after a moment, I put down my drink, feeling low in my spirits, and wandered out into the hall. I heard a bellow of voices coming down the passage and thought I recognised Angus, so on impulse I picked up my skirts and ran swiftly up the stairs.

It was peaceful on the dimly lit landing, the noise of the party receding, and I took a deep breath, recovering myself. The meeting with Al had shaken me. I kept hearing him say that Angus looked reliable. *Reliable? I'm too young for reliable. I need passion. I need love.*

Another voice in my head:

The man you love is married.

'It's hopeless, just like Al said,' I whispered. 'Hopeless.'

A sound came to my ears, a man's voice singing gently. I followed it along the carpeted landing to a door that stood open. There I could hear it better. James was in there, singing, I supposed, to his children, a low, sweet and comforting noise. I stood behind the door, listening until it stopped.

'Are you feeling better now?' he asked.

'Yes, Daddy,' said a childish voice.

'Why are they making all that noise?' asked another, even higher.

'It's our party. They're just having fun.'

'I don't like it, it's scary,' said the littler voice. 'Will you make them stop?'

'I can't make it stop, but I promise that if you go to sleep, it will be gone in the morning. Why don't you pretend that it's like the wind? You hear that all the time and you go to sleep.'

'It's too noisy,' said the little voice obstinately. 'The wind doesn't laugh!'

James chuckled. 'All right, wee chaps. I have to go now. I'll come and check on you in ten minutes. Try and get to sleep now. You're snug as bugs in rugs. Night night.' I heard him stand up, drop kisses on their cheeks. 'Sleep tight.'

I realised that of course he'd be coming out and I turned to run for the stairs but too late. He was there. 'Tigs?'

I turned slowly and faced him. The glitter on my hair and dress sparkled in the half-light.

He looked astonished, and then overcome. 'My God,' he said in a choked voice. 'You're a vision. A vision.'

Under the influence of something I didn't understand but didn't want to fight, I walked towards him, my gaze fixed on his. It was as though we were seeing one another properly for the first time.

'Have you come here for me?' he asked in a wondering tone.

'Yes,' I said simply. 'I've come at last.'

And I kissed him.

PART NINE

Chapter Twenty

HELEN

2018

I didn't sleep well the night that we returned from our dinner at Tremewan with Daphne and Lars. The children were fine, tucked up in bed as usual. I suspected that Josephine had been able to oversee their bedtime, and then had knocked herself out with a bit more of her Coke and vodka after they were asleep. Not that it made the situation any better.

It wasn't just that. The whole evening had disturbed me. The alarms that had started going off a few days ago were blaring even louder than before. It was as though some kind of protective film had been removed from my eyes and suddenly I was seeing things as they really were, not as I'd imagined. When had it begun to change? Not before we left Stourhaven, surely. No. Back then, life had seemed so straightforward.

Even so, Stourhaven had been such an artificial world, more like a commune than anything else. Surrounded by the beautiful parkland with the school at the centre of it, we'd lived in our neat little houses, all in service to the institution that protected and provided – and took. It took plenty. Hamish had been overwhelmed at first. His working days stretched late into the night and over the weekends too. Lessons – with all the associated planning, marking and exam setting – were just the start of it. If he wasn't teaching, he was coaching sports or running clubs or driving minibuses full of schoolchildren here and there. He had a boarding house to assist in, pupils assigned especially to his pastoral care, and a department to contribute to as well. He had junior members of staff to mentor, senior members to placate, and a housemaster to help. There were parents to report to, meet with, reassure. It never stopped. Then the holidays came and he collapsed, exhausted, desperate to sleep and rest and recuperate to be ready for the next tranche of term that was inching towards us hour by hour. Like a boxer, he was thrown into the ring for a fierce bout, and then out for a while to get his breath, and then back in again.

There were upsides. The atmosphere was busy and energetic. There were lots of friends about, and a ready-made social life to step into. Many of the other families had young children too, and I was soon in a gang with other mothers, helping out at the preschool, running the children's social lives and activities, and keeping up to speed with all the gossip. We were newbies for a while, and then slipped into being old hands, knowing the routines and the traditions.

The shock of it all being taken away, just like that, was enormous. We didn't stay the full two weeks after Hamish was sacked, it was too painful to be in the house knowing that surely everyone must be aware of what had happened.

I knew enough about the way gossip travelled around the school to be sure of that; in fact, I now thought with shame of the relish with which I'd passed on titbits about others, not always sure of their veracity. I wanted to put a sign outside our house, a big banner that read IT ISN'T TRUE. It was the only way I could think of to defend ourselves. Of course, I didn't. All I could do was swallow down the whirling feelings of rage and indignation and try to keep my dignity.

I had messages from my closest friends, some of them just sad-faced emojis and hearts, as if actual words could not be trusted. Tessa – famously straight-talking – was one of the few who wrote.

Sorry, Helen, this is unutterably shit for you. If you need to talk, let me know. I've got wine and I'll come right over. Keep me posted on your plans. Strength and love.

At first, I was touched she had written. Nearly everyone else had vanished, as though we were now untouchables. When I took Lilac and Jamie to school the day after Hamish was sacked, intending to be brave, I nearly burst into tears as people's gazes slid away from me, and mothers I knew well suddenly had to walk off in the opposite direction. Even the teachers focused on the children and couldn't meet my eye. They all knew. And they all thought Hamish was guilty.

I read Tessa's message again and saw it in a different light. She also thought Hamish was guilty. It was shit for me, because my husband was a sexual predator. I guessed they were all waiting to see if I would stand by him or not. She probably wanted to bring wine over so that I'd drunkenly spill all the details. I sent a message back:

Really kind but we're getting through it. Obviously it's a pack of lies. Hamish didn't do it. Let's hope the truth comes out. xxx

It was the equivalent of my official statement and I hoped Tessa would pass it round and that it might go some way to putting my side of the story across. Half of me couldn't bear to think about it, and half wanted to know what everyone was saying about me, and what they all thought, and what was happening to Kaya as a result. Was everyone rallying around her? Of course, they must be. Fine. I was on my own in this, but I was standing by my husband and that was that. Tessa replied.

Okay. I'm wishing the best for you, Helen, no matter what. You don't deserve this crap. Good luck. xxx

'That's you off the Christmas card list,' I said aloud, when I'd read it. She couldn't make it clearer that she thought Hamish was guilty. Fine. Let them think what they wanted. I deleted the message and didn't reply.

Hamish, meanwhile, was so low I wanted him to see a doctor, but he refused. Instead, he lay for long hours in the dark on our bed, unable to get up or do anything much at all. He'd only eat when I forced him to.

While he was falling apart, I was considering what we could do next. I stopped taking the children to school after that awful first morning. I wasn't having them in an environment where everyone thought their father was a criminal. Instead, I started searching for places we could go in the short term. Our flat in London was rented out and was only just paying for itself in any case. Ironically, we could not afford to live in it ourselves and if we sold it, would probably make a loss with the amount we owed on it, as we had remortgaged to free up some money. But there were only two weeks before we were homeless . . . It was urgent.

I drove into the nearest town to visit the estate agents and arrange viewings of any rental properties that were in our budget. Whatever we could get would have to do. I was heading down the high street on my way to another branch of estate agents when I saw her. Kaya was walking up the road towards me, her blonde hair bright in the sunshine. I stopped short, my heart racing and my breath coming fast. A horrible whirring filled my mind and a dizziness took over. As I stood there, horrified, she looked up and saw me and her own expression changed, her mouth dropping open and her gaze darting away in panic. The next moment she had turned around and was hurrying back down the street away from me. I started to stride after her, not sure what I'd say if I did catch up with her, aware only of boiling fury rising up from my core. She had ruined our lives. Perhaps I would do something awful: cause a huge scene, scream at her, call her names. Would I go for her, pull her hair, scratch her face? Perhaps I would. It was almost a delicious thought to imagine attacking her, letting all my rage and hurt free and not trying so hard to keep control, keep civilised and calm.

I stopped abruptly in the middle of the high street, tears suddenly falling down my face. I would not do those things. Of course I wouldn't. I could not afford to get into trouble, perhaps be arrested for assault or affray. And I would not do them anyway. I'd never hit anyone in my life and never wanted to. Even if I did act so contrary to my character and instincts, I would hurt no one but myself.

Kaya had disappeared. I stood there, with people weaving past me on their way to wherever they were going, some eyeing me curiously, most ignoring me, and I let the tears fall until they stopped. Then I took a deep breath, wiped my eyes, and carried on to the estate agent.

My friend Katie came to our rescue. Many of the staff, with school accommodation, had permanent homes elsewhere where they went to escape the institution out of term time. Katie and Giles had a home by the sea. We could use it until the Christmas holidays.

'I'm not going to ask you anything about all this, it's your business,' Katie said, when she came round. 'But the offer is there. No matter what's happened, it's hard on you and the children to lose your home. So we'd like to help.'

'What does Giles think about that?' I said dryly.

'He knows it's not in his interests at the school to do this. But he's going to do it anyway.'

I felt ashamed. Katie was right. So many people had failed to stand by me, but could I really blame them? They could be tarnished by association with us. They would be staying on at the school after we had been banished and then forgotten. Why risk their futures here by consorting with us, even if they thought Hamish was innocent? 'I'm sorry, Katie. Really. It's very kind of you both. I appreciate it and you'd be saving our lives.'

She looked sympathetic. 'We've been here a long time, we've got plenty of credit with the powers that be. I'm not about to judge anyone for anything. You're my friend and I want to help you.'

'Thank you.' Tears sprang to my eyes again. They seemed to come very easily these days. 'I'm so grateful.'

'You'll get through this.' She took my hand and squeezed it comfortingly. 'I promise. And if you and Hamish can sort it out and rebuild, then I'm happy for you.'

She thought he'd done it too. They all did. Well, I couldn't fight everyone. And if Katie wanted to help me, then I was glad to accept.

'Thanks, Katie. I mean it.'

Even with the stopgap of Katie's house, it was obvious things were not going to resolve very quickly. Hamish was completely undone by what had happened, barely able to make a cup of tea without asking my permission in a plaintive voice and then doing it with shaking hands.

'My teaching career is over, full stop,' he said weakly, once he was able to start coming down for the day instead of lying in bed. 'I can't get another job with today's safeguarding regulations. I'll have to start all over again.'

'We can do it,' I said sturdily, but in my heart, I was doubt-ful. Another career change? What was he going to do this time? Would this assault be on his record? He was vague about it. When I asked him to show me the agreement he'd signed, he said it was in his files somewhere, now all boxed up and in storage with most of our possessions.

It was a huge relief when Katie said we could stay until the New Year after all, as they were going abroad for the holidays. I managed to see us through Christmas, putting on my bravest face for the children, and then Hamish announced that we were going to live at Ballintyre, at Charlie's invita-tion. I didn't even protest that I should have been consulted, I was just so pleased that he at least had enthusiasm for that. And a place to live would take the financial weight off us until Hamish knew what he wanted to do. Of course, every-thing took longer than it was supposed to. But eventually, with most of our things still stored away, we packed up everything else, got into the car and made the journey here.

So, when did I start to doubt?

I was annoyed with myself. What did I doubt? There was no question that Hamish had lost his job. And I didn't think for a moment that he had sexually assaulted Kaya. It just wasn't in his character, I was certain of it. The worst that could have happened was a misinterpreted action, perhaps a bit of tipsy flirting at some staff do. What didn't make sense was why Kaya would take it so badly wrong. She'd seemed so straightforward and plain-speaking. So Australian. Not likely to faint at a misplaced hand on an arm. More likely to brush it off with a scoff and a laugh and a warning not to do it again.

So, what happened?

The alarms had started going off after I'd seen Daphne. She had said that Hamish had a Facebook page, though I wasn't aware of it. With just that tiny chink in my faith in him, things were flipping over in an unexpected way, as though I'd blinked and woken up in an alternate reality where everything I'd previously believed now seemed ridiculous.

He shouldn't have brought me back to Ballintyre.

The thought fell into my mind as though dropped there by an outside force. I almost laughed. *What? Why not?*

And it all began to whirl around my mind. Everything that happened here years before, and what it all meant now.

He's the same as he was back then. He's still the same. He's never changed. But I've changed. And now, everything is different.

Hamish went down to the lodge to discuss the Diet Coke affair with Josephine. I didn't go with him. I didn't trust myself not to lose it. It seemed the height of irresponsibility to get wasted while in charge of two small children and I was worried that if she started making excuses, I'd lose my temper. Besides, I thought, as I scrubbed dishes in the sink, I didn't want to humiliate her.

You're letting her off easy again.

It was Sylla's voice in my mind.

You always let them off too easy. All of them.

'Maybe I do,' I muttered. I remembered how I'd thought just that the previous night: that Hamish knew I wouldn't blow his cover when he lied about his leaving teaching. 'Are you becoming my spirit guide, Sylla?' I said jokily out loud. 'I think you have to be dead for that, and you'd better not be dead!'

'Who are you talking to?' It was Hamish coming into the kitchen.

'No one. Myself,' I said honestly. 'How did your talk with your mother go?'

'Fine. She woke up early this morning and took herself back to the lodge. When I told her we knew about the Coke, she was very apologetic. She won't do it again.'

'That's it?'

Hamish looked exasperated. 'What did you want? A pound of flesh?'

'No.' I turned back to the dishes. 'I don't know. I suppose that's fine.'

'I don't know what else she can do.'

'Is she going to apologise to me?'

'Does she need to?'

I let out a long breath and said, 'No.' I breathed slowly again, then said, 'Listen, Hamish, I had a go at that brochure this morning and I'd like to take it round this afternoon, with a thank you for dinner. Strike while the iron's hot and all that. Is that okay?'

He looked interested. 'I could come, if Daphne's there.'

'I don't plan to see her. I'll just drop it in and come back.'

'Oh. All right. I'll stay here then.'

'Okay.' I dried my hands. 'Then we'd better check on the children, I think they've just had a whole hour of TV. They must have got Charlie to turn it on when he went out.'

I drove back up the coast after lunch, the annotated brochure on the seat next to me along with a file of notes and text to go with it, and a pretty thank you card. It had been so odd seeing Daphne and Hamish laughing the previous evening, and remembering the last time I'd seen them together, twenty years before. Then, he'd left me standing while he went off to answer her siren call. I could still see her, that vampish beauty with her red lips and black hair, drawing Hamish to her like a bee to honey.

'I don't trust him,' I said out loud. Then half gasped, astonished at myself. I had never said it so firmly before. After the business of the hidden loan, I'd made a point of giving Hamish back my trust. He said he wouldn't abuse it. I had believed him. He hadn't suddenly become perfect, of course. It was still hard to get him to be forthcoming without being asked, but I thought he did tell me the truth when I made him talk about it. Had I been stupidly naive?

I had, though, always trusted him sexually. It never occurred to me that he would stray. Possibly he was flirtatious, but that was just an aspect of being charming and good-humoured. Wasn't it?

Why then did I feel so uneasy about his attitude to Daphne?

Because I was beginning to realise he had hidden something from me. Nothing huge. A Facebook page. Contact with an old friend. But if he hid that, what else might he hide?

I stared out at the coast road curving away in front of me, feeling as though I were having a revelation. The morning had been so strange. My intuition seemed to have been turned up to full blast and it was bombarding me with information, as though it had been bubbling up very slowly through my consciousness and was now bursting free for me to see as clearly as if someone were holding up signs.

'Oh my goodness, what does it all mean?' I said out loud again.

I think it means I don't know the full story.

I drove straight ahead in silence now. I couldn't help thinking that if I didn't know the full story, it was because I didn't want to. At least, I hadn't wanted to. Until now.

Amy the receptionist greeted me with a sunny smile and a familiar hello. 'Back again!' she said.

'Yes, hello, Amy.' I held out the file. 'I'm getting to be a regular. Can I leave these for Daphne and Lars? They know what they're for.'

'Of course,' Amy said. The front door opened behind me, and she looked at whoever was coming in and flushed bright red, suddenly very flustered. 'I'll . . . er . . . I'll give them to Daphne, that's no problem.'

'Something for Daphne?' said a voice behind me. 'I'm seeing her in a moment, I can take it over.'

I turned and saw someone standing at the door. The light that was streaming through the inner door put a white glow around the figure, so that he looked only like a shape to me until my vision cleared and then I saw him properly. He was startlingly good-looking, much more than he'd been as a young man. I should have known he was the kind who'd mature well. 'Sebastian?'

He stared at me blankly. 'Yes.'

'Helen Ballintyre. Hello. It's been a very long time.'

His expression cleared and transformed into a smile. 'Helen! I wondered when I'd see you. Daphne told me you'd been here.'

'Did she?' I felt ridiculous as I flushed slightly. I was not far off forty, a mother, a grown-up married woman. I had barely thought of this person in years. And yet here I was, awkward, suddenly remembering the sulky boy who had flirted with me and been so annoyed when I'd rejected him for Hamish; as vivid in my mind as if it had all happened yesterday. 'She didn't mention you.'

'I'm disappointed you didn't ask!'

I laughed awkwardly. 'Of course, I should have . . . How are you?'

'Fine. You?'

'Very good. You look well.'

He looked absurdly healthy, a light tan to the skin I remembered as pale, his eyes bright and his hair still dark, though with a sprinkle of grey running through it. He was wearing jeans and a dark zip-up top over a white T-shirt and looked both casual and elegant at the same time. He looked like someone who ate carefully, slept well and looked after himself. 'Thanks, so do you.'

I knew that wasn't true. I looked how I felt – tired out. I hadn't taken time to look after myself for a long time now and there seemed to be no point when I was invisible anyway. The children didn't care what I looked like and Hamish didn't seem to notice. In the week before we moved, when I'd been working flat out to finish my copywriting, get everything packed, the house cleaned, and keep Hamish going, I'd worn the same jeans and jumper for seven days and barely washed my hair. While I wasn't quite in that state now, I wasn't far off. Even getting ready for our smart dinner hadn't really altered my grey complexion and general washed-outness. Certainly no one had commented on any apparent change. I felt depressed by my own condition.

Sebastian seemed to sense the swoop in my spirits. 'Do you have something for Daphne? Would it help if I give it to her?'

I picked the file of papers off the countertop and held it out to him. 'Yes. If you can give this to her, I'd really appreciate it.'

He took it. 'I'll do that.'

'Thanks.'

There was a pause and Sebastian said, 'Are you dashing off? Do you want to have a coffee with me?'

'Oh.' I was startled, about to say no. Then, realising I really had nothing to hurry back for, said, 'Yes, please. That would be lovely.'

A few minutes later I found myself sitting with him in the beautiful room where I'd first seen Daphne a week ago. Amy brought the coffees over a moment later, and I stirred my cappuccino, self-conscious and awkward. I wished I'd at least put on some make-up before I'd come out, so that I wouldn't look quite such a miserable specimen. I might be one in real life, but I still wanted to put on a good front if I could.

'How's life been treating you, Helen? It's funny, isn't it? We spent so little time together all those years ago, and yet I feel like I know you. I have a theory that if we meet in those formative moments in our youth, we never forget each other. We know one another no matter how long passes.'

'Yes. I know what you mean. And it was a very formative moment.'

'Of course. You met Hamish. And then married him.'

'Against your advice.' I smiled.

Sebastian burst out laughing. 'Oh no, what did I say?'

'Don't you remember?'

'No! I mean, I know I wasn't that keen on him. But I hope I wasn't too foul about him.'

'Oh, you just said he was a prize twat, I think. And a waste of time. And . . .' I frowned jokily. 'I *think* you said that he was an idiot and not to go falling for the Ballintyre charm. Yes, I'm fairly sure that's what you said.'

His black eyes danced with amusement. 'How rude of me. I'm sure I put it very pleasantly too. Well, it's a good thing you didn't listen to me. You did fall for the Ballintyre charm, didn't you? Unless you're regretting it and are very sorry now that you didn't listen to me!'

My smile started to fade and I dropped my gaze.

He leaned towards me, his voice concerned. 'I'm only joking, Helen.'

To my horror, my eyes were filling with tears. Sebastian saw them.

'What's wrong? I've put my foot in it, haven't I? I'm so sorry.'

'No . . . no . . . it's not you. It's just . . .' The pent-up stress of the last few days hit me hard suddenly, and the tears began to roll out despite my best efforts to keep them in. 'I can't explain.'

'Wait there.' He jumped up and hurried out of the room, coming back a moment later with a box of tissues. 'There's no one else here,' he said, looking around at the empty room. 'Cry your heart out. I don't mind. Whatever you need to do.'

This kindness made me cry harder and to my own horror, I started to sob, grabbing some tissues from the box and covering my face with them. The worst was over in a few moments, and I mopped up the tears, sniffed and felt I'd got myself under control.

'I'm so sorry,' I said, when I could talk again, managing a watery smile. 'Really. I'm just feeling a little emotional today.'

'It's fine. You don't have to explain yourself to me.' He gazed at me, his expression sympathetic. 'I know what it's like when you get jumped by hurt. And seeing a blast from the past can do that. Bloody nostalgia. It should be banned. How about we drink up our coffees and go for a walk down to the beach? That always helps, I find.'

I nodded. 'Yes. That sounds good.'

As we drank our cappuccinos, I told him a little background about our lives and our time at Stourhaven, and that Hamish and I had returned to live at Ballintyre just a few weeks ago. 'Not because we wanted to. We had to. Hamish got sacked, we lost our home, our old life. He fell apart. We're trying to put our lives back together. It's not been easy.'

'It sounds immensely tough. No wonder you're a bit tearful. You've been through a lot.'

'Not as much as Hamish,' I said. 'He's really been through the mill.'

Sebastian stared at me and said nothing.

'Shall we go for that walk?' I asked, draining my coffee.

'Yes. Let's.'

We got our coats and Sebastian let us out through one of the huge pairs of French windows that gave onto such a stunning view: the strip of golden beach and the silver blue sea glittering beyond it. We walked down across the lawn, then over the sandy scrubby dune and onto the sand. The afternoon was expiring in a last shimmer of light before the cold night took over. Sebastian led the way to a big rock on the shore with a smooth level ledge near the top, just right for sitting on and staring out to sea. He took a tin out of his pocket, extracted a rolled-up cigarette, and lit it.

'You're still smoking!' I said in mock disapproval.

'Not really.'

'You're smoking now, so you are.'

'I have the odd one. I'm allowed to when I'm on a stunning Scottish beach with someone I haven't seen in years. That's one of my passes.'

I smiled at him. 'Ah. I see.'

'So.' He put his hand on his knee, as if to stop it fidgeting. 'So, Helen. Why the tears? Do you want to tell me?'

'It's very complicated. Very. I don't know if I'm ready yet.' I sighed. 'I really don't know you, after all, and it's all very personal.'

'That's why it might be easier. I know Hamish, but only vaguely. I haven't seen him in years and we were never friends.'

'True.' I squinted out over the water. It seemed to be turning grey and shadowy as I looked. 'But I can't go into it now. It's a very long story. And I don't think I even know the half of it. I feel at the moment like I'm being pulled in a dozen different directions and it's wearing me out horribly.' I sighed. 'But I mustn't start. It's getting dark. I must go home.'

'Yes. Of course. Two more minutes.' He smoked his little roll-up.

'Are you living here too?' I asked. 'Like Daphne?'

'I've only just come back, to stay at Tighglachach with Dad. It seemed like a good time with Daphne here. And you remember my other sister, Eve? She's promised to come back to visit – she lives in America now, she's a successful photographer.'

'You're all so creative. What about Sholto, what's he doing?'

'Not so good. Too sensitive for this rough old world. He's in and out of psychiatric hospital, living in a nice place in Glasgow with helpers to keep him going. He likes it. He wouldn't want to be here.'

'I'm sorry to hear that.'

Sebastian shrugged. 'Every family has its sadness.'

'What do you do?'

'Oh, this and that. I keep busy.' He smiled at me again and stubbed his little roll-up out on the rock. 'Let's head back, I can feel the temperature dropping, I don't want you to get cold. And I expect your kids are wondering where you are.'

'Yes.' I knew he was right and I had to leave, but I didn't want to. There was still so much to find out. Just in those few words we had exchanged, Tighglachach and its inhabitants had come back to me in all their colour and vivacity. I had felt alive there, just for those few days. Alive and part of something real, despite the fantasy surroundings. It had been bewitching.

We got up and began to walk back up the beach towards the house. Just before we reached the French windows, he stopped. 'Helen?'

I turned to him and saw the way his cheeks had hollows in them that caught the shadows and held them, and that his dark eyes were unreadable in the gloom. 'Yes?'

'I want to know why you were crying. Will you come back and tell me?'

I was awkward again. 'You don't need to hear about my woes . . .'

'All right. Come in any case. As a favour to me?'

'Well . . . if you want me to . . .'

'Good. Come soon. I'll get your email from Daphne and will be in touch. Take care till then.'

'I will. Goodbye, Sebastian.'

Chapter Twenty-One

When I got back, Hamish said, 'You took your time! Did you run into Daphne?'

'No. I had a coffee and went for a walk on the beach,' I said truthfully. For some reason, I didn't want to mention Sebastian. I had a feeling it would cast Hamish down to know I'd bumped into him. I felt guilty, though: wasn't this lack of transparency exactly what I was upset about with him?

And yet, I thought, I would never have hidden anything from him. Not until now, when I was beginning to realise how much had been hidden from me.

Hamish poured me a glass of wine from the bottle on the kitchen bench. 'Nice for some! I was on child duty all day. We really ought to look into a school for Lilac and Jamie next week, you know. They can't keep spending seven days a week in the house.'

'Thanks for looking after them, I appreciate it. And you're right – I'll look into schools on Monday.'

*

I lay awake that night beside Hamish, thinking over how it had felt to see Sebastian again. The truth was, I barely knew him. He'd been kind, though. It had been nice that someone had seen me and asked how I was, and appeared genuinely interested in the answer. And I liked the idea of seeing him again. It would be a relief to talk to someone, a relative outsider but who still knew the protagonists, who would listen to my side of it all and perhaps act as some kind of confessor. He might see where I'd gone wrong or what I should have done. Perhaps he could advise me. I nearly laughed at the thought of that sulky boy, the one who enjoyed mucking up a reel, being a fount of wisdom now.

Yes, that was it. He would listen, not judge, and would advise and sympathise. That was all I wanted. And the prospect was a pleasant one.

So go to sleep, I told myself firmly. But it was some time before I finally dropped off.

Josephine came up the following morning, acting as though nothing had happened and saying not a word about passing out drunk while babysitting. She was, in fact, her normal self, bumptious and unrepentant, actually telling me that she thought the children ate too many biscuits and it wasn't good for them.

'Thank you, I'll keep an eye on it,' I said, with just a touch of sarcasm, as I handed her a cup of coffee. 'The good news is, I might have a job,'

'Oh? Where? What job?'

'You mentioned that hotel. They might be interested in using me as a marketing consultant.' It was almost true and that was good enough right now.

Josephine gulped her coffee. I watched her, realising she was often thirsty for coffee in the mornings. That made sense if she was always hungover. When she could speak, she said, 'And I suppose that means Hamish will have to look after the children.'

'I thought you wanted me to get a job.'

She ignored this. 'You ought to put them in school, so he has time to recover.'

'I'm going to visit the primary near town tomorrow actually, to find out about places.'

'Oh.' Josephine considered and couldn't see a way to criticise me, so was prepared to be gracious. 'That's good. For everyone.'

'Yes. More coffee?'

'Please.' She held out her mug.

The primary school in Lanceston was charming – modern and well built, warm and bright inside with plenty of outside space. There were places for the children if we wanted them, and I arranged for some taster mornings to get Lilac and Jamie accustomed to the new surroundings and, I hoped, to make some friends.

'They've had a bit of disruption lately,' I said to the head teacher as she showed me round. 'So they might need time to settle.'

'But you're staying here now?' she asked.

'I think so. Yes. We are.'

I drove back alongside the loch, heading for home, thinking about how beautiful it was and how, if we could, staying here would be a wonderful thing, when I heard my phone beep with an incoming message. I pulled over into a lay-by to check it. It was a message from Sebastian.

Great to see you yesterday. I gave the folder to Daphne as requested. Are you free tomorrow? We could meet up and have that talk if you like. S

I texted quickly back:

Yes please. Tomorrow is great.

His reply followed almost at once:

Good. Come to the hotel for 12 p.m. See you then.

My spirits rose. He had meant it, he wanted to talk to me. It was something to look forward to. I'd felt a bit like my old self with Sebastian, and it would be nice to feel like that again. A pleasant anticipation filled me as I drove and it was some time before I noticed a tell-tale bumping on the right side of the car.

I slowed down. Another car overtook me, beeping, and the driver pointed at my front right tyre as he went past. I pulled into the next lay-by and got out to examine the damage. I had a nail deep in the tyre and it was now very flat. I rang home to tell Hamish.

'Bad luck,' he said. 'Do you want to have a go at changing it?'

'Not really. I've never used the jack and I'm sure the bolts will be on too tight for me to loosen.'

'Okay. I'll call Mackay's and get them to go out to you. They'll get there sooner than I would. Charlie's not here so he can't bring me. Where are you?'

'In the lay-by opposite the ferry port.'

'I'll let them know now.'

'Thanks.' A few minutes later, his text arrived to say Mackay's were on their way. I sat in the car watching the ferries come and go until their old red pick-up truck came up and parked behind me. Mackay's men were delighted to find they only had to change a tyre and were affectionately patronising about my feminine inability to do it myself. I couldn't really blame them; I was always telling myself to practise it and never had.

'You're all done now, missus,' said the older man, as the young one dismantled the jack. 'All good as new. You'll need to get that damaged tyre seen to; I think it'll mean a new one. Come up to us as soon as you can for a replacement. I'll need to order it, though . . . Can I check your specs so I get the right one?'

'Of course. I'll get the manual.' I went to the passenger door and leaned in to open the glovebox. The car manual was stuffed inside so I took it out, and handed it to him. He leafed through, found the information, and handed it back.

'Thanks. You can never tell what these newer models might require, it's best to check. We'll see you then, and you can settle for the callout at the same time.'

They drove off and I went to return the manual to the glovebox. As I did, my eye was caught by a flash of white in the footwell, quite far back, in the shadows. It could be paint, perhaps, and my first thought was that one of the children had smeared something on it. But how on earth would they do that? I leaned forward to inspect it and saw that the blob of white was a piece of paper. I reached for it.

The white blob was, in fact, a name badge in a slip of plastic with a pin on it. The kind stuck on people's fronts with their names on when they attended events. Like lectures. Or parents' evenings.

I pulled the badge into the light and looked at it. There was a name in pen, in black marker capitals:

KAYA STONE
Business and Economics

I gasped and my hands began to shake. There was only one explanation for this. She had been in our car. Why?

Panting and confused, I walked away from the car to the side of the lay-by, staring out over the loch or down at the badge in my hand, each time astonished anew to see that name again.

How had it got there? How long had it been there?

Be calm, I told myself. *Think about this. It's just like the badge Hamish wore for parents' meetings.*

At the beginning and end of each term, one school year would have its parent–teacher meetings, held then so that boarders being dropped off or picked up would have their parents present.

Think, think.

The last one Hamish went to was at the beginning of that autumn term. That was when Kaya started. He didn't know her then.

All right. Not parents' evening. When else did they wear the badges?

Something else came into my mind. The sixth-form options fair. When the youngsters started thinking about their A-level subjects and the various departments tried to recruit students to their subject. The more A-level students, the greater the prestige of the department. Hamish had been determined to get plenty of pupils signed up to Business.

'Kaya's going to help,' he told me. 'I reckon between us we'll make a good team, my brains and her looks.'

'Very modern thinking you have there,' I'd joked.

'It's going to go on quite late, I think, and we'll probably all go to the pub afterwards. Giles will drive us all in the minibus, he never minds not drinking.'

Going to the pub meant going off campus, so it would take a while and, as a result, it was a fairly rare occurrence. 'You'll all deserve it after an evening of hard recruiting. I'll see you when you get back.'

'Don't wait up. Just in case the infamous darts competition gets going.'

I hadn't waited up. He'd been there when I woke up in the morning, full of beans when the alarm went off despite his late night. So full of beans, he wanted to spend twenty minutes in bed with me, before dashing off to school.

Why did I remember that?

It hadn't been like him. It hadn't been like normal.

That morning had stuck in my mind because he hadn't quite been himself. He'd made love to me . . . differently. Not very. Just a bit. I'd noticed. And then forgotten it.

Until now.

I held the badge in my hand. She had been in our car, probably after the options fair. A few weeks before Hamish lost his job. Was this when he assaulted her? Had he lured her in somehow? Why hadn't they been in the minibus with Giles? What was she doing in our car?

Everything whirled around my head and then, to my surprise, a calm dropped down on me, like a heavy blanket. It lay like a snowfall over my panic and suffocated it. All I needed to do was ask Hamish one question. I would go home and I would do that now.

I got into the car, turned it on and drove home, silent, my eyes fixed on the road ahead.

I would ask him one question. That was all I had to do.

At home, everything was normal. Charlie was back from his morning's work and was bellowing across the table at Hamish about the latest activities on the estate and his plans for investing in a solar farm. The children were finishing up their fruit yoghurts while Josephine chivvied them and went back and forth between them, wiping chins and fingers, as though one speck of stray yoghurt anywhere was not to be tolerated.

'Hello,' Hamish said, as I came in. 'How was the school?'

'Great. Very good. Hamish, can I have a word with you?'

'Sure.' He got up. ' 'Scuse us, back in a moment.'

We went out of the kitchen together and he followed me down the passage until we reached the library. I opened the door, beckoned him in and closed it behind us. I was sure no one would hear us in here. In my pocket was the badge, carefully put there. Not that I intended to show it. Not yet.

Hamish looked interested but very slightly edgy, as though this could go any number of ways, some of them not very pleasant. 'What's the summit in aid of? Did everything go all right at the school?'

'Yes, it went fine.'

'The tyre then. Don't tell me – we have to have four new tyres at a cost of a grand each.'

'No. We do need a new tyre. But we can talk to Mackay's about that.'

'Then what is it?'

'I was just thinking on the way home.' A story rose easily to my lips. 'I was thinking it all over – what happened at Stourhaven and what it might still mean for us. I know you resigned on the condition that Kaya didn't report you for the assault . . .'

He looked wary. 'The assault that never happened.'

'Yes. But what if she reports you anyway? Have you thought about that? She might, if she's feeling vengeful. Or someone talks her into it.'

'I don't think she will. If she hasn't already, it's unlikely. It was ages ago now anyway.'

'People get arrested for assault years and years later.'

'I don't think that's going to happen in this case.' He frowned. 'So what's your point?'

'I suppose I want to be ready if I have to support your story. From my side of things, you had a perfectly normal friendship with her. Like colleagues.'

'Yes.' He narrowed his eyes. 'Why are we talking about this now?'

I took a deep breath. 'You said you never touched her – not in any meaningful way. And I wondered . . . did you ever cross any lines with her that could be misinterpreted? How close were you? Were there times when you were alone with her?'

'Of course there were.' He looked exasperated. 'I was alone with her all the time! Talking about pupils, arranging timetables, discussing stuff. She was always popping into my classroom.'

'Okay . . . but that was on school premises. Were you ever on your own together off premises?'

'No,' he said firmly.

'Never?'

'I said no, didn't I? That means never.'

Here it was. 'So she was never . . . for example . . . in our car?'

Hamish looked me right in the eye and didn't hesitate. 'She was never in our car.'

'You never drove her anywhere? Or sat with her in the car?'

'I told you – no. I didn't.'

389

'You promise?'

'Yes, she was never in our car. Satisfied? If you don't mind, I've got to bring this particular interrogation to an end, Charlie's making me a cup of tea.' He shook his head as he turned for the door. 'I don't know why you're bringing this up now, Helen. It's water under the bridge. Finished. Over.'

I watched him leave, sadness welling up inside me. So now I knew. I couldn't trust him. Not one bit. He would look me in the eye and lie to me. Not just over money but over this. And if he was lying that she hadn't been in our car – what else was he lying about?

The shock of Hamish's blatant lie was so great, it left me numb and, as a result, I was able to carry on almost as normal. All through the afternoon, I would pull that little tell-tale badge from my pocket and look at it, as if to remind myself of what I knew.

Kaya had been in our car, in the passenger seat. There was no other way to explain it.

I hadn't realised how much Hamish's lie had been weighing me down until I pulled out of the driveway the next morning and felt it lift a little from my shoulders. I offered to take Lilac and Jamie out with me for lunch, to give Hamish a break. He'd happily agreed.

They sat in the car behind me as I drove, listening to the audiobook I'd put on the stereo system, and I glanced at them from time to time in the rear-view mirror. I hadn't wanted to leave them at home, I realised. I'd been away from them too much lately, working or else escaping into my thoughts, to get away from Hamish or Josephine. I'd been happy to do that before but now – in the wake of the babysitting debacle and Hamish's untruthfulness – I felt uneasy about it.

I wasn't sure how Sebastian would take to having my children with us, but in the event he didn't seem to mind at all.

'Hello there,' he said as they came up with me, each holding a hand and suddenly shy. He kneeled down to their level to greet them. 'This is a nice surprise. I like making new friends. What's your name?'

They introduced themselves and he won them over at once with a lollipop each from the jar in reception.

'I hope it's okay to bring them,' I said, glad he seemed so amenable.

'Not a problem at all. I was going to suggest a drive up the road to a little place I know but as you've got the children, we can stay here if you like.'

'If it's child-friendly, we could go in my car? I've got their seats in there.'

Sebastian thought for a moment. 'Why not? Let's have a change of scene.'

We climbed into the car. 'Where are we going?' I asked.

'A little pub on the way to Gillygantry.'

'That's the big estate in the north.'

'Yup.'

'Owned by a Swedish billionaire, I heard.'

'Owned by a Norwegian actually. Called Lars.'

I turned and looked at him in surprise. He was laughing at my expression. I looked quickly back at the road. 'Lars owns Gillygantry? Is he buying up all of Scotland?'

'Not all of it. But a fair-sized chunk.'

'He's rich then.'

'Yes. Filthy.'

'Oh.' I said nothing more as we drove and neither did Sebastian.

He seemed to be listening to the recording of *Charlie and the Chocolate Factory* I'd put on for the children and I was taken by surprise when he suddenly said: 'Turn right here, it's up this road.'

The pub was a low, white building with empty hanging baskets outside that would be full of flowers in the summer but now looked a little sad. Inside, though, it was warm and bright with a blazing fire. A quick word from Sebastian and we were put on a family-sized table with a bucket of crayons and colouring books for the children. We ordered food, and the waiter brought our drinks.

'This is really nice. The kids are great,' Sebastian said, watching them colouring in and talking to one another. 'And as you're driving, I get to have a pint.' He took a gulp from his beer and wiped away the foam around his mouth. 'Result.' He smiled.

'You don't have any of your own?' I asked, stirring my lemonade with my straw, although it didn't need it.

'No. That hasn't happened. And I'm single right now, so it's not likely to. But I like children. I'm always on at Daphne to get on with it; I'd love a pack of nephews and nieces.'

'That's nice.' I smiled back, thinking how relaxing it was to be with him. 'I felt I had to bring them.'

'Why?'

I told him about Josephine getting drunk while looking after them, and how it had made me uneasy about leaving them in her care, even with Hamish there.

'That's not good at all,' he said seriously. 'I always thought she was barmy but I didn't think she was irresponsible.'

'I forgot you knew her.'

'I didn't exactly know her, but we all thought she was strange. It was one of Dad's jokes that she was trying to raise boys with Oedipus complexes – you know, that was her goal. We all saw how much she fussed over them. That's why I'm surprised she was that careless with her grandchildren.'

'She still fusses over her boys. Other people . . . not so much.'

'Ah. Okay. And you don't trust Hamish to sort her out.'

'I don't trust Hamish at all,' I said more emphatically than I'd meant to.

Sebastian raised his eyebrows at me. 'Is that anything to do with why you were upset the other day?'

I glanced at the children but they were absorbed in their crayons and sucking on the straws of their orange juice cartons. I lowered my voice anyway. 'It's been so difficult. When he . . . ' – I didn't want to name Hamish in front of the children even if they weren't listening – 'when he lost his job . . . well . . . it was pretty awful. I had to take his version on trust and I did. I completely believed him. Even though he hadn't been entirely straight with me in the past.'

'What had happened?'

'Lies about money. A hidden loan.' I shrugged. 'Not so bad really.'

'What?' Sebastian laughed disbelievingly. 'Did you just hear yourself? What's not bad about that? It sounds pretty awful to me.'

'Does it?' I felt surprised. I'd grown so used to Hamish telling me that I was exaggerating things. Going over the top about them. Overreacting. Taking it too much to heart. 'You expect perfection,' he'd said, 'and I'm afraid I'm only human. I make mistakes.' He'd downplayed everything I was upset about to the point where I thought I must be doing what he said: refusing to forgive. Punishing him. Not moving on.

Sebastian took another drink of his beer and sat back in his seat, regarding me with a serious gaze. 'You're telling me that he concealed debts from you.' He glanced at the children. 'I can see why this is hard to discuss in front of them.'

'It's hard to discuss with anyone.' I looked at him sadly. 'And it's only the start.'

'You'd better tell me later,' he said as the waiter approached, loaded with plates. 'Okay, folks, who wants fish fingers, eh?'

Over lunch, while I oversaw the children and ate my own food, Sebastian told me that he'd never gone to art school after all. To his surprise, he'd got into the other side of it. He ended up running galleries, representing artists and finding new talent, and when I asked if I might have heard of any of them, he named several well-known modern artists.

'Impressive!'

'Lucky for me, I've got an eye. And I love my work. Now I go all over the world, dealing in art. I've got a gallery in New York, where I show Eve's work, and one in Hong Kong. Another in London. It keeps me busy.'

'It sounds so glamorous. I can't think what you're doing back here.'

'Spending time with Dad. And I'm doing some work with Lars. He's quite keen on some kind of gallery here in Scotland. There's a move away from just having art in the big cities, and towards using it as a way to reinvigorate rural economies. A smart gallery out here could serve as a way to draw tourists here – to stay at Lars's hotel or on his estate. Gillygantry is going to be turned into a very luxurious retreat, to be used by the sort of people who spend big money on art. The house itself will be a kind of gallery – everything you see for sale.'

'Sounds exciting.' I smiled at him. 'Who would have thought when you were desperate to escape all those years ago that you'd be so happy to be back?'

'And now you're the one who's desperate to escape,' he said softly.

'Me? No! I love it here. I didn't think I would, when we arrived in such awful circumstances. But I'm really falling in love with it.'

'I don't mean Scotland. I mean something else.'

I coloured. 'Oh. I see.'

He said easily, 'I want to say something. I don't know the whole story yet, nothing like it. But what I do know isn't great. So let me say this. It's a saying, I can't remember where I first heard it. It goes like this: if someone shows you who they are, believe them. Just think about it, okay?' He looked over to the waiter. 'Could we have our bill, please?'

*

In the car on the way back, Sebastian suggested we make a detour. 'There's a place nearby with an amazing view. We should stop and see it and walk off some of that lunch.'

'Sure. Just tell me where to go.'

Ten minutes later he directed me to take a turning towards the coast. Before long we were taking a gentle slope down towards a long white-sanded beach. I parked up and we got out, the children running ahead squealing, delighted to be out despite the wind coming off the sea.

We followed, hands in pockets, chins tucked down into coats, and talked. I told him the story of leaving Stourhaven, why we'd had to go and how I'd believed Hamish completely.

'Until when?' Sebastian asked.

'Until Daphne said that Hamish had a Facebook page. I didn't know about it. When I looked, I couldn't find one. I guess that's how she knew he was a teacher, before he said anything.'

'I'll ask her about it,' he said briefly. 'I'm not on it. But she'll tell me.' He glanced at me as we strolled along the sand. 'Was that why you were crying?'

I nodded. 'It's a lot of things. Not just Hamish. But it all seemed somehow to be interconnected. All based on lies. On people not saying things. On deception of all kinds. I felt I'd based my life on something I'd thought was so secure and so reliable. What could be more unshakeable than a place like Ballintyre? And Hamish. I thought he was . . . unshakeable too. And then . . . well. It felt like it was all shifting, moving under me. My life was not . . . safe.' My hand went to the badge in my pocket. 'And then yesterday, I found this.'

I held it out to him and he squinted to look at it. 'That's the name of the girl who said Hamish assaulted her?'

'That's right. It was in our car. She had to have been in it for her badge to be there. And when I asked Hamish, he swore she had never been there.'

'Does he know you have this proof?'

I shook my head. 'If I'd told him, he would have explained it away. It would be innocent. But if he doesn't know I have it, and says she was never there . . .'

'Then what else is he hiding?'

'Exactly. My whole version of events came from him.'

Sebastian stopped and looked at me. His black hair rippled in the wind like little dark feathers. 'This is serious, Helen. You don't really have any idea of what went on.'

'I know. And I feel like I have to find out. But I'm also afraid. What happens when I know the truth?'

'I think you already know the truth,' Sebastian said. 'You want evidence, that's all. The proof. But it's like knowing who committed the crime – you just need to find the weapon.'

'What do you mean?' I asked, half fearful.

'You already know he lies. And that's all you really need to know. What the lies are is just the detail.'

I turned away, my heart sinking and yet a kind of clarity filling me. He was right, of course. I knew. The voice in my head had been telling me something like this for a long time now. I just hadn't wanted to listen.

The children were down at the edge of the sea, throwing stones into the oncoming waves.

'Look at that,' I said, pointing out towards the islands that lay off the coast. In between them was a churning mass of white and green, as though something huge were about to burst through the surface. 'The water out there is going crazy!'

'Don't you know it? That's Crithcorrey. The famous whirlpool.'

'What?' I whispered. I felt suddenly faint and dizzy. I staggered slightly and Sebastian put out his arm to grab me.

'Are you okay? What's wrong?'

'Can we go, please? I . . . I can't be here.' Panic filled me. 'Lilac, Jamie, come here!' I yelled. 'Come back here, right now!'

They turned and started making their way back towards me, trotting across the sand.

Sebastian gripped my arm tighter. 'What's wrong?' he asked urgently. 'What is it? Have I made a mistake bringing us here?'

'I have to leave,' I said breathlessly, tears in my eyes. The children were almost with us, so I spoke rapidly. 'My niece, Rose. She died here. In the whirlpool. Her . . . her boat was taken down and she died there.' I clutched at him. 'Please, Sebastian, I have to go!'

'Christ. Of course.' He let go of me, strode to the children and picked them both up. 'Come on, kiddoes, we're off now.'

We went quickly back to the car.

'I'm driving,' he said briefly and I didn't argue. Instead, I sat, numb and shocked, all the way back to Tremewan

House. I had never been on that beach. I had never wanted to be there. Sebastian was not to know that.

'I'm so sorry,' he said, when we'd pulled to a halt in the car park of the hotel. 'Do you want to come in?'

I shook my head. 'No. We'd better go home. It wasn't your fault. You didn't know.'

'I feel like an idiot because I did know.' His black eyes were blazing almost as they had all those years ago but his fury was directed at himself.

'What? How?'

'I knew a girl had died there a while back and I think I also knew that she was connected to Ballintyre. I didn't know she was your niece. I'm so sorry, Helen.' His eyes had softened now, and he was looking at me with infinite sympathy. 'I can't imagine how awful that was.'

'It was terrible. But it was a million times worse for Sylla, her mother. My sister-in-law. That's the other thing that's been troubling me so much. Sylla wasn't here when we arrived and no one knows where she is. I'm the only one who seems to care, or even miss her. I think she must be somewhere nearby but sometimes I worry the grief was too much and she's killed herself. I really want to find her. I think that's partly why I reacted so strongly today.'

'Sylla?' Sebastian said thoughtfully. 'Of course. I remember her, now you say. And I'm sure I remember . . .'

'What?'

He started the engine. 'Let me think about it. But for now, let's get you home.'

PART TEN

Chapter Twenty-Two
TIGS
1977

'Poor Angus. I don't understand it.' Mumma was shaking her head sadly as she sewed by the fire. 'Why have you finished it with him, Tigs?'

'It wasn't working.' I stared into the flames, sitting bolt upright. I was full of dancing energy now, alight with excitement.

'Working!' Dadda shook his head. 'What on earth does that mean? He's a good man, you liked each other. Of course it was working, if you put the effort in.'

I said nothing. He didn't understand. How could he, at his age? Had he ever felt like this for Mumma, or Mumma for him? I doubted it. This feeling, fierce and all encompassing, was beyond anything anyone had ever known before, I was sure of it. It gave me power, raising me to heights I hadn't known I could reach. I felt capable of anything. I'd been able to go to Angus's cottage on New Year's Day and tell him that we were finished.

'But why?' he'd said, still pale from the previous night's excesses and clearly both confused and struck with sorrow by my ruthless pronouncement.

'I don't love you. I'm sorry. You're marvellous and you've been wonderful for me but you deserve better. So we should split up now before you do anything silly like propose to me.'

He looked so hurt that my heart swooped momentarily and I felt sorry for him and ashamed of myself. I hugged him goodbye, full of remorse for what I was doing to him, but the moment I walked out of the cottage, my spirits took flight again and I was back in my state of rapture, my emotions a rhapsody of joy.

I drove home in that state. Even the dullness of the winter morning couldn't pierce the shine that touched everything I saw. My thoughts were in a whirl of delight. *I kissed James. He kissed me. It was wonderful. It was perfect.*

That moment on the upstairs landing at Ballintyre on New Year's Eve, while the party caroused beneath us, had been everything I'd ever dreamed of. I'd melted into his arms, the Winter Queen surrendering to the fisherman, and our mouths had met as though they had been designed expressly for the purpose. His touch made my body sing, my head whirl and life had taken on a meaning it had never had before.

When at last we parted, breathless, astonished by one another, he'd stared at me, mirroring my own astonishment, and said, 'Oh Tigs. What is this?'

I'd known what it was at once. But it wasn't time to say it yet. 'I don't know,' I said. 'But it's wonderful.'

A burst of laughter from below brought us back to our situation.

'I have to see you again,' James said urgently. 'We have to talk about this. Not here, though. Not tonight.'

'Come to the house tomorrow. I'll meet you on the beach,' I said.

'I can't tomorrow.'

'The day after.'

'Yes, I can get away then. Ten in the morning. On the beach.'

Our lips met again and the sweetness of it suffused me as though I'd sipped some kind of heavenly wine. Then we parted and James hurried down the stairs, greeting the people at the bottom with a hearty hello. I caught sight of myself in a mirror. My eyes were bright, my cheeks flushed and I seemed transfigured. Not like myself at all. I knew at once that everything had changed. I had been waiting all this time, and the moment had come. At last.

I was on the beach at ten o'clock on the appointed day, at a section out of sight of the house. There was no one about on this freezing day, no boats on the horizon. The sea and sky melted into one another in a moody grey, as though joining forces in the misery, and the waves were choppy. My mood, though, was sunshine and stars, everything bright and good. I had suppressed the memory of my interview with Angus the previous day, and now walked impatiently back and forth on the wet sand, sometimes picking up a stone to lob into the sea or checking my watch.

Then at last, I saw him, coming towards me across the sand, his eyes half closed against the buffeting wind. I ran towards him and he held out his arms. I fell into them, gasping, and then we kissed again. I tasted the salt on his lips, the warm interior of his mouth and felt the unutterable deliciousness of his arms tight around me.

'What are we doing, Tigs?' he murmured into my hair.

'What we're supposed to be doing,' I said firmly, and covered his face in kisses.

We walked towards the rocks, where we could shelter from the wind.

'But there's Josephine. And Angus.'

'I've finished with Angus. It's over.' Our hands were clasped firmly and I held his in both of mine. 'It wasn't serious, I didn't love him.'

James looked down at me with that expression of wonder again, as though he was just beginning to see me properly. 'You seem very determined.'

'We've been waiting for each other, you must feel it too.' I beamed up at him. 'Or it wouldn't be like this.'

We sat down on some rocks, as close together as we could be.

'Yes.' He smiled and hugged an arm around me. 'I don't understand it. Two days ago you were just young Tigs, my childhood friend. Someone who had retreated to the edges of my life. And now . . . everything's changed. Suddenly, you're the centre of everything.'

I leaned my head upon his shoulder, soaking in his nearness, full of happiness, his hand tight in mine. 'It's all fallen into place. That's what's happened.'

'Oh Tigs.' We kissed again and after a long while, he pulled away. 'But . . . there is Josephine. I'm a married man.'

'Do you love her?'

He paused and squinted out to sea, his expression a grimace. 'I thought I did. I loved her when I proposed, when we first married. She was different then. But life has become so difficult.'

'How?'

'I can't explain it entirely. So many, many tiny ways, all of them adding up to something impossible. I can't please her no matter how hard I try. At first, I was her sun and moon, and she couldn't do enough for me. She loved everything – Ballintyre, the loch . . . me. But after we married, it changed. Sometimes she seems to despise me, and then love me again, until my head is spinning. She hates Scotland after all and wants to live in London. It took all my strength to persuade her to move back here, and she demanded total control of the house in return. By then, we'd had the boys. Nothing I do with them is right. They're never allowed to be dirty or to play rough games, and she fusses over them as though they're little princes, or gods, when she isn't shouting with anger. They're rarely punished, but often threatened with it, so they quickly learned not to take her seriously. And then she's so mercurial. They're angels on Monday and devils on Friday, even though in reality they're no different. They never know if they'll get a kiss or a slap. And me too – I'm her hero or her burden. A saint or an irredeemable sinner.' He shook his head. 'I've tried to make her happy. But I can't. I feel like I'm trying to fill an empty lake with one cup of water at a time. It's an impossible task. No matter what I do, I will never make her approve of me.'

'I'm sorry.' I leaned against him, trying to press my love and comfort into his body with mine.

'I used to feel like I could still love her if I could only find out the secret to making her happy. But now I know I will never find out that secret and I can't make her happy. I wonder if anyone could.' He turned to me, his expression agonised. 'She's so cold, Tigs. It's like there's a ring of ice around her heart. Nothing really seems to touch her. I don't think I've ever seen her cry with real emotion, with real pain. She cries with anger and with self-pity but I've never seen her weep in sympathy or in genuine remorse. I've never seen her sad for me.' He hugged me tight. 'At the costume party, you were the queen of ice and snow, and she was the queen of heat and love. But the reality is the opposite. She's frozen inside and you're warmth and joy.'

I reached for him and we kissed again, embracing with all our hearts. When we parted, he said, half mournful, half frustrated, 'I wish I'd known it before.'

'We can't change the past. But we have our future.'

'I don't know how,' he said unhappily. 'I can't divorce her. I can't do that to the boys. I owe it to her to stay. I've married her, she's given up so much for me.'

'Don't think about that. Just think about what we have now, and what it gives us both. You don't have to leave her. Let's just be happy in any way we can.' I gazed into his gentle blue eyes. 'Please, James. Please.'

He looked back, tenderly. 'I can't resist this. You. It's too late. I can't live without it now.'

'And neither can I.'

We sat as long as we dared, the wind buffeting us, and soaked in each other's presence, home at last.

James knew of a cottage on the edge of the Ballintyre estate, once let and now standing empty between tenants. We were afraid of telephone calls between our homes, in case my parents or Josephine answered the phone, and made our arrangements beforehand, planning each time we could meet at the end of the last.

The cottage was bare and basic, not much more than a shepherd's croft, but I loved it for that. The ancient stone floor and thick walls, the two basic rooms with a small bathroom tacked on the side, were simple and elemental, and all we needed. James would arrive before me, light the stove and prepare something hot to drink. Gradually he brought bits and pieces to furnish it a little: some chairs and cushions, blankets and a rug.

The first time we went there was the first time we made love, on the stone floor with only our coats to protect us from the chill, but that didn't matter. If sex with Angus had been rambunctious and fun, then the experience with James was on another plane. I had been worried about being self-conscious but when it happened it was so unbearably natural and so exactly right and glorious that when it was over, I burst into tears of emotion, and we held each other tightly, unable to speak for a long time.

We met there twice a week if we could, and before long I stopped crying afterwards. Now we took our time, finding infinite pleasure in making our cushioned bed before the stove and exploring one another slowly and joyfully, learning everything we could about each other. This was love, I knew that. Real love. It had come at last.

No one knew. I didn't breathe a word to a soul. It was my most treasured secret and I was prepared to keep it for the rest of my life. Nothing mattered but those stolen hours in the cottage, making love with James, being with him and loving him.

My parents noticed I was different – Mumma commented on the light in my eyes, and the way I was painting with greater skill and creativity, and Dadda said I must be taking some special vitamins to be so charged and energetic – but I was sure that they hadn't guessed the cause.

'Does Josephine suspect?' I asked, nestled against James's chest under the rough wool blanket he'd brought there for us. The flames danced inside the stove and I watched them leap and wave behind the sooty glass.

'No. I don't think so.' He kissed my hair and nuzzled my neck. 'I want this to go on forever.'

'So do I. As long as she doesn't know.'

'You can't really give your life to me like this, though – you'll need to find someone else eventually.'

A stab of cold went through me. 'No . . . no! I don't want anyone else. Ever!'

'You can't be my mistress all your life, Tigs.'

'Not mistress. It's more than that. Your love. Your true love. I'm happy to be that all my life.'

He wrapped me tighter in his arms. 'Yes, you're that. I didn't know what love was till now. And I don't know if I can live without you.'

'You don't have to,' I said, happy again. The threat of his setting me free seemed to have passed. 'I'll always be here for you. With you.'

He sighed happily. 'And me for you.'

'I know.' I kissed his chest and laid my head against it so that I could hear his heartbeat, thudding slow and constant beneath his skin. 'We'll always be together. No matter what.'

Chapter Twenty-Three

'Josephine Ballintyre has just been on the telephone,' Mumma said, coming into the ballroom where I was painting.

My brush froze on the canvas. My heart seemed to stop for a moment and a wave of cold goosebumps flew across my skin. 'Oh?' I said, as casually as possible. James and I had been seeing one another for six months now and, if anything, it was more intense than it had been in January. Our hunger for each other seemed to grow the more we saw one another, and it could never be sated. We missed each other desperately even while we were still saying goodbye. When the season started and the guests began arriving, it was harder to get away. James was still working in Edinburgh three days a week and to be free when he could escape from home was a constant juggling act. Carina was now working at Tremewan almost full-time, chambermaiding and doing as much as I could pass over to her, even though she was claimed too by Tighglachach where they had welcomed a new baby boy. 'What does she want?'

'She's heard that you paint portraits of children,' Mumma said, 'and she wants you to do the little boys. Hamish and Charlie.'

My brush began to move again, and I hoped I'd maintained my composure, enough to escape Mumma's eagle eye in any case. 'Of course, I'd be happy to. Can you ask her to send some photographs? I'm sure I can fit them in before I do the next big commission from the States.'

'She wants you to go there and do them from life.'

My brush stopped again, but only for an instant. I took a breath, pretending to be assessing my work but really allowing my racing heart to slow a little and my thoughts to calm down. 'I don't do children from life. They can't keep still.'

'Then I suggest you go and photograph them. She isn't going to do it. I did say, but she was adamant.' Mumma shook her head. 'She is a very *adamant* person.'

I said nothing but wiped my brush on a rag. I knew all about how adamant Josephine was. James often told me what she was like to live with, and the more I knew, the more I disliked her. Right from the start, I'd known she was not what she seemed and I'd been proved right. I hated her for making his life so hard even while I was grateful that this released him from her bonds and meant that we could be together. It meant, too, that I was not sorry for having such a wild love affair with her husband. If she had been kind and good, it would have ripped me in two. As it was, there was a justice in it. She had won James by deceit, pretending to be what she was not, and now she had lost him to me, who had not pretended anything but had instead loved him sincerely and truly, right to my very depths.

'I'll go over there then,' I said at last. 'Or I suspect we won't hear the end of it.'

I'd warned James and we made sure that I visited Ballintyre on a day when he was in Edinburgh. I drove up with Dadda's old camera and a roll of film, plus some sketchpads so I could do some life drawings of the boys.

Josephine answered the door, a vision in pink ruffles with cherry-coloured high suede boots that climbed her legs in interesting ruches. 'Hello. Where's your easel?'

'I didn't bring it, I'm not going to paint them today.'

She looked disappointed. 'Why not? I got them all ready.'

She led me into the drawing room, where two boys sat on the sofa, both fair and blue-eyed, polished within an inch of their lives and buttoned up in matching white shirts and green ties, their hair gummed down with something that made it look solid and shiny like leather. 'Here they are. Say hello, Charlie.'

'Hello, Charlie,' said the older one before bursting into giggles.

'Say hello, Hamish.'

'Hello, Hamish,' echoed the younger one, who also burst into giggles.

'Aren't they terrors?' she said fondly, but she did not correct them.

I smiled at them. They had Ballintyre blue eyes and a look of James in their face shapes and cowlick hairlines, and I felt close to him when I saw them, even though Josephine's proximity made me uncomfortable. Seeing Charlie reminded me of how I had been there when she was in labour all those years ago. She clearly didn't recall me in the slightest. That was a relief.

'They're ready for painting!' Josephine said with a dramatic flourish of her arm in their direction. 'I don't really understand why you're not getting on with it.'

'You seem to want something quite formal?'

'I want them to look their best. That's natural, isn't it?'

'Of course. My portraits tend to be just of their faces, not much in the way of clothes and things, and I try to capture their personalities, as they are. Children have a natural beauty, they don't need to be too washed and brushed.'

She frowned at me. 'Mine do.'

I produced the camera from my rucksack. 'If it's all right with you, we could let them watch television, and I'll do some sketches, and then we'll take their photos. I'll work from those to create the final portraits.'

Josephine consulted her watch. 'What on earth is on at this hour?'

'Let's just try them with whatever is there. It's more of a focal point, I suppose.'

'All right.' She didn't seem very happy but we went down the hall to a small television room where a colour set was sitting on a low table, with a sofa in front of it for family viewing. Josephine went over and switched it on while the boys got excitedly into place, obviously delighted by the treat of daytime television watching. I sat down on a chair by the wall, and when the television had warmed up and the day-time drama had come on, I got out my sketchpad and started working quickly.

'I'll leave you to it,' Josephine said. 'Come and find me in the kitchen when you're ready.'

I nodded and concentrated on my sketching. Each boy kept moving and shifting but sometimes stayed still long enough for me to catch the shape of a nose and the curve of a forehead, or a turn of the lips. After about fifteen minutes, though, they were bored, so I ruffled their hair into something like a natural shape, and took their photographs before they wriggled down and ran away.

Josephine was in the kitchen and looked round as I came in with my things packed away in my rucksack. 'Finished already?'

'Finished for today. But I'll make a start on the portraits as soon as I can.'

'How long will they take? Two days? Three?'

'Perhaps a little more. I need to get the film developed. I'll let you know.'

She smiled at me. 'I'm rather impatient, I'm afraid, particularly when I'm paying for something.'

We hadn't discussed a fee and I wasn't sure how to bring it up even now, when she'd mentioned it, so I just smiled back and said, 'It's worth waiting for something you'll treasure forever.'

'I'm sure that's true. I'm going to have my portrait done, actually. By a proper artist.' She touched her hair self-consciously as though mentally putting herself into a gilt frame. 'He's done Princess Michael of Kent and he's very expensive, but I'm told he's worth it. It's a gift for James, so he can remember me in my prime.'

'How lovely,' I said politely, and thought of James as he'd been with me last time, very much in *his* prime.

She was only half listening to me, but switched on the kettle and was, I thought, about to offer me tea. 'I expect you'll want to be on your way then. So you can make a start,' she said with faux sweetness.

'Yes,' I said, half relieved that she didn't want me to be there any longer. 'I'll head off. I'll be in touch about the pictures.'

'Please do. Can you let yourself out?'

Driving home, I felt a sort of delayed shock at having spent time with Josephine. It was obvious she didn't have the faintest clue what was going on, and that she had felt no need to impress me or suck up to me. As result, I'd seen her as her real self. Rude. Inconsiderate. She hadn't even offered me a cup of tea. I'd only been of interest to her as far as I was useful, and she didn't even consider me a proper artist. No doubt she thought she was getting portraits of the children done on the cheap.

No wonder James hates her. And I hate her too. If only he could leave her – or she would leave – then we'd be happy. But she'll never allow it. And he will never do that to her, or the boys.

If that was the price I paid – being concealed, his secret – then I didn't mind.

*

I started work on the portraits right away. Dadda took the film to the chemist in Lanceston to be developed while I worked from my sketches. I'd learned that most children shared certain characteristics in proportions and the ones I'd done so far had taught me a lot about skin tones and eye shapes. I brought my knowledge, along with my sketches, to these portraits – a matching pair, each boy looking out in an opposite direction so that they could face one another on a wall. Mumma admired them as I progressed quickly, feeling close to James when I was working on the faces of his children. I tried to think of them as his, rather than hers, and that helped me to enjoy the work and make it the best I could.

When James and I managed to meet again on Friday, we were more concerned for the first hour with our physical reunion. When we were lying in one another's arms afterwards, I told him about my visit to Ballintyre.

He tightened his hold on me as if protecting me. 'Was it all right?'

'It was fine.' I turned my head so I could gaze fully into his eyes. 'James, you can't stay with her. You must see that. She's awful. She'll suck the life out of you. And if you want to rescue the boys, you need to get them out of her clutches, at least some of the time. They seem very good children at heart, but they're more than halfway to being spoiled by her.'

He sighed sadly. 'I know. I've wanted to fight her on it, but she's so powerful.'

'I can see that. She's unstoppable.'

'She gives no ground. Doesn't listen. Won't compromise.'

'You can't spend your life with someone like that, you really can't!'

He looked at me with something like despair in his eyes. 'You don't understand, Tigs. I can't do that to the boys. And even if I could, there's something else.'

'What?'

'I've got a financial crisis on my hands. We renovated the lodge for my parents at the same time as Josephine did her huge and very expensive redecoration. I was expecting the cost of the renovation. But Josephine spent five times what we'd planned on the interior of Ballintyre.'

I gasped. 'Five times?'

He nodded. 'I didn't think it was possible. I also had no inkling she would spend so much without telling me. She's enrolled the boys at the prep school on the other side of the loch and that's costing a fortune too.'

'What's going to happen?'

'I don't know.' A frown had furrowed deep into his forehead. 'I'm keeping things on track for now but it's a huge burden. My head is only just above water. My father's more or less stopped managing the property so that's on my shoulders too. I may have to give up my work in Edinburgh in order to look after this place, and without that income stream, we're going to be right up against it.'

I felt a bolt of hot rage against Josephine. Of course, there was no question that she would earn anything, or even do anything to help by managing the property for James. Instead, she had spent money recklessly and expected him to magic up more for an expensive private school. 'How can I help?'

'Tigs, you're so sweet, but there's nothing you can do. I'll manage, though it's going to take a little while to find my way out of this. Until then, there's no way I can break up my marriage. I couldn't afford to.'

I lay there, in his arms, thinking about it and wishing with all my might I could wave a wand and make it all right for him, and for me.

'Well, these are lovely.' Josephine inspected the portraits carefully and then looked up at me smiling. 'Yes. I like them very much. How clever you are. I thought that if you painted from a photograph, they'd be rather stiff, but you've caught them well. Congratulations.'

'Thank you.' I hoped I was hiding the fury I felt towards her as we sat in her flounced drawing room, where the curtains alone had costs hundreds of pounds. 'And I'd like to make them a present to you.'

'Oh?' She seemed startled. 'Why?'

Because I'm not taking more of James's money for these, that's why.

'Because you're friends of the family,' I said easily. 'Please think of them as late wedding presents.'

'Very late,' she said with a laugh. 'But very welcome. Thank you.' She frowned and stared closer at the portrait of Charlie. 'Is this your signature?'

'Yes, that's the mark I put on all my work.'

'What are these initials? The front one looks like an L. I thought your name started with a T?'

'Tigs is my nickname. L stands for my actual name, though no one uses it. It's Leonora.'

'That's very pretty. I think you should use it. Tigs is very ugly.'

'I suppose I'm used to it.'

'Well, I like these,' Josephine said, evidently having talked enough about me. 'I know where I shall put them. In my bedroom above the chest of drawers. They'll look just right there.' She looked at me and smiled again. 'Thank you, Leonora. I appreciate it.'

I hoped I would never have to see Josephine again. Instead, I made love fiercely to James whenever I could, desperate to give him all my love, my cherishing, my nurturing as if it was some kind of armour against her poison. Our times together were sweet respite for both of us. James's burden was weighing ever more heavily, as the amount he borrowed to pay for Josephine's spending grew larger with time, not less. He didn't want to talk about it but I made him tell me, hoping that just confiding it to me would make the burden lighter somehow.

'I love you so much,' I said. We were sitting on the bench outside the cottage, in the afterglow of being together, soaking in the summer sun and the scents of the cottage garden: hollyhocks, roses, lavender and honeysuckle. James had poured us glasses of cold white Sancerre, as stony as the granite of the hills around us, and we sipped it, holding hands.

'I love you too.'

'Tell me.'

'I love that I've known you since you were a child. You were my friend, first. That funny, big-eyed girl, coming on adventures with Al and me. So keen to learn everything, so fearless. My companion before you were my lover. I love that you know this place in the same way I do, and adore it as much as I do. We know it, you and I. It's in our bones and blood. We share all those things: our past, our home. But I love you on the outside too: those eyes of yours, that long dark hair, the way you raise one eyebrow without knowing it. And then there's the way you feel, the way you sigh when I make love to you. I love the way you talk so freely, say whatever's in your heart; I never know what you'll say next. You speak like you see – with colour and poetry and humour. I love your impish smile and your cross pouts. I love it all.' He squeezed my hand. 'Do you love me?'

'I love you,' I said, 'from top to toe. You've always been my hero, the centre of my life. For as long as I can remember. I need you like I need food and air and water. You're my lifeblood, and all my joy.' I squeezed his hand in return. 'Can we stay like this forever?' I always asked this. He always said the same thing in reply.

'We can try, Tigs. We can try.' Now he smiled at me. 'Josephine told me how you gave her the portraits. That was good of you.'

'It was the very least I could do.'

'I love them, I think of you every time I see them. It means so much, as though you're close to the boys as well.'

'I felt close to you while I was painting them.'

'She called you Leonora.' James raised my hand to his lips and kissed it gently, each knuckle in turn. 'Is that your name?'

'Didn't you know?' My whole body was thrilling to the touch of his lips even though we had just been to bed. 'I thought you did.'

'I suppose I must have once, but you've been Tigs for as long as I can remember.'

'Because I was so bouncy. Like Tigger.'

'Of course. But you're really called Leonora.'

'Only when I'm naughty.'

'And what about when you're nice? When you're very, very nice?' He kissed my hand again, turning it over and placing his mouth on my palm. My heart began to race with pleasure. He spoke against the skin of my hand, which warmed under his breath. 'I'll call you Nora. That will be my name for you. Nora.'

'Yes,' I said. 'Nora.'

It felt right.

How long could we go on like this?

I wanted it to go on forever. Our affair was bliss. It was the light in my life. It was all I thought and dreamed about. It was like hope springing eternal – I was always to be blessed, but never quite getting there. I tasted joy with James but each time it was temporary and each meeting came with the knowledge of its inevitable end. Although we always planned another, we could never be completely sure that it would happen. Something awful might occur before we could see one another again.

And so, when I said to him, 'Can we stay like this forever?' I also wanted him to say, 'This affair won't last forever because I'm going to leave her and marry you. And that will last forever.'

A summer passed, a winter and a Christmas came and went. Our stolen moments continued and the possibility of parting got ever more remote. We were deeply in love. The only thing that Josephine's relentless self-obsession guaranteed was that she couldn't be bothered to be suspicious of James. It never seemed to occur to her that he might be seeking comfort elsewhere and that was why he had the resilience to face her.

'We've had a terrible row,' he told me one spring day. The cottage was cosy from the wood fire. I had arrived an hour before James and lit the stove so that the place would be warm when he arrived.

'What about?' I pressed the kettle on the hotplate of the stove to make it boil faster.

'Money. I told her we need to take the boys out of school. She was furious. She won't accept that her spending is to blame. She says it's my parents leeching off us and they need to give me the money to clear our debts.' He sighed. 'She doesn't understand. They don't have any ready cash. It's all tied up in the property and in trusts. She more or less told me to hope that they die soon.'

'James!'

'I know. She's a fright.' He kissed me as I sat down on the old sofa with him. 'If I didn't have you to talk to, I don't know what I'd do.'

'Talking is all very well but how does it solve the problem?' A thought occurred to me. 'What if she gets so annoyed that she leaves you?'

'You know what would happen then. She'd force me to sell up and give her half of everything. It would break my parents' hearts. We'd lose Ballintyre and even though I sound like a ridiculous old feudal relic, I'd really like to be able to pass it to the boys if I can.'

I sat thoughtful next to him. Then I said, 'I can give you some money.'

'What?' He looked at me, startled. 'What do you mean?'

'My parents have been talking for ages about making the house over to Serena and me. They were going to sell it not so long ago, but it's made us a good income over the last few years as a guest house and now they see that there's a way they can retire. They want to buy a smaller house down the road, and leave me to run the main house as a business until Serena and I decide to sell it. The idea is to take out a small mortgage on Tremewan to release funds to buy their cottage. The point is – I can raise money against my half of the house.'

'You can't do that, Nora! I won't let you. You can't give me money.'

'All right, not give. Lend.' I looked at him obstinately. 'I want to. And you won't talk me out of it. Can't you see it's the answer to all our problems? If you lose Ballintyre, I lose you, so I'm only acting in my own interests!'

Of course, he wouldn't hear of it. It was madness. He would not allow it. I couldn't be asked to take the risk. I went home and talked to my parents seriously about the future of the house and the business. A week later, we were in the Edinburgh offices of a lawyer who specialised in property.

A month after that, with many discussions between us and Serena, my parents made the house over to my sister and me, and we applied for a mortgage against it. And I secretly enquired into the possibility of getting a further loan against my half of the house.

None of the main lenders wanted to know. I was an unmarried woman under thirty, I had no permanent job and no one could understand why my father wasn't taking charge of the whole affair. I refused to give up and my investigations led me away from high street banks and building societies to a small finance company running out of basement offices in the middle of Glasgow. And that is where I signed up to a large loan secured by my ownership of half of Tremewan House.

'I can't take this!' James was aghast.

'It will get you out of trouble,' I said, full of pride that I had the wherewithal to hand him a sum large enough to clear all his debts, and to save Ballintyre. 'Without Josephine knowing.'

He stared at the cheque I was trying to press on him, appalled and yet also admiring. 'How did you do this? How?'

'That doesn't matter. The point is that you only need to get out of trouble. I can help you in the short term, and you can pay me back.'

He stared at the cheque, then he looked up, directly in my eyes. 'Nora, I can't pretend that this wouldn't be an answer, because it is. And here's the thing. I'm considering selling a bit of land – to the Gillygantry estate. They're not that keen – no one has ready cash right now and land is so cheap – but they're thinking about it. If I can sell, I'll give the money right back to you. But if you can really spare this – and it isn't going to put you into dire straits – then I'll take it. As a loan, not as a gift.'

I didn't want to tell him the truth about how I'd come by it. I only wanted him to take it. It didn't matter that the interest rate was exorbitant. It would buy him peace, and a sort of freedom. And it would buy us more time to be in love.

'Please take it.' I put my arm around him. 'It would make me so happy.'

'You're my queen.' He kissed me, and I was completely and utterly content.

We decided to make a change to our usual routine.

'I have to go to the dentist in Edinburgh, when you're there working,' I told him. 'Why can't we meet?'

He was reluctant. 'It's much more dangerous in the city. I might easily run into someone I know.'

'But I'm a friend! What could be more natural than to meet for lunch?'

He smiled at me. 'Do you think that we hide it that well?'

'Of course!' I said stoutly. 'We're masters of disguise.'

He looked around the cottage. 'I love it here, but I can't pretend it wouldn't be wonderful to see you somewhere else.'

'Anywhere else,' I said feelingly. I loved the cottage too, but I wanted to live something like a normal life with James, a life where we could wander freely, hand in hand, letting everyone know about our love for one another. An afternoon in Edinburgh suddenly seemed like the most wonderful opportunity to be free with one another.

I took the train there on a sunny May morning, excited to be visiting the big city, despite the dentist, and seeing James. All our lives, trips to Edinburgh had been great occasions and full of rituals of where we would have tea, of what we would see and where we would go. Holyrood was a regular jaunt for us, trailing around the rooms after Mumma and Dadda, being cajoled into looking at art with a promise of buns afterwards. This time, though, there would be no museum and no stroll down Princes Street. I had my dental appointment and then James and I were meeting at a bistro high on the hill behind the castle, a reward for having my teeth inspected.

James was waiting for me when I arrived, sitting outside at a table with a brightly coloured umbrella over it to keep off the morning sun.

'I thought we could enjoy the sun while it makes a rare appearance,' he laughed, and I kissed him happily then sat down.

Anyone watching would have thought we were just an-other happy couple as we ordered our lunch and then ate it, talking easily, laughing and enjoying each other's company. We were clearly more than friends. The way we gazed into one another's eyes, or touched one another's hands, reaching across the table to connect every few minutes.

'I want to spend the rest of the day with you,' I said, as the waiter brought our coffees at the end of the meal.

'I know. Me too.' James regarded me with a mixture of love and sadness. 'But it's not possible. I have to work – now more than ever.'

'Are you any closer to getting the Gillygantry sale?' I tried not to sound anxious but the repayments for the loan were depleting my savings at an alarming rate and I was beginning to be keen for James to repay the money. I knew that he would at the first possible moment and I had faith that he would find the money before too long.

'It's looking promising,' he said. 'I'm having a meeting with them next week and I'm very hopeful we're going to come to some arrangement. They want a parcel of land going along the whole of the north side of our property. It includes our cottage, I'm afraid. I don't know if we'll be able to use it after that.'

'Oh!' I was dismayed. I'd grown to love the little cottage where we had spent so many happy hours. 'What a shame.'

'I know. I feel the same. But we'll find somewhere else, Nora, don't worry about that. Nothing will stop us being together, I promise you.' He leaned across the table and pulled me gently towards him so that we could kiss, a sweet and lingering kiss that would have embarrassed me, as we were in public, if I were not utterly unaware of anything but him.

'What is going on?' The voice was chill as ice and as sharp as a blade. 'What the *hell* is going on?'

We flew apart. I already knew who it was. My stomach turned fierce somersaults of fear as I saw Josephine, smart in a green coat, her handbag clutched by knuckles white with tension. She was staring at us with a mixture of surprise, realisation and disgust. There was no way she could not know what was going on. James released me and stood up.

'Josephine,' he said. He had gone dead white, but he seemed determined to be strong.

She was looking at me, fury on her face, her eyes narrowing into slits. 'So this is the way you repay me. I put work your way – work that you, as a very mediocre artist, should be thankful for – and you seduce my husband in return.'

James took a step towards her. 'This is not about Nora,' he said firmly. 'This is about us. You and me.'

'I don't think so!' she snapped back. 'You and I are married. We are husband and wife.' Her voice began to rise and people on nearby tables turned to look. 'Marriage is a sacred bond! *Sacred!* How dare you come between us, you slut!'

I was mortified and full of horror, feeling desperately guilty that Josephine had discovered our affair and for the pain it would cause her. And yet, as she stood there, the embodiment of the wronged wife, I couldn't help feeling that, on some level, she was enjoying this. She seemed to be acting a part that she was almost delighted to have been handed. And I sensed, too, that this was giving her yet more power over James. This situation would make him forever her vassal and possession. As I thought this, a new horror began to rise in me.

This wasn't Josephine's tragedy at all. It was mine. And James's. She would not suffer, not really. How could she, when she had no real emotions? She might be outraged and furious, she would certainly feel wronged, but hurt? No. Only her pride. But we would suffer. I saw it, entirely and completely, in just a few moments as she began to rant so loudly that passers-by stopped to see what the fuss was about. A slew of insults exploded from her mouth. She ignored James and turned her torrent on me. I was a slut, a marriage wrecker, a tart. I had seduced her innocent husband and betrayed her. I had revealed myself for the slattern of low morals she had always suspected I was. I had slept with her husband behind her back and this was how she had to find out about it.

James tried desperately to quieten her. It was only when he physically led her away that her shouting finally stopped, and I was left, shocked and humiliated, still sitting at the table, the object of scorn and derision from those around me, realising that my world had just broken into pieces.

I knew she would do everything in her power to keep him from seeing me ever again.

PART ELEVEN

Chapter Twenty-Four

HELEN

2018

The night that I saw the Crithcorrey whirlpool, I dreamed of Rose.

She was as I remembered her just before the accident. We had celebrated her thirteenth birthday here at Ballintyre, a picnic lunch on the lawn with some of her friends to stay. It had been a bright, sunny day, full of laughter. Bottles of wine for the grown-ups – Charlie sat with several empties on the table right in front of him, kept busy popping more when we ran out, his belly rounding out under his navy polo shirt – and fizzy drinks for the youngsters, along with birthday cake conjured up by Sylla: lemon and elderflower sponge bursting with whipped cream and sweet curd.

'Please, Dad, can we take *Kitty* out?' she'd begged, kneeling next to her father's chair. She was tall now, as tall as Sylla almost, and her long red hair flowed down her back, glinting in the sun.

'Ask your mother,' Charlie said, gesturing to Sylla.

'I can't believe *Kitty* is still going!' I'd exclaimed. 'She's ancient. I thought she would have been retired to a home by now.'

'She's still going,' Charlie said placidly.

'Barely.' Sylla looked at Rose, who was gazing at her pleadingly. 'Where do you want to go?'

'Just round the cove to the beach. *Pleeease?*'

Sylla thought and then said, 'No, darling, not today. There are too many of you. *Kitty* really isn't that reliable anymore. She's all right for fishing, but not for going round the coast. Why don't you girls get into your swimming things and I'll drive you round to the beach?'

'All right,' Rose said with a sigh, but she was instantly cheerful again, rounding up her friends to get their things.

That was Rose. Sunny. Adventurous and pushing boundaries, but accepting the limitations. I could see her now, running away across the lawn with her friends. That was how she was in my dream: laughing and alive and full of spirit and vigour. She was a risk taker but she was always obedient. That was why it never made any sense that she'd taken *Kitty*, against Sylla's express orders, and gone around the headland in it to the whirlpool. Someone at school – some boastful boy – had told her he had put a boat across one of the pools and ridden it on the spot for ten minutes. He had dared her to do the same. It was safe when the sun shone, he'd told her. That's what Rose had told Sylla.

'Don't be silly, Rose!' Sylla had said. 'You can't take *Kitty* to Crithcorrey, even in the calm. It's completely unpredictable!'

'It's not, I've watched videos on YouTube. The tourists go out there all the time. Why can't I?'

'Because I said.'

Rose kept pestering. Sylla couldn't understand why it mattered so much. She took Rose herself on one of the tourist trips, bouncing out over the waves to the churning circles of water, to show her how dangerous it was.

'You're braver than I am,' I'd said when she told me, hardly able to repress a shudder. I hated the whole idea of the whirlpools and had no desire to go anywhere near them. Storms at sea were magnificent to watch as long as you were safely on the land.

'Well, it's backfired. She's keener to go than ever. It was calm when we went and now she thinks it's perfectly safe.' Sylla had smiled, shaking her head. 'She's irrepressible.'

But she was not disobedient. What possessed Rose to go out there that day? It had been calm enough, Sylla said, but the forecast had been for a blustery afternoon. Rose knew the loch and the sea well and she was familiar with a sunny morning that turned murky by lunchtime, the grey-yellow light a harbinger of a storm coming in from the sea. And yet, she had gone out despite it.

When I woke from my dream, I had tears on my cheeks. It was still early. I got up and walked through the house, remembering Rose, stopping to look at her photographs, weeping when I thought of how badly I wanted to hear her capering down the stairs, her laugh in the corridors, her shouts echoing through the rooms.

I wondered desperately if Sebastian had remembered what he'd heard about Sylla.

I was drinking coffee in the early morning calm of the kitchen when my phone beeped with a text. It was Sebastian.

Lovely to see you and the children yesterday. I'm so sorry about how it ended. I've found out something you might be interested in. Can you come up to the house for lunch today? Sx

I texted back to say of course I would come.

Hamish took the children to the first of their taster mornings at their new school, so on impulse I got one of the old bikes out of the shed, pumped up the tyres and oiled the chain, and cycled up to Tighglachach for my lunch with Sebastian.

'You look about eighteen,' he said, coming out to greet me. 'Turning up on a bike like this.'

'The youthful qualities of cycling,' I said, unbuckling my helmet, shaking out my hair and hoping it didn't look flat and awful. 'That must be why it appeals to middle-aged men.'

'I'm sorry the children couldn't come.'

'Yes, they would have loved it but it's just me, I'm afraid.' I looked about, taking in the vista of the house: its ancient grey walls, the old windows with uneven glass that reflected the light in strange ripples, the ivy climbing one side in a dense green curtain, the roof mossed and bare in patches. The fountain in the middle wasn't playing and the pond was half full of stagnant brown water with an oily khaki-coloured covering of algae. The drive was thick with weeds growing through the gravel. 'Goodness, I haven't been here in such a long time!'

'It's looking a bit tired,' Sebastian said. 'Dad's found it tricky to handle on his own.'

'It's a big place for someone alone. I remember how full of people it was when I visited – all you brothers and sisters.'

Sebastian nodded. 'It was quite a place to grow up. Come on in, let's find Dad. He's looking forward to seeing you.'

I leaned my bicycle against the wall and followed him through the front door, feeling as though I'd been taken on some kind of time-travelling event. Twenty years ago I'd walked with this man across this piece of ground. I remembered how he'd gone off and left me. He stayed with me now, as we went into the hall.

'The menagerie is still here, I'm afraid.' He gestured at the cases of stuffed animals, all as frozen in time as they were when I first saw them.

'The only things that haven't changed,' I said wryly.

'The advantage of being stuffed. But it's a rather tedious existence.'

'True.' I looked around at the hall. It was as chaotic as ever, with papers on every surface. There was dust and cobwebs everywhere but the beauty of the house's old bones shone through. 'I didn't see that minstrels' gallery last time. How wonderful!' I pointed up at the carved balcony tucked at the top of the room. 'You should have a party. Great spot for the DJ.'

'There used to be an annual ball here. But it hasn't happened in years.'

'Imagine a ball in this room! How fabulous! You should do it.'

'We'd need to do a bit of tidying up first.' Sebastian grinned. 'But it's a good idea. I'll think about it.' He went to the back of the room where the passage led down to the reception rooms. 'Dad! Are you around?'

There was no answer.

'He's a bit deaf,' Sebastian said apologetically, and he picked up the hammer that sat on top of the gong stand, and gave the brass disc a good solid thwack.

The room filled with a shimmering boom and as it faded away there was a distant shout: 'Who the bloody hell is that? Sebastian?' Rapid footsteps in heavy boots approached. 'Why are you ringing the gong, you blasted child?'

'He still thinks I'm sixteen,' Sebastian said with a smile.

Mr Drummond burst into the room, an oily rag in one hand and an unidentifiable piece of machinery in the other. He looked much the same: tall and broad, but a trifle more stooped and thinner too. His hair was a shock of white and his beard was gone, revealing a sagging jaw with a red tinge that travelled down his neck. His black eyes were still fierce although not quite as intense in colour, but he had great white beetling eyebrows that exploded above them and made him look simultaneously surprised and furious. He stared at me. 'Who's this?'

'This is Helen Ballintyre, Dad. Do you remember I told you she was coming? She stayed here once, years ago. And then she married Hamish.'

'Did she? I do remember that we had a house guest who got seduced by that young rotter, then went and married him. I always felt terribly sorry for her. So that was you, was it? You've survived the experience?'

'So far,' I said, smiling. 'Hello, Mr Drummond.'

'You may as well call me Alastair,' he remarked. 'Now we're all older and wiser.' He glowered at Sebastian. 'You didn't need to bash the gong, you vandal. You could just have called me. Now, are you going to offer our guest some sustenance? Or should she just die here in the hall?'

He turned around and stomped off.

'He's a little more crotchety these days,' Sebastian said as we followed him. 'He doesn't like being deaf and old.'

'Understandable.'

'We'll have lunch with him and I'll get him to tell you what he knows.'

'About Sylla?' I felt a flutter of anxiety and apprehension, but also hope that for the first time, I was on the verge of finding out what I longed to know. I'd become certain that when I discovered the truth about Sylla, I would also get to the bottom of why Rose had disobeyed Sylla that awful day. But I would still need to be patient, I told myself as I followed Sebastian down the passage.

The kitchen was also chaotically untidy and piled with papers and whole collections of miscellaneous objects: machinery, garden pots, books, pottery, light bulbs and tools.

'I try to tidy up a bit, but it's such a huge task, there doesn't seem much point,' Sebastian said. 'But I've kept on top of cleaning up after meals and keeping it all hygienic. And I got the lunch at the hotel this morning.'

'It's fine,' I said, quite glad to hear that our food had been prepared elsewhere.

Sebastian cleared off the table, and Mr Drummond came stomping in with the oil now cleaned from his hands, and we sat down to a lunch of sandwiches and salad. We talked about the house and Mr Drummond told me proudly how he was keeping it going all on his own, despite the size of the place.

'It's not easy,' he said sadly. 'I want one of my offspring to take it on, but none of them shows much interest.'

'Sell it to Lars, Dad, he's very keen.'

'I don't want it to be a hotel,' he said. 'I want it to be a home. I want some grandchildren here! If you would pull your finger out and find a nice girl, you might be able to bring her here if she were the type who wanted a place like this.'

'It's in the middle of nowhere, after all,' Sebastian said ironically.

'It's beautiful here!' I said. 'I remember the garden and the walk down to the cove. I thought I'd never seen anywhere lovelier. And what a place to bring up children.'

'Exactly,' said Mr Drummond. 'That's what this kind of place is for. I loved growing up here, all the adventures. I had my friends, a boat, some fishing things, and all of this to roam in. What more could a child want?'

'I thought you were miserable, growing up here all on your own,' Sebastian said. 'What friends were these?'

'Other local children.' Mr Drummond looked at me from under his beetling white brows. 'Hamish's father was one. We were friends when we were boys.'

'Really? What was he like?' I asked, interested. It had been hard to get a picture of James Ballintyre in my mind. Josephine spoke of him with reverence, as though he'd been too good for this wicked world. Hamish rarely mentioned him at all.

Mr Drummond fidgeted, picked up a sandwich and ate it slowly. At last he said, 'He was a decent man. I rather worshipped him as a boy, but we grew apart. I suppose I envied him in some ways. He seemed to have so much. Still. I wouldn't have changed places with him. Josephine was too strong meat for me, that's for certain. And, of course, his end was very sad.'

'You've been happy here, though, Dad?' Sebastian said, as though needing reassurance. 'It might not be as grand as Ballintyre, but it's all right?'

Mr Drummond nodded vigorously. 'Of course! This is our place. And I've been happy enough, writing my books and keeping the whole thing going.'

'Dad's a cult author in the US,' Sebastian said proudly.

'All over the world, actually, through the miracle of self-publishing,' Mr Drummond said. 'It keeps me busy.'

'I'll have to read one of your books,' I said politely.

'Polycarp the mystery-solving medieval Greek monk. You must. They're terrific, if I do say so myself. Yes, I'm quite

happy with everything except for the lack of grandchildren.'
He glared at Sebastian. 'You've all been disappointments in
that respect. Daphne won't breed. Eve is too busy taking her
snaps. Sholto won't, poor lad. It's up to you, Sebastian!'

Sebastian shot me a look, rolled his eyes and mouthed,
'Sorry!'

Alastair was still muttering to himself. 'I don't know what's
wrong with you lot. You've all got money. You're all successful. I don't know what you're waiting for. Get on with it,
Sebastian! There's no time to lose.'

'Dad, Helen really wants to hear about Sylla. Remember?'

'Oh. Sylla.' He looked wary. 'I promised her, you know. I
promised her that I wouldn't say anything.'

My heart began beating faster and I leaned towards him
across the table, speaking fervently but, I hoped, respectfully.
'Please, Alastair. Can you please tell me what you know? If
it helps, I promise to keep it entirely to myself. I've been so
desperate to know that she's safe. After what happened to
her daughter, Rose, I've been worried that she's been overwhelmed. I'm the only one who seems to care. Her husband
won't help me find her.'

'Well, he wouldn't,' Alastair said solemnly.

'Why not?'

Mr Drummond sat back in his chair, balancing it on the
back legs, put his hands in his pockets and stared at the ceiling. 'I promised I wouldn't tell *him*. Or *her*. I don't suppose
that's the same as not telling you.'

'It isn't the same,' I said quickly. 'She would want you to
tell me, I'm sure of it!'

He looked thoughtful for a moment. I pushed my plate away, unable to eat any more now that my stomach was churning. I felt trembly, convinced I was on the brink of finding out what had happened.

'It was a little like being Polycarp myself,' Alastair said slowly, staring into space as though remembering. 'Polycarp is always telling the monks that they each hold only one piece of the puzzle and all the pieces are needed to make sense of it. So every monk needs to offer his version exactly as he himself remembers it in order for Polycarp to solve the mystery. I thought of that when I found that poor woman on the beach, looking ready to swim out to sea and never come back; I made her tell me her side of the story. And then I told my side. Together, our two pieces seemed to make a whole. There may even be a third perspective that might elucidate things even further. But perhaps we don't need that. We seemed to find our answer as it was.'

'Yes?' I asked tremulously, casting an anxious look at Sebastian, who was listening hard.

'Was that Sylla you found on the beach, Dad?' he asked slowly, as if wanting to direct his father's thoughts without invading them.

'That's right. The Scylla. The beautiful nymph transformed into a monster. There she was, weeping. "I can't bear it," she told me. "I can't bear to be me anymore. I need to escape myself." "Why is that?" I asked her. She told me how she'd lost her girl. I knew about the tragedy, of course. I thought, that family is touched by disaster. James, killed in his car. Now that poor girl, lost in the whirlpool. I believe it was in the local papers, though I don't pay much attention to all that.'

'What happened?' I whispered, fearful again. So Sylla had been overwhelmed. It was terrible to think of. Poor, poor Sylla. My heart ached for her.

'You did stop her, didn't you, Dad?' Sebastian asked almost nervously.

He glanced around at us. 'If she'd been determined, in her right mind . . . I don't think I would have. It's every person's choice to live or die. I don't say I would have helped her. But if walking out to sea was what she wanted, then I would not have stood in her way. I sensed, though, that she was in tumult and confusion. She didn't want to die; she wanted an answer. *Why did my girl go out in the boat on her own when I told her not to? Could I have stopped her?* And living with that uncertainty was becoming too much.'

'And did she?' I asked, desperate. My fingers tightened into a fist with the tension coursing through me. 'Did she walk into the sea?'

He paused, and then said firmly, 'No. She did not. She came home with me, I made her a cup of tea and I told her my side of the story.'

'What was your side?' Sebastian asked warily.

'Very little happens without being seen by someone. If you go out in a little white boat and motor around the headland, then someone will see you. Probably someone taking a long amble along the coast road and making a note of the ships going by. Especially if they know that little boat. *Kitty*. If they know it well from their own childhood.'

I drew in a breath, but said nothing, not wanting to break his stream of thought.

Alastair went on: 'You see, I saw it and thought to myself, I wouldn't let any child of mine out there in that boat. *Kitty* must be fifty years old. Even if she's been well looked after, she's going to be past her peak. I wouldn't take her out beyond the loch towards the wild water, not with a breeze blowing up and the sky going dark.'

Sebastian said quietly, 'You saw *Kitty* on her way to the pool.'

'I did. And I thought, perhaps they don't know about how fast the weather will change. I felt uneasy. I went back to the car because I'd driven up to the headland. I decided to drive along the road and follow the boat, just in case.'

'You said *they*,' I said.

'What?'

'Perhaps *they* don't know about the weather. But Rose was on her own.'

'No, she wasn't. That was the thing, you see. She wasn't on her own. That was my piece of the puzzle. She was with her father.'

I gasped. 'Charlie?'

He nodded. 'That's right.'

I was confused. 'No, Charlie wasn't there. That wasn't the story at all. He went out in his car to meet her when she texted him to tell him that she was in the boat, the weather was bad and she was frightened. But he got to the beach too late to rescue her.'

Alastair Drummond regarded me through grave eyes. 'No. I'm afraid that is not the truth. I saw it all, you see. And it was I who raised the alarm.'

'Oh my God,' I said brokenly. 'I can't believe it. I had no idea.'

'And nor had Sylla.'

'What did she do when you told her?'

An expression of sadness settled on his face. He looked suddenly very old. 'She wouldn't believe it at first. But when she did, she was possessed with fury as cold as ice. I knew she was no longer a danger to herself unless her anger put her in the way of it. I told her not to go back until she was calmer. But she wouldn't listen. So I let her go. The same night, she came back. It was two in the morning when her car roared up the drive. She banged on the front door till I opened it. She said she'd left and I told her the same thing I'd told her earlier that day: I had a place for her if she needed it.' He stared straight at me. 'And that is where she still is.'

Sebastian led me to where the cottage was tucked away, hidden down a track-like lane on the border between the Ballintyre and Tighglachach estates. It was easy enough to see it at this bare time of year. I could imagine that in the summer, it would be almost invisible, hidden among the mass of trees and foliage.

'It used to belong to Ballintyre apparently,' Sebastian had said. 'Until the eighties when Josephine Ballintyre sold off bits of her land after her husband died.'

I stared at the slate roof of the single-storey cottage, a skein of grey smoke emerging from the chimney. So here she was. I'd suspected she was nearby from the time I'd seen the flowers on Rose's memorial plaque. Sylla would never leave Rose. But I hadn't guessed she was so close. The journey round by road took almost half an hour but as the crow flew, she was probably only five minutes from Ballintyre, except that you'd have to fight your way over the hill, through the forest and cross the coast road to get to her. I wondered how hard Charlie had looked for her, and I suspected that he had not. He had been busy since the day we'd arrived, bustling around with his estate work, driving here and there for meetings, hardly at home, never stopping, as though he didn't want to pause and think.

No wonder.

'Do you think she'll mind me coming to see her?' I asked Sebastian nervously.

'I don't know. You've got her best interests at heart. It's her husband she doesn't want to see.'

'I suppose it's a risk I have to take.'

Sebastian nodded. 'I don't think you can turn back now. I have a feeling she needs you.' He took my hand and squeezed it with a smile. 'I hope it goes okay. Call me if you need me. I'll be at home with Dad, waiting to hear that you're all right.'

'Thanks so much, Sebastian.' I felt the warmth of his concern and it comforted me.

'You're welcome.' He turned and headed back the way we had come. I turned back to the footpath to the cottage and made my way down it, letting myself through the small iron gate that opened with a rusty screech. A kind of natural doorbell, I thought, as I went through. The cottage was very small, and looked no more than two rooms wide. A vase of flowers sat on the sill behind one of the windows. I walked up to the wooden front door and knocked loudly. Then I waited, my heart pounding with anticipation. I thought I saw the flash of a face at the window. A moment later, I heard a bolt go back and the latch lift. Very slowly, the door opened and I saw her at last.

'Hello, Sylla,' I said.

She looked so familiar: fair skin pulled tight over high cheekbones, a sprinkle of freckles across her nose, the deep navy eyes with their child-like clarity. A slow smile turned up the edges of her mouth. 'So,' she said, 'you've come. I had a feeling you would.'

'Oh Sylla! I'm so glad you're safe!' I threw my arms around her and pulled her close, filled with relief that, at last, I had found her.

Chapter Twenty-Five

Inside, Sylla sat the kettle on the hotplate of the wood-burning stove.

'There is electricity,' she said from the kitchen area, where she was putting teabags into mugs, 'but I quite like heating the kettle up in the old-fashioned way.'

'It's very sweet here,' I said, looking around. 'You've made it so cosy.'

'Sweet but small.' She smiled. 'A bit of a change after Ballintyre.'

There was only one large living space, with the kitchen at one end and the sitting area opposite, with a small table and chairs against the window, then the front door and then a sofa and armchair facing the stove which was tucked into the old fireplace. Beautiful thick and warm patchwork curtains hung at the windows, a large deep-pile rug covered the stone floor in front of the stove, and the wooden bookshelves had been painted a cheerful turquoise. Sylla had stacked colourful china on the shelves in the kitchen area, and the general effect was cheerful and welcoming.

'Where do you sleep?'

'There's a bedroom through that small door on the other side of the fireplace. And a tiny bathroom tacked on to that, a later addition.'

'I'm so glad you're safe,' I said. 'I've been so worried about you.'

'I'm sorry you worried.' She put the tea caddy back on the shelf.

'You didn't answer your phone or any messages.'

'It's mainly been switched off. I've been seeing a therapist for a while now and she counselled a break for me. I needed to focus on myself and Josephine was texting and emailing constantly – nasty abusive messages often late at night.'

'When she was drunk?'

'Probably. Drinking certainly doesn't make her nicer.'

I was indignant on Sylla's behalf. 'What on earth was she abusing you about?'

'How I was treating Charlie, mainly. Why wasn't I kinder? Couldn't I see how he was suffering? You can imagine the kind of thing.' Sylla brought the mugs over to where the kettle was beginning to whistle.

'And you?' I shook my head in disbelief. 'Didn't you deserve kindness after everything you'd been through?'

'That's what makes me so sad,' Sylla said thoughtfully. 'She could have been a force for good, helping us through the grief, bringing us together. A wiser, warmer person might have seen that. Instead, she tried to get her way by criticising and bullying.'

'Warm and wise are not words I'd associate with her.' I watched as Sylla made the tea. She looked much the same, her long blonde hair drawn back into a ponytail, but she was certainly thinner and grief had sucked something from her face. Her cheeks had sunk and her eyes were deeper in their sockets. She moved with a kind of slowness, as though things were an effort and nothing came easily. 'Has the therapy helped?'

'It is helping. But it's a long journey that will never be over.' She spoke with finality and I understood it was not something she wanted to share with me, not right now in any case.

After a moment, I asked, 'How long have you been here?'

'For about four months.'

'Charlie never said it had been so long.'

'What has he said?'

'Not much at all. If anything, he's dodged the question. The strangest thing to me is how unconcerned he is about where you might be or what you're doing. '

'It's no surprise to me,' she said, picking up a jug from the windowsill and adding milk to our tea.

She brought over the mugs and handed me one.

'Sylla,' I said almost hesitantly. 'Alastair told me the most terrible thing. He told me why you left Charlie.'

She went still for a moment and then said, 'I see. So you know.'

'Not everything. But I do know that Alastair saw Charlie in the boat with Rose that day.'

'Yes.' She looked grave. 'Thank goodness he did. It saved my life that he did. Even so, it was the most terrible shock. But there was more than that. Have you got time for a walk? I'll find it easier to talk if we walk.'

We took our tea and went out into the overcast day. Spring was coming but the frost and chill were still dominant, biting at the shoots and flowers trying to appear. I was glad of my warm boots and coat as we tramped through the undergrowth near the cottage, before coming out on a clearer walk as we approached the cliffs. Sylla talked as we went.

'When Rose died, it hit me like the force of a giant landslide. I thought I'd never come out from under the terrible grief of it. In fact, I never will, but that's something else. The only comfort was that she didn't go away. It felt as though she was with me and Charlie constantly – at every meal, on every journey, throughout every day . . . She sat between the two of us all the time. Except for him it was agony. His guilt, you see.'

I nodded, listening as we walked. Sylla said nothing for a while, then seemed to start from another tangent.

'Rose was such a soaring spirit. She knew no fear. I told you that she wanted to take *Kitty* out to look at the whirlpool, even after I'd taken her on the tourist trip. I said no, of course. *Kitty* was not seaworthy enough, she was an ancient old thing, and Rose had no experience of really rough sea, nothing more than a few squalls and windy days. She said she'd go on a calm day; the tourists went out, why couldn't she? I forbade it absolutely.'

I said softly, 'But Charlie took her there.'

'Yes. She talked him into it. I suspect he was drunk. In fact, I'm pretty sure he was. Full of ridiculous bravado, unable to make a sensible decision. They went together. Even when the weather turned as they went around the coast, he didn't change course. They would go close, he said. Not too close. Enough for her to get a look.'

I felt the familiar chill of horror. I knew the ending but still couldn't help hoping for a different one, where they made the right decision and turned back and everything was all right. 'And that was when Alastair saw them.'

'That's right. He knew at once that they were getting into a dangerous situation. So he drove to the beach and waited, just in case. He saw what happened, and told me most of it. Charlie gave me some details when I confronted him but I don't think he could remember it very well. Either through drink, or blotting it out.'

'Sylla . . .' I took her hand and held it. 'This is frightful. I can't believe it.'

She gave me a small smile. 'It's appalling, isn't it? Things went wrong as they got closer. The water was much fiercer than Charlie had guessed it would be. He'd never been out there himself, only seen it from a distance. *Kitty* wasn't up to being buffeted like that, and the engine was suddenly spliced clean off. Gone. Charlie panicked. Neither of their mobiles got reception out there. They tried to row out of trouble and managed to get away from the wilder water. He decided to go for help. He would swim for the shore and find someone to call for help, she should wait for the coastguard. He told her to keep rowing towards the islands, but mainly to keep out of the pull of the wild water.'

I gasped. 'He left her?'

'It was a crazy, stupid decision. He was panicked. He thought it was best.'

'He swam for shore?'

'He couldn't make it. He ended up on a rocky outcrop on the edge of one of the islands. He watched Rose struggling with the oars. He saw the boat pulled back into the wild waters, and he saw it go down. By then, Alastair had called the coastguard. And I got a message too, on my phone, telling me to get to the Crithcorrey beach as fast as I could. They rescued her from the water but it was too late to save her.'

'And Charlie?'

'They brought him back from the rock before I got there. He'd discarded his life jacket by then. In the flurry, he told me that Rose had gone on her own. He said she'd texted him from further round the coast, when the weather turned bad, but hadn't listened to his advice to turn back. He raced down to the beach to see her approaching. He'd tried to swim out to her but he hadn't been able to get close – the tide took him over to the rocks. In the horror of that day, I didn't ask myself the obvious question. Where was his car? How had he got to the beach without it? It didn't occur to me until much later.'

'And you didn't see Alastair?'

'He left when he saw the coastguard arriving. And they never traced his call because he uses one of those pay-as-you-go phones. He wasn't called to the inquest because they couldn't find him. And he was so close all the time.' She shook her head. 'He really had no idea of what had gone on. I think he lives in medieval Greece most of the time.'

We were standing now on the edge of the cliffs above the beach and the stretch of sea that contained Crithcorrey. The water out there was fierce, a bubbling torrent as usual, full of the vigour of early spring tides. It was a majestic and yet chilling sight.

Sylla said, 'You know, that whirlpool has been called the Scottish Charybdis. And I'm Sylla. Isn't that odd? What are the chances? Sometimes, I wonder: what chance did Rose have, caught between us?'

'That's all in your head,' I said. 'It means nothing. It's coincidence.'

'Yes. Of course it is.' She sighed. 'I come out to this spot often. I feel close to her here.'

We stood for a while in silence. I thought of Rose with infinite sadness. Then Sylla turned to me.

'When Rose was lying in front of me on the beach, I was full of so much anger, despair and disbelief. I couldn't believe that this catastrophe was actually happening. I didn't believe that she was dead; I thought life would go into reverse, like a spool of film being rewound. She would open her eyes, breathe again. Talk to me. Say, "What a stupid thing to happen, I'm glad that's over." But my worst nightmare had happened, the worst thing in the world.'

My eyes filled with tears. The rawness of it. The horror. I knew that every day I was spared such an experience, such a torment, was a blessing. I could hug my soft warm children close, feel their beating hearts, smell their sweet hair. I felt the loss of Rose again, with that desperate pang. I whispered, 'It's so terrible.'

'She lay there on the shore. The paramedics had stopped their resuscitation efforts, even though I begged them to go on. I was her protector, her mother, the one who made everything right. I couldn't let her die. She couldn't go without me.'

I bit my lip to hold back my tears. This wasn't my grief, it was hers. I had to respect it by restraining mine.

'But she had gone. I had to accept it and find the strength to continue. The longer I lived without Rose, the more I realised that I could no longer go on as I had been, living with those hollow people. Charlie and Josephine. I know they're in pain, but it was killing me to live with them. I couldn't honour Rose any more by staying, though I did for a while. Until I was sure it was time. When I reached my nadir, I thought I might have to leave life altogether. Then Alastair Drummond released me with the revelation of what Charlie had done. It explained everything. It took away Rose's responsibility for her death. It made her Rose again. And it took away my dreadful guilt. Or, at least, some of it. Enough to make life bearable.'

'Did it have anything to do with us coming?'

'No, I left a good while before that. Although when you messaged I knew I couldn't see you as you would be bringing your own pain and I wasn't ready for it. But I am now.'

She took my hand and wrapped it in hers. I looked into those wise, navy eyes.

'I left Charlie because he lied to me. He took Rose to the sea that day. He pretended he hadn't, but he had. He knew I'd forbidden it but he took her anyway, then lied about it. And if that wasn't bad enough, he let Rose take the blame for her accident, when it was really his fault.'

'That's awful, Sylla.' I shook my head, shocked again at the realisation of what Charlie had done.

'I saw him for what he really is: a coward. Spineless. I couldn't love him after that. There was no question. It was over.'

I nodded. I understood.

'I think you may be suffering in your own way, Helen. And I want to tell you: the lies don't end. You have to know that. The only way to prevent them is to walk away and stop this here. Stop your children learning that this is the way to cope with life. Put your hand up and say enough. That's what we can and must do.'

I nodded. I'd thought often of Lilac and Jamie, and what they were learning from Hamish. I knew I wanted more for them than that. I wanted them to be braver, truer and stronger. That was what I needed to focus on now. 'Yes. You're right. But I haven't suffered what you have.'

We watched the sea in silence for a while. Then Sylla turned to me. 'I'm going to stay in my little cottage for now, Helen. I don't want you to tell anyone where I am yet. But before you go I think we need to talk.'

'About Hamish?'

'About Charlie, and Hamish and Josephine. About all of it. About us.'

*

We went back to the welcome warmth of the little cottage.

'Look at this,' Sylla said, and showed me a shelf full of books about psychology. 'I've been doing a lot of reading and learning. I've felt an overpowering urge to understand what's happened and why.'

We sat down on the sofa near the stove, and Sylla poured us each a glass of wine from the bottle on the little table in front of us.

She went on. 'You see, this whole thing is about more than just someone being a bad man. A bad husband. A foolish, silly man, who makes a mistake. Or a bad woman, or an imperfect mother. And you'll understand that, because I think you're experiencing the same thing. It's what we've both shared all these years, though we didn't know it.'

'What do you mean?'

'I think they have a personality disorder. You see, Charlie is supremely unconcerned about anything outside his immediate needs. Josephine is the same. And so is Hamish.'

I nodded. 'All three of them are of the same stripe.'

'They have learned to survive in a certain way,' Sylla said, passing me my wine. 'Once you understand that their behaviour is a particularly unattractive defensive mechanism, it begins to make sense. I've had a lot of time to consider and read and make notes. I may even do a degree – I find it fascinating.'

'And you've made the Ballintyres your subject?'

She nodded. 'I realised I had to understand why they did what they did. It was driving me almost mad, living with Charlie and Josephine and trying to understand why they were so impossible. No matter how flexible or accommodating I was, it was never enough. Sometimes it's called blending. Most of us learn how to blend with others: have discussions, make arrangements, come to agreements. Imagine I ask you out for lunch. I suggest some days. You tell me honestly which days suit and which don't. We come up with a time and a place, and we meet there at the time and place. Now . . . take Charlie. I could ask him that question and somehow nothing about it would be straightforward. He would have issues with all the days and all the places. He'd insist on one day – because it suited him, my needs wouldn't matter – then change his mind and make it another. Then suggest dinner instead. Then change that. He would discover that he has double-booked himself and can't do that day after all. Or he would agree to one time and when he arrived, make it clear it had been a terrible stretch for him to fit it in. I'm trying to say . . . nothing runs smoothly, even when you offer all the options.'

'Yes! Hamish is just like that. Things are always so confused. They're never what I thought they were. And . . . ' – I frowned – 'he's always changing the facts, so if I say we agreed something, he'll have a different version I don't remember. If I make a suggestion, he either acts like I've given him an order he must obey without question, or he simply sweeps it away and suggests something else entirely. All or nothing.'

Sylla nodded. 'Yes. It's a form of power play. With Charlie, it's disruption. But he does that revision of history too. I learned to keep detailed notes of what he said so I could check when he denied things and I thought I was going mad. And he also has a sort of learned amnesia. If anything doesn't suit him, he simply forgets it. And I knew that as soon as I walked out of the door, he would forget all about me. I just wouldn't really matter anymore. As though I'd served my purpose; and if I didn't have a role in his world, then I was as good as not existing at all.'

'That's harsh.' I shook my head slowly. 'Do you really mean that?'

'Yes. I mean it entirely.' She sipped her wine, staring into the stove at the flames dancing there. Her face was very solemn and still. We were quiet for a moment. Then she said, 'How about you, Helen? How are you?'

'I'm all right. No. That's not true. I'm not all right. You know what happened, I'm sure – how Hamish lost his job.'

'Yes. You told me a little last year. Charlie told me a bit too. Josephine was outraged that someone had accused Hamish of something she assumed was false. You were in the process of leaving the school.'

'That's right. We moved into a temporary place and came here after Christmas. The whole thing was awful and Hamish simply collapsed under the pressure. I've held the family together in every way since then, until, I suppose, we got here, which took some of the pressure off us financially. But I'm not sure how quickly Hamish will recover or what he'll do.'

'And that's the problem?'

I looked down at my hands. 'No. That's not it.' I looked up at her, comforted by the wise, calm gaze that met mine. 'I'm beginning to doubt it all. Everything. I believed Hamish.

462

I said that I didn't think he was capable of assault, and I still don't. He's stupid sometimes, but not that stupid. He's not the type to force himself on someone.'

'Because he needs to be adored.'

As soon as she said it, I knew it was true. Hamish craved approval. He needed it like air, and so he'd not risk doing anything that would incur disapproval or wrath – he hated that. He would never let me be angry with him. If I ever was, he would collapse, or walk out of the house. But mostly he would attempt to prevent it by doing all he could to avoid provoking anger. I frowned to myself. But if he was so eager to please, then why were we in constant low-level conflict? What kept going wrong?

Something was tugging at the edges of my mind.

'I used to think he had to be right all the time,' I said slowly. 'But that isn't it. He doesn't mind being in the wrong, or doing wrong. That doesn't bother him.'

Sylla said quietly, 'He doesn't want to be *found out*.'

'That's it! He can't be found out. That's why he concealed that debt from me. He thought it would make me angry with him, so he simply hid it.'

Sylla stared at me. 'What did he tell you when things went wrong at school?'

'That he'd been sacked for assaulting Kaya. And he hadn't done it. I believed him.'

'And what have you found out?'

I told her quickly about the badge. 'She must have been in our car, but he lied about it.'

'So he's protecting himself,' Sylla said. 'You've learned that he'll tell lies to protect himself, right?'

'Why would he protect himself by telling me he'd been sacked for sexual assault?' I asked, confused.

'Because . . .' Her gaze was candid and strong. 'Because the truth would be something worse.'

At home, it was strange to be the one with the secrets. I held my private knowledge close to me – that Sylla was living nearby, that Kaya Stone had been in our car – and I felt suddenly like Sylla: the calm at the heart of things, as the Ballintyre storm blew around me. When I got back, I found Hamish lolling around in his pyjamas, having reverted to his old ways, and Josephine fussing around him as if he were an invalid.

'Nice bike ride?' he called out as I came in and put my bag down.

'Yes, thanks. Where are Lilac and Jamie?'

'Watching the television.'

I checked my watch. It was late afternoon, and Hamish had said he would do some art with them, and perhaps some reading. 'How long have they been doing that?'

He sighed. 'Does it matter? They were at school all morning and I'm not really feeling up to an art and craft session.'

'If you're so concerned,' Josephine said from the stove, where she was stirring soup, 'then I don't know why you go off gallivanting leaving Hamish to oversee your children.'

I metaphorically shook her off. She was, I realised, losing

her power over me. I didn't care what she thought anymore. I said, 'Is Charlie here?'

'No, he's out.'

'I'm going to check on the children.'

Passing the television room, I looked in on Lilac and Jamie. They were sprawled across the sofa in the stunned way of children who'd had too much screen time, hypnotised and yet not really appearing to take it in. I told them we were going for a walk later and then went slowly upstairs to Charlie and Sylla's bedroom suite at the front of the house. Their rooms were the largest: a dressing-room-cum-sitting-room, a large bedroom and an ensuite bathroom, all looking over the loch and the hills beyond. I had been in there, but only as far as the sitting room. I'd only ever peeped into the bedroom that lay beyond. It was their private enclave, and there was hardly ever a reason to go inside. But I had one now.

Sylla had said, 'There's one thing I want you to do, if you will. You can say no if you're not comfortable with it. I left something special behind and if you can get it for me, I'd be very grateful.'

I hadn't hesitated and now here I was on the threshold of her bedroom, feeling like an intruder. I stepped quietly through the door and into the dressing room area. It was a mess, with Charlie's discarded clothes all over the sofa and floor and the wardrobe door standing open. Dirty laundry lay on the floor by the washing basket, balls of pants and socks screwed up together and tossed down. I picked my way across it and went into the bedroom where the large bed was unmade and there was more evidence of carelessness: empty mugs on the bedside table which was littered with piles of books, papers and assorted junk, as was the floor around the bed.

'Sylla would hate this,' I said out loud. She liked calm and order in her environment, and here was chaos. I felt uncomfortable there myself, and went quickly over to her dressing table. She had told me where to find it and I opened the smooth green leather jewellery case to see neat rows of earrings, rings and a pile of necklaces. On the top was what I was looking for: a simple watch with a black leather strap. Rose's watch.

'I don't know how I forgot it,' Sylla had said. 'I must have it. Charlie wouldn't care, unless he knew I wanted it. Can you get it for me?'

'Of course.'

I picked it up now and looked at it, my heart full of sorrow. Gorgeous Rose, so vibrant and happy and full of life. She should be wearing this now, on her way to some great adventure, or another day packed with friends and laughter and learning. She had been so inquisitive and curious, so open to the world, so full of charm and excitement. Not like a Ballintyre at all.

I looked up, sighing, and in the mirror my eye was caught by two portraits of children, each facing the other, across the top of a walnut chest of drawers. I turned slowly, then moved towards them, frowning. They looked familiar although I'd never seen them before. They must be Hamish and Charlie, at very young ages, and they were delicate and beautiful, catching their childhood innocence in a way I felt I knew.

Their Ballintyre blue eyes and fair hair, the curve of their noses and chins – it was all exactly right.

I stood in front of the two portraits, staring, a strange feeling building up inside me. I had watched exactly this kind of painting emerge on canvases for years. I had seen the careful addition of pastel to bring that childish flush to a cheek, and the coloured pencil used in the hair for that soft, almost fuzzy effect. And there in the corner were the initials. I knew them so well.

'Why do you sign with an L?' I'd asked years before, sitting in the studio.

'Because my name is really Leonora,' she'd said. 'But no one calls me that. I'm Nora. That's my name.'

Here, painted unmistakably by Nora, and with her signature in the corner, were Hamish and Charlie. I was bewildered. She'd known them. She must have known the family. I tried to remember what she'd said all those years ago: she'd grown up near here. She knew the house. She'd known the Drummonds. I'd not understood the set-up here then. I'd never thought to ask if she'd known the Ballintyres themselves.

'But she must have known Josephine,' I said out loud, astonished.

Why had she not told me?

The sudden sound of an engine and the crunch of wheels on gravel startled me, and I glanced out of the window to see Charlie's car coming up the drive. I slipped Rose's watch into my pocket and hurried out of the room.

PART TWELVE

Chapter Twenty-Six
TIGS
1978

It was no surprise that Josephine told everyone what she had discovered: a frightful betrayal by a wanton hussy who had shamelessly attempted to steal her husband. James was an innocent, a man who had only behaved as men do, the Adam tempted by the wicked Eve. He had not been able to control himself, but that was understandable, he was only human. And now he was sorry. He was repentant. She had taken him back into the heart of their wholesome and happy family home. He was forgiven.

The slut, though, must be punished.

I was immediately not only the object of frenzied gossip, but an outcast. Shirley Mahon in the village shop, who had known me since I was a child, turned her back on me and wouldn't serve me. Others were more civil but not friendly. I felt the awful chill and hated it, so I stopped going anywhere unless absolutely necessary. The humiliation was terrible. I could not challenge Josephine's version of events. She was the wife, I was not, therefore she was wronged and I was the wrongdoer. It was indisputable. Could I explain to every person I met that she was a tyrant, hateful and cold, and that James suffered every day of his marriage to her? Could I persuade them that we were truly in love, each other's happiness and solace in life? Of course I could not. Josephine had won and I had to retire, completely vanquished.

I could have lived with the disapproval of my community, hard though it was and unjust though it felt. But I could not bear the disappointment of my parents. They had not yet moved to their cottage, planning to go when the holiday season was over and they had finished the preparations in their new home. I hoped against hope that they would not hear of my disgrace, but I had known in my heart that somehow they would find out.

I was doing the only thing I could think of: painting in the evening light of the ballroom. It was midweek and we had no guests until the weekend. Inside I was in desperate pain, though trying my best to hide it. I had come back from Edinburgh in a frenzy of despair and pretended that I felt ill from my dental appointment so that I could retire to bed and weep. The next day, I'd kept my distance from my parents, attempting to conceal the floods of tears that continually surprised me by erupting without warning, but also trying to keep close to the telephone in case James called me. There was nothing from him, no call and no message. I could hardly stand it. I longed to drive to Ballintyre so that I could at least see him, beg to know what was happening and whether there was any hope for us. I wanted to do battle with Josephine on his behalf because I was sure of one thing: he was being terribly punished. Her wrath would be awful. She would use everything in her arsenal to extract maximum suffering from him, and in particular I was sure she would be using their children as her weapon of choice. Guilt and shame would be heaped upon his head, and he would be made to promise to give me up forever, and probably live in a state of permanent remorse, in order to be allowed to keep his family intact. I could hear her screaming: *If you ever see her, you will never, ever lay eyes on the boys again, do you hear? Never!*

My heart was ripped into bloody pieces inside me. I felt his suffering and longed to alleviate it but I was powerless to protect the man I loved so dearly. And there was my own pain and suffering. I had lost the thing most dear to me in the world, apart from my family. I had no idea if it would ever be restored to me. And under all this, I had to keep my sorrow concealed.

'Tigs.' Mumma came into the ballroom, her face so solemn that I knew at once she was aware of everything. She sat down on the chair near my easel. 'I have just been talking to Josephine Ballintyre.'

My insides felt as though they had plummeted away from me. I put down my brush and palette, hot shame flooding my cheeks, and could not look at her as she gazed at me. Her voice, though, was not harsh. It was questioning, concerned.

'You can guess what she told me. Is it true? Have you been seeing James?'

I bit my lip, wanting the floor to open up and swallow me and my shame whole. Eventually, I managed to say, in a low voice, 'Yes.'

'Oh Tigs.' Her voice was full of sadness and disappointment and I could not bear it. 'How long for?'

'Just over eighteen months.'

'What?' She was astonished. 'That long? It must be serious then!'

'Yes, it is. Very.'

'My dear girl. This is awful.'

'I'm sorry,' I said, in a choked voice, looking up at her through a blur of tears. 'I really am very sorry. We couldn't help it.'

'You've always loved him, haven't you?' I could hear that she was trying to understand something that went entirely against her system of values and beliefs. A married man was out of bounds. He was not to be loved. He belonged to someone else, tied with sacred bonds to another. 'And he loves you?'

I nodded, trying to stop the tears from falling but a hot shower began to run down my face.

'Oh Tigs.' She got up and came over, enveloping me in a hug that made me sob on her shoulder, desperate for release, consoled only by the relief of my grief and the comfort of her closeness and pity. 'You poor child.'

'I thought you would hate me!'

'I can never hate you, my darling girl. I'm so very sorry this has happened. People get themselves into terrible tangles sometimes and you and James have got yourselves into a great deal of trouble because of what you feel for one another. It's a great blessing to love where you're allowed to love. But to love what can never rightly be yours . . . that suffering is not what I would ever want for you.'

Mumma rocked me gently as I wept, the storm subsiding a little as my raw grief passed. Eventually I was able to say, 'What did Josephine want?'

'She is very angry. She said some nasty things and spoke to me about you as she has no right to. If it's any comfort, Tigs, she is not someone I like. For that reason, I have sympathy with James. I can understand why he would love you instead of her. But that doesn't make what you have done right. I don't have to tell you that it's wrong and must come to an end.'

I began to weep again, not stormily but in the grip of utter despair to which I could see no end.

Mumma said, 'Dadda must know.'

'Yes. I understand.'

'I don't think Josephine has kept this to herself and that will make things impossible for you.'

'She's told everyone. It's so humiliating.'

'She's hurt and angry and she feels very badly betrayed.'

I pulled away from Mumma's embrace to look her in the eyes. 'You know she deserved it!'

Mumma looked, just for a second, angry, and then the anger vanished and she was kind again, but stern. 'She did *not* deserve it, Tigs. You must never tell yourself that. You and James have betrayed her. You have done wrong. I can't pretend that isn't true. It doesn't make you wicked but it means that now you must act in the right way. Do the right thing. As I would expect of you. You must give him up.'

'No!' I cried. 'I can't! I'll die without him!'

'You won't die. You feel like that now but you'll get over it. You must. You promised me once to stay away from James and Josephine.'

'I tried, I really did. It happened by accident,' I said miserably, ashamed again, feeling like the lowest of the low.

'One way or another, your promise was broken. So I want you to make another promise to me: that you will not attempt to see him again. He is married. What happens to his marriage is his business now, and you must allow him to make that choice unhampered by you. He loves you, that is clear, but that doesn't mean he shouldn't give you up and stay with Josephine. If he makes any other decision, that must not be because of you clouding his judgement.'

I nodded sadly. I knew she was right. I hated what she was saying, but there was no other way. 'Then I'd better go away.'

'I'm so sorry, Tigs, but yes, I think that's best. Now, come with me. I'll make some tea and we can talk all this through with Dadda.' She kissed my forehead. 'My darling child. I know it doesn't feel like it now, but you will be happy again. I promise.'

Over the next few days, with much discussion, we came to some decisions. We would honour the remaining bookings for the year, cancel the rest and take no more. Mumma and Dadda would delay their move until the end of the season, and Carina and another helper would be recruited for more hours, so that they could cover the cleaning and laundry and some of the cooking.

My parents put on a brave face for me, but I knew they were deeply disappointed by what had happened even if they did not blame me for it. They both had an air of sadness that made me desperately guilty. How many people was I hurting? I didn't deserve their love and kindness, but I needed it to my core.

Worst of all, though, was missing James. His loss was agony. It was so painful, I had to cling to Mumma and Dadda as a way to bear it and it felt so harsh when we discussed my departure, even though I knew it was for the best.

'I don't want to leave you,' I said in a small, miserable voice. We were in the study, the fire lit as usual despite the warm weather outside, and Dadda was puffing away on his pipe in the old familiar way.

'I know,' Dadda said. 'But it's for the best.'

Mumma said, 'Serena is happy for you to live with her for now. In fact, she wants you to go. She has her hands full with the baby and you'd be company and a help for her.'

'A cleaner again,' I said, with a wan smile. 'A cleaner for Serena. It rhymes.'

'A friend. A sister. She wants to comfort you too.'

'I know. I'm not being serious. I'm grateful to her and Richard.' Serena had rung me, obviously brought up to date with events by Mumma, and for once she had been all sympathy and understanding. 'I don't blame you,' she'd said. 'He is very dishy,' and that had made me laugh because it was so like her to see it like that.

'It's the right decision,' Dadda said firmly. 'I don't want you to be treated like an outcast here. People have no right, but they will make judgements. You don't have to endure that, on top of everything else.'

My parents could not say that they sympathised with how I was suffering from my separation from James, but I could tell that they understood and also that they wanted to protect me, and I loved them for it.

'Yes,' I said at last. 'It is right. I can see that. I'll go soon.'

'The sooner, the better,' Dadda said.

I nodded, knowing he was right, though my heart was breaking all over again. I had lost James, and now I would lose my home.

The letter came after three long weeks, not long before I was due to leave. Mumma picked it up from the mat but said nothing as she put it by my plate, even when I gasped at the sight of James's handwriting. She evidently guessed who it was from.

I also said nothing but finished my toast and coffee, and then took the letter down to the beach, where I could sit on my rock and read it in peace. It was not long but I read it very slowly so that every word could sink in and I could make it last. The sight of his handwriting alone was huge comfort to me. His words were now my only tie to him.

My darling,

   I am sorry. I can hardly think of what to say that can express this more fully. I'm more sorry than you can know. I'm sure you're suffering as I am. I miss you desperately, I love you desperately and all of this is sheer agony.

Dearest Nora, you know we will have to part. Josephine is, of course, deeply hurt and betrayed and she has told me that unless we part forever, she will divorce me and take custody of the boys, and ensure I have no more to do with them. She will, as I suspected, force the sale of Ballintyre. She will do everything she can to destroy what is dear to me. I cannot allow this to happen, not for my sake, but for the boys and for my parents.

We have no choice. We must separate for good. It breaks my heart and I know it will break yours but it is for the best. You must stop loving me, and find someone who can make you happy. You deserve it, my sweet Nora. You deserve everything I cannot give you: a marriage, children, a home.

Please forgive me for visiting this disaster on you. You've made my life worth living for the time we've been together, and I will live on that for the rest of my life. Thank you, my darling.

I have not forgotten the money I owe you and I will repay it as soon as the land sale is confirmed, as I promised.

Please try to forget me, my sweet Nora, even though I can never forget you for as long as I live.

All my love,

James x

When I had finished reading it twice, I sobbed until the tears falling on the page began to make the ink run. Then I put it away and walked for a long time on the beach until I had the composure to face my parents again, and finish the preparations for my departure.

They never asked me what was in the letter from James but I think they guessed from my tear-stained face what he had said. They didn't ask either if I had written back to him. I had. I poured out my heart to him, I told him I understood and that this was the right decision, that I loved him and always would, and nothing would ever change that. I wrote down all the love in my heart – enough, I hoped, to protect and comfort him – and sent the letter marked 'Personal' to his office in Edinburgh, hoping that there it would escape Josephine's eye. Not that I cared if she read it, there was nothing in it I was ashamed of. She might as well know that I loved James with true, honest emotion that would sacrifice itself before it hurt the loved one. Perhaps she could, for a moment, glimpse what it meant to be a whole person, not a hollow crucible of self-interest.

That was cold comfort, though. The reality was the daily wakening and realisation that I would never see James again, and the rush of pain and despair that brought me. It was packing my suitcase for my stay at Serena's house, not knowing how long it would last or when I would see my dear home again. I missed it already even though I had not left. I was still busy looking after guests and managing the house while they were there, but soon I would be handing that over to our helpers and to Mumma and Dadda. That made me feel even more guilty. At a time when they'd been looking forward to retiring to their cottage, they had a busy summer of work ahead of them without me to help. And they were not immune to the vicious gossip that was still travelling around our small community; they knew what was being said about me and it hurt them. It hurt them too when friends and neighbours avoided them at church and in the shops. But they bore it all without complaining for my sake.

The day of my departure grew ever closer. Beyond it, I had no idea of my future. It was a dark, unwelcome place I had no desire to live. I knew it would be blighted by loneliness and misery and the lack of James, which in itself made the prospect next to unbearable. I hoped that Serena and the new baby would prove enough of a distraction to provide me with a reason to go on getting up in the mornings.

On the day I was to leave, I woke very early. It was a glorious day outside, with the purest blue sky that was rich with white clouds scudding in the summer breeze. The sea stretched away in dazzling silver blue, dancing with waves that broke and burst along the shore in floods of foam. Nature seemed young and vigorous, while I felt old and sad, not just because of the pain in my heart but because I was leaving all of this.

I breathed in the salt-edged breeze and tried to pull the sunshine into my lungs too, as if to illuminate myself and banish the dark of my despair. I needed to store this magic Scottish air to help me through the days ahead. The wind blew around my head, buffeting my ears so that I didn't hear the voice until it was quite close to me, then I realised a man was calling and I whirled round in great excitement, hoping wildly that it was James.

'Hi, Tigs! Hello there!' It was Al, walking towards me across the sand. When he came level, he said, 'Your mother said you were down here. I wanted to see you before you go.'

'Hello,' I said, happy at his arrival. 'You're still talking to me then.'

He looked surprised. 'Of course.'

'Last time I saw you, you said you couldn't be my friend anymore.'

'Well . . . yes. You know what I meant. We couldn't be close. But we'll always be friends.'

We fell into step with one another as we wandered along the waterline. It was nice to see him: a familiar face looking at me without judgement. 'You're flying in the face of fashion as usual,' I said wryly. 'Just as everyone else has decided to cast me out and send me to Coventry, you're calling round for a chat.'

'Yes.' He stared at the sand, frowning in that furious way I knew so well. 'I've heard. You've got yourself into a sticky situation and I'm sorry about it.'

'I know, I've been a disgrace and a trollop and everyone is glad to see the back of me, you don't have to say it.'

He looked up at me, his black eyes serious. 'I didn't come to say that, Tigs, and I'm surprised you think I would.'

'I don't think you would.' I sighed. 'I'm sorry. I'm being ungenerous. It's been hard, that's all. Everyone hates me.'

'Well, they don't but that's beside the point, because I don't. If you think I'm on anyone's side, you're quite wrong.

482

I'm no fan of that dreadful woman – she's a monster, anyone can see that. But I'm no fan of his, either, and I'm sorry you got mixed up with him.' He shook his head. 'I tried to warn you, Tigs. You wouldn't listen.'

'I love him.'

'You don't love him. You only think you love him.'

I burst out laughing. 'Oh Al, you never change! You're just the same! I think that's a good thing.'

He laughed too, a little uncertainly, as though nonplussed by my reaction. 'I'm glad to see I've cheered you up so quickly and, I must say, so easily.'

'I'm very happy to see you, thank you so much for coming. It means a lot. But I'm afraid it doesn't change how I feel about James. I still love him, and I always will.'

'You think you always will. But you won't.'

We walked along in silence for a moment. For the first time, I wanted to believe him. I wanted a bit of his certainty to help me go on. We stopped and looked out at the glittering water, and the waves rising, curling and breaking in an unceasing roar on the shore.

'I want you to know I'll always be your friend, Tigs. If you need me. No matter what's happened, and what will happen. I'll be right here. You're always welcome at Tighglachach.'

I took his hand and squeezed it, smiling up into his face. 'Thank you, Al. That means so much. I can't tell you how much. I'll miss this place.'

He squinted out at the sea. 'It'll always be here. And so will I.'

*

'Tigs, you do a good bit of polishing,' Serena said admiringly, looking over at the sideboard in her little dining room, where her photograph frames were shining. 'You haven't lost it!'

'Thanks.'

'The silver has never looked so good. Richard's very impressed. I'm afraid you're revealing the truth about my talents as a housekeeper.' Serena jiggled baby Susie on her knee. She had settled very happily into her role as a wife and mother. Richard caught the train each day into town and returned at seven p.m. just in time for gin and tonic before his dinner, and Serena passed her days at baby groups and coffee mornings, and cooking Richard's meals. She also did a bit of housework and a lot of shopping, and she had grown plump and content in this sedate and yet busy life of hers.

Sometimes I watched her and Richard talking over dinner, discussing Susie and her progress and what they would do at the weekend, and which dinner parties they were attending, and I would wonder if they had ever known the kind of passion that James and I had shared or if it had simply worn off in the routine of married life. Could all married people have felt wild passion for one another at some point? Was there that much passion in the world? Surely not.

Privately I was convinced that people rarely felt what James and I did. And as a result, they did not have to go through this daily pain, the constant ache of separation, and knowledge that it would go on like this indefinitely.

'You don't really seem yourself, Tigs,' Serena said, looking sympathetic. Susie was staring up at me too, her big eyes enormous over a button nose and cupid mouth. I wondered about getting out my sketchpad and drawing her but then decided against it. I had stopped drawing. 'You don't smile anymore and you used to be really quite cheerful most of the time. You don't tell half as many jokes as you used to.'

'I suppose I am a bit muted.' I didn't know how to tell her that it was hard to smile and joke when I was crying inside.

'It must have been a joy to get one over on that bitch Josephine,' she said confidentially, leaning towards me. 'I never liked her.'

'I thought you did.'

Serena wrinkled her nose. 'I don't think so. Anyone could see she was on the make. Horrid. No wonder James preferred you. So.' She raised her eyebrows. 'What was he like in bed? Do tell.'

I managed to avoid telling Serena my woes, or what James was like in bed, by dodging her questions. She meant well, but she didn't seem to have a clue of what I'd been through or why I was staying with her, and why I was so very miserable about what had happened. She acted as though I'd had an ill-advised fling and come down here till the heat of discovery had cooled and I could go back to my old life. I would have loved a confidante but Serena was not it. Perhaps that was for the best. Instead, I was forced to talk about baby food and baby clothes and how wonderful Susie was – although she was adorable and I loved her – and that kept me from dwelling all the time on my situation.

Each day I went eagerly for the post when I heard the letter box snap and the drop of mail on the doormat, hoping that James had written to me again, but there never was anything. He had no doubt promised Josephine that he would not contact me and was sticking to his promise. I, too, had made a promise to Mumma and I could not break that, not after what I had done last time. And so I didn't write to him either. I knew he must be suffering as I was. That was my only consolation when I lay awake at night, weeping and thinking of him, hoping that tonight I would see him in my dreams because that was better than nothing. I just didn't know how long I could go on like this, and I yearned with all my heart, day and night, for him.

I prayed, against everything I knew to be true, that one day soon he would come for me.

The telephone rings, and I wake at once. I leap out of bed and dash across the hall to the upstairs landing, where the table lamp casts a soft glow across the shrieking phone. I grab the receiver. 'Hello?'

'It's me,' he says.

My breath catches in my throat. I can hardly believe I'm hearing his voice. 'Yes?'

'I can't do this anymore. I want to be with you.'

Suddenly exhilarated, I see the life I've longed for drop into my hands like a gift from heaven. Will he actually leave? Come to me, into my arms? Then . . . grey reality consumes it. 'You can't leave. The children . . . they need you.'

'It's too late for that. I can't undo the damage. I can't bear to see it. I've been weak, stupid . . .'

He sounds utterly bleak, desperate.

'They still need you,' I say, but less firmly. The truth is that I agree with him. He's right – the damage has been done.

'But I need *you*,' he says, his voice low. 'I see that now. Forgive me. Is it too late?'

The gift is still sparkling in my hands. Its promise has not been doused. My heart is racing. I glance at the hall clock and see that it is one o'clock in the morning. 'Perhaps you should wait until tomorrow. Sleep on it, darling. Don't make any hasty decisions.'

'That's not what I mean. Is it too late . . . for us? Will you still have me?'

I close my eyes, standing there in the hall in my nightdress, everything in me rejoicing that, at last, I've heard the words I've longed for. 'You know I will.'

'Then I'm coming, darling. Right now. Tonight.'

'Are you sure? Do you mean it?'

'I've never been more certain. Wait for me.'

'Always.'

When the phone is replaced, I cannot go back to bed. I go down to the kitchen, wide awake and bubbling with happiness, my very fingertips feeling full of magic, and I make tea. I will wait. How long will it take? Six hours? Seven?

If only I could sleep, then I would wake to find him here with me. I can almost feel it now: the warmth of his touch, the slight roughness of his stubbled skin on mine, his lips pressing against my mouth as he murmurs. He likes to do that: to place words of love onto my lips as though pressing them into my soul. He'll reach for my hair with those hands I love so much: broad, the palms almost square, the fingers long, blunt-ended and capable; he'll wind my long hair around them and say, 'You're my sea witch, my Beira, my queen.' I'll feel the soft wool of his faded, holey jumper and inhale the scent of woodsmoke and cedar, and then those strong arms will wrap around me and never let me go. Because he's going to leave her, he's going to come to me. Whatever awaits us in the future, we can face it together. Her wrath will be terrible. She's already taken whatever rage has possessed her since birth and used it to terrorise him and their children. When she knows he's finally broken free, what will she do? To him? To me? What form will her revenge take? What will she destroy?

I pace the kitchen, wondering where he is now on his journey. I will wait for as long as it takes. And when he arrives, I will give him all the strength that comes from my love and, together, we will face her.

I wait for the dawn, longing only for him.

Chapter Twenty-Seven
TIGS
1979

Nine months after James was killed, I went back to Ballintyre.

I drove in absolute silence, stopping only for petrol, the lavatory and enough fuel in the form of coffee and biscuits to keep me going. I had no interest in food and drink anymore, so didn't care what I ate just as long as it gave me enough energy to do what I needed to do. Sometimes I considered not eating at all, and just waiting for life to end. I didn't think I'd mind that very much. Driving along, consumed by my thoughts, I had a certain recklessness, almost hoping that something might hit me, suddenly and unexpectedly, and put me out of my misery. I never did anything dangerous – I couldn't bear the thought of hurting anyone else, of putting some other family through what I was suffering – but I hoped someone else might and that I might be there when they did.

Fate had other ideas for me. I travelled the length of England and into Scotland without mishap and soon I was leaving the city and the motorways behind, and making my way along the narrow winding roads through the hills towards home.

I had not known what to do with myself in the wake of the disaster. Misery and guilt had consumed me so violently, I thought I surely must die of it, and I hoped that I would. I had waited all night for James to arrive, and then all the next day. By the evening, my prayers had changed. Where I had been longing for him to arrive, now I only hoped that he had changed his mind and decided to stay with Josephine after all. Better that than the alternative.

On the evening of the next day, my parents called to talk to Serena but I guessed they must know something. When Serena, solemn and scared as I'd never seen her before, asked me to sit down and took my hand. She told me that on the road from Ballintyre to Glasgow, in the early hours of the morning, James had rounded a bend at speed and veered suddenly to avoid a van travelling in the middle of the road. He had skidded off the road and hit a tree. He had been killed instantly. I felt as if I was walking into a nightmare.

That nightmare lasted months. Mumma came down to stay with us, to help me through the worst of it, to hold me when I was screaming and shouting, telling her it was all my fault because if it weren't for me, he would not be dead, and I'd rather he lived with her than not at all.

'There is nothing you could have done, it was not your fault,' Mumma told me over and over. 'You must endure it and you will survive. But it was not your fault.'

It was impossible to hear it. I was trapped in my personal nightmare. I couldn't even think of Josephine and her two boys. It was beyond my capability.

And now here I was, returning. I would not do it, unless I had to, but there was no other choice. It was a bitter pill that I must swallow.

It was late afternoon by the time I approached Ballintyre, following the curving road at the side of the silvery loch. I passed the kirk, where James had married Josephine and where he now lay in the cemetery. I had not been invited to the funeral, of course. There had been no farewell for me, only the memory of that final phone call and his last words to me. At least they had been of love and need. I could hold that close to my heart.

I turned the car through the gates of Ballintyre and climbed the long, sloping drive towards the house at the top. It looked exactly as it had before, although there was a kind of emptiness, a sense of something missing. But perhaps that was my projection.

A shiny new car stood outside the house. I supposed that the one lost in the accident had been replaced. It was yellow, which was no surprise given Josephine must have chosen it, and the sight of it chilled me, so I looked away and concentrated on approaching the house and keeping my feelings of sickness and fear in check.

My knock on the door was answered by a housekeeper in a blue pinny and with a duster in her hand.

'Aye?' she said enquiringly.

'I'm here to see Mrs Ballintyre. I think she's expecting me.'

She nodded and opened the door for me so I could walk into the hall. 'She's in there.' She waved her duster in the direction of the drawing room.

'Thank you.' I went slowly to the drawing room door and pushed it open. I saw Josephine at once. She was standing by the window, staring out over the loch, and she turned as I came in, her eyes icy cold and her face set in an expression of disdain.

'So you came.'

'Yes.'

'Well, I admire your nerve.' She came around the armchair by the window and moved to the lemon-yellow sofa. On the coffee table was a silver tray laid with tea things and a pot. 'Do you want some tea?'

'No thank you.'

She sat down and gestured at the sofa opposite for me. 'Make yourself comfortable.'

I sat down, wishing I could stand but I needed at least to appear docile, until I found out how the land lay. I watched as she poured herself some tea into a porcelain cup, added her milk and sat up to look at me. 'You wanted to see me,' she said. 'About an urgent matter.'

'That's right.'

'I can't think what it could be. What could be so urgent after nine months? Unless you've got a baby stowed away somewhere!' She laughed mirthlessly, then said in a stony voice, 'You haven't, have you?'

I shook my head, trying to quell the pain inside me. I had dreaded this. I had told myself it would not be so bad. But now I feared it would. I had come too far to turn back now. 'I need to talk to you about the money I lent to James before he died.'

'James. My husband. My dead husband. You lent him money.'

'Yes. A sizeable sum that I borrowed against our house and which he promised to pay back as soon as he could. He was going to sell some land to the Gillygantry estate and repay me from that money. I've heard that the sale has gone through.'

'That's right,' Josephine said. 'It's no secret. I've sold off rather a lot, actually, and it's brought in a very nice sum. What with the money from James's life assurance policies, and the compensation I've claimed . . . things are going to be all right. The boys will go through school. I can keep this place and live very well.'

'Then you'll be able to repay the money,' I said, with a wash of relief. It was now a matter of urgency that I find the money to pay off the loan.

'What money?' She stared at me, her face impassive.

'I just said – the money I lent James.' I named the sum.

She gave a derisory laugh. 'That's a lot, isn't it? I'm surprised you've got the front. Coming here, after sleeping with my husband behind my back, and now trying to extort money from me!'

'I'm only asking for what's mine.'

She snorted. 'Oh please! Spare me that. Where is the proof of this loan? Tell me that! Where's the proof?'

'I . . . we . . . nothing was signed,' I said in a faltering voice.

'How convenient!'

'It was a loan given and accepted in good faith. It saved the house for you – after you spent a fortune redecorating.'

'It's my fault, then. I see. You're jealous. You've always been jealous of me. My lovely house, my family, my husband! You are just a sad, single woman with nothing of her own and you decided you wanted my life. You did your best to steal my husband and destroy my life but everyone knows the truth! He chose me. He chose to stay with me and his family. And here you are, wanting money from me. Well, you can't have it!'

'That's not true, none of it. And you know it's not. He was coming to me. He loved me. We were going to start a life together.'

'That's your story, but I say it's not true.'

'Then where was he going?'

'I don't know! A man can drive his car where he likes, it doesn't mean he was going to you.'

I was shaking hard, but determined not to crumble in front of her. I needed to stay strong, for everyone's sake. 'All right,' I said at last, my voice tight with tension. 'Let's say he had decided to stay with you. I still lent him that money. I'm sure I can find proof of the transfer. And I desperately need it back.'

'If you chose to give James a gift of money, that's nothing to do with me.'

I stared at her, desperate. 'Please, Josephine! You know I would never come here unless it was vitally important. We must repay the loan or lose our house. The sale will be forced. I lent James the money because he assured me he would repay it as soon as he could.'

She lifted her chin loftily. 'I'm very sorry for you. I'm sure it's a terrible thing to lose your house. But if you make such bad decisions, I'm afraid the responsibility is entirely your own.'

'Please, Josephine. I'm going to beg you. You know I'm telling the truth and that I lent James the money you needed. It kept your sons at prep school and your house in your hands. For that, I may well now lose my beloved family home forever. I know that what happened between James and me was terrible for you and you have every right to be angry about it. We both lost him that night, and it has broken us both. I'm not asking you to like me, I'm only asking you to be fair. Because it will not just be me who suffers, but my family.'

Josephine rose slowly to her feet, like a monster emerging from the deep. 'How dare you!' she said in a terrible voice. 'You are not just a slut but a charlatan! How dare you attempt to perpetrate this fraud on me, a grieving widow!'

I rose too, feeling a growing sense of despair and helplessness. Just as on that day in Edinburgh, I felt I had somehow handed her a role she relished, where she could occupy a pleasing moral high ground that meant something to her despite the fact that it was all wrong. Meaningless. Empty. Like her. Like her entire life. 'Then you won't,' I said in a cold hard voice.

'Of course I won't. Do you think I'd help you? Get you out of trouble? Give you money you don't deserve?' Her voice dripped scorn and hatred. 'I'd rather die. I'm glad you're going to lose everything. I never want to see you here, or even near here again. You tried to wreck my life. You've succeeded. You can be happy with that, and rot in poverty for all I care.'

I wondered why I'd come. Why I had put myself through this. Had I really believed that Josephine – with everything I knew about her – would do the right thing, the honourable thing? Of course she would not. I had given her the opportunity to enjoy a great triumph over me. I might as well have just sold the house and denied her the satisfaction. But it was too late.

'I see. I'll leave.'

'Leave! You're not leaving! I'm throwing you out!'

I turned and started to stride for the door. She followed me, out of the drawing room and down the hall, her voice rising with hysteria as we went.

'You disgust me! You're revolting, the lowest of the low. James never loved you! He loved me. He never wanted you. I hope you burn in hell!'

Her voice was still ringing in my ears as I reached my car and climbed in, my heart pounding and panic coursing through me. I had to get away from her. She was still coming for me, advancing out of her house and towards my car, a malevolent, unshakeable force. I turned on the engine and was seized with a violent longing to reverse hard, hit her and squash her flat, to roll back and forth over her until I'd squeezed the life out of her.

I breathed hard. *Don't let her turn you into a creature like she is.* I reached out in my mind to James. *Help me.*

I heard him speak. *I love you. Forget about her. I'm with you and always will be.*

I let go of my shaking breath, and turned the car, avoiding her, and drove away.

Never again. I swear I will never come here again as long as she is here. I never want to set eyes on her again.

PART THIRTEEN

Chapter Twenty-Eight

HELEN

2018

I walked across the hill to the fairy ring and back again, trying to untangle it in my mind and make sense of it.

Nora never said.

All the times Nora had met Hamish since we married. She'd never said, 'I painted your portrait when you were a boy.' And she had never appeared at any event where she might have met Josephine. She had not been at our wedding or the parties to celebrate the births of the children. She had never crossed paths with my mother-in-law. Could that be a coincidence or did she make sure they would never meet? There was little chance of Hamish remembering her if he'd only seen her as a small child – and that was the only time I could be certain they'd met – but no doubt Josephine would. Then why would Nora want to avoid her? If they were acquaintances, or even friends?

No. I could not imagine Nora friends with Josephine. They were polar opposites. Nora was warm and wise, loving and kind. She loved life and art and had exquisite taste. Josephine was not at all like that.

Why didn't she say anything?

I thought of Nora as she was now. After my father died, I'd sold his house and Nora and I had shared the proceeds as he'd wanted. Nora had moved to the Isle of Wight, to a small house near Cowes overlooking the sea.

'It's good to be close to the sea again,' she said. 'I've missed it.'

I'd once asked why she hadn't gone back to Scotland.

'Oh, lots of reasons. It's very far away. I feel the cold more than I did. Sometimes it's best to let memories lie.'

I hadn't asked her more about it, accepting that she was happy in her bright little house, painting, making friends and taking up new hobbies and pursuits. She was still young, after all, only in her mid-sixties. She knew her own mind and was not hampered by any false sense of guilt or martyrdom in the pursuit of what made her happy.

Despite living on the south coast and not that far from the ferry port that would take me across the Solent, I had not gone to visit as often as I should have. Now I felt a desperate need to see her again. During my early twenties, she'd been like a mother to me, cheering my successes and comforting me in my woes. We had supported one another through the loss of my father. Then I had let myself drift away from her, much more than I should have. Part of it was that I'd wanted to conceal the truth about Hamish from her. She'd warned me, gently, from the start and I hadn't listened, convinced I knew better. She had stayed discreetly away, never prying or judging.

502

But what did she know? Was she really intimately involved in my life the whole time, without my realising?

I thought of that portrait of Hamish, catching him in the bloom of early childhood. I thought of Sylla's theories of why the boys had turned out the way they did, shaped by Josephine and their own predisposition.

Did Nora already know that? Even then?

I have to see her, as soon as I can. I need to know the answers. Only then can I really decide my future.

I raised it the same day, intending to leave almost at once. Hamish thought it was a ridiculous idea.

'All the way to the Isle of Wight? From here? For the weekend?'

'A long weekend,' I said obstinately. 'I think it will be lovely. We'll fly from Glasgow to Southampton and get the ferry from there. It's not that difficult. I haven't seen Nora for far too long.'

'You didn't go much when we were just a couple of hours away at Stourhaven.'

'You know why. We were so busy.' I changed tack. 'I'll take the children with me and you can have a break from looking after them.'

He looked mournful. 'Leave me here all alone with my mother for company? Great.'

I bit back my exasperation. Nothing was ever right. I couldn't make him happy unless I devoted myself entirely to his welfare. Why hadn't I seen it before? But now I was seeing a lot of things more clearly than I ever had. I looked

503

at him and saw a stranger: a deceitful, weak, needy stranger who had taken everything I could give him and not been satisfied with it. I saw someone who had met their own needs all along the way, but not cared about mine. Memories kept floating to the surface of my mind and replaying there, illuminated by my new knowledge. I recalled my father's illness and how little Hamish had seemed to be affected by it. He said sympathetic things, but he himself appeared untouched by Dad's suffering or by his death. At the funeral, he'd played a not-so-quiet game of hide-and-seek with the children in the cemetery during the service. I'd hissed at him to stop it and stand with me.

'I was just trying to keep them occupied!' he'd protested when I'd told him off for it. 'It's a sad occasion, I didn't want them to be miserable.' He'd made woeful eyes at me. 'And I wanted to give you the freedom to concentrate on your dad.'

Give you the freedom . . .

So often his thoughtlessness had been dressed up as something he was doing in my best interests. So often the way he isolated and abandoned me was done in the name of giving me time and space to myself – as a gift.

It was not that. It was abnegation of responsibility. It was a refusal to consider me and put me first. It was childish evasion.

Why have I never seen it before now?

'We're going this weekend, as long as it's all right with Nora. The children have got the rest of their taster mornings next week, so it won't be so easy to get away.'

Hamish considered. 'All right,' he said at last, with a sigh. 'If you really want to.'

'Yes. I do.'

He did not, I noticed, even consider that he might come with us.

I had a brief telephone call with Nora.

'That would be a marvellous treat,' she said, evidently surprised by my eagerness to visit. 'I'd love to see you all.'

'Not Hamish. He's not coming.'

'All the more time for us to chat in peace. How lovely, darling, I can't wait.'

She did not seem sorry that Hamish wasn't coming. *She doesn't like him*, I realised. Another of my little revelations. I laughed wryly to myself as I put the phone down. I was getting to be a regular prophet, with all the revelations I was having these days.

I got on to the computer to make all our reservations for the flight and the ferry. I would drive us to Glasgow so we'd need to set off very early to make a mid-morning flight and arrive with Nora in the late afternoon. As I was finishing off our bookings a text came in from Sebastian.

I've been thinking about you. How did it go? Are you okay? Did you and Sylla get on all right? Let me know. Love Sx

I blinked at it, feeling absurdly moved by such an ordinary little message. It was those words: *I've been thinking about you.* I'd heard them so rarely in my marriage, I'd grown used to coping alone. I wrote back:

It all went fine, thank you so much for making it happen. Can we meet? I'll tell you all about it. I'm away this weekend with the kids but back next week if you're free.

His reply came back a few minutes later.

That's great. I'm really pleased. I want to hear everything. Whenever you're ready. Bring the children too if you'd like to, it would be lovely to see them.

I believed him. I believed that he wanted to talk to me. I believed he wanted me to bring the children. That was a good feeling too.

Trust.

That was what I'd been missing. It was what I longed for in my life.

Lilac and Jamie were beyond excited by everything about our journey, from getting up in the dark, to eating breakfast in the car, and then our plane trip. I wished Hamish was there to see it. We had always enjoyed the children. He was a good father who adored his children and they loved him fiercely in return. I also missed him when they had their mid-afternoon slump, worn out by the long day and grizzling, asking when we were going to get there. The ferry would once have been a highlight but it lacked the thrill of the plane, and they were bored and tired.

It was a relief when we pulled into the port at Cowes where Nora had come to meet us in her little car.

'Good journey?' she said, enveloping me in a warm hug.

'Yes. Good.'

She hugged the children hello. 'You all look bushed! Come home for tea and cake and that will perk you up a little.'

Her house was full of Nora-esque touches: a collection of antique flower pictures hung in a charming arrangement on one wall; a lamp made of an old Indian tea caddy. It was light and bright, comfortable and modern inside, with a stunning view of the sea through the sliding glass doors. She looked the same too, although she now eschewed the tweed skirts and vintage sweaters she had once worn. She was instead casual and relaxed in loose trousers and a tunic top, her now grey hair short and neat, spiked on top in a way that made her look quite edgy. She made me tea and gave the children orange squash and biscuits and a cartoon to watch, so they could rest for a while.

'You look so well, Nora,' I said, happy to see her and full of fondness for her. She had been such a comforting presence in my life. I hadn't realised how much I'd missed her.

'I wish I could say the same for you, little Hélène.' She sat across from me on the white sofa with its bright Mexican throw across the back, and regarded me with concern. 'You look drained.'

I glanced at the children who were sitting in a little connected snug; Lilac was gripped by the television and Jamie was curled up asleep on a bean bag. 'It's been a tough ride.'

'Tell me about it.'

I gave the whole story from the beginning of the previous term, even though she knew some of it, and she listened carefully, sometimes interjecting with a question, but mostly just paying attention as the tale unfolded. When I got to the point of the discovery of the badge, she looked grave, and when I told her what Sylla had said – that Hamish was probably hiding something worse than I knew – she nodded and gave a heavy sigh.

'Oh Helen. I'm sorry. I'm afraid she's probably right. I've said very little about your relationship with Hamish because you're your own person and needed to make up your own mind about things. I'm not necessarily right about people even when I think I can see danger signals. And if you love someone and want to be with them . . . well, nobody's perfect and love is the thing that makes that all right. We can love someone who makes mistakes or has a lot to learn because we are the same. As long as they are sorry for the mistakes and try their best to learn from them.'

I nodded, looking into her kind eyes. 'I hear a "but".'

'Yes. But. There comes a time when you need to make a decision. Are you wasting your time waiting for lessons to be learned? Does your partner really have the intention of learning them? Do they even accept they have made mistakes? Is their remorse real, or assumed – in order to keep you close and invested in the relationship? When you have forgiven and forgiven and forgiven, and all the future holds is more of the same . . . and if you have realised that you will not receive kindness and care and respect in return for that forgiveness, and for the kindness and care and respect you offer . . . well . . .'

Sadness was welling up in me at her words. I knew they were true and every one of them was falling like molten iron into my soul. 'Are you saying my marriage is over?'

'Dear Hélène, I can say no such thing. Some marriages, some partnerships, last wonderfully well. Two people spend their lives together and most of the time they are happy. My parents were devoted to one another. My father died one week after my mother, he couldn't live without her. Your father and I weren't married but as good as. And while he drove me mad in many small ways, in the larger ones, he was all I wanted: kindness itself, loving and supportive, and always my best friend. He came to me at a time in my life when I needed him desperately. Not everyone is so lucky. There are many types of cruelty and not all of them are physical. Just because you are not beaten up, or insulted or kept prisoner – those ideas of cruelty that we accept – doesn't mean you're not suffering. An unfaithful partner, or a deceitful one, or a damaged and sick one, can make our lives unutterably miserable. We are taught it's right to forgive, and that it's our duty to stay faithful ourselves, and to nurture and care for someone who's sick.' Suddenly her eyes flashed. 'But we only have one life. One *precious* life. It is *not* right to sacrifice it for someone who isn't worthy of the sacrifice. Believe me on this. Do you understand?'

I stared back at her, my eyes round. 'Yes.'

She leaned over and took my hand. 'Life is too short to be thoroughly miserable when you are certain beyond all doubt that you cannot be happy with someone. No one wants you to make that sacrifice – no one who loves you, anyway. Even your children will understand because one day you'll be able to tell them why you couldn't do it and why you had to show them that personal integrity mattered more than keeping up appearances. The ideas of service and honour and duty and self-sacrifice are all too often used as a tool by people who do not have those things, to keep those who do in their power, doing what they want.'

I gasped. She had said something important to me, something that chimed and resonated. Hamish knew that I took my marriage vows seriously. That was why he felt he could do what he liked. 'Are you asking if I think I should leave him?'

Nora looked me full in the face, her expression more serious than I had ever seen it. 'No. I'm asking you a different question. Do you think, with all you know, that you can stay?'

The children woke up enough in the evening to go for a scamper on the beach, and Nora and I walked with them, reminiscing about Dad and our lives years ago. Then we came home, gave them supper and put them to bed, before Nora and I sat up late over the meal she had prepared for us and a bottle of good claret.

As we were sitting together afterwards, replete and expansive from the wine, I gathered my courage. I had to ask her now. The time was right.

'Nora, you told me years ago that you grew up around Ballintyre, or, at least, not far away. And yet you never came up to visit us there.'

She looked away, nursing her glass in her hand. 'It was a very long journey. And that was Hamish's territory really. I never felt comfortable invading it. You were only there in the holidays, in any case. You wouldn't miss us.'

'You could have come up for Christmas, we did invite you once or twice . . .'

She shook her head. 'No. It was Hamish's home. His place.'

'You didn't want to go there.'

'To be frank, I didn't.' She looked suddenly sad. 'I did know Ballintyre as a girl, and it has a lot of memories for me. I didn't go back for a reason – it was too difficult.'

I paused, thinking. Was it right to ask her about something she clearly hadn't wanted to tell me? But what was the point of secrets now? 'I want to ask you something, Nora, but you don't have to tell me if you don't want to.'

She was perceptibly more alert, although outwardly just as relaxed as before. 'Yes?'

'I was in Sylla's bedroom last week. It used to be Hamish's parents' room, I think. I'd never been in before and I saw two portraits for the first time. One of Hamish and one of Charlie. And they are by you.'

Her mouth opened but no sound came out. Her cheeks reddened and she looked away, blinking rapidly.

'You don't have to tell me, of course, but . . . how did you come to paint the pictures? Because you never said you already knew Hamish.'

She was silent and I said no more, waiting for her to regain her composure. When she turned to look at me, her eyes were so sad that I almost begged her to stop right there, not wanting to hurt her by any unwelcome recollections. But she started talking before I could say anything.

'I never told you because it's a sad and complicated story that happened many years ago. I thought so hard about it, Helen. But there was no reason why my past should influence your future. When you were invited to Ballintyre for New Year, I could hardly believe it! That invitation with Josephine's name on it . . . I was astonished. But the past seemed far away then, and I thought you would go and have fun, come home and tell me what it had been like to dance at Ballintyre, just as I had years before. I would get a glimpse of my old surroundings and have a furtive, secret look at the lives of those I'd left behind. I never dreamed that you would fall in love with Hamish but once that happened, it was too late to tell you the truth. And besides, if I told you, it would change everything in a way I had no right to do. You're right, of course: I did paint him, when he was a boy, and Charlie too. I knew him then. And I knew his mother.'

'Josephine. So all those years of me telling you what she was like . . .'

'I tried to counsel you in many small ways. I wanted you to protect yourself as best you could against her, and keeping your distance was best for that. I thought that if you and Hamish built a life well away from her, you had a chance. The fact she lived in Scotland while you were in London . . . well, I thought that was fairly safe in terms of allowing you to develop without her. But I didn't count on her being with you all along.'

'What?' I half laughed. 'What do you mean? Was she hiding under the stairs or something?'

'No, my dear child. She was with you all the time – in Hamish. The longer you were married, the more I saw it. He had grown up in her image. I was so sorry for you. I hoped he would grow out of it, that time and fatherhood would mature him, but the longer it all went on, the more certain I was that he was too like her, deep within himself. Perhaps he would have had a chance if his father had lived. But for whatever reason, he wouldn't change.'

I was amazed. 'You knew all along it was doomed?'

'I hoped not. I hoped I was wrong.' She looked very sad.

I shook my head. 'But I don't understand, Nora – how did you know Josephine? Why did you never want to see her again? Because I assume you were also avoiding her when you didn't come up to Ballintyre?'

'It's a long story. Too long for tonight. I'll tell you tomorrow. All of it. I promise.'

It was bright and brisk the next day. Nora took us to Osborne House, and we walked through the house, then went down to the beach past the Swiss Cottage playhouse where Queen Victoria's children had played at being normal little people. As we went, she started to tell me her story, which began nearly fifty years before, conjuring up for me a house on the coast of Scotland, bare and beautiful, where she grew up with her parents and her sister, and she told me of a passion she'd had for as long as she knew: a deep and wild love for James Ballintyre.

'I was only sixteen when he married Josephine, but it broke my heart. He never knew how I felt. I was just a child as far as he was concerned. I knew there was something wrong with her, though I couldn't say what. It was an instinct.'

Down on the beach, she told me how she'd gone to art school in London and how her path had crossed with Josephine's again.

'That disaster sent me hightailing it back to Scotland, back home. But they returned, eventually, as everyone always did. To my relief, she didn't recognise me at all. But it was clear that James was ever more unhappy. I'd promised my mother, who'd guessed my feelings, that I wouldn't go near him, but events brought us together and in one of those magic moments that come only occasionally in our lives, we discovered that we loved one another.'

Her face was transfigured when she said it, illuminated by her remembered happiness. How strange it was that we had both fallen in love at Ballintyre.

'Childhood friends who fell in love,' I said wistfully. 'It's beautiful.'

She nodded. 'But it came too late. He was already married when I transformed from his tomboy friend into the woman he loved. He knew what Josephine was by then, but he couldn't leave.'

We went back home for lunch to warm ourselves up. Over coffee afterwards, with the children amusing themselves with toys and books that Nora magically provided from a huge basket – 'my niece Susie has small children, so I'm well prepared for her visits' – she continued her story.

I was half afraid to hear it. I already knew what the ending of it must be. I knew from Hamish what had happened to his father but he never said that his father had left his mother.

Nora said, 'We were so happy for a while. We had enough happiness to fill my soul until I was lucky enough to meet your father, much later. But it was still not enough. If Josephine hadn't found out, we might have gone for years like that.'

'She found out!'

'Yes. It was terrible.' An expression of pain crossed her face. 'I knew it was a disaster when she caught us together. But I never dreamed that day would be the last time I would see him. I'm glad I didn't. I couldn't have borne it.'

'Nora, I'm sorry. And I know Josephine. She wouldn't have asked why. She would have punished him.'

Nora nodded. 'That's exactly what she did. We were in the wrong, but he knew that, he stuck by her and tried to make it right. She would never forgive. Nothing was enough. I don't believe she was truly wounded by our affair either. She was insulted and angry, but not hurt in her heart that James loved someone else. He had handed her a weapon that she had no intention of putting down. James did what he believed to be right, by standing by her, but he had chosen a lifetime of recrimination and regret.'

'No wonder you couldn't bear to see Josephine. And she never knew our link! I talked about you but she never connected us.'

'She wouldn't have thought about me again, despite what she did to me.'

'Do you mean keeping James?'

'No. I could have understood that. After James's death, I saw her one more time. Then I swore I would never see her again.'

'Will you tell me about it?'

'Later. I can't say more now. It's been exhausting, all this remembering. But I want to say this.' She looked at me seriously. 'James didn't do the wrong thing when he stood by Josephine. He did the right thing but with the wrong person. If she had been capable of what I talked of yesterday – understanding, growth and forgiveness – then it would have been different. But she wasn't. And so, he realised he had made the wrong choice.'

'He made the wrong choice,' I echoed. I frowned. 'And he knew that? He realised that?'

She looked at me with infinite sadness. 'Yes. He realised that. And, in the end, he chose happiness. He chose me.' She took my hand in hers. 'And you should choose happiness too.'

*

As we left Nora to return home, I resolved to see much more of her in the future. She had been so kind, and wise, and I came away feeling renewed and strengthened. I had a lot to think about, but nothing could be done lightly and hastily.

We landed at Glasgow, and I drove us back along the road that wound through mighty hills and beside great lochs, to the beautiful place where we belonged. From the moment I'd arrived at Ballintyre all those years ago, something in me had chimed in response to this landscape with its space, grandeur and austere beauty. This was our home now, and I loved it.

We pulled up to the house late in the evening, the children exhausted again. But I seemed to have shaken off the fatigue that had weighed me down so often lately. Hamish came out to greet us, scoop up the children and take them in for supper. Afterwards, when they were in bed, and Charlie had gone to watch the football on the television, he said, 'So, how was Nora? I haven't seen her in a long time.'

'She was fine. She's made the house look really lovely. She seems happy there.' I had wondered what I would tell him. Nora hadn't told me I mustn't say anything about the past, but it didn't seem my place to reveal secrets about Hamish's parents. What good would it do to tarnish the memory of his father? It was, I decided, up to Josephine to tell him if she ever wanted to, and she hadn't so far.

'Did you have a nice time? Did you enjoy yourself? What was it like?'

I looked up at him, surprised. He wasn't usually so interested in me, yet here he was, asking questions with a faintly anxious air. 'Yes – I had a wonderful time. We loved the seaside, Osborne, the beach. And it was great to see Nora again and talk about Dad.'

He nodded, seemingly satisfied. Then he took my hand and stroked his thumb across my knuckles. His expression was tender. 'I missed you.'

'Really?'

'It was lonely here without you and the kids.'

'Just you, your mother and Charlie.'

Hamish nodded. 'I realised how much I need you.' He lifted my hand to his lips and kissed it softly, raising his eyes to me as he did. Then he said gently, 'I love you, Helen. I don't say it enough, but I do. You're my rock. You're a fabulous mother, a wonderful wife . . . you're everything to me.'

I stared at him, bemused. He hadn't talked like this to me in a very long time. I wanted to believe in it. It was all I had longed to hear from him.

For a moment, I wondered if I'd been too harsh. Perhaps we could be happy, if I just tried a little harder to be forgiving. Life with him wasn't exactly unbearable. We had this marvellous place to raise our children, we had our health, we had so much. And I loved him, despite everything. He was my husband. Maybe a little perspective was all I'd needed.

But as I looked into his eyes, I realised that nothing he said was touching me.

I just don't believe it anymore. And I don't think I ever will again.

Chapter Twenty-Nine

Hamish continued to be angelic towards me the next day, bringing me coffee in bed and asking about my time away. He took the children off for the entire day, promising them a trip to a funfair down the coast, so when a message came in from Sebastian suggesting a walk, I accepted. I cycled down and met him by the Tighglachach gates. From there we wandered slowly down through the woods towards the cove while I told him about my visit to Nora and her connection with Ballintyre. He listened intently, taking it all in.

'So Nora is like a stepmother. Where's your real mother – if you don't me asking?'

'She left when I was little. I never see her now. She's never seen my children. We've not been in touch for a long time.'

'I'm sorry to hear that. You must miss her.'

'I don't really. That's the thing. Nora filled that place in my life. And she still does. I saw her this weekend, and it was wonderful. But what about you? What happened to your mother?'

'She ran off when Eve was a baby. She and Dad had a very volatile relationship – you can imagine what he'd be like to be married to.'

'A tricky customer.'

'Putting it mildly. She also hated the weather here. One day, she just cracked, packed a bag and disappeared back to Greece. She lives there now, happily married again. We visited her most holidays; she never came back here.'

'Really? Then we're the same.'

'Not really. She still loves us, and sees us and takes an interest. You don't have that.'

'No. That's why it's so good to have Nora.'

We walked on for a while, stamping through long grass where the path was overgrown, and Sebastian said, 'If Nora grew up here, then she must have known Dad as well. Shall I ask him?'

'I don't know . . . I suppose it can't do any harm. Perhaps they did know one another. She didn't mention him.'

'It would be weird if they did. But it seems like Nora's been involved here right from the start without you knowing.' He smiled at me. 'I'm glad you've got her to support you.'

I looked at him suspiciously. 'Do I need that right now?'

He sighed. 'We're nearly at the cove. Let's sit down and I'll tell you everything.'

We found a sheltered spot on the grass at the back of the beach and Sebastian took out his phone. 'I promised you I'd talk to Daphne. I saw her yesterday. While you were away, Hamish got in touch with Daphne and suggested a drink with her on Saturday night. He spent the evening with her at the hotel.'

'What? He didn't say!'

'Daphne isn't interested in him, she never really was, even when they were young and she snogged him fairly often. She's very happy with Lars. Even so . . .' Sebastian gave me an apologetic look. 'I'm afraid she said that he was pretty flirty with her.'

I thought of Hamish telling me how bored he'd been at home with his mother and brother, and how much he'd missed me. 'Oh,' I said blankly.

'But that isn't all. Daphne gave me her log-in details so you can take a look at her Facebook page. You wouldn't be able to see otherwise.' He tapped on an icon, and a page sprang to life on the screen of the phone. He handed it to me. 'Daphne said she thought it was odd that he had so few friends. See what you make of it.'

The screen showed Daphne's list of friends. I took it and looked at the profile he was indicating, with a silly cartoon avatar and the name 'Bally H'.

Sebastian said, 'His privacy settings mean you can see his friends, and a few interactions.'

I clicked on the avatar and it took me to a profile. I clicked on the list of friends. There were a dozen or so, and I knew hardly any of them. They were mostly women. Daphne herself was one, of course.

And there, near the end of the alphabetical list, was a smiling photograph of Kaya Stone.

'Oh my God!'

'What?' Sebastian looked concerned as my face flooded scarlet.

'This is the girl he was accused of assaulting! He's friends with her!'

Hamish might have protected his account with some security settings, no doubt so that I could not stumble upon him and see his friends list, but Kaya Stone had no settings. Her timeline and photographs were there for me to see.

Underneath a photograph of Kaya wearing a pair of slippers in the shape of sheep, with black pompom tails on the back, was a comment from Hamish: **Love the slippers, lambkins! H xx**

There were some jokey interactions: emojis back and forth that had to mean something to the two of them. A little dialogue about listening to the same music at the same time.

The most recent thing Hamish had put on Kaya's timeline was to wish her happy birthday. **Wish you were here to celebrate with me!** she wrote.

Maybe one day soon xxx

He had written that two weeks ago.

This was only what I could see. I knew there would be much more that was hidden.

Sebastian read it with me, his face grave. 'I'm so sorry. You're obviously devastated.'

'I am,' I said simply. 'This changes everything.'

'I thought it was better that you knew.'

'Of course it is. This is a shock. But it's not a surprise.'

He put his hand on my arm, his face sympathetic. 'Let me know what I can do to help.'

'Thanks, Sebastian. That's very kind.' I stood up. 'We're close to Sylla's cottage, aren't we?'

He nodded and pointed. 'It's about ten minutes' walk that way.'

'I'd like to go there. I want to talk to her, if I can.'

'Of course. I'll point you in the right direction and leave you to it.'

I smiled gratefully. 'Thanks. I'd appreciate that.'

Sylla was at home, and welcomed me in with a smile.

'Helen, how wonderful to see you. I've been thinking about you. I was going to break my rule and put my phone on to call you. I'm glad you've come round.'

'I wanted to give you this.' I took Rose's watch out of my pocket. I'd put it there just before I left Ballintyre on the off chance I might call round.

'Oh, thank you.' She picked it up and gazed at it lovingly, tears in her eyes. 'I'm so grateful, Helen. Really. It means so much to me.'

'You're welcome. I was glad to be able to get it for you.'

She looked at me questioningly. 'What's happened? Something has.'

'I've found out the truth about Hamish. I think . . . it's the end. It must be.' I shook my head, still disbelieving. 'I feel like everyone – you, Sebastian, and now Nora – you're all telling me to open my eyes.'

'Ah. I see. I'd better make some coffee and you can tell me all about it.'

While she did that, I filled her in on everything that had happened since we last spoke. Her expression was grim as I told her what I had now learned from the Facebook page. We had finished our coffee and had a second cup before I'd finished explaining it all.

'It's obvious that whatever went on then was quite different from what he let me believe. He let me lose my friendships over it. He left me to cope with the fallout from whatever it was he did without even knowing the full story. It's obvious there was no assault. So he must have lost his job for another reason and the only thing I can think of is that he had an affair and got found out.' I closed my eyes in appalled disbelief. 'And he managed to make me believe a completely different version of events.'

'So there you are,' Sylla said. She was sitting across from me on the sofa, her legs tucked up underneath her, listening carefully. 'I've thought very hard about this, Helen, because as you already know, Hamish and Charlie are cut from the same cloth. And here's the rub. They won't change. Because they can't. They can't analyse what they do and why; they act instinctively in their own best interests – or what they think are their interests, even when they are clearly not. I think you're right, Hamish had an affair. Hamish, if he was wise, would have seen that a dalliance of any kind with Kaya was not in his best interests – professionally and personally. But instead he thought, it's what I want and it makes me feel good, so I'll do it, and I'll conceal it in order to protect myself. When the time came to confess, he decided that was not in his best interests. Wise Hamish would have thought, I need to tell Helen everything, be sincerely remorseful and promise not to do any such thing again. Foolish Hamish thinks, I don't want Helen to be cross with me, so I'll lie about this to protect myself.'

'He's always telling me he's doing things for my sake.'

'That's a delusion. Another form of self-protection. Your feelings will not have entered into it.'

'That's what I suspected.'

'Zero empathy. Like Charlie.'

I put my mug down on the table and regarded her solemnly. 'What do I do? Confront him?'

'You can if you like. And I'll tell you exactly how it will play out, if Hamish is what I think he is. But honestly, Helen, you know everything you need to know.'

'It's just another story about a silly unfaithful husband, I suppose,' I said sadly.

She leaned forward, looking at me intently. 'That's where you're wrong. Your story and my story are the same, though mine might sound worse. These are not stories of events, they're stories of character and how character *shapes* events. As long as you have that character in your life, bad events will keep happening. That isn't to say that bad things don't happen in any other circumstances, but with these characters, misfortunes are worse and harder to handle. And they make bad things happen – not on purpose but because they can't help it. Some will be tiny, but others will be huge: a marriage destroyed, a daughter needlessly lost. And always you'll be lied to. Because that's what the character does to protect itself.'

'Then I don't have a choice.'

'No. Once you know, you go. It's the only way.'

'Choose happiness,' I murmured. 'That's what Nora said. She wants that for me, because the choice came too late for her.'

'She's right. Don't wait until it's too late for you.'

When Hamish came home with Lilac and Jamie, he was in a good mood. The children had enjoyed their day but were tired and ready for a quiet afternoon. I put on the television for them and when they were settled, I went to find Hamish. He was in the kitchen, leafing through a newspaper.

'Can you come upstairs with me, Hamish?'

He looked over, instantly alert. 'Ooh, that sounds ominous! Am I in trouble?'

'I need to talk to you.' I turned and walked out, making my way to our bedroom. Hamish followed, still cheerful but very slightly breathless as though he had a touch of nerves.

'What's all this?' he asked as we went in. I sat down on the bed and faced him and he sat in an armchair by the window.

'You went to see Daphne on Saturday night and didn't say anything about it.'

'Oh!' His face cleared. 'Yes, sorry, I should have said. I popped over and we had a quick drink. Nothing to be jealous about.' He grinned.

'I'm not jealous. But you didn't tell me the truth.'

'I never lied!' he protested, injured innocence all over his face. 'I just forgot to mention it.'

'What else have you forgotten to mention?' I fixed him with a firm, unflinching stare. He looked uncomfortable, shifting in his seat.

'What do you mean?'

'Is there anything else you've forgotten to tell me that you should have?'

He looked even more awkward. I could almost see the cogs in his mind working, as though he was assessing what I might have found out and what he could admit to without incriminating himself. I guessed that he dare not say anything.

Sylla had said, *He will act innocent right up until you show him the evidence. Then he'll change position.*

As I looked at him, I suddenly realised that, just as Sylla had said, everything had been about Hamish keeping out of trouble. He was like a naughty schoolboy nicking sweets and eating them in his room and hiding the evidence. That was all it really was to him. Getting what he wanted and avoiding consequences. But it wasn't that to me. To me, it was truth and fidelity and loyalty. It was comfort and kindness. It was the bedrock of things.

'Daphne tells me you're her friend on Facebook.'

He looked simultaneously wary and relieved. 'Oh, that! It's very silly. I should have told you about it. I signed up one day on a whim. I think all of that social media is ridiculous, you know that, and I didn't want to be inundated with friend requests and what have you, so I put in a pseudonym. I hardly ever look at it, if I'm honest.'

That's not true. 'So why did you friend Daphne on it?'

'It was after you met her.'

That's not true either. 'And so you went on Facebook then?'

He shrugged. 'I was just browsing. I hardly ever do that.' He frowned. 'I think it was a pal's birthday actually, so I went on to wish him a happy birthday.'

That's a lie but I can't be bothered with it right now. 'Do you have many friends?'

'A couple. Some old university friends.' He looked at me with a clear and frank gaze. 'Do you want to have a look? I'll show you if you like.'

Oh, this old trick. The honest, open behaviour and the offer that you gamble I won't take up. He had done this with the loan. 'Do you want to see my bank statements?' he'd asked. 'I'll show you right now if you want.' And I had thought, well, he wouldn't offer if he had anything to hide. So I'd said no.

'All right. Show me now.' I stared at him.

'My phone's downstairs,' he said quickly. 'But I can get it if you like.'

And that will give you enough time to delete Kaya as one of your friends. 'No. There's no need right now. That isn't actually what I wanted to talk to you about.'

'What isn't?' he said, looking baffled.

'Daphne. Facebook. That's not what I wanted to talk to you about.'

'It isn't? Sorry, I'm confused now.' He screwed his face up in a frown. 'What's all this about?'

I've seen this before too. Acting confused. Looking as though my questions are so relentless, I've churned up your brain and you don't know which way is up. You want me to stop this interrogation right now and give you some breathing space. But I'm asking reasonable questions. Only someone who was lying could possibly be confused by them.

I said again slowly, 'I don't really want to ask you about Daphne and Facebook. I want to ask you about something else.'

The wary look was back, underneath the innocent confusion he'd affected. 'Okay . . . ?' He shifted awkwardly. Then said suddenly, 'Is this really the time? I've got to get the children's supper on.'

'It can wait.'

'I don't think so, Helen! Do you really want to punish the children by refusing them their supper, just so you can have a go at me?'

He was bringing out all the weapons in his arsenal of manipulation, just as Sylla said he would. *There'll be emotional blackmail, denial, avoidance, a shifting of blame. Watch and see . . .*

I guessed that he wasn't ready for a big confrontation if I had, by some awful chance, found out the truth. Well. That wasn't my problem. I wasn't going to help out by giving him the breathing space he wanted. I had the upper hand for once, and I was not going to surrender it.

'I want to know the truth. I don't expect you to tell me, but that's okay. I do, though, want to hear what you've got to say. Because I still want to hear your side of it. So. Tell me. What happened at Stourhaven? Why did you lose your job?'

Hamish went dead white. He stammered, then went silent. He stared at the floor and began to twist his hands, and then, to my surprise, his eyes filled with tears. 'I told you.'

'You told me that you were falsely accused of assaulting Kaya Stone. Was that true?'

'Yes.'

'Was it?'

'What do you want me to say?' he exclaimed, his eyes still glistening with tears.

'I want you to tell me the truth!'

'I'm trying to, but you won't accept it!'

I shook my head, feeling more sad than anything. He didn't see how pathetic it was. He didn't see how weak it looked to cling to lies and excuses like a child. Why had I not seen it clearly till now? He'd always been like this, just never on this scale. Had I let it happen? Was I responsible? Did that even matter?

'All right. We don't have to go on like this. I know what happened,' I said simply. 'I know it all.'

'Know what?' he demanded.

'I called Katie today. She told me everything.' I had rung her on the way back from Sylla's cottage. She'd not been able to believe that I hadn't known. *We all thought you were standing by him. We thought you knew. And he told you something else?*

Hamish said nothing, staring at the floor and looking agonised.

'I know that you and Kaya Stone were having an affair. I know that you were discovered together and reported. Your employment was terminated not because she accused you of assault, but because you were guilty of having an inappropriate sexual relationship with someone who was in your professional care, someone years younger than you. She resigned as well but you were forced to go. And you gambled that no one would tell me, because everyone would assume I knew the truth but was standing by you. None of them spelled it out to me because they didn't think they had to. And I never guessed. I suppose if that ruse hadn't worked, you'd have come up with some other story.'

He continued to stare at the floor with a fixed expression somewhere between anguish and fear. He looked like a child being carpeted by a stern parent.

'What do you say to this, Hamish? Am I right? Did you have an affair with Kaya?'

'Not an affair,' he said weakly. 'Nothing as serious as that. It was just a friendship that got out of hand. It was flirty, playful. I shouldn't have done it. I regret it and it was a mistake. I'm sorry.'

'So just like that . . . you've denied it but now you admit it. Now you know I know. And you're sorry. That's it?'

'What do you want me to say?' he cried. 'I was ashamed and I tried to hide it. But, yes, I shouldn't have done it! It's just difficult to deal with you when you're so angry.'

'I'm not angry – at least, I'm not acting angrily. I'm not shouting, I'm not swearing or throwing things.'

'You are angry, though,' he said.

'I suppose on some level, yes, I am angry.'

'There you are then.'

I took a moment to breathe, then said in an even tone, 'And this playful friendship – is it over?'

'Of course.' He sighed as though he was exhausted and beaten. 'I haven't seen her since Stourhaven. She's gone back to Australia, I think.'

'And you haven't been in touch at all?'

'No.'

I let out a long breath. This would never end, I could see that. As long as he could deceive me, he would. 'You wished her a happy birthday on Facebook two weeks ago. I can't see your private messages. For all I know, you're in touch all the time.'

'So you're spying on me! Fine! Look at my messages then!' he shouted. 'Look at them! Look at everything, I don't care! This is like some kind of police state! Yes, I'm in touch with her, but only because it's nice every once in a while to talk to someone who doesn't hate me! Is it so bad that I like to be appreciated every now and then?'

I stared at him, a feeling of immense sadness welling up inside me. He wasn't really ashamed, he was just annoyed to be caught. He wasn't remorseful, he was just embarrassed, and he was doing all he could to turn the tables and make himself the victim. He'd had a relationship because I was mean to him. He'd lied because he had to. And one feeble apology was supposed to make all the lies and all the deception and all the shattering of trust just go away.

'I made a mistake, I told a lie and I'm sorry.'

'You lied every day for months, right up until a moment ago. Every day you let me believe things that weren't true, you were lying to me. And you took that decision, day after day. You were never going to make any other decision, as long as you could get away with it.'

'I was trying to protect you,' he said in a broken voice. 'I thought it would be easier for you if you didn't know.'

'Easier for *me*?' My voice was rising, despite my intention to stay calm. 'Easier for *you*!'

Abruptly, his face crumpled and he started to weep. 'I'm so sorry. I know it's awful. Please, Helen, what are you going to do? You can't leave me. What about the children? What about our lives and everything we've meant to each other?'

I thought of what Nora had said just two days before, about how fidelity and forgiveness were used by people who didn't have those qualities to keep those who did under control. I regained my calm with an effort.

'You didn't think about those things when you had your little fling. When you were caught and lost your job, you only tried to protect yourself.'

He was sobbing hard now, knuckling at his eyes like a child. 'I wanted to protect you! And us.'

'It's too late for that now. I never thought you'd do such a thing.'

'We're just friends!' he said desperately. 'You're reading too much into it!'

'If you're friends, why lie about it? Why hide your Facebook profile? You act guilty! You look guilty! And you still want me to disbelieve the evidence of my own eyes.' I stood up. 'No, Hamish. I can't take this anymore. This isn't the marriage I want. I can't trust you. I'll never trust you again. Without trust, there's nothing.'

He stared at me, his blue eyes burning through his tears. He looked indignant, angry and . . . thwarted? Was that a cross look I could see on his face? Like a child who wants to stamp his foot because he can't get his own way.

'No apology is ever good enough for you! Fine. Have it your own way!' he shouted, and turned on his heel. He stormed out, slamming the door behind him. A minute later I heard the front door, a crunch on the gravel and then the engine of our car start up and grow fainter as it went further away.

The last thing he'll do is withdraw, Sylla had said. *When it all gets too much, he'll go.*

She was right.

He had gone.

I was bringing our luggage down into the hall, Lilac and Jamie upstairs playing, when Charlie came out of the kitchen to see what was going on.

'What are you doing?' he said suspiciously, looking at our luggage in the hall.

'We're going off to stay with some friends for a while,' I said, brushing past him to get up the stairs. I had texted Sebastian to ask him if he knew somewhere we could stay for a while, and he messaged back at once that he was on his way to collect us. 'Excuse me, I'm getting the last of our bags.'

'Does Hamish know about this?'

'Not yet. But he will.'

'Where is he?'

'I don't know. And I don't care.'

Charlie stared for a moment longer, then went back into the kitchen. I guessed he must have phoned Josephine when I came down with the last of the luggage and saw her through the window, hurrying up the drive towards the house, going as fast as she could, her face red and her eyes staring. I was piling everything up when she came in.

'What are you doing, Helen?' she demanded, seeing our piles of things. 'Where's Hamish?'

'He's gone, I'm afraid, Josephine.'

'Gone? Gone where?'

'I don't know. But he's rather selfishly taken the car along with the children's seats. Which is annoying.'

'Where are you taking them?'

'Away for a while.'

'Without Hamish?'

'That's right.'

'And you don't know where he's gone? That's terrible! How can you be so uncaring?'

I turned to face her, taking in her stocky, barrel body in its sensible skirt and cardigan, her furious expression, and the reddened hands on her hips. She was staring at me with accusing eyes and righteous indignation. I thought of all the pain and misery she had caused in her life and how it had spread out: to Nora, whose life she'd ruined, and whose money she took and never returned, leaving her penniless. Perhaps I should thank Josephine for that. Without that,

Nora would never have moved to our town and met my father. But it was a high price to pay. She'd lost her love, her house, her money, her reason for existing.

'And on top of everything else, I lost all my hair,' Nora had laughed.

'Your wild tawny hair in its mad bandanas?' I'd asked.

'A wig. My long dark hair fell out in handfuls until I only had bits of fuzz and fluff left, and didn't grow back for years. And the strange thing was, I didn't mind. With the wig, I became someone else. Not Tigs, who'd lost James. But Nora: colourful, happy, new. It helped me survive. I don't know what would have happened to me otherwise.'

I thought of Alastair Drummond telling me what Sylla had said on the beach. *I don't want to be me anymore.*

I stared at Josephine. *You nearly killed Nora*, I thought. *And you nearly killed Sylla.*

'You knew, didn't you?' I said suddenly.

'What? What are you talking about?'

'You knew all along that Charlie had been in the boat with Rose that day. I bet you covered up for him, didn't you? Did you tell him to lie about it, lie to the coroner, to the police, to his wife, to protect his own miserable skin? You knew how much Sylla suffered, believing Rose had gone out on her own when she'd been told not to. Even when Sylla disappeared, you still only wanted to protect Charlie. You didn't care what might have happened to her.'

Josephine had gone pale, her jaw set except for a muscle twitching in her lower cheek. She had a look in her eyes I didn't recognise. And then I realised what it was. She looked afraid.

'I'm right, aren't I? You both lied. Charlie, because he's a coward. And you, because nothing matters more than your boys, whatever they do, however low they stoop. Not even your precious granddaughter mattered more. How can you look at yourself in the mirror? How can you sleep at night?'

'Don't you dare speak to me like this!' she retorted but without her usual ferocity. I had struck a nerve at last. The last vestige of feeling she had. It was still, I suspected, self-protection and protection of Charlie. But lying to the police and the coroner was a serious matter. Not just the feelings of two hysterical and silly daughters-in-law. It could mean a fine. Prison.

I smiled bleakly. There was pleasure in this triumph but it was still bitter. 'I have a witness who saw Charlie in the boat, and what happened afterwards. I'm sure the authorities would like to hear about it. It would make quite a story, not just here, but everywhere.'

Charlie had come out of the kitchen and was listening in the corridor, his eyes terrified.

'You are a vile and unspeakable woman,' Josephine declared. 'Hamish should never have married you. I told him you weren't right. I said you weren't suitable for a life in a place like this but he insisted. And now you've ruined his life. Who knows where he's gone to get away from you?'

I laughed mirthlessly. 'Attack, attack. It's the best form of defence, isn't it, Josephine? You can attack me all you like but it doesn't change a thing. I know the real reason Hamish has gone: because he can't face what he's done, any more than you can. But we know. Sylla. Me. Nora. We know who you are and what you are. And it all stops now.'

'Nora? *Nora?*' Josephine looked appalled. 'Who?'

'Leonora. Tigs. Nora. My stepmother. She told me the truth about you. She told me everything.'

Josephine howled, her eyes stretched wide. 'How dare you? How dare you say her name to me!'

'Mum!' Charlie came hurrying along the corridor and grabbed her. She collapsed heavily into his arms, panting and sobbing. 'Mum, calm down. Control yourself.'

'Good luck with that,' I said scornfully. I cared nothing for either of them now. I just wanted to get as far away as I could as quickly as possible.

Just then, there was a knock at the door and Sebastian put his head around it. 'Hello?' he said loudly over the sound of Josephine's bellowed sobs. 'Helen, is everything okay?'

'It's fine,' I said. 'Thanks for coming to get us. Would you mind putting this stuff in the car? I'll get the children. Then we can leave.'

'Sure.' He came into the hall, picked up some bags and went out.

'Where are you going?' demanded Charlie over his mother's crying, which was beginning to subside as she realised something was going on.

'That's none of your business,' I said. 'I'll talk to Hamish about that, when he decides to get in touch. Right now, we're leaving. And I suggest you think hard about what you want to happen next. If it were up to me, we wouldn't hesitate to report you to the police. We'll see what Sylla wants.'

'You know where she is?' he said.

'Yes. She's safe and well. Not that you care.'

Charlie looked suddenly broken. His life was collapsing around his ears. His beloved daughter was gone, his wife was gone, he was left with only his impossible mother in a house full of memories.

Don't feel sorry for him, I cautioned myself. I remembered what Sylla had said: *Feeling sorry for them is your greatest weakness. Just remember that they never feel sorry for you.*

Sebastian came back in to get the last of the bags. 'Ready when you are, Helen.'

I smiled at him. 'Thanks. I'm getting Lilac and Jamie now. Then we leave.'

When I came back with the children, Sebastian took them to the car. Josephine was quieter now, sitting in the hall chair, her cheeks wet, breathing hard as if with the aftermath of shock. Charlie stood, his shoulders slumped, by the front door.

'Helen,' he said as I picked up my bag and went to leave. His eyes were pleading. 'Tell her I'm sorry, will you? I mean it. I'm sorry. It was the worst thing that ever happened. I hope she'll forgive me.'

'I'll tell her,' I said as I headed out. 'But I doubt you'll see her again. You and Josephine deserve each other. Good luck, Charlie. And goodbye.'

'What about me?' screeched Josephine. 'You can't take those children, they're all I have left!'

I turned slowly to face her. My anger faded away as I looked at her hunched form and the tears on her face. I didn't need to punish her. She punished herself every day just by being herself. 'Goodbye, Josephine.'

Then I turned on my heel, and walked out of Ballintyre. I would never go back as long as Josephine was there.

I walked out into the open air, breathing it in deeply, feeling free at last.

PART FOURTEEN

Chapter Thirty

NORA

2019

Helen collected me at Glasgow airport, her bright face smiling at me as I emerged from the arrivals area.

'Nora! Here I am!' She was waving at me, jumping up and down for my attention, which made me laugh.

'You seem very happy to see me,' I said, putting my arms around her for a hug.

'I am.'

'In fact, you seem happier all round,' I said as we went to find her car. She was so much more at ease than during her visit to me in the Isle of Wight, before things finally resolved. For years now, I'd seen her weighed down with worry and anxiety, trying to cope with so much. I'd always known that Hamish wasn't capable of supporting her in the way she needed. I had feared from the start that he would slowly suck her life and energy away until she was left hollow and bitter. To see her like this again – light and free and happy – was a joy. Whatever she had been through, it was probably worth it to get her old self back again.

'I am. Much happier.' She smiled at me. 'I'll tell you all about it as we go.'

I listened as she chattered on, mostly about the children and how they were getting on at their new school, what they loved to do in their spare time and how Jamie had caught his first mackerel. It was lovely stuff but eventually I asked apologetically if she would mind if I dozed off for a while. The journey had been long and I was tired.

'Of course! Rest. We have all the time we need.'

So I closed my eyes and slept.

When I woke, the landscape was familiar: the grand, unchanging hills of Scotland, soft yet fierce and austere, and her lochs. What a land rich in stone and water she was. I had missed this solid, mournful landscape. I had stayed away now for nearly forty years, unable to return to the place I'd been happiest.

How strange it had been when Helen received that invitation to Ballintyre, all those years before. The memories were bittersweet by then. Her father Gordon had come into my life when I was ready, at last, to love again, after many years of mourning for James and blaming myself for his death. I blamed myself too for the loss of Tremewan. We had been fortunate. The Gillygantry estate had bought the house from us before the foreclosure of the loan, and we had been able to repay what we owed. My parents already had their little cottage, thank goodness. Serena took her half of the purchase price, and I had what was left after my loan to James had been repaid – enough for a down payment on a tiny house in a quiet town and a life that was small enough to bear.

It had taken a long while to heal. First, I had started to paint, and then I had found I could love, not just Gordon but his daughter too: a suspicious young woman who had finally relaxed and learned to trust me when she was sure I would not run off as her mother had done, and break her father's heart all over again. When Helen had inadvertently brought Ballintyre back into my life, I'd assumed it would be short-lived. Her long association with it had been entirely unexpected. Her marriage to Hamish was a turn of events I could not have foreseen but there was an odd happiness in it. In a strange way, James and I shared grandchildren, and I often thought of another unrealised life, where we enjoyed the pleasure of them together. It gave a poignancy to my role in their life as surrogate grandmother. I knew how much he would have loved them. How touched he would have been that Hamish's son was named after him. I was glad he was spared the tragedy of losing Rose.

But all this was just a dream. He had not seen his grand-children. He had died in a crash on his way to reach me. I could never know what he was thinking or how it happened, or what might have been my life if he had not left this world on the road that night.

What was not a dream was that, through Helen's marriage, Josephine became a part of my life, and I was part of hers, though I stayed hidden in the shadows, never showing myself at family occasions or breathing a word to anyone about our shared past. I had taken my vow. I would never see her again. No matter what.

'This is all very familiar,' I said, as we took the road along the loch, the one that undulated gently for miles until eventually it reached Ballintyre.

'How are you feeling?'

I considered. 'All right, really. But the biggest challenges are yet to come.'

'Of course.' Helen gave me a sympathetic look. 'Just say any time you need a break, or a moment.'

'I will.' I rested my head and watched the loch slide past the window. There was the great ferry – larger and more modern now – and the sailing boats bobbing at their moorings. Little fishing smacks were pressed up against jetties, tied fast with coils of rope, and motorboats puttered gently through the grey water on their way here and there.

At last, knowing where we were, I looked up. Helen was slowing and a moment later we were turning through the gates of Ballintyre, then climbing the drive, before coming to a stop in front of the house.

My heart beat hard as I remembered the last time I'd been there, for the dreadful interview with Josephine. And the time before that, when I'd come to paint the boys. And the night I'd come as the Winter Queen and stolen James's heart.

'Are you okay?' Helen said, taking off her seat belt.

'Yes. Yes. I'll be all right.'

'I promise there are no nasty surprises. You're going to be fine.'

I got out of the car and looked properly at the house. The grey granite front, the turreted towers and the gracious old windows. It was still the same, on the outside at least. 'Come on then. I'm ready.'

Helen led the way, and opened the arched front door for me. I stepped inside.

'Oh. It's different.'

'It certainly is.' Helen smiled. 'Come into the drawing room.'

I followed her and gasped. All of Josephine's frills and flounces were gone. Her fitted carpet and fancy lights with the dripping crystals and fake wax had vanished. The ruched and draped curtains with their tiebacks and tassels had disappeared. The room reminded me now of the ballroom at Tremewan: classic and beautiful. The floorboards were polished and covered in faded antique rugs. There were shutters at the windows and long elegant curtains in plain linen. The walls were the palest blue and the paintings had been rehung to their best advantage. The sofas were covered, the chairs reupholstered in plain and simple fabrics with bright cushions to enliven them. An Ottoman in a Turkish kilim provided a small riot of pattern and colour.

I turned to Helen. 'It's lovely. Ballintyre never looked like this before.'

She smiled. 'It isn't down to me. It's all Sylla's work, I can't take the credit.'

Just then, a woman came in through the drawing room door. 'Hello,' she said, her expression bright and friendly. She was a little older than Helen but looked timeless with her pale hair back in an elegant bun and her skin tissue-fine over the good bones beneath. 'You must be Nora. I've heard so much about you.'

'And I about you.' I smiled back at her. 'How very nice to meet you at last. And you've wrought this transformation on the house?'

'Yes.' Sylla looked around, pleased. 'It was good to be able to get my hands on it properly after all these years. Josephine wouldn't let anyone change her decoration even though it was well past its sell-by date.'

'We all paid a high price for those frills,' I murmured but the others didn't hear me.

'Sylla's done such a good job that other people want her to decorate for them!' Helen announced, clearly proud of her sister-in-law. 'Lars and Daphne think her aesthetic is just right for Gillygantry. And perhaps for Tighglachach.'

'Tighglachach?' I raised my eyebrows. 'Do they own that too?'

'No.' Helen coloured a little. 'But Sebastian is thinking about bringing it temporarily into the business. It's so big. Alastair won't hear of a hotel, but he might be open to the house being used as a sort of holiday home. A retreat. There are lots of ideas washing around. But the house needs a big makeover in any case.'

'Alastair is still there, is he?'

'Oh yes. I hope you'll come with me when I go up tomorrow.'

I gave her a warm look. 'You and Sebastian spend a lot of time together.'

'Of course.' She coloured still more. 'We work together.'

I nodded. 'Well, that makes sense.' Sylla and I exchanged knowing glances. 'Now, where are the children? I want to say hello! And a cup of tea would not go amiss either . . .'

I spent a happy afternoon in the Ballintyre kitchen, enjoying the company of Lilac and Jamie, and still taking in the transformation of the house. It looked far more beautiful than I'd realised was possible. Not only that, but there was a newly acquired ease about it, as though problems had been addressed and solved, and the house was now fit for a family to live in comfortably. It was in service to them, not them to it.

Helen took me out for a walk around the garden while it was still light, and showed me the walled garden where Sylla did all her growing. 'And there's a workshop behind the house, a little unit really, where she does all the making and bottling.'

'Oils?'

'Botanical oils and potions and salts. Salves and candles. Lots of wonderful things for skincare and wellbeing. It's just a little business for now, but who knows how it will grow? Things flourish so well in the walled garden.'

'It's a wonderful idea.' I looked around at the neat, well-kept garden, the polytunnel running along one wall, the greenhouse along another, and the raised beds and borders. The place buzzed with life despite the cold and the season. 'I admire what you girls are doing here. You're really making a go of turning Ballintyre into a business.'

Helen nodded. 'We can't rely on subsidies forever. The land brings in a certain amount, and we got the payment for the wind farm across the way. But we have to keep moving in lots of directions.'

'Well done to you both. This part of the world has a buzz about it suddenly.'

Helen laughed. 'A newly acquired chic. Lars is putting a lot of money into his hotels and retreats, and marketing them in Germany and Scandinavia. That's going to bring in tourists and raise the profile, which is all good for us.'

We stopped on the other side of the walled garden. Below us, shielded by ridges of pines, was the old kirk. Helen put her hand on my arm, her expression sympathetic and enquiring. 'Do you want to go down?'

I shook my head. 'Tomorrow.'

We walked together back to the house.

'I like this new version of Ballintyre,' I said.

'The one without any Ballintyres in it?' she laughed.

'I admire the way you managed to extricate them, let me put it like that.'

Helen's expression grew solemn. 'We laugh about it, but it was very hard for all of us.'

'Have you heard from Hamish?'

'Sometimes. He has online chats with the children every few days. He seems to be enjoying life in Australia.' She shook her head. 'I had him down as a lot of things, and I certainly knew he was capable of running away from problems, but even I was surprised when he actually ran away. Properly away. About as far away as he could possibly get.'

'And is he with that girl, the one from the school?'

'No, that didn't last. But he's got a girlfriend – young, active, outdoorsy. He seems happy. The downside is that he's too far away to see the children regularly.' She gave me a sideways look. 'That's both good and bad, as you can imagine. They miss him. But he can't teach them his own particular brand of life lesson and I'm relieved about that. I suppose they'll want to see him more in the future, which will be interesting. They might want to go there. But he might come back.'

'And by then, you'll have given them enough armour to protect them.'

She smiled at me. 'That's the idea.'

I hesitated a moment. 'And Josephine?'

'Gone with Charlie. Hamish and Charlie surrendered their interest in the house – in return for us giving up our interest in their pensions and all the other trusts Josephine had set up for them. Various investments have paid off and she's been squirrelling it all away for herself and the boys, but she didn't factor in that we'd be entitled to our share. So quite a lot of bargaining had to go on. She was furious that Sylla and I got this place but she'd made the mistake of putting the house in the boys' names. And . . . well, we had a certain leverage over them. Josephine screamed and complained and threw the most almighty tantrum, but she knew she didn't really have a choice. So she packed up and went with her golden boy. Charlie's managed to convince an estate in Inverness to take him on as a manager, goodness knows how. They went there.'

'Then it's all worked out.'

Helen said slowly, 'Better than I could have imagined. If you'd told me that my marriage could end so painlessly, I would never have believed you. To be honest, I think I had all the pain beforehand in the miserable years of confusion. I didn't know how unhappy I was, or how difficult life with Hamish was. Everything is so much easier now. I'm happy. And so are the children.'

I squeezed her hand. 'I'm so glad.'

'So am I. And there's something else I managed to persuade Josephine to do.' She pulled a slip of paper out of her pocket and handed it to me. I opened it out and saw, to my astonishment, a cheque for a sizeable sum, Josephine's signature at the bottom. 'The money she owed you. She's made it back several times over from her investments. So it's only fair.' Helen grinned at me and said, 'You can imagine how well that went down with her!'

I laughed wryly, imagining how it must have tormented her to hand back my money. 'I appreciate this, Helen. I don't think I can accept it, though.'

'Don't think about it now. You can think about it later, and decide then. There's no hurry.'

I slept very well in my lovely bedroom at Ballintyre. I had worried that I would be haunted by all the ghosts of my past that must surely reside in the house, but Sylla's remaking of it seemed to have banished them. Besides, Josephine was gone, kicked out screaming by the women who were strong enough together to take her on and vanquish her.

That brought me a peace I hadn't known in a very long time. It was as though when she'd yelled at me that day, all those horrible words she'd flung at me had stayed ringing in my ears for all these years. Until now. She was silenced. It had been a long time coming but I was, at last, free of her and, in some small way, thanks to Helen and Sylla, triumphant.

Over breakfast the next morning, Helen said, 'Where do you want to go? Tremewan or Tighglachach?'

I considered. 'You know . . . I think Tremewan first. It was always so wonderful first thing and last thing. Yes. Tremewan first, I think.'

We set off, just the two of us, along that familiar road to the coast, where my old and beloved home looked out over the strip of sand and sea, its dear white face still turned outwards to that spectacular view.

'It's certainly different,' I said, as Helen pulled the car to a stop in front of the house. 'Much smarter than when we were here!'

Tremewan looked like an old friend who'd had quite the makeover. The white render was fresh and clean, immaculate window boxes on every sill, well-behaved climbers trained up neat trellises, beautiful border and box hedges lining every neatly gravelled path. Discreet signs pointed to spas, tennis courts, terraces and gardens.

'Do you like it?' Helen said anxiously.

'Very much,' I said firmly. 'It still feels welcoming. The spirit is still here. And I loved sharing this place with people, so I'm delighted it's doing that today, and so well.'

'Shall we go in and look around?'

'Yes, but . . . would you mind if we go to the beach first?'

We skirted around the house, past what was obviously now a very smart and professional kitchen, and took the path down to the sea, over our sloping lawn, across the rough grassy dunes and down to the sand. Then we walked along the shore where the waves broke in their ceaseless roar, to my thinking rock.

'This is where I used to sit and dream,' I said to Helen.

'It's a wonderful spot.'

'Just the place for imagining.'

We sat on the smooth hollow area, like a natural seat, where I used to tuck my legs up under me and gaze out to sea. I did the same now, thinking about those who were once here and now were gone.

'I suffered very much when we lost this place,' I said thoughtfully. Helen listened in sympathetic silence. 'It was ridiculous really. My parents had been ready to leave it for years, and my sister didn't care about it in any case. Only I cared. I'd appointed myself its saviour, whether everyone else wanted it or not, and when I was then the reason for our losing it, I was devastated.' I glanced at her. 'It came at the same time as other losses.'

'I understand,' she said quietly. I had told her that weekend on the Isle of Wight about how I'd lost James. She knew what I meant.

'And I thought I couldn't bear it. But I could. And now here I am again. My rock is still here, the house is still here. The people I loved are gone.'

'What does that tell you?'

'Love people – they are the ones who are so briefly here. Love while you can. The places pass from one hand to the next, from one generation to the next, and are remade. But we only have one life, one precious life. We must do all we can with it. Love all we can.'

Helen nodded. 'Forgive our own mistakes. Forgive others. Move on.'

'You've got it.'

After a moment, she said, 'Shall we go inside?'

'You betcha,' I answered. 'Before my fingers fall off from the cold.'

Daphne Drummond came to say hello to us as we had our coffee in what had been my ballroom, the place I'd spent so many hours painting.

'I saw you as a child,' I told her. 'You were at a fancy dress ball, a tiny angel with wings, in your father's arms. I knew you'd grow up to be a beauty, just like your mother.'

Daphne looked touched. 'Thank you, Nora, what a lovely thing to say.'

She sat and chatted to us for a while and then went off to oversee the business of the hotel.

'She's a force to be reckoned with,' I said thoughtfully, as her elegant form disappeared.

'I know,' Helen said, draining her cappuccino. 'I'm in awe of her.'

'If her brother is anything like as good-looking, then I can understand his attraction,' I said dryly, and was pleased to see Helen blush and call quickly for the bill.

'Let's go to Tighglachach,' she said.

'Yes. I'd like that. I'm ready.'

It wasn't a long drive back down the coast road to Tigh-glachach. The old gate pillars looked more decrepit than ever as we drove through them, Helen's ease with their narrow dimensions betraying how often she'd negotiated them in the past. A moment later, we'd pulled up in front of the old house I remembered so well. It was looking better than I'd feared.

'We've been slowly sprucing it up,' Helen said. 'Alastair is very resistant, though. He wants to do everything himself and he's not really up to as much as he thinks he is. Sebastian has forbidden him to go on the roof but he's always trying to get up there. We've had to hide the long ladders.'

I smiled at her, loving the way she was betraying her in-timacy with the family in every sentence. She was still trying to pretend that nothing was going on with her and Sebastian, as though she had to go through a certain period of mourn-ing for her marriage before she could love again, like a Victorian widow wearing her crêpe for a year.

'And Al is here?' I asked.

'Yes.'

'Good. I want to see him.'

We got out of the car and walked across the drive to the front door. Inside, the hall looked fresher and cleaner than I was expecting.

'We've been clearing out, bit by bit,' Helen said. She indi-cated some taxidermy in glass cases. 'There was quite a lot of that. We've moved it around, as it was a bit overpowering otherwise. And finally getting Alastair to throw some things away. He's rather a hoarder.' She walked to the middle of the room. 'Hello? We're here!'

A moment later, a very handsome man came striding into the room, his face beaming as soon as he laid eyes on Helen. 'Here you are!' He hugged her quickly and then turned to me. 'And you must be the famous Nora.'

I looked him up and down, seeing Al there, and the legacy of Dimitra's dark beauty. He had expressive dark eyes, full of intelligence and warmth, a strong jaw and a full mouth. 'I am. And you're the famous Sebastian.'

He looked pleased. 'Am I famous?'

'I've heard a lot about you.'

'All good, of course,' Helen said hastily. 'Now, I think we're supposed to be tracking Alastair down . . .'

'He's in the garden,' Sebastian said, 'if he hasn't made a break for the roof again.'

We walked through the hall and out via a shabby old drawing room to the garden. I saw him at once: a tall but stooped figure sitting at a wooden table, fidgeting, one leg jiggling up and down. And then, he jumped up and went over to one of the beds, where he began scrabbling about.

'Dad!' called Sebastian. 'Our visitor is here.'

He turned around, saw me and froze.

'Come on,' Helen said, and we walked down the stone steps to the lawn.

Al, finding his power of movement again, was staring at me, and began walking towards me. 'Well!' he exclaimed. 'Well, well. Here you are.'

'Here I am,' I confirmed, smiling. His hair was quite white and he had bushy eyebrows, also white, over his dark eyes. He looked older. But so did I.

'Back so soon,' he said, and smiled at his own joke.

Helen and Sebastian helped arrange us at the table, promised to bring out tea, and then disappeared.

'Those young people seem very fond of one another,' I said, watching them go.

'Yes.' Alastair beetled his brows. 'I'm pleased about it. It's keeping him here, and she's a delight. I just hope it all works out. I try not to interfere.' He leaned towards me confidentially. 'If anything, I play up being a bit of a useless old man. It gives them a mission, a reason to work together. Part of my grand plan.'

'It's a very good one.'

'How are you, young Tigs?'

'Young! I'm sixty-seven, Al! I'm not young anymore.'

'You'll always be young to me,' he said firmly. 'Young Tigs. Not Nora, or whatever they call you now.'

'Well . . . all right.'

There was a pause. 'I know you've had some pain in your life, Tigs. I was so sorry when James died. Very sorry for you.'

'That's generous. I know you didn't rate him.'

'I loved him too, though you won't believe me. I was desperately jealous of him because you loved him best of all. It was a great shock when he died, and I imagine much worse for you.'

'It was terrible,' I said simply. 'But also a long time ago.' After a moment, I said, 'And you've known sadness too. It didn't work with Dimitra.'

'I'm impossible,' he said shortly. 'I've always known that. She couldn't stand me. No one could. Well, perhaps my children can, in very small doses.' He looked over and smiled. 'You could once. From time to time.'

'We were always good friends.'

'Yes. Always that. One of the few who understood me.' He made a wry face. 'My tragedy was that you didn't love me.'

'Perhaps mine was that I couldn't.'

He laughed shortly. 'Maybe you're right.' He reached in his pocket for something. 'Knowing you were coming, I looked this out for you.' He took the object out and put it on the table in front of me. It was a dull coin.

'What is it?' I said, squinting at it. 'I need my glasses.'

'It's a coin. Half a crown. I won it off you by reciting the Book of Obadiah by heart.'

I laughed heartily. 'Oh my goodness, I remember that! My half-crown! I was keeping it for a souvenir when they brought in the new money.'

'Why don't you have it back?' he said and pushed it towards me.

'No. It's yours. You won it. I'm impressed that you kept it all this time.'

'I suppose that it meant something to me.'

'Well, that's nice.'

We sat in companionable silence for a few moments.

'So you're back?' he asked.

'For a while.'

'But you'll come back again?'

'I'm sure I will. Often. Helen is my daughter. Not the daughter I never had, but the daughter I did have.'

Al looked satisfied. 'Good,' he said. 'Good.'

'And I suspect she'll be a daughter to you too. In time.'

'So do I.'

We smiled at each other, finding pleasure in the knowledge that our two young people were finding love with one another.

'Yes,' I said. 'I think I will come back. Often.'

'I know.' He looked at me, his black eyes warm under his beetling eyebrows. 'You see, everyone always comes back. In the end.'

Epilogue

TIGS

2019

Before I left Ballintyre, I took the walk to the kirk that I'd been promising myself. It was a stern grey day, when the land and the sky made a pact to share the same colours of steel and mud. I had a bunch of late roses, though, that Sylla had gathered for me from the garden.

I stood at his grave in the churchyard alone. Tomorrow I'd go home, back to my cosy house. But I had to do this first.

'Here I am, James. I'm back at last,' I said aloud. 'I wanted to come to you before now, but I couldn't. I couldn't as long as she was here, like the angel at the Gates of Paradise, holding up the sword to stop me. But she's gone and I've come home.'

I waited as though expecting an answer but there was nothing.

'I know you were coming to me. I know you wanted us to have a life together and that our love was everything to you. It was for me, too. I still dream about what life would have been if you'd arrived safely that night.'

I stopped, thinking of those years of dreaming and longing and grieving. How glad I was that they were over.

'I'll never know what you were thinking at the end. But I believe you were thinking of me, as I was thinking of you. I'll always love you, James. You were my great love. My life was built around you for so many years.'

There was no sound in the graveyard. I listened, as though hoping I might hear his voice, as I had sometimes, at times when I'd needed it.

Perhaps I did not need it now. Not in the same way I once had. I still had a life to live. Years to fill. Things to do.

'Life is good,' I told him. 'I'll always miss you, my love. But life is good. We only have one life, one precious life. You live on in me. And in your children, and your grandchildren. I'll look after them, you can be sure of that. For as long as I'm here.'

I heard a cuckoo in the pines, a sweet sound echoing over the loch. Spring was coming. Winter was nearly over.

I carefully put down the flowers, blew a kiss to his grave and started the walk back to Ballintyre.

Acknowledgements

Thank you, as always, to the marvellous team at Pan Macmillan, who've been so patient, kind and supportive over the somewhat delayed writing of this book. My wonderful editor, Wayne Brookes; Alex Saunders, now powering on to his own author list; Samantha Fletcher and Charlotte Wright; publisher Jeremy Trevathan. Rosie Wilson is my wonderful publicist, Lucy Wai masterminds the marketing, Stuart Dwyer and his team do brilliant sales combat. Neil Lang designed another stunning cover. Thank you all so much.

Lorraine Green went above and beyond to help me restructure this book, and edited with all her usual skill and wisdom. I appreciate her encouragement more than I can say. Thank you, too, to Pippa Wickenden, who proofread with an eagle eye.

Over the last year and a half, we have all had testing times and challenges to cope with. This book should have appeared in 2020 but I didn't finish it until this year. So many people helped me over this time. My superb agent Lizzy Kremer, and Maddalena Cavaciuti and Kay Begum, at David Higham.

ACKNOWLEDGEMENTS

Paul Laikin and Lucie Donahue, who read and encouraged and advised and took sincere interest in my progress. Ophelia Field, Helen Robertson, Emily Hamilton, Charlotte Ceccato, Emma-Jane Kirby: the kindest of friends. All the Swans – the South West authors – particularly Veronica Henry, Sue Mongredien, Harrie Evans and Rosie Walsh. Maddy Wickham is always an inspiration. Thank you to you all.

Thank you to the Macintyres, whose beautiful home in Argyll supplied some of the inspiration for a house in that magical part of the world.

Thank you to all the readers who love books, buy books, read books and send messages of encouragement, and to the booksellers in all their many guises, but particularly the independents, who have had to weather the storm of lockdowns.

Thank you to Nick at Snell Print, who printed and bound my first draft for editing in super quick time.

Thank you to my family for their support – over computer and phone rather than in person, of course. And thanks and love to James, Barney and Tabby, who make it all worthwhile.

THE WINTER CHILDREN

Behind a selfless act of kindness lie dark intentions . . .

Olivia and Dan Felbeck's dreams of a family are finally fulfilled on the birth of their twins. The longed-for babies mark a new and happy stage in their lives.

Soon after, Dan's oldest friend, Francesca, offers them the chance to live at Renniston Hall, an Elizabethan house she is renovating. They can stay rent-free in a small part of the unmodernised house, which was once a girls' boarding school.

The couple accept, and just as they are enjoying the family life that they have craved for so long, Francesca arrives at the Hall and doesn't seem to want to leave. What exactly happened between Dan and Francesca years ago at Cambridge? As Olivia wonders how well she knows her husband, she starts to suspect that her perfect life could be built on a lie.

Meanwhile, Renniston Hall holds dark mysteries of its own, and slowly the old house starts to surrender its long-held secrets . . .

THE SNOW ROSE

*I know they think I shouldn't keep her . . . That's why I've
escaped them while I can, while I still have the opportunity . . .*

Kate is on the run with her daughter Heather, her identity hidden
and their destination unknown to the family they've left behind.
She's found a place where they can live in solitude, a grand old
house full of empty rooms and dark secrets. But they're not
alone, for there are the strange old ladies in the cottage next
door: Matty and her sister Sissy. They know what happened here
long ago, and are curious about Kate. How long can she hide
Heather's presence from them?

When an eccentric band of newcomers arrive, led by the
charismatic Archer, Kate realises that the past she's so desperate
to escape is about to catch up with her. And inside the house,
history is beginning to repeat itself . . .

THE WINTER SECRET

'My dear boy, the place is cursed. It always has been and it always will be . . .'

Buttercup Redmain has a life of pampered luxury, living in beautiful Charcombe Park. Her older husband, Charles, is wealthy and successful, and proud of the house he has painstakingly restored. Buttercup is surrounded by people who make her life delightfully easy. But the one thing she really wants seems impossible.

There are other discomforting realities: her husband's ex-wife Ingrid still lives nearby, although Buttercup has never met her. And it soon becomes clear that all the people who make Buttercup's life so carefree are also watching her every move. Does she actually live in a comfortable but inescapable cage? And what is the real story of her husband's previous marriage?

Xenia Arkadyoff once lived in Charcombe Park with her father, a Russian prince, and her mother, a famous film star. Life seemed charmed, full of glamour and beauty. But behind the glittering facade lay pain, betrayal and the truth about the woman Xenia spent her life protecting.

Now Charcombe Park is calling back people who were once part of its story, and the secrets that have stayed long hidden are bubbling inexorably to the surface . . .

A Midwinter Promise

The embrace of the past can never be broken . . .

The past

A lonely and imaginative child, Julia loves her family's beautiful and wild Cornish home with all her heart. But, marked by dark troubles, she enters her adult years determined to leave and seek a new beginning in London. It's there she meets the handsome David. They fall in love, but when Julia becomes pregnant, even he can't stop the terrible echoes of the past from ringing in her ears. The only sound to be heard above the noise is the old Cornish house, calling her home . . .

The present

For Julia's adult children, Alex and Johnnie, the house hides the history of their family within its walls. For Alex, it is full of memories of her late mother. For Johnnie, it is the house that should have been rightfully theirs after Julia died but has been stolen from them instead. With their father now lying in a hospital bed, time is running out for Alex and Johnnie to uncover the secrets of what happened to their mother all those years ago. Can they discover the truth before the house closes its doors to them forever?